BEAUTIFUL BOUNDARY

CAROL SPIVEY

To Mary Anne.
Be blessed !
C Spivey

First paperback edition October 2021

Cover design by Kelsey Kukal-Keeton with K Keeton Designs

Edited by Jessica Nelson with Rare Bird Editing

Edited by Karen Robinson

Edited by Tiffany White with Writers Untapped

❀ Created with Vellum

This book is dedicated to
Taylor, Cole, Blaine, and Kaylee,
my gifts from above.
I love you,
Mom

BEAUTIFUL BOUNDARY

CHAPTER ONE

DENVER

Sulfur and death sting my nostrils as we slip down the dark alley, following the stench of demon. We're getting close. The fur along my back stands on end and my insides tingle. Mitch and I have been tracking this creature for half an hour. I suppose he thinks he's gotten the best of us. Stupid, stupid demon. The Stone family of wolves *never* give up on a good demon fight.

With a slight swing of my snout, I gesture toward the dumpster. Mitch's blue eyes lock on mine. He lets out a snarl, revealing a razor-sharp canine. I'd say he's itching to sink his teeth into the neck of our little friend. I know I am. Other than stalking this "stray dog," tonight's patrol has been pretty uneventful. With an hour to go until daylight, we spotted this guy lurking outside my favorite hamburger joint. Not sure what he wanted with Mr. Hagerdy, who had just gone into his restaurant for the morning, but his mission is now survival. Not gonna happen.

The pavement is slick from an earlier rain. Our paws make no noise as we inch closer to the dumpster. Thirty feet to go and I pause. It's not like a demon to hide, so his tactic has me second guessing myself. What is he doing back there? I'm on the verge of giving Mitch the signal to proceed when a loud screech resounds into the night. Nails scrape against the dumpster, causing me to grind my teeth. Behind the metal trash bin, bones crack and one growl erupts into several.

What the crap was that, Denver? Mitch's voice in my head says right before not one, but four scraggly dogs greet us from the back of the alley.

Cloning demon. Nice. More of a fight. What do you say, Mitch? Two for you, two for me?

Hell yeah!

The demons almost match our wolf form in size, but they're sickly looking: matted hair, protruding ribs, red eyes, and foam dripping from their snouts like rabid dogs. Make no mistake—those teeth are full of poison. One cackles like a hyena and the others chime in. Mitch and I cover their cries with growls of our own.

They go for the element of surprise and storm forward. I jump to the side and shove my attacker into the bricks with my hind legs, his body landing with a thud. The second one lunges at me, but I meet him head on and wrestle him to the ground. In the scuffle, his teeth scrape into the flesh of my shoulder. He tries to pin me down, but I get the upper hand and shove his muzzle to the pavement with my paw. His beady eyes bore into mine. A hiss escapes him as I squeeze my teeth into his jugular. The demon makes one last attempt to free himself, but it's too late. My jaws close down for the kill, and the demon dissipates beneath me, leaving his nasty slime behind.

Blood drips from my lips onto the pavement. I take quick stock of the situation. Mitch took out one demon and is grappling with his second. My first attacker rises from his run-in with the wall and sprints toward me. I meet him halfway and we slam into one another. His scrawny body is no match for my brute strength. He's feisty, though; I'll give him that. In seconds, I have him pinned and go in for the kill. The demon releases a screech before he returns to his hellish home.

I spin around to see if Mitch needs help.

That was fun. Mitch shakes demon blood from his fur as he pads toward me.

Damn straight. Overhead, the sky is pale gray. *We need to get back to the warehouse. It's almost daylight.*

Rie-man, you there? Rieder is not only an integral part to our team, but my friend as well.

Yeah, boss. What's up?

Time to wrap it up. Send word to the others.

You got it.

Once we're at the warehouse and everyone has gone home, Mitch rolls up the maps and organizes the conference room while I enter the night's events in the logbook. Dad requires that we keep a record of our patrol so he can monitor the demon activity. I scan over the last few weeks and am thankful the sightings have been few and far between. The job of protecting our families, wolf clans, and the surrounding community is our number one goal. After jotting down the run-in with our little cloning friend, I switch to the computer and review the patrol schedule for the rest of the week. Teams and leaders are assigned and are spaced out to give the proper rest between shifts. Wolves don't require a ton of sleep, but too many nights on patrol will wear out even the strongest of men. And women.

I swivel the leather chair to face the myriad of television screens, checking for any last-minute signs of lurking evil. The whopping four thousand people of Forrest City have no idea the lengths we take to keep them safe. Hardly anyone is moving about at this early hour, and there's no foul play to be found.

"Bro, you about ready to go?" Mitch leans on the doorframe of Dad's office. He has a full day of high school ahead, and I'll be writing a paper for my online business class.

"Check all the doors and get the lights. Oh, and run by the security room to make sure the morning shift manager is here to take over. I'll meet you at the car."

"On it."

Our father is a man of many talents. He's not only the pack leader, but he also runs a security company. We sell, install, and monitor security systems for personal homes and businesses alike, at a very reasonable cost. Mitch hopes to take over that side of things when he's out of college.

As for me...I'll be the next pack leader. Dad continues to groom me to follow in his footsteps, and honestly, it's all I've ever wanted. My main focus right now is a business degree and learning all I can from the man I call Father.

The single missing piece to my future is meeting my mate. With six months left until my twenty-first birthday, there's a hint of apprehension that haunts me when I give it permission.

HOME SWEET HOME. Mitch and I pull into the driveway, but instead of parking inside the six-car garage, I leave the Porsche outside.

"You gonna wash your car?" Mitch tosses our bag on a bench in the garage.

"Thought I might."

"You need something better to do with your time than wash your car and polish your motorcycle. Didn't you wash it like three days ago?"

"Maybe."

Mitch snorts. "Anyway, Dad and Mom are going out tonight. I'm gonna ask Dad if I can have some people over. You in?"

"Sure."

Mitch pauses before turning the handle to the kitchen, his squinted eyes honed in on my wrinkled brow. "What's with all the short answers?"

"Nothing. Let's get some food."

"Nice try, bro. Something's bothering you."

"Dude, I'm hungry. Let's go inside before I die of old age."

"Ah. I get it. You're going to be twenty-one soon. It's gonna happen, man. Don't sweat it."

"Yeah, yeah." I shoulder Mitch out of the way and push the door open.

Mom and Dad are in a lip-lock by the stove. I inwardly groan but say nothing.

Mitch is not as gracious. "Seriously? It's way too early for that."

Dad pats Mom on the bottom. "It's never too early, son." He turns to the coffee pot. "How was your patrol?"

Mitch slips around the corner to get ready for school, leaving me to answer Dad's questions.

"Pretty quiet. Mitch and I took out a cloning demon, but that was it."

His eyebrows rise in question. "It took two of you to kill one cloning demon?"

"Well, no. We didn't know he was a cloning demon until he multiplied. Even then, it was like a Sunday stroll."

He nods his approval. "And the rest of your team?"

"Nothing."

"Excellent." Dad takes his coffee to the table and grabs the newspaper. He's like the only person I know who still reads the paper.

Mom reaches in the cabinet for the pancake mix.

"I'm going to run up and get clean before breakfast, Mom. Be back in ten."

"All right, Denver." She ruffles my hair.

I'm almost around the corner when my dad calls my name.

"Yes?"

He smiles. "I'm proud of you, son. You're a great team leader."

"Thank you."

I run upstairs and take a hot shower. My dad tells me at least once a week that he's proud of me. I can only hope to be half the man he is some day.

Mitch and I return to the kitchen, greeted by blueberry pancakes and bacon. We fill our plates and join my parents at the table.

The usual morning conversations float around the room. How is school, what's new with the pack, everyone's plans for the day, etc.

Dad mentions he's taking Mom out for dinner and a late movie. They're going up to Diamond Hill to stay the night, but will be home early in the morning because Dad has an area pack meeting.

Mitch looks at me and winks. "Is it okay if I have some friends over? Denver will be here to supervise."

Dad glances at Mom and then back at Mitch. "That's fine. We trust you boys."

"Thanks, Dad. I'm gonna grab my stuff and head to school." Mitch takes his plate to the sink.

I rinse my plate so I can load the dishwasher.

Mom kisses Mitch and then me on the cheek. "You boys have a good day. I will be with the pack wives this morning planning our next family event."

I give her a hug. "Love you."

She squeezes my arm. "I love my boys more than anything. Except your father of course."

I smile. "Of course." *Your mate comes before anyone or anything. I hope to someday know what that's like.*

Once everyone is out the door and the dishes are done, I climb in bed for a nap. I have that paper due later, but I'll function better with a couple hours of sleep. Lord knows I'll need it to spend my Friday night babysitting Mitch and his friends. Not like I've got anything better to do. My life consists of online college courses, demon patrol, and learning to take over the family business as pack leader. My family is everything. My dad is my hero, Mom is my—well, you can't describe a mom in one word—and Mitch is my best friend.

Maybe this party will end better than the last one did, with a drunken brawl and hours of clean up. One can always hope.

CHAPTER TWO

JADA

I try not to stare at the way he places his hand on her back or touches her arm. She laughs at something he said and my insides tighten. Her back is to me, so I see the way he smiles at her. He used to smile at me that way, but I ruined my chance and pushed him away. I realize, too late, that I shouldn't have. He's still my best friend, and I try to be thankful for that, at least. I spin back to my locker and grip my English book harder than necessary. Forcing my eyes closed, I take three long breaths. Once I'm more centered, I open my eyes to find Emily sauntering my way. I ignore the urge to slam my locker closed and instead close it lightly while grinding my teeth. I lean against the cool metal and wait for Emily to join me. She stops four times on her way down the hall, being the social butterfly that she is. I talk to no one as they pass. I'm not in the mood.

"My God, Jada, you look like crap."

"Gee thanks. Exactly what I needed. A little pick me up."

"Shut up. You know what I mean." Emily sneaks a peek down the hall to where *they're* standing and back to me. "Stinking tell the boy you're crushing on him."

"No. Absolutely not."

Emily rolls her eyes. "Whatever. You're both ate up with each other, but neither of you have the guts to admit it."

I glance at him once more. Not that I need to. I know everything there is to know about that handsome face. Where the cowlick is in his thick dark hair. How his eyes change color depending on the day or what he's wearing—they're a deep blue today. I know he has one tiny freckle above his lip. How he got the small scar on his forehead. Where the muscles in his jaw jump when he's flustered or angry. I know which tooth is fake because I was there when he lost it. I know...

"Earth to Jada. Hello?"

I pull my attention back to Emily. "Sorry. Can we go to class and forget about this conversation?"

Emily loops her arm through mine. "Isn't that what we always do?"

We start down the hall arm in arm. Two more classes and this day is over. I can't wait to be free of these stifling hallways. Even if it is only for the weekend. We've almost reached the door to English when Emily stops short.

"I almost forgot. Mitchell invited us to a party at his house tonight—seniors only. His parents are out of town."

"No thanks. I'd rather stay home."

Emily twists her hair around her finger. "That is not an option. Get beautiful and I will pick you up at seven."

"I don't want to go. You know Grainger will be there. With her. I can't watch that all evening."

Emily stomps her foot. "You're about to make me swear. Either tell him he's the chocolate to your peanut butter or move on, but my God, do something. You can't walk around pouting all the time. It's our senior year. Have some fun. There's a ton of hot boys in this high school to flirt with. But don't hit on mine. I'm picking you up at seven."

She turns and saunters to the classroom, leaving me speechless in the hall.

. . .

I'M CUTTING across the grass to my car after school when a familiar voice calls my name. It's Grainger. I want to keep walking and pretend I don't hear him, but realizing how childish that is, I stop and turn. My abrupt spin surprises him, and he almost plows me over.

"Whoa. Sorry about that. I didn't know you were going to pull that ninja move."

I smile and bite my lip. He's so close I'm enveloped by the woodsy cologne I bought him for Christmas last year. For a moment the scent pulls me back to a simpler time when Grainger and I sat beneath the pine trees between our houses. An unwanted memory creeps in of the day my dad left and Grainger held me while I ugly cried. Don't want to go there. "It's okay. What's up?"

"Nothing really. Haven't seen you today. Are you going to Mitchell's party tonight?"

"Emily insisted, so yes. What about you?"

"Yep. Candy and I will be there."

I knew it. "Great. Should be fun." Either he didn't pick up on the sarcasm or he's ignoring it.

"Sweet. I'll catch you later." He kisses the top of my head before walking away.

Gah! I hate this. How did my life get so complicated? Maybe Emily is right. Tonight I'm going to have a good time. I'm going to move on and find someone else to occupy my time and thoughts. I call Emily on the way home and tell her the plan.

"Will you stop screaming?" I hold the phone away from my ear until Emily calms down.

"I'm sorry. I'm legit excited that you've decided to move beyond the Grainger universe."

"So will you help me?"

"Of course I will. What time do you want me to come over?"

"How long will it take you to make me beautiful?"

"You're already beautiful."

"I just threw up a little."

"That's gross. You are beautiful. But tonight we need extra special. I'll be there at five. Can we order pizza?"

"Sure."

"Awesome. Be there soon."

"Love you, bye."

OUR THREE-BEDROOM RANCH isn't that big. If Mom's not in the living room, she's in the kitchen. I find her sitting on the counter beside the sink, the dishes half finished. Her thumbs fly over her phone, and I catch an eye roll before she shoves it in her apron pocket.

"Oh, hey, sweetie. How was your day?"

"Normal. How were the angel first graders?"

She harumphs as she slides off the counter. "Nobody puked, so I call it a win. Although angel Andy did punch a second grader in the face."

"I don't know how you do it." My weight shifts as I hoist up my slipping backpack. "Who were you texting?"

"Oh, you know, one of the girls. We can never decide where we're eating dinner."

Uh huh. "I'm going out with Emily. Her sort-of boyfriend invited us to his party."

"I must be getting old. What is a sort-of boyfriend?"

"They're talking, but he hasn't asked her to be his girlfriend yet."

"Makes sense. Any sort-of boyfriends for you, or are you free to roam the buffet table?"

"Um, just no. I need to shower before Emily gets here. Have fun tonight."

She laughs as she goes back to the dishes waiting to be washed. "You too. Be careful and don't stay out late."

"I'll give it my best shot."

.   .   .

AFTER HALF AN HOUR in the steamy shower, the water begins to cool. I've washed my long brown hair twice, shaved my legs for the first time all week, and scrubbed off every dead skin cell. I could do a Dove bodywash commercial, my skin is so soft. Emily will help me pick out clothes, so I don some underwear and a tank top. I swipe my phone off the bed and check the time. Dang, Emily will be here in thirty minutes, and I still need to dry my hair.

As I lay the dryer on the counter, my bedroom door clicks open. "I'm in here," I call.

"Good Lord, it's hotter than Hades in here."

"That's doubtful." I notice Emily is holding two bags full of makeup and hair stuff. "Did you bring enough stuff? I thought I was already beautiful."

She places the bags on the counter. "You are. This is for me."

"Haha. For real though, what's the plan?"

Emily studies me for a moment. "I don't think we'll change your makeup that much. I want to add some wow to your brown eyes to make them pop. We should definitely curl your hair, which will take forever, but we've got plenty of time. As far as clothes go, I've brought some options."

"You didn't bring me a dress did you?"

"Well, I can't have you wearing jeans and a T-shirt now can I?"

"I changed my mind. This is too much work."

"Quit your whining and order us a pizza while I get everything set out."

"Fine." I stomp over and grab my phone off the nightstand to order a meat lovers pizza. I flop across the bed. "Do I really have to do this? I'm totally fine with staying here."

Emily sticks her head out of the bathroom doorway. "Get your butt in here now."

My lips vibrate as the loud puff of air passes through. "I hate you."

"Whatever." She drags my desk chair to the bathroom, placing it in front of the sink. "Sit down."

"You're so dang bossy."

She squats in front of me and twirls her hair around her finger. "I think we'll start with makeup."

Emily works her magic on me until the pizza arrives. We take a break to eat and watch TV, all the while debating the hottest boys and who I should talk to tonight. Her only objective is Mitchell. I'm to ignore Grainger at all costs. Which should be easy since he'll be with his girlfriend. All the boy conversation makes my stomach hurt, so I finish my Coke and take the leftovers to the kitchen. My mom has already left to hang out with her Friday night girlfriends.

When Emily is done curling my hair, she tells me to turn back to the mirror. I hardly recognize myself. All I can do is stare.

"I know, right?" She rests her chin on my shoulder. "You have the most gorgeous, big, brown eyes ever."

"Thanks." I stand up beside her. We're so opposite—my brown hair and coffee-colored eyes next to her blonde hair and hazel eyes—yet we're both masterpieces in this moment.

"You're pretty smokin' yourself."

She squeezes my hand. "Let's get dressed. It's time to hit this party."

THE STREET IS LINED with cars, with Grainger's truck amongst the vehicles in the driveway. The colossal home is lit up like Las Vegas. Apparently the light bill isn't an issue. Or any other bill for that matter. I glance around for the jet that shot me over to Malibu. Homes of the rich and famous. My awe is short lived when I remember why we're here. Emily is oblivious to my inner turmoil. She blabs on and on about winning Mitchell over tonight, which I don't doubt. The boy has it bad. We park and step out into the cool March night.

I run my hands down my dress. I would love to put on a pair of jeans right now. I'm more comfortable with a lot less leg showing.

"I don't know if I can do this."

"Don't be ridiculous." Emily comes around to my side of the car and grabs my hand. She practically drags me to the front door. "You remember what to do?"

I take a deep breath. "Yes."

"Good. Get in there and kill it."

The odor of alcohol assaults me as soon as Emily swings open the door. And sweat. The music is bumping and bodies are grinding. We force our way through the dirty dancing in the massive living room and find a much quieter kitchen. Some of our classmates are hanging out by the counter, others passing through to grab a beer. No sign of Mitchell or Grainger.

Emily takes a beer from the cooler. "You want one?"

"No thanks. I'll have a Coke."

"Here." She hands me a beer anyway. "You're going to need this to loosen up. You're tighter than my dad's wallet."

I roll my eyes but take the beer. She's right. I'm pretty wound up.

"Let's check out the rest of the place."

She means "Let's find Mitchell." Emily weaves through a family room, where Grainger and Candy are nestled together on the sofa watching a movie, his arm slung over her shoulders. Something twists inside of me and I want to go sit between them. Grainger must sense me staring because his head rotates in my direction. His eyebrows rise as he takes me in, and his smile makes my heart jump. I need to get out of here.

"What are you doing, Jada? Come on."

Emily saves me as she pulls me in the opposite direction of Grainger. We walk out of an open set of French doors onto a deck that can only be described as the Garden of Eden. A fountain gurgles nearby as we walk through a path lined with every flower, plant, and bush imaginable. The path opens at the end to a pool. The area is lit with torches and deck lights hanging from wooden beams. Some kids are actually swimming. At a house this nice, the water is probably heated. Emily spots Mitchell and continues to drag me along. Mitchell is talking with a couple of guys from school and a boy who's an older version of him. A few girls linger nearby trying to catch the attention of the group. Emily acts as if they don't exist and struts up to the boys.

"Hey, Mitchell."

"Hey, gorgeous." His arm curls around her waist.

For the life of me I can't figure out why they aren't a couple already. Mitchell introduces us to his brother, Denver, who is quite the fine specimen. A definite yes on the buffet table. His blond hair hangs across his forehead, almost touching his eyes. His turquoise-blue eyes. He's muscle all over. A short sleeve T-shirt reveals the edge of a tattoo. I find myself examining his beautiful features with no hint of apology. He studies me with the same interest. I take that back—his stare is intense, yet...

"May I?" Denver reaches in my direction. I have no idea what he wants. I gawk as if his hand is a foreign object.

He laughs and my insides flutter. "Your beer. You want me to open it?"

I glance down and realize I never took off the lid.

"Sure." I pass it to him, and he snaps off the cap and gives it back.

"It's easier to drink that way." His face lights up and a dimple pops up on his right cheek. His blue eyes sparkle.

"I suppose it is. Thanks."

I take a long pull on my beer. Emily is engrossed in Mitchell, and it's awkward being the third wheel. Denver laughs at something Rieder said. Rieder and I have a class together, but I don't know him well enough to join their chat. I scan the deck for anyone from school I can chill with. Most of the kids are swimming or sitting in intimate groups, but a fire pit across the way looks like a welcoming place to sit.

I tap Emily on the shoulder. "Hey, I'm going to sit over by the fire pit, okay?"

"Are you sure? Why don't you stay here with us?"

"Someone made me wear a dress and my legs are cold. I'll be fine."

Denver is suddenly interested in our conversation. "I'll keep her company."

"You don't have to do that. I'm sure you have better things to do."

I can't imagine for the life of me why this gorgeous college boy would want to sit with me.

He shrugs. "Actually, I can't think of one single thing I'd rather be doing."

Emily pinches the back of my arm. That's her nice way of telling me not to say anything stupid. "I'm sure she would love the company. *Right,* Jada?"

"Of course."

Denver places his hand on the small of my back for me to lead the way. His touch is warm and comforting, and the strangest sense of knowing consumes me. I couldn't tell you what I'm supposed to know, but something hides under the surface of his fingertips. Other kids sit around the fire pit, leaving one bench seat open. I plant myself on the cushion, holding my hands out toward the heat. Denver sits close beside me and crosses his feet at the ankles.

"So, Jada, you're friends with my brother?"

"Friends might be a stretch. Honestly, I don't know much about your brother except what Emily tells me. She's my best friend, so I came for her."

"Ah, the best friend sacrifice. I get it. So what would you rather be doing tonight, instead of hanging at this fine establishment?"

I let out a breath. "The truth isn't that exciting."

"Tell me, Jada."

My name drips off his lips like sugar-sweet maple syrup. I pull my gaze from the fire to study him. The flame flickers in his blue eyes. I've never imagined myself with anyone other than Grainger. I didn't consider it a possibility that my heart could make room for someone else. I might be able to clear some space for this boy. For a split second his cool demeanor slips and his eyes portray something akin to longing. It's gone so quickly, I tell myself it was nothing.

"I'd probably be in sweats and a T-shirt, curled up on my bed, eating popcorn and watching a movie that I've already seen. Lame, right?"

"Sounds perfect. What are you doing tomorrow night?"

"Excuse me?"

"You know, tomorrow? The day after today? Do you have plans?"

My God what is happening right now? Is this some kind of twisted joke? Have I been transported into the Twilight Zone?

I play with the hem of my dress. "No plans. In the evening anyway. My mom and I clean the house on Saturday morning and then I like to get in a run. Sometimes Emily and I hang out, but we haven't made any plans yet."

"You like to run?"

"Yeah. It's a good stress reliever. Do you run?"

"Only for getting in my cardio. I like strength training, lifting, sparring, stuff like that."

My traitorous eyes scan his biceps. No doubt the boy works out. The edge of his tattoo still taunts me. I grip the edge of the bench to keep my hands from running up his arm to push up his sleeve.

Denver sits up from his relaxed position on the bench. "Are you curious?"

He nods in the direction of his shoulder.

I angle my body toward him, brushing his thigh. He jerks his leg away, which is odd considering he wants me to touch his shoulder. "Yes."

"Go ahead."

My hands tremble as I slide them along his skin. The tattoo takes my breath away. It's an intricate scene of a tree-lined lake at the foot of a mountain. A bird soars near a crescent moon, and on the shore of the lake sits a canoe. I run my fingers over the flesh of his shoulder, causing goosebumps to rise up on his arm.

"Denver, it's beautiful. What is this place?" I don't want to stop touching him, but I replace his sleeve and put my hands in my lap.

"It's the Boundary Waters up in Quetico, Canada. My dad's been taking Mitch and me up there since we were like ten and eight. It's in my blood. I love it up there.

"I bet. You have any pictures?"

He chuckles. "About a million. You want to see them?"

Don't sound desperate. Don't sound desperate. "Sure."

There's this awkward moment of silence. The fire becomes my

focus as I try not to die of embarrassment. I inwardly groan at my attempt to be cool.

"How old are you, Jada?'

"Eighteen. My birthday is in August, so I'm older than a lot of my friends. How old are you?"

"Twenty."

Denver leans forward and takes my hand. I'm so surprised by the gesture that I jump, and he immediately lets go.

"Sorry about that. I was testing out a theory."

"What does that mean?"

"There's this dude over there staring at me like he wants to kill me or take me out at the least. He clenched his fist when I touched your hand. You have a boyfriend you didn't tell me about?"

Has to be Grainger. No one else would care who I'm sitting with. And what does he care anyway? He's with his girlfriend. An odd and foreign indifference to Grainger's opinion overwhelms me. "No. No boyfriend."

"What's his deal then?"

I follow his gaze to Grainger. As soon as our eyes meet, he shifts his attention elsewhere.

"That's my friend Grainger. We grew up together, so he's a little overprotective. "

"If you say so." Denver stands and stretches. He extends his hand, so I let him pull me to standing. "You still up for pictures?"

"Absolutely."

"Well come on then."

MY PHONE CHIRPS three times in a row.

Emily: Where are you???

Emily: I can't find you anywhere??

Emily: Grainger says you left with some boy?!

Me: I didn't leave. I'm in Denver's room, upstairs.

Emily: What???

Me: Just come upstairs.

Denver and I are sitting on the floor of his room. There are pictures and albums everywhere. He's been showing me pictures and telling me stories of his trips to Canada for over an hour. I've loved every minute of it. Peculiar notions continue to trickle into my system. The fact that I want to spend time with Denver is strange enough, but the raw landscape of these photos pulls at something deep in my core. I suddenly have the urge to run through a field, barefoot.

Denver nudges my knee with his. "Everything okay?"

"Yeah. Emily was worried because she couldn't find me. She's on her way up."

"Gotcha. Is Mitch with her?"

"Why do you call him Mitch? Everyone at school calls him Mitchell."

"It's my right as a big brother. I've called him worse, believe me."

I laugh. "I'm sure you have."

Mitchell and Emily come barreling though the door. Emily's shoulders slump forward.

"Sorry. Emily was worried about Jada," Mitchell says.

"Well, as you can see, she's fine." A strange stare passes between the brothers.

"I'm sorry, Em. I should have texted you."

"It's okay. Grainger had me freaked out. He said you left with some college boy. That didn't sound like you, but he seemed to be a little distraught."

Oh my gosh, what is his deal? "It's none of his business who I leave with."

"You're right, but it worried me when I couldn't find you." Emily notices the pictures all over the floor. "What's all this?"

"Denver is showing me photos from his trips to Quetico, Canada. They're pretty amazing."

Denver slides over, making more room. "You guys want to join us?"

"Can we, Mitchell?"

"Sure, why not."

For the next few hours, we look at photos and the guys tell stories that make me laugh and cry. When we've exhausted the Canada albums, Denver drags out other family vacations and of course the baby pictures. We make trips down to the kitchen for popcorn and other snacks. By midnight, we've migrated to a TV screen. Emily and I pick the movie while the boys check on their guests and make sure the house is in one piece. At 2:00 a.m., we call it a night. The best night I've had in forever. Denver wants to meet up later, so I give him my number. When Emily drops me off at my house, I thank her for the hundredth time for making me go out tonight. We hug and say goodnight. For the first time in a long time, I fall asleep *not* thinking of Grainger Nelson.

CHAPTER THREE

DENVER

"What in the hell am I going to do?" I say to the pillows on my bed as I punch them repeatedly. Jada is my mate. My parents tried to prepare me for this moment, but now that's it's here I'm acutely aware of how unprepared I truly am. In my ignorance, I thought her life would revolve around mine. That was horse manure. The defining moment of watching her walk toward me was like Thor's hammer to the gut. I would do anything, change anything, become anything for this woman.

To make matters worse, she's not a wolf. At least I don't think she is. Her scent is unique and unlike anything I've experienced. And it's absolute hell trying to keep my emotions in check and reigned in when I'm bursting at the seams to release them.

The power she has over me is disturbing. My thoughts are caught up in a tornado that won't freaking stop spinning. I want to protect her, touch her, kiss her, stand beside her, encourage her, support her, and be with her all day, every day. The distance from her now makes me a ravenous and crazed man.

My body is completely exhausted, but my mind is unrelenting. I need a couple hours sleep to combat all the running I did last night but don't know if I can stop thinking of her long enough to fall asleep. Like I told Jada, I don't like running—in my human form. I couldn't very well tell her how much I love to run when I'm not in human form.

There's a soft knock at my door.

"What do you want?"

The hinges creak in protest. "It's me, man. Can I come in?"

"No."

Mitch comes in anyway. The edge of the bed dips with his weight. I'm lying on my back with my arms behind my head, staring at the ceiling.

"You were gone all night. Are you okay?"

I don't know if I'm ready to talk about this yet. "What's the big deal? I went running. It's not like we don't do that."

"Sure, but the fact that you blocked me out had me worried, and I could still sense your stress. You kept me up most of the night too."

The dark circles under his eyes are proof of his worry. "Sorry about that, bro."

"I don't care about that, but tell me what's wrong with you. Or better yet, tell me why you didn't come and get me? We could have run together."

I pinch the bridge of my nose. "I needed to be alone last night."

"Is there something going on I don't know about? Is there another pack in the area?"

"No, Mitch. It's nothing like that."

He stands up and paces the floor. "Then what the hell is wrong with you? The emotions rolling off of you are hitting me like waves. I'm getting seasick, dude."

I blow out a long breath. "Jada is my mate."

Mitch stops walking the floor and stares at me. He doesn't speak for a solid minute. "Shit, Denver."

"I know."

"She's not even…"

"Dude, I know."

"We need to tell Dad. He'll know what to do."

I sit up on the bed. "I will, okay. Give me a little time to process. I'm losing my shit right now."

Mitch plops down on my desk chair. "Is it as bad as Dad said it would be?"

"Worse. So much worse." I fall on my back again, waiting on the ceiling to give me all the answers I need. "When will Dad be home?"

"Not sure. He left early this morning. Something about a pack meeting."

"Couple of days then. I can make it a couple of days."

"Are you guys gonna hang out?"

"I don't know if I should, but if I don't I may stop breathing."

"Wow. That's much worse than Dad ever let on."

"You have no idea." I recall sitting next to her last night. "Her scent drives me crazy. She smells like rain and pine and earth, and I want to bury my nose in her hair. And oh my God, when she touched my arm—I had to bite my cheek until it was bleeding because my whole body felt like it was going to combust. Being near her is almost torture, but it's euphoric at the same time. And her lips." I moan at the memory of her pink, full lips. "The urge to kiss her is unbearable."

"I think I'm going to throw up."

I jerk upright on the bed. "Hang on, little brother. It's going to happen when you least expect it and you'll go to shit like I have."

"I hope it's not for a long time. You're a freaking mess."

"Get out before I punch your lights out. I need some sleep."

"Yeah, well that makes two of us."

I flop back across the bed once more and close my eyes. Mitch's steps leave the room, and the door clicks shut. I get it. He can't understand because I didn't understand either until it hit me like a freight train moving faster than the speed of sound. Does sound move fast? I have no idea. My thoughts are so jumbled up. I force the airflow slower in and out of my lungs. I seriously do need some sleep. If I'm going to attempt to be around Jada later, I'll need my wits about me to keep myself in check. I use the same breathing and mind exercises Dad taught us to use to control the change. My incessant thoughts eventually calm and I fall asleep.

. . .

TWO AND A HALF HOURS LATER, I'm a new man. Sort of. My thoughts still radiate all things Jada, but I'm a bit more in control. Maybe after lunch I'll be in the right frame of mind to decide whether or not to text Jada.

My mom is in the kitchen making triple meat sandwiches. The aroma so tantalizing to my wolf nose, my mouth waters. I walk over to the fridge and get a pop. Before sitting at the bar, I kiss her on the cheek. She grins at me like it's Christmas morning and she can't wait for me to open my presents.

Thanks for snitching, bro. "Mitch told you."

"Don't be mad at your brother. He was concerned."

"I'll show him concerned."

Both hands plant on both hips. "Denver Stone, do not hurt your brother. He's not as strong as you are."

"I won't kill him, just maim him a bit."

"Denver…"

"Geez, Mom. I'm kidding."

She points to the stool behind me. "Sit down and eat. I know you were out running half the night. You're going to need your strength."

I take a few bites of my sandwich while my mom makes hers and joins me at the bar.

"I have so many questions."

"Don't talk with your mouth full."

"Sorry." I finish chewing and swallow. "What am I supposed to do? How do I handle all of these rolling emotions and urges? Does it get easier?"

"Oh, Denver. When we find our mate, it's the strongest of all wolf desires. Stronger than the need to run, fight, or protect. It's not like a human love that can be thrown away. It's forever. The connection will never diminish."

"I'm so miserable. It's like a slow death by chihuahua bites."

My mom laughs. "I know sweetheart. I know."

"If you know, why are you laughing?"

"Because we've all been there. You'll be fine."

"I don't know if I agree with that. What about the fact that Jada's not a wolf?"

She gazes out the kitchen window for a moment and then back to me. "That part I'm not sure about. It's rare, Denver, to connect with a human. We'll talk to your dad when he returns. Are you sure she's not a wolf?"

"Pretty sure. She's eighteen. And even if she were a late shifter, I would be able to pick up her scent. Although…"

"What is it, Denver?"

"I'm not sure. I sense something different about her, but I can't quite place it." I shake my head. "Maybe it's nothing more than part of the pull."

"Maybe."

Neither of us talk as we finish our lunch and then clean up. I have so many more questions. Some can wait for Dad, some can't.

"Mom?"

"Yes?"

"Do you think it's okay to see her? Last night I told her I would be in touch today, you know, maybe hang out tonight."

"I think that's fine. You're strong enough to handle yourself. You're the pack leader's son."

"It's so hard to be near her."

She puts her hand on my cheek. "You will never practice as much restraint as you will need to do these next weeks and months. But I know you can do it."

"Thanks, Mom. I love you."

"I love you too, and I'm so proud of you."

I take a few steps toward the hall and stop. Questions bombard my mind. Her being completely human makes everything different. I start to turn around but then decide I'll keep my thoughts to myself. At least until Dad gets home.

MY BARE FEET shuffle across the wood floor of my room as I pace back and forth. It never occurred to me until now that she may not want to hang out. She may not care one iota about me, and I'm over here crazier than a new changeling on a full moon. I can't think that way or I'll go mad. My entire body itches like hives. I send a text and wait. She doesn't immediately respond, so I go out in the garage to tinker with my bike. I fear what I might do if she declines my invite...or doesn't text back at all. It's best if I stay outside.

CHAPTER FOUR

JADA

I reek of Clorox. I always end up with the stupid bathrooms, my least favorite chore. Oh well, at least we're done cleaning now. As I change into my running shorts and tank, I check my phone again. No text from Denver, but one from Emily. I don't know why, but I'm disappointed over his lack of contact. What was I thinking? I text Emily that I'm going for a run and will call her when I get back.

While I'm stretching my legs, I gaze over at the pines. I can't even begin to count the number of times Grainger and I have met under those trees. The memories parade in my mind, causing a stab in my chest. I stretch my neck from side to side and do a few jumping jacks to clear my head of all thoughts that contain boys. Doesn't work. Maybe this run will help me to get my mind on track. I take off on my usual route and let my feet and legs carry me away.

Four miles in and I've got a good sweat going. It's at least sixty-five degrees today. The sun is bright and daffodils are in full bloom. Spring is so refreshing after the long winter. Everything that has been dormant is coming back to life. Makes me think of my life and how I need a fresh start. At that very thought, I receive a text. It's from Denver. A huge, goofy grin materializes on my face. Anticipation has me running faster. I make the loop around my school and start back toward the house.

I sprint the last few feet and can barely breathe by the time I reach the yard. I double over to catch my breath. When my side stitch fades, I raise up and notice Grainger waiting for me on the steps. I smile as I join him on the porch.

I nudge him with my shoulder. "What are you doing?"

"Waiting for you." Grainger's lips are in a tight line, his eyebrows scrunched together.

"What's wrong? Is everyone okay? Your mom?"

"Yeah, everybody's fine."

"Okay, then what's your deal? You're being weird."

He turns toward me then. "Jada, I don't know how to say this except to just come out and say it."

I throw my hands in the air. "Say what you came to say, Grainger."

"I don't trust that guy you were with last night. Something about him is off. I mean, maybe you weren't planning on seeing him again, but I don't think it's wise."

My whole body goes stiff. Who does he think he is coming over here telling me who I can and can't see? What does he care anyway? He's dating Candy. "Are you serious right now? Who are you, my dad?"

"Someone needs to be."

That was a low blow and he knows it. I jump to my feet.

"Jada, I'm sorry. I care about you, you know that."

"I know you used to. I'm not sure anymore." I try to get to the door, but he grabs my wrist.

"How can you say that? We've been through so much together. Of course I care about you. I always will."

I shake him loose and walk over to the porch rail. "Things are different between us. This last year has been—"

"Has been what, Jada?"

The branches of the pines sway in the breeze. Our fort was hidden in the center of the grove, the floor a bed of sticky needles. We were so close our parents had probably planned our wedding. I know I had. Yesterday morning I was sick watching him and Candy together, but now I'm conflicted. My heart is torn and I'm at a loss as to what to do. I love Grainger. He's my steady rock, and until recently, I thought we would end up together. But last night changed all that. Meeting Denver has done something to me. Touching him felt like magic. I tell myself how stupid that sounds, but I can't think of a better way to describe it.

Grainger places his hands on my shoulders and turns me to him. "Jada, tell me what's going on. You've always been able to tell me anything."

"Did you think we would be together? You know, when we were kids?"

"Of course I did."

"Me too."

Grainger releases me and leans over the rail. He's quiet for so long I wonder if he's going to shut me out.

"What do you want from me, Jada?" His voice a shaky whisper.

"I don't know. I thought I did, but now I'm not sure."

He stands up tall, his face puckered in disgust. "Because of that guy?"

"You have no right to say anything to me about that. You're dating Candy."

His angry steps cause me to stumble back. "Because you told me we could never be in that kind of relationship. You didn't want to ruin our friendship. Remember that, Jada?"

I lurch away from him, my arms tight across my middle. This is too painful. I am so confused. How can a few hours with Denver make me question what I thought I wanted my whole life? And is Grainger saying he'd end his relationship with Candy to be with me? Is that what I want? Tears begin to flow down my cheeks.

Grainger's arms encircle me from behind. "Hey, I'm sorry. I didn't mean to make you cry. But you did push me away. I moved on because I thought that's what you wanted. Is it not what you wanted? Do we have a chance, Jada?"

"I said those things because I thought it was the right thing to say. I didn't want to ruin our friendship. My head told me that if we tried dating it would screw everything up, but my heart wanted something different."

"And what do you want now, Jada? Tell me the truth, because I want to be with you."

"I don't know."

Grainger goes rigid behind me. He lets go of me and paces back and forth across the porch.

"Shit, Jada. I don't get it. You're hesitating because of a guy you've hung out with one time? That doesn't make any sense."

He's absolutely right. It makes no sense at all. When I don't answer, he swears again.

Grainger's boots clomp down the stairs. "I have a date to get ready for." He stops in front of me. "You know where to find me if you want me, Jada, but I won't be hanging around forever."

I can't speak around the lump in my throat, so I simply nod.

AFTER HALF AN HOUR OF CRYING, I remember the text from Denver. I need a clear head, so instead of reading the text, I go take a shower. Emily has called three times, but I can't deal with her right now either.

I spend an hour in the bathroom. I'm not sure why I'm getting beautiful, but I am. In anticipation of Denver's text maybe? I suppose I should actually read the text. He may have made other plans by now. If he was even offering to hang out with me in the first place. I grab my phone and walk to the window. Right past those pines is Grainger's house. He's probably leaving soon to pick up Candy. My gut twists at the thought, but at the same time, I can't pledge him my love. I pull up my texts and hit Denver's name.

Denver: Hey Jada. So did you make plans today? You know, the day after yesterday?

I think of his relaxed position on the bench last night when he said those words and my insides flutter. The way he says my name. I can't explain it, but I swear it sounds like music. Sexy, beautiful, soul searching music.

Me: I did not make plans.

It's been two hours since he sent the message. He may have changed his mind. I call Emily to kill some time. She answers on the second ring.

"What the heck took you so long?"

"Sorry, I ran into a bit of a...well, I ran into Grainger. And we had a pretty serious talk. I don't know, Emily, but I'm all sorts of messed up."

"I'll be right over. Oh and by the way, Mitchell and Denver want us to come over later."

She hangs up before I can give a response.

I curl up on my bed and turn on the television. There's a baseball game on. I don't like baseball, but I stare at the screen. My phone chirps with a new text.

Denver: I understand you may have plans now.

Me: It seems that I do.

Denver: Are you happy about those plans?

Me: Yes

Denver: Good

I laugh to myself. He's so different. I'm fascinated and baffled by the magnetic tug in my soul.

I finally have the brains to change the channel to something worth watching and wait for Emily. My mom pops in to tell me she's going out with "a friend." Could be a date. I think she's been seeing someone but afraid to tell me. I'll give her some time to hash things out. I don't blame her for wanting to have someone in her life. It's been the two of us for so long, but I'm eighteen now and a senior. I want her to be happy. I inform her of my plans with Emily and she tells me to have fun and be careful.

I've really made it too easy on her as a parent. I don't have a rebellious bone in my body. Well, maybe a couple, but not as many as most teenagers. I barely drink, never smoke, almost never cuss, and I do not, under any circumstances, sleep around. Not even a kiss. I've been on a few dates, but I have no interest in giving myself to someone that isn't my forever. When my dad left, it did something inside of me. I will not trust my heart, soul, or body to just anyone. They'll have to earn it. In fact, Grainger and I were saving ourselves for each other. We made a pact when we were twelve. I don't know if he's stuck to his end of the bargain. Maybe he and Candy have slept together, but I don't think so. Crap, I don't want to worry over this right now. Thank the skies above, Emily comes in to distract me from my own screwed up head.

Not even a hello. Emily pounces with both feet. "Wow, Jada. What did Grainger say to you?" She sits crossed-legged on the bed beside me. "Wait, don't tell me yet. First off, I need you to know how hot you are right now. What's going on with that? Oh my God, is it Denver?"

I hug my fuzzy pink pillow to my chest. "Where do you want me to start?"

"Oh geez. Start at the beginning."

"Here's the abbreviated version. Grainger handed me, on a silver platter I might add, everything I've wanted for weeks now. Himself. And for the first time in my life, I'm not sure that's what I want because of a guy I spent one evening with. How convoluted is that?"

"Pretty convoluted. And not like you at all. The universe has shifted dramastically."

"Dramastically is not a word, and you're being a little over the top don't you think?"

"I made it up." She peers at me thoughtfully. "No, I don't think I'm being over the top. This is real shit. I mean, what is it about this guy?"

"It's hard to explain. Honestly, there's nothing I can say that doesn't sound crazy."

"You and crazy don't mix."

"I know." I shrug. "I'm totally aware of how this must look."

"I'm not speechless very often, but I don't know what to say."

"You and speechless don't mix."

"I know."

"I don't understand what's happening." I lean over and place my head in my hands.

Emily rubs my back. "I told you. The universe has shifted."

I jerk my head up. "That's nonsense."

"Well, it's all I've got." She unfolds herself and gets off the bed. "Maybe tonight will hold some answers."

I let out a sigh. "Maybe."

She holds out her hand. "Let's go, hottie. You've got a date waiting."

"What about you? Has Mitchell sealed the boyfriend deal?"

"No. I get the weirdest vibe that he either won't or can't."

"He cares for you, I'm sure of it."

"I thought so too." She shrugs. "Maybe he's not the one for me."

I give her a hug. "I love you so much. You are the most beautiful person I know. If he can't see what he has right in front of him, then that's his stupidity."

"Thanks, Jada. I love you too."

WE ARRIVE AT THE BOYS' house twenty minutes later. Their swanky neighborhood is tucked away by itself, outside the city limits. It's the strangest place for a gated community now that I think about it. All the houses are huge. I don't know what his dad does, but they obviously have plenty of money. Emily rings the doorbell. Last night this place was full of life. Tonight, it's eerily quiet. Mitchell answers the door.

"Hey, beautiful." He pulls Emily in and kisses her cheek. "Hey, Jada. Come on in. Denver's in the living room."

Denver is sitting on the couch next to the most gorgeous woman I've ever seen. Her golden hair hangs in waves past her shoulders. Her eyes are a shade of hazel with a hint of gold. She's wearing a simple black top with dark skinny jeans, but on her model body the outfit is stunning. She stands when we walk in. Denver hovers beside me but stays at a distance. The woman's brows scrunch together and her intense stare is like standing before an x-ray machine. My fingers drum on the sides of my legs.

Mitchell clears his throat. "Emily, Jada, this is our mom, Aurar.

She wanted to meet you since, you know, we'll be hanging out tonight."

Even when she speaks to Emily, Aurar doesn't take her eyes off of me. Her embrace lingers and she inhales the scent of my hair, causing my spine to tingle. As I separate from her hug, she keeps hold of my hand and searches my eyes with a severe but passionate stare. What is it with this family and their ability to stir up unknown waters in my soul? I don't get the sense that she doesn't like me, but I can't begin to comprehend what just happened. She smiles warmly and excuses herself to the study. I'm dumbfounded by the whole thing and stand immobile with my mouth hanging open.

Denver touches my back and a shock runs through me. He jerks his hand away. "I'm sorry about that. She can seem a little intense, but I promise she's one of the most loving people you'll meet."

I bob my head, my lips sealed shut.

Denver is not as cool and collected as last night. He stumbles around his words and eventually leaves the room with Mitchell to get some snacks, while Emily and I pick out a movie.

I whisper to Emily. "Are you as freaked out as I am?"

"What, why?"

She's oblivious, or I'm overreacting. "Never mind."

The guys come back and we settle in to watch a movie. Denver sits next to me but continues to leave a fraction of space between us. I realize we hardly know each other, but he was so warm last night. I don't know what to make of this Denver. As the credits start to roll, Denver jumps up like a jack-in-the-box.

"Jada, you want to go for a ride?"

Mitchell gets up as well. "Brother, are you s…"

"I'll be fine."

Mitchell nods and takes Emily up to his room.

My nerves fizzle like Pop Rocks. Denver waits for my response. "Um, sure."

I follow him out to the garage and gawk at the line-up of vehicles. "The cars in here are more expensive than my house. Are you guys drug dealers or something?"

Denver laughs for the first time all night, and my whole body responds to the sound. He's smiling at me and I want to run over and kiss that beautiful mouth. Oh my God, did he put drugs in my drink? I can't think straight. I've never kissed anyone but Grainger, and we were thirteen at the time. Denver's lips are so inviting right now I take two steps in his direction. His smile falters and he staggers back.

"Come on, Jada." He walks to the other end of the garage to a motorcycle. "I'm glad you wore jeans. You look really good by the way." He swallows hard.

"Thank you."

"Here, put this on."

I stare at the helmet like it's going to bite me. "I've never been on a motorcycle."

"I won't go too fast. I think you'll really like it."

I take the helmet but fumble with the strap.

"Come here, let me."

As quick as a flash, he has me buckled and pushed away. I'm pretty sure I caught a swear word spoken under his breath.

Denver hops on the bike with ease and motions for me to sit on the back. I climb on, clumsy at best, and search for something to grab ahold of.

"Sit closer and put your arms around my waist."

As soon as my arms go around him, he shivers. His chest rises and falls with several deep breaths before he starts the bike. The engine rumbles to life and he revs the motor.

"Hold on."

I tighten my grip and he glides out of the garage. He turns in the opposite direction of town, taking me further in the country. The winding road dips and climbs and my belly does the same. We pass several houses then the dense forest overtakes the view. Trees are full of new spring leaves and several dogwoods are blooming. I suck in a lungful of fresh air and release it slowly. I'm probably cutting off his breathing capability, but I'm too scared to lessen my hold. After a few minutes I start to relax and enjoy the freedom of the open road and the wind hitting my face. We've only been riding for maybe ten minutes when he pulls up to a dock.

We climb off of the bike and take off our helmets. Denver is silent as he places them on the handlebars and ambles out on the dock. I wish I knew what he was thinking. He's been so distant today. Maybe Mitch coerced him into inviting me over so he could be with Emily. I stroll out on the dock and am fascinated by the comforting lull of the still, dark water.

"It's a beautiful lake."

Denver rubs the back of his neck. "I love coming out here to think. It's so peaceful."

"Did you stumble upon this place while out riding?"

Denver invades my space and reaches for my hair. I stand stock still as he rubs a strand between his fingers. His face is so close my breath catches. God, he's so gorgeous. The moonlight makes his blue eyes glow and his jaw more defined. I find myself mesmerized by his lavish lips. He catches me gawking and stumbles back.

"This is my family's land."

I shake my head to clear the fog. "What?"

"You asked if I found this place while I was riding. It's my family's land."

"Oh."

Denver leaves me by the rail and sits at the end of the dock. He doesn't invite me join him, but I do anyway.

"You know, if Mitchell wanted to be alone with Emily, he should have said so. You didn't need to be the sacrifice tonight."

"Is that what you think? I'm making a sacrifice by being with you?"

"I'm not sure what to think."

"I wish I could tell you, but it's complicated."

"Wow, that's original." I hate those two words. It's complicated. Anytime I've tried to bring up my dad and what happened to him with my mom, that's the answer I get. It's like they think you're not smart enough to comprehend or you're too immature to deal with the truth. It ticks me off. I grip the deck rail and pull myself to standing. I don't really need this *complication* in my life right now.

Denver jumps up and gently grabs my wrist. "Jada, please don't be angry. I'm sorry. Shit, I'm so sorry. I know I'm messing this all up. This is all new to me, and I'm trying to take it slow."

"I understand slow. I'm the queen of slow. I've had one bad kiss at thirteen, very few dates, and I'm still a..."

"Still a what, Jada?"

Oh my gosh, why am I telling him this? My face heats as I answer. "A virgin."

I'm totally unprepared for what happens next. Denver pulls me in his arms and hugs me. "Jada." My name falls off his lips in admiration. My arms slip up around his shoulders, and I snuggle against his chest. The rhythm of his heart builds and pounds next to my cheek. His embrace is warm and comforting, and his aura is that of fresh air and sunshine. My eyes flutter closed as I bask in his presence.

As we're wrapped together, something pinches at a deep-seated place inside of me. It's like a dormant seed was fertilized in my soul. A dead part of me come to life. I'm not sure whether to be excited or afraid by the alteration, and I don't have any indication of what it might be. There's an urging to know more about the mystifying Denver.

At his nudging, I lift my head. He's grinning from ear to ear.

"What's the goofy grin about?"

"Nothing. I'm happy, that's all." He puts his chin on my head. "Jada, believe me when I say I want to spend time with you. It's scary how much I want to spend time with you."

My hands go to his chest. "Your heart beats so fast."

"You do that to me, Jada."

My gaze once again falls to his lips. "Can I say something that will sound crazy?"

"You can tell me anything."

"Your lips, Denver. It's like they sing siren songs to me."

He grabs my face in his hands. "Everything about you sings siren songs to me. Which is why I should let you go."

He releases me and takes a step back to create distance. For a brief moment, a flash, Denver's eyes spark and glow, and a ripple of want cascades over my skin. I'm beginning to question my sanity.

The warmth of his touch recedes, and I'm left with a void in its stead.

"We should head back. Mitch is probably worried."

I want to ask him why Mitch would be worried, but all I can think about now is being in his arms again. It freaks me out the effect he has on me. Not enough to stay away, but it freaks me out all the same.

CHAPTER FIVE

DENVER

As soon as Jada leaves there's an emptiness in my soul. I haven't decided which is worse—touching her or not touching her. Both are torture. Life was definitely much easier before she walked in here last night. You hear stories, but nothing prepares you for finding your mate. A part of me wants Mitch to take me out back and put me out of my misery.

"I'd be glad to." Mitch strolls into the kitchen where I'm sitting at the bar.

"Get out of my head."

"Believe me, I want nothing more. It's like you're screaming. Sheesh, man, chill."

"I'm sorry, but you seriously have no idea how hard this is."

"You'd be surprised, big brother. I'm getting a pretty clear picture."

"Shut the hell up."

"Make me."

"You want to take this outside? I could use a good wrestling match right about now."

"Nah dude, I just took a shower. I don't want to get all dirty rolling around in the yard."

Mitch pulls leftovers out of the fridge and piles two plates high with food. He warms them in the microwave and passes one to me. "Here. I assume you're going to need some fuel for the night."

"Damn. I'm never going to be able to sleep again. I'll be up running all night, every night."

Mitch shovels in a huge bite of potatoes. "Well, I hope you can get your shit together, because I may never sleep again either."

"Mitchell Dean, don't talk with your mouth full. And both you boys need to stop swearing in my house."

"Sorry, Mom," we say in unison.

"You boys are going to have to work through this. Mitchell, try to be a little more compassionate. You'll be experiencing the same thing before long; then Denver will have to deal with all your thoughts. Although..."

I know better than to say anything until I've swallowed my food. I take a sip of water to wash it down. "What is it, Mom?"

She props her hip on the other side of the bar facing us. Her eyebrows pinched in thought. "Things could change with Jada in the picture. I don't hear you boys like I do your father. Our connection is much stronger. But if Jada is fully human, will she have the ability to hear you at all?"

I push my empty plate to the side. "I've wondered that too. What do you mean, *if* she's fully human?"

"She does have a peculiar scent. I'm not familiar with it. I went to the study to search through your father's notes but didn't come up with anything. She has a hint of shapeshifter, but I don't know for certain what it is."

"I wish Dad were here."

"Oh right, that's what I came in here to tell you. I called him tonight and told him what was happening, and he's coming home a day early. He'll be here in the morning. He said to tell you he's happy for you, and that you'll survive."

I roll my eyes. "He would say that."

After ruffling our hair, Mom retires to her room. If I know her at all, she'll be up half the night like the rest of us, trying to figure this all out. I am so thankful Dad will be home in the morning. I love my mother dearly, but I'm extremely close to my dad, and I have a boat-load of questions for him tomorrow.

Mitch and I clean up our plates and put them in the dishwasher.

"You want company tonight?"

I shake my head. "No, that's okay. I don't think I'm very good company right now. I'll try to keep my thoughts to a minimum."

"All right. Let me know if you change your mind."

I slap him on the shoulder. "Thanks. I will."

I RUN the perimeter of our territory for as long as I can. It's not my night to patrol, but I'm bored out of my mind. I weave my way closer to town and sniff out Jada's neighborhood. It takes me no time at all to find her house. Her scent is so strong I go lightheaded. I walk around her house for nearly an hour. I want to see her so bad I ache. Mitch is in my head telling me to stop torturing myself. He's right. I can't go inside, and there's no point in wearing a path in the yard.

Eventually, I pull away from her home and head for some hot spots in town. I run into Rieder and we take out a couple of demons together. I can't remember the last time it felt so good to rip some-thing apart. Mitch has gone quiet, so I assume he's been able to get some rest. Dawn is approaching. I need to get home and get cleaned up since Dad will be there soon, but the drive within me is too strong not to go by her house one last time. I sit near her window in the shadows and breathe her in. Once I'm drunk on her scent, I sneak out of town and sprint the rest of the way home.

Mitch and I keep a stash of boxers by the back door. I yank out a pair and slip them on before entering. The house is silent, all but Mitch's snoring. If Mom's awake, she's not yet in the kitchen. I tiptoe to my room and turn on the shower. I scrub off the stench of demon and then stand in the hot stream for another good twenty minutes. My body is wearing down. I'm going to need a nap, but I hope to speak to Dad first. I grab a pair of sweats and head back down to the kitchen for food.

My stomach is going to eat itself. The aroma of bacon wafts

down the hall, calling my name. I round the corner to find my mom and dad making out. You'd think after all these years they would slow down, but they still act like teenagers.

"Get a room." I walk to the stack of bacon and snatch a couple off the top.

My dad stops kissing my mom long enough to give me a high five. I walk around them to get to the juice.

"Can you do that after breakfast? I'm ravenous."

He slaps my mom on the bottom. "Duty calls."

"Fine, I'll feed your boy."

"Boys." Mitch strolls in, and he too nabs a couple pieces of bacon.

"Stop eating the bacon. Breakfast will be ready in a few minutes."

I fill two cups with juice and give one to Mitch. My parents are drinking their morning coffee. Mom moves around the kitchen with a dancer's grace. Dad is drooling. Good Lord, is this my future? Does it never die down?

"No, son, it doesn't."

"You in my head too?"

"Not on purpose, but you're pretty loud."

"Told you, bro."

I let out a groan. "This sucks. Does everyone in this house know how bad I want this girl, because some of my thoughts have not been —very clean."

"Yes!" says everyone.

"I'm moving out."

My dad gives my shoulder a squeeze. "It's all good. We get it."

Mitch grunts. "I don't get it, and I'm kinda sick of his daydreaming. His mind is a constant stream of how hot she is, and how soft her skin is, the sexy sway of her hips, her full lips…"

I slug Mitch harder than necessary. "Shut the hell up!"

"Boys, that's enough. Denver, apologize to your mother for swearing and to your brother for punching him."

"I'm sorry, Mom. Mitch."

My dad sighs. "Let's eat breakfast together, peacefully please. Then you and I will go to the study and talk."

"Sounds good. I'm starving. Ran around with Rieder last night. We took out a couple of lower demons."

"Were you on patrol?"

Oops. "No. I needed to get out of the house and thought I would help out for a bit."

"All right. I'll accept that for now. Don't make a habit of it. We take turns for a reason. You'll run yourself ragged."

"Yes, sir."

Around the breakfast table, the tension rolls away and we're able to laugh again. Mitch and I never stay mad for long. The bond between us is too great. I do hate he has to share in my thoughts about Jada. If I could contain them, I would, but she has turned my whole world upside down.

Mitch helps with the dishes while Dad and I head to the study. He closes the door and sits behind his desk. I begin pacing. I have so many questions, I don't know where to begin.

"Denver, sit down."

"I don't know if I can sit."

"Well try, son. Between the pacing and your racing thoughts, you're giving me a headache. I drove all night, and I'm tired."

I light on the edge of the chair. "I'm sorry, but I'm losing my damn mind." I jerk my head up because I've said a swear word. "I'm sorry. Again."

He laughs. "It doesn't bother me as much as it does your mother. I know you're going through a lot."

"What am I supposed to do, Dad? I mean it's different right, because she's human? I can't tell her what's happening. She has no idea what she does to me. What if she doesn't fall in love with me? What do I do then? Be miserable for the rest of my life?"

I jump out of the chair and begin to pace once more.

"Your mom was right. You're in a bad way."

"What is that supposed to mean?"

"Stop pacing and face me for a second."

"What?"

His finger taps on his chin while sizing me up. "Are you working out more? Eating more?"

I shrug. "Not really. Why?"

"Have you gotten stronger?"

"Um, I don't know, maybe. I mean, now that you mention it, killing those demons was like chasing down a possum."

"Hmm. Could all be related. You appear thicker, bigger in the chest and arms. I'm not sure what it all means."

"Okay, we can cover how sexy I am later. Why am I in a bad way?"

"Poor Mitch."

"What the heck, Dad? Why are you avoiding my questions?"

"I'm not. I didn't mean to say that out loud."

I take a deep breath and attempt to sit down. "What does this have to do with Mitch?"

"He's right, your levels are through the roof. He used the word waves, and I'd say he's completely accurate in his assessment. I've never in all my years known anyone to experience their mate with this intensity. I should have known though, with the crazy bond you have with your brother, that this would be so much stronger. We'll work through your questions the best I can, but I am going to need to do some research."

"Awesome. So I'm some kind of freak?"

"Being in tune with your emotions in no way makes you a freak."

I slump back in the chair. All of a sudden I am completely drained. "I'm really tired. Can we please cover some of the basics?"

"Of course." He moves some papers around on his desk for a clear spot to prop his feet. He steeples his fingers and stares out the bay window. "I spoke with a couple of the elders after our meeting. There's no way to comprehend fully, at least for now, why you've been mated with a human. Your mom suspects there's something under the surface still waiting to get out. More for me to research. Anyway, you are navigating through rare territory. It has happened before in our history, but not often. And there are horrible stories of betrayal and great heartache."

"This isn't the pep talk I was hoping for."

"Let me finish. Your young lady, Jada, should at the least sense a tug between the two of you. She won't understand it because she's not a wolf, and she could essentially blow it off as any other romance. When I mated with your mom, we both knew and were married in weeks. It's extremely hard to fight the attraction. To stay true to our ethics, most marry quickly. You're going to need to win her love and affection. It will be way more difficult on you. You're going to need to be strong and very careful."

"What will I do if I can't win her over? I need her more than the air I breathe."

"Let's not worry on things that haven't happened yet, all right?"

I let out a sigh. "Right."

"So when can I meet this young lady?"

I smile thinking about her beautiful face. "Maybe tonight. I'll see what she's doing later. She's special, Dad. There's something so pure and innocent and loving inside of her. Her heart holds a sadness, but at the same time, so much love. The connection is there, but you're right, she's not sure what it is."

"I look forward to it." He shifts in his seat. "Not to make this weird, but you may have to deal with the fact that Jada hasn't saved herself for marriage. Our standards are quite different from those outside of the pack."

"Actually, we're on the same page where that's concerned."

"Happy to hear it." He removes his feet from the desk and stands to stretch. "I need to get some rest, and so do you."

"Yeah, I'm beat." I walk around the desk and throw my arms around him. "Thank you, Dad. I love you."

He engulfs me in strong arms. "I love you too, son. You can do this, I know you can."

I drag my heavy limbs across the room.

"Hey, Denver."

"Yeah?"

"We need to have a family meeting tonight. The elders have concerns about a shift in the spirit realm."

"How bad?"

"Go get some rest for now. We'll discuss it later."

"Okay."

By the time I get to my room, I'm like the walking dead. I reach out to Mitch in my mind and offer a sincere apology for what I've put him through.

What are brothers for?

I'm going to owe him big time before this is all over. He sends suggestions of how I can make it up to him until I tell him to shut up. Within minutes of crashing across the comforter, I'm asleep.

CHAPTER SIX

JADA

Denver. I've known the boy for two days and he's consuming my thoughts. If that's not weird enough, there's also the fact that it's eleven o'clock and I'm still in bed. But I'm a little sluggish this morning. Mom invited me to go out for breakfast, but I couldn't muster the strength to get up. She felt my head, said I don't have a fever. Maybe I needed some extra rest. I wonder if Denver wants to hang out later. I hope so. I roll my eyes. Every train of thought chugs back to him.

I stare out my window at the clear blue sky, watching robins fly back and forth carrying twigs. It's a beautiful day full of promise. I find it interesting that animals need not worry about their purpose. They know what to do from birth. Maybe we humans make things harder than they have to be. Maybe we too have a purpose from birth, but we're not in touch with our inner selves. Or there's a higher power that knows what we're meant to do, but we don't pay attention. I wish he would speak to me if he's out there. I have no idea what I want to do after high school or whether I have any gifts or callings.

"Gee whiz, Jada. Where did that come from?" Great, now I'm talking to myself.

As I debate whether or not to go get coffee, there's a knock at my door.

"Mom, is that you?"

"No, it's me. Can I come in?" Grainger's familiar voice greets me from the other side of the door.

"Just a sec." I pull the covers over my chest. "Come in."

Grainger pushes open the door and stops in the doorway. "Hey. You okay?"

"Why are you here?"

"Your mom called earlier and said she was going out and you might be coming down with something. She asked me to come check on you."

"Oh. That makes sense. I'm better now, thanks for checking."

"Yeah sure."

I hate that it's awkward between us. "You want a cup of coffee?"

"I'd like that."

"Let me get dressed. I'll meet you in the kitchen."

"Okay."

Grainger shuts the door and his steps trail off down the hall. I jump out of bed, throw on some clothes, and pull my crazy hair in a bun.

The coffee is brewing when I stagger in. Grainger regards me from his seat at the table.

"You want some toast or something?"

"I'm good. I ate earlier."

I grab the bread from the pantry and shuffle to the toaster. "What are you up to today?"

"Nothing. I wondered if you wanted to do something later."

"You're not going out with Candy tonight?"

"We broke up."

I snap my head up and examine his demeanor for sadness or regret. Nothing. "Grainger, I'm sorry."

He shakes his head. "It's all good. She's not the girl for me." His long legs make quick work of the distance between us. "You are."

His proximity makes my heart do funny things. I take a step back. "Grainger…"

The muscle in his jaw clenches and releases. "I know. You're unsure of us now because of this Stone kid."

"His name is Denver."

"I don't really care what his name is. What I care about is the fact that he's trying to swoop in here and steal my girl out from under me."

"I'm not your girl."

He laughs. "That's not what you used to say. We promised each other forever."

"We were twelve."

He steps in and it sucks up the air left between us. "We were thirteen. And I know it's what you wanted up until a couple of days ago. I notice you watching me, Jada."

Oh my God, I can't breathe. This is what I want, isn't it? Why am I doubting it now? Grainger puts his hand under my chin and makes me look at him.

"You are so beautiful." His fingers run along my jaw and go into my hair. My eyes flutter closed. "You remember when we were sitting in the pines and I tried to kiss you?"

I swallow the lump in my throat. "Yes."

"I've been thinking lately how I'd like to get a redo. I'm pretty sure it will be a heckuva lot better now than it was then."

I don't have asthma, but I sure could use an inhaler right now. His hand on the back of my neck is possessive, and he pulls me closer. Our lips brush and I push him back. "Grainger wait."

"What the crap, Jada." Grainger turns his back to me and leans on the counter.

The distance gives me clarity. "I'm sorry. Grainger, I'm so sorry. You know how I want to wait until I'm sure. Please don't be angry."

He spins around to face me. "I'm not angry, I'm hurt. I thought we *were* sure. I thought we were forever, and if I gave you time you'd be ready to admit it." His hand slams on the counter. "I take that back. I am mad. I'm mad at myself for playing games, for pretending to be interested in someone else. And I'm mad as hell at this Denver guy for messing with your head."

"He didn't do anything to me. We've barely hung out."

"Exactly my point. But you want to hang out with him, don't you? I'm telling you, something's not right about all this. The guy gives me the creeps."

"He's a nice guy."

"Whatever. I'm going home. I'll let your mom know you're alive and well if she calls."

I reach for him, but he jerks away. "Grainger, please. I need you in my life."

"But not the way I want." He slams the door on the way out.

My God, could that have gone any worse? Someone may as well have punched me in the gut. My jelly legs force me to the floor. I can't live without Grainger. He's been by my side for as long as I can remember. He'll come around, right? Maybe not. Maybe this time I've pushed too far.

Toast all but forgotten, I nab my cup of coffee and go back to my room to crawl in bed.

Somehow I manage to doze off. When I wake again, it's one in the afternoon. I lay my hand across my forehead. Am I sick? I'm not hot to the touch, but something is definitely off with my body. I grab my phone off the nightstand and have several texts.

Mom: Jada Brooks. Let me know you're okay. I've called several times!

Me: Hey Mom, sorry. I'm fine. I fell back asleep.

Emily: Dang girl, are you awake yet or what? Are we hanging later??

Me: I'm awake now. I'll let you know shortly.

Denver: Hey. I'd really like to see you tonight. Can you come over? My dad's back in town and I want you to meet him.

Me: I would like to see you too. Your dad, huh? Sounds scary. Lol. What about Emily, is she coming over?

Denver responds as if he's been waiting on my text.

Denver: Lol. My dad is cool, promise. Can you do dinner? Say maybe five? I'm not sure on the Emily thing. Mitch didn't say.

Me: I can do dinner. I've been in bed all day. Glad to have a reason to get ready.

Denver: Me too. Been in bed. I'll c u at five.

Me: C ya then

No word from Grainger. He's super pissed, so I'm not surprised. The rift between us makes me hurt. I do love him. Only thing is, I'm not sure what that love looks like anymore. The mere idea of spending time with Denver later fills up my soul with energy and promise. I throw off the covers and sprint to my closet for clothes. What do you wear to meet a guy's dad? Emily. Shoot, I need to text her back.

Me: Have you heard from Mitch?

Emily: No. Why did you call him Mitch?

Me: I guess cause that's what Denver calls him. Denver invited me to dinner.

Emily: Oh. Well, have fun

Me: Em, I'm sorry. He didn't know what Mitchell was doing tonight.

Emily: It's fine. Tara texted earlier. I'll hang with her.

Me: Ok. Sorry

Emily: No biggie

Ugh. Is it possible to piss off everyone you love in a single day? I don't think I've made my mom mad. Yet.

I take a long hot shower and apply my makeup to perfection. Emily would be so proud. I take the time to curl my hair as well. I try on a couple of dresses, but in the end I can't do it. I opt for my dark skinny jeans and a cute tank. I'm wondering what to do with the next hour when my phone rings.

"Hey, Mom."

"Hey, baby. How are you?"

"Much better. Where have you been today?"

"I met up with an old friend. What are your plans for the evening?"

"Denver invited me to dinner."

"He did, huh?"

"With his family. I'm going to his house. He wants me to meet his dad."

"Wow, Jada. This sounds serious. Didn't you just meet this guy?"

"Yes, but it's not like that."

"If you say so. I know my baby girl and she doesn't waste her time on someone that's not worthy of it."

"Mom."

"What? You know it's true. I think you like this guy."

"Well, like you said, we just met."

"Sometimes that's all it takes."

"Are you a romantic all of a sudden?"

"Maybe. Be careful and have a good time. I love you, baby."

"I'm always careful, and I love you too."

"Should I wait up?"

"What? No."

"You might have something to tell me. First kiss possibly?"

"Oh my God, Mom. Stop. I love you and I'll talk to you in the morning."

She's laughing on the other end of the line. "Fine. Bye, Jada."

Has the whole dang world gone topsy turvy? Anyway, I have some time to kill and don't know what to do. If I leave now for Denver's house I'll be half an hour early.

Me: So, I'm ready and would like to get out of this house. Could I maybe come a little early?

Denver: Absolutely

Me: All right then, be there soon

I waste no time grabbing my stuff and getting out the door. I jump in my Jetta and take off toward Denver's house. I said I would never be one of those lovesick girls that spend every waking moment with their boyfriend, but I can envision myself spending all my time with Denver. Good Lord, what is wrong with me? Maybe Grainger is right.

Denver has done something to me. That's absurd, right? You can't make someone fall in love with you. OMG, now I'm throwing around the L word about a guy I met two days ago. What I can't figure out though, if there's something wrong here, why does it feel so right? A revival takes place in my being the closer I get to his house. Like his absence is what had me sick this morning. This is all kinds of screwed up.

By the time I pull in his driveway, I've decided I don't care how messed up it is. My body hums with excitement as I wait at the door. The timbre of his sexy voice greets me before he does.

"It's okay, Mom, I've got it."

He opens the door and stares. I need to say something, but no words will form on my lips.

"Jada, I mean holy sh…"

"Denver Stone!" His mom yells from the hallway.

"You look beautiful. Is what I'm trying to say."

I swallow. "So do you."

His eyebrows go up as he smiles. "I look beautiful?"

"Yes, actually, you do."

Denver is staring at my mouth. "That thing you do when you roll your bottom lip under your teeth is very sexy."

"I wasn't aware I did a thing with my lip. Can I come in?"

He laughs. "Yeah, sorry."

I follow him through the living room and up the stairs. He yells at his mom to let us know when dinner's ready. I sat in his room with him the other night at the party, but the electricity in the air suggests this time is different. My body tingles from head to toe. Denver sits on the edge of the king-size bed. I'm not sure what to do, so I lean against his desk and take the opportunity to consider his room.

The pictures hanging on the walls remind me of his tattoo. I point to a cluster above his bed. "Are those from the Boundary Waters?"

"Yeah. Last year's trip."

"Those are amazing. Did you take them?"

"I did. It's so gorgeous up there, I don't think you can take a bad picture."

"I'd love to go."

"I'd love to take you there."

My heart beats as if I drank ten energy drinks. I walk over and sit by him on the bed. I don't know what makes me so bold, but I push up his sleeve to get another peek at his tattoo. He inhales a sharp breath and shudders. I trace the intricate design. "Have you been here, in this exact spot?"

"Yes."

"Then this is where I want to go."

I explore his shoulder with my fingers, but they grow a mind of their own and trail down to his bicep. His very strong bicep. Denver sits so still I wonder if he's breathing. His eyes close, so I take the opportunity to study his handsome face. His chiseled jaw is working overtime. His long eyelashes are to die for. His blond hair hangs down near one eye and I want to push it out of the way. I start to touch his face when his eyes flash open. We're so close I breathe in his minty-fresh toothpaste. My hand freezes an inch from his hair. His eyes glow, reminding me of a fluorescent jellyfish I saw at the aquarium last summer. He stares at my mouth and I realize I'm biting my lip. I let my fingers finish the task at hand and push aside his hair. A sound comes from inside of Denver that surprises me and I flinch.

"Did you…growl?"

His breathing is erratic. "This is harder than I thought."

"What is harder…"

The door to his room swings open and Mitchell appears. "Hey guys, it's time for dinner."

Denver seems relieved by the interruption. I'm perturbed. He stands up and holds out his hand. "Come on, let's go downstairs."

"Sure."

On the way to the kitchen I realize the universe is sure enough in disarray. What in the heck has come over me? I pushed Grainger away, but I can't stop touching Denver? How far would I have gone if not interrupted? My mom may have been right. I wanted to kiss him. I wanted him to kiss me. The thought alone makes me lightheaded.

His mother has outdone herself with the meal. The table is set to perfection with cloth napkins and all the fine touches. Candles are lit in the middle of a magnolia flower centerpiece. The massive roast with all its garnishes is like something off of a cooking show. And there must be five different sides on the table to go with it. Denver pulls out my chair. He sits next to me and grabs my hand under the table. Mitch sits across from us and his mom is on one end.

"Your dad is coming. He got held up on a conference call. How are you today, Jada?"

"I'm fine, thanks. And thank you for having me over for dinner. The table is lovely."

"You are welcome anytime, Jada. I don't know if Denver told you, but after Sunday dinner we try to have game night."

I glance at Denver. "He failed to mention that, but I love to play games. My mom says I get too competitive."

"You'll fit in perfectly. These boys of mine don't know when to call it quits."

"I'm sorry to hold up dinner." Denver's dad goes straight to Aurar and kisses her cheek. "The table is stunning as always."

Denver clears his throat. "Dad, this is Jada."

He takes my hand, kissing it ever so gently. "It is a great pleasure to meet you, Jada."

"It's nice to meet you too…I'm sorry, I don't know your name."

"It's Bolivar, sweet princess."

"Bolivar, it's nice to meet you."

His smile makes me blush. Not in a weird way, but it's like he sees something in me I don't see in myself. And he called me princess.

Bolivar takes his place at the head of the table. "Jada, it's tradition that we hold hands and pray."

I nod my head. "Of course."

We take each other's hands and he says a prayer over his family and for the food. He even mentions me. The warmth of this family, their kinship and their love is a new experience for me. My mom and I are close and I love her dearly. It's my long-lost father and the lack of his support and affection that causes me insecurity and pain.

When the prayer is over, it's every man for himself. Denver and Mitch put away more food than I thought humanly possible. There's so much laughter. I can't get over how close they are. After dinner is cleared from the table, the games commence. They teach me a couple of new card games, one of which I win, and a new board game. I don't remember the last time I had this much fun. They are so in tune with each other, I swear they can communicate without words. I glimpse a side of Denver that makes me like him even more. He loves his brother. Not the "I love you man" kind of stuff, but the "I would lay down my life for you" stuff. By the time we're done playing, my jaw hurts from smiling and laughing.

At nine o'clock, Denver offers to walk me out to my car. I was hoping to spend some alone time with him, but he ushers me out the door.

He hesitates on the porch, grabs my hand, and pulls me to a swing.

"I thought you were trying to get rid of me."

He lets out a short breath. "Never. I wish you never had to leave."

My tongue is tied up by his confession.

"I shouldn't have said that."

"No, it's okay. Denver, what is happening, because I don't get it. I've known you for three days."

He stares out over the rail into the night. The clear sky showing off the brilliance of the stars. "I can't tell you anything that would make sense."

"But you know something, don't you?"

His glowing eyes hold mine. "Yes."

"Will you tell me, eventually?"

"Yes."

I don't know why that last answer makes him nervous. I take his hand in mine. "It's going to be okay."

"I hope so. I need you like I need air. That's probably more than you wanted to know, but it's the truth."

"Yesterday when I said I'd never been kissed, that was true, with the exception of the time Grainger kissed me when we were thirteen.

It was terrible, by the way. Grainger tried to kiss me this morning. We've been best friends our whole lives, and we thought we would be together. The crazy thing is, I pushed him away. All this time, I thought I was waiting on him to kiss me, but it was you. I was waiting on you."

I'm over here spilling my guts, and Denver is scowling like he wants to punch something. I take his face in my hands to get his full attention. "Hey. Did you hear me?"

"Why was he trying to kiss you?"

"Are you…jealous? God, were you not listening to me? I want you to kiss me, Denver. You."

His face softens and he suddenly realizes our proximity and swallows. "Jada, I don't know if I can."

"Why not?" I inch closer, gauging his response. He doesn't move away, but his whole body begins to tremble. His eyes are so intense and full of passion my core heats like lava come to life. Waves of emotion roll off him and it's more than I can bear. I let go of his face and slump back. My face heats from the rawness of the exposure of who he is and how bad he wants me.

"Denver, oh my God. What was that, and how can you care for me that deeply?"

He springs off the bench. "I'm sorry. I try to keep it reined in, but when you get that close, it's so hard."

The door opens and Bolivar walks out on the porch. "Denver, why don't you go cool off and let me see Jada off tonight."

"Probably a good idea. Goodnight, Jada."

"Goodnight."

Bolivar extends his hand. "Will you allow me, princess?"

I give him my hand, and he leads me to my car.

"I am unable to answer all your questions at this time. Please understand that our family is different. When we love, it's fierce, and it's raw, and it's real, and it's forever. Your presence alone is a dragon to slay for my Denver. Your touch is almost unbearable. A kiss. Well, it's hard to come back from that one."

"Are you saying your son is in love with me?"

"Yes, my dear, that's what I'm saying. I'm saying he would offer up his life for you at this very moment if it were necessary."

"Why me?"

"He'll have to answer that one."

"My head is spinning."

"I know, princess."

He opens my car door to let me in. I pause, not sure if I should ask the question that's been bothering me all day. "Bolivar?"

"Yes, dear."

"I felt bad this morning. Tired, weak, kinda yuck. Was that because of Denver?"

"I'm afraid so. You two need each other now. It only gets harder from here."

"What am I going to do? I still have to go to school. Will I be sick all the time?"

"Don't worry. We'll figure something out."

"Okay."

"Goodnight, princess. Go home and get some rest."

"Goodnight."

I drive home in a deep fog. I'm not sure what's real anymore, because tonight felt anything but. The idea of going to school tomorrow holds no appeal, but I know I have to. I drag out my stuff for school and crawl into bed. Tomorrow is going to be a long day.

CHAPTER SEVEN

DENVER

I pace the yard while Dad speaks to Jada by her car. I want so badly to tell her goodnight one last time, but it's best if I stay away. She has no idea how close I came earlier to going all wolf on her. She was sitting so close, her hands on my face. Her luscious lips were right there. The lingering thought of it, mixed with the smell of her on my skin, has me shaking. But the mental picture of this Grainger guy laying even a finger on her almost pushed me over the edge. I wanted to rip him apart.

"Calm down, boy. You're gonna go all dog."

I kick a clump of grass left by the mower. "Thanks, bro for saving me earlier in the bedroom."

Mitch punches my arm. "No problem. Maybe you should consider your bedroom off limits. The girl can't keep her hands off you, and you're not doing much better yourself. You owe Dad one too for saving your ugly butt."

"You're probably right about the bedroom. Anyway, what did he tell her? I was so consumed with trying not to wolf out, I couldn't concentrate on what Dad was saying."

"He pretty much said we're a weird family, and that you're in love with her and it's all downhill from here."

"Mitchell Dean, that is not what I said."

"Why does everyone use my middle name, but never yours?"

"I'm the good son."

"Let's go inside, boys. We need to have a family meeting before your patrol tonight."

"Yes sir," Mitch and I say in unison.

We meet in the study. Dad's pinched face has me worried. Mitch and I sit in our usual spot on the couch. Mom always pulls up a chair beside Dad. No one speaks, and the silence is driving me crazy.

"What is it, Dad?"

"We have multiple situations to deal with, son. First things first, let's talk about you and Jada." He rubs the stubble on his chin. "Even in her human state, the progression in your mating process is accelerated. It's something I have only read about. After being with you for two days, she was ill this morning."

"What? What does that mean? I make her sick?"

He shakes his head. "No, Denver, that's not it. In your absence she gets weak. It will only get worse. We'll have to work out some sort of schedule. She will need to spend time with you every day in order to function properly. To get her through the school day, you will need to pick her up in the morning and then take her home after. The more time in the evening together, the better."

"Why have I never heard of this?"

"It's more common in wolves that try to wait more than a few months before getting married. Your circumstances are very rare. We will start with this schedule for now and evaluate in a week."

"Yes, sir."

My dad lets out a sigh. "There's more going on here I don't understand, but we don't have the time to hash it all out tonight. That Jada is special. Her scent befuddles me. It's strange yet somehow familiar. She's smart and perceptive. She experienced you, all of you, and didn't run. And why are you getting stronger? Why are your emotions heightened? You two are an anomaly. I wish I had more time to figure it out, but we have other concerns."

Dad shuffles around some papers on his desk. Mitch and I lean in get a better look. Mom bites her nails. When my dad finds what he's searching for, he points at a map.

"This area right here. It's a field near town. The elders believe the demonic activity is beginning to shift drastically. They suspect a greater demon will be paying us a visit. Before that happens, there could be an increase in the lesser demon release. We will be working harder than ever."

Mitch and I exchange a glance. Neither of us have seen a greater demon. "Why on earth would a greater demon come here?" I voice what Mitch and I are thinking.

"Why indeed. The elders and leaders don't always know why things happen, but we can be prepared, and we can vow to protect our loved ones and community. You boys will be on tonight and Wednesday night, and I may have to add another. Know where your team members are at all times, and have each other's back."

"Yes, sir."

"Denver, this could be taxing for you with your new development. Be careful, son."

"I will, Dad, promise. I'm ready to go kick some demon butt."

"Mitch, you keep your brother's head on straight out there. I'm counting on my boys, as the next in line, to lead our pack."

Mitch flops back on the couch. "Geez, Dad, give me the most difficult task of all. Ain't nobody gonna be able to keep his head straight right now."

I thump Mitch in the ear. "Shut up, pup."

"I'll show you 'pup.'"

Dad abruptly stands and shouts, "Boys, this is serious! Your lives and the lives of others are in danger. Never forget that we are in a battle. It's been easy up until now, but I'm telling you, things are shifting and we have to be aware."

Dad never yells. Never. The severity of the situation settles on me like a boulder. And now I have Jada to protect. "We're sorry. We accept our assignment and will fight to the finish to uphold the Stone name."

He comes around to the front of his desk. "I'm sorry too, I have a lot on my plate. I know I can count on you both."

I rise up and we are toe to toe. This giant of a man that I admire is counting on me. I will do everything possible to make him proud. He's heard my thoughts and grips my shoulder in approval.

"Let's go, Mitch. We better head to the warehouse to meet up with the others."

"You got it."

We grab our duffle bags and walk out to the garage.

Mitch stops by the keys hanging on the wall. "What you want to drive tonight?"

"I don't care, you pick."

"Sweet. I'm thinking grandpa's truck."

"Works for me."

The ride to the warehouse takes about thirty minutes. All my thoughts have been consumed with Jada lately and I hate it for Mitch.

"It's fine. I just like to give you a hard time."

"Would you stop."

"I can't. I swear our bond gets stronger every day."

"I was thinking the same thing. So much crazy shit happening."

Mitch agrees with a nod. We're both quiet for a while, lost in our own heads for a change.

I tap my fingers on the steering wheel. My thoughts spin like a tornado, swirling around so I can't pick out one thought long enough to give it serious consideration. The longer I try to stop the spinning, the worse my head hurts. It's best not to try to solve all the world's problems tonight.

"So, what about you and Emily?"

I see Mitch shrug out of the corner of my eye. "I don't know, man. It kinda sucks because I actually like her, but if she's not my mate…."

"Yeah that does suck. That's why I avoided relationships. It's easier that way. No nasty break-ups if you don't date."

Mitch grunts. "It's so stupid. I like her and I'm drawn to her, but I shouldn't date her because I might wake up some day and find my true mate. And if she doesn't happen to be the one, then I hurt her. Why don't we get to choose?"

"I don't know, brother. It's the wolf way. All I know is, I couldn't have chosen any better if I tried. I love Jada in every way. She's perfect for me."

"That she is." Mitch is quiet for a moment. "Should I end whatever is going on between Emily and me?"

"Follow your heart and do what you think is right for you. Just be careful. You don't want to go too far."

"Yeah, I know. We haven't kissed or anything, but I for sure think about it."

I chuckle. "Dude, you don't have to tell me what I already know."

"Shut up."

"It's not as fun being on the other end, is it?"

"Okay, okay, I get it."

"We're almost there. Probably need to get our thoughts on more pressing matters, like killing some demons."

"Now you're talking. What do you make of all this greater demon stuff?"

"Blows my mind. Why would a greater demon bother with our little redneck town? Seems like there would be bigger assignments than our wolf community and the town we protect."

"Agree. Makes no sense."

"I trust Dad, though. If he says something is coming, then something is coming."

"Agree again. Are you scared?"

I let out a breath. "Not for myself so much as I am for my family. Which includes Jada now. If something happened to her, I don't think I could handle it."

"At least if we die, you will have had the chance to find her."

"Shit, Mitch, don't talk like that. We're gonna get through this. I've got your back."

"Same, brother, same."

I pull into the parking lot and kill the lights. It's eerily quiet here tonight. I grab our duffle and we walk to the entrance. Mitch has his key out, so he unlocks the door.

"Looks like we're the first ones here. I'll get the lights, you grab the maps."

"On it."

Mitch and I have the maps laid out and ready to give instructions by the time everyone else arrives. After Mitch, Rieder is my best friend. He walks in with his brother Layne.

I slap Rieder on the back. "What's up, yo."

"Not much, man. Question is, how are you?"

I'm the oldest in this particular pack and the only one to have found a mate. Good news is, I won't be the only one for long. Most wolves mate between eighteen and twenty-one. This ragtag crew are all close to eighteen. Our youngest being fifteen—a girl, Kalika, but a heck of fighter.

"Never better. It's a piece of cake."

Mitch slides in beside me. "He's full of shit. Poor dog is falling apart."

Rieder laughs while punching me in the arm. "I knew it. You're such a softy."

I growl. "Better watch it, Rie-man. I can still take you down."

He rolls his eyes. "Whatever. Why don't you give our assignments for the night?"

Everyone gathers around the table, and I give out orders for each pair of wolves. I stress the importance of being extra careful and calling out to the others if you need backup. Once we have our sections memorized, we head out of the warehouse with our patrol partner. Mine is always Mitch.

Before Rieder and Layne go their separate way, Rieder calls out to me. "Hey Denver, can we call you Whipped Puppy?"

"Only if you have a death wish."

I hear him laughing right before he changes to his wolf form.

"You ready, brother?"

"Always."

Mitch and I both transform and take off in the direction of our beat. We slip through the streets and alleyways of town. We know the places safe to patrol in the open, and where you need to hide in the shadows. We know where every wolf family lives in town in case we need immediate shelter or cover. We know every hotspot for demons. Those are the places we check first. Then we stroll neighborhoods and even outlying properties. So far it's been quiet, and I'm thankful for that.

We circle through town twice and then stop in an alley to check in with the others. Everyone says the same thing. It's still. I should be happy about that, but this foreboding deep in my gut tells me something's not right. It's two in the morning on a Sunday night. What can go wrong? Mitch and I make another sweep and then decide to meet Rieder and Layne in the middle of town.

I reach out to Rieder. *Hey, Rieder, you hearing me?*

Loud and clear, what's up?

I'm getting a weird vibe. Meet us on Chestnut Street behind the burger joint.

Be there in ten.

The four of us meet in the dark parking lot for employees of Hagerdy's, a local burger and soda shop. I pace for a minute, trying to figure out the source of my unease. There's a tingling in my chest and my hackles rise for no apparent reason. A foul odor drifts in on a breeze from our left. It's all I can do to warn the others before a swarm of something comes ripping out of a tear in the sky above us.

Mitch and I immediately back up to one another and begin to circle. *What in the hell are those things, Denver?*

I have no idea. They look like locusts.

Yeah, if locusts were the size of buzzards and had fangs and a stinger.

They circle over our heads. Rieder and Layne stay close.

Rieder growls. *What are they waiting for?*

Not sure. Sizing us up? I know that's what I'm doing.

What's the plan, brother? Mitch says as we continue to watch the sky.

Stay together. Try hitting them with your paws. Let's see if we can get them on the ground. Once it's down, pounce and go for the throat. Don't get near that damn twelve-inch stinger.

The swarm descends. There must be at least a dozen of the hideous things. The closer they get, the more foul the air becomes, and the uglier they appear. Their red eyes bulge from a bumpy, green face. One finally swoops close enough for me to get my paw on, but I swing and miss.

A second locust demon dives down. This time I don't miss, but the creature recovers before hitting the ground. The wingspan is greater than I thought, and the edges slice like knives grazing my skin.

Shit! Watch the wings, they're razor sharp.

A trickle of blood runs down my side. Now they've done it. I'm pissed.

I don't like the cramped quarters of this alley. Come on, Denver— think. The park.

Hey guys we're going to take this party to the park. On my word, we'll dart around the corner and take every turn possible to slow them down. Use the park equipment as protection for yourselves. Rieder, call out to the others and have them meet us there. You guys ready?

Let's do this. Mitch voices his agreement.

Go! I yell before taking off at a full sprint.

I lead the guys toward the park, taking every side street, alley, and back road there is. The locust demons follow, like I knew they would. The winding path gives us the edge that we need to stay one step ahead. When we reach the park, I sprint to the back side of the bathrooms so that they have to circle around, facing us. One flies down at me, screeching and hissing, and this time I swing with all my might. The demon hits the ground and I'm already in the air planning the kill. I land on the creature, one paw on its body and one on its head. Sharp wings cut into my paw, but it doesn't stop me from closing my massive jaws around its neck. The demon lets out a high-pitched scream, releases its last breath, and deflates beneath me.

One down! The throat is definitely the sweet spot.

Make that two, Rieder reports.

Our backup runs up, growling, ready to jump in.

We have more help. Spread out, but don't leave your backside exposed. Mitch, stay with me.

Mitch and I once again back up to one another so we're protected. A locust demon swoops by, swinging its barb in our direction. The darn thing is dangerous as the tail of a stingray. It darts down again, this time near Mitch, and he swats it down to the ground. Mitch has the thing by the throat before it knows what happened. We battle down two more before I'm able to assess the situation.

I take in the scene around us. There's been a few yelps, but nothing that sounded serious. Every wolf is accounted for with only two locust demons left. They circle for a moment, then fly back up into the sky and disappear. Hopefully back to the pit where they came from.

Everybody good?

Layne got the worst of it. Most of us have a few scrapes from the wings, but Layne got a swipe from a locust's barb. He's bleeding pretty badly. Our shift is over, so I disband the group, and Mitch and I run back to the warehouse. We quickly throw on some clothes and pick up Rieder and Layne at the park. I throw Rieder some shorts, and he puts them on as we load Layne in the backseat of the pickup. I lay a blanket over Layne and jump in the driver's seat.

My scrapes prickle like a sleeping limb as they heal. Layne groans. His wounds are much deeper.

"Is he doing okay back there?"

Rieder examines his brother. "He's gonna be fine. That barb in the side might as well have been a knife. The bleeding has almost stopped."

"Good to hear. Make sure your dad checks him out."

"Sure will."

No one speaks the rest of the way. Mitch closes his eyes and lays his head against the headrest. We let Rieder and Layne out at their house. Layne is limping but walking on his own. As soon as they're inside, I speed off toward home.

I pull in the garage and kill the engine. "I'm exhausted. I'm gonna take a nap before I have to pick Jada up for school. I'll clean up the truck later."

"Sounds good. I'm gonna take a hot shower and drink about four cups of coffee."

"Save me a cup for when I wake up."

Mitch and I part ways in the hall. "Can't make that promise, brother."

"Fine, I'll make my own."

After setting my alarm, I drop on my bed and fall asleep within seconds.

CHAPTER EIGHT

JADA

Monday mornings are the worst. I hit my snooze three times and have waited until the last possible minute to get ready for school. I take the quickest shower in history and throw my wet hair up in a messy ponytail. Mom yells from the kitchen to come get breakfast. Problem is, I'm weak and nauseous this morning. Bolivar said he would work something out, but I don't know what he's planning. Mom calls for me again.

"I'll be right there," I say in my annoyed teenager voice as I grab my things from the desk.

"There's a boy at the door for you. A very nice-looking boy."

I rush down the hall. When I reach the living room, Mom is holding the door open talking to Denver.

"Sweetheart, you didn't tell me Denver was stopping by."

"Uh, I didn't know he was."

Mom steps aside to let Denver in. He glances to my mother and then to me. "Sorry about that. I thought maybe I could give you a ride to school?"

"Yeah sure. Let me grab some coffee."

We all three go into the kitchen. Denver leans against the bar while he waits.

"So, Denver, do you go to school?" Mom says.

"Yes ma'am. I'm a sophomore in college. Business major."

"Why aren't you at school?"

"All my classes are online. I wanted to stay home and help Dad with the family business."

"That's nice of you. What kind of business does your dad run?"

"Mom, give the guy a break. It's not even eight o'clock in the morning."

Denver smiles. "It's fine, Jada. My dad is a diverse businessman. He has his hand in several pots, but his main focus is security. He wants me to take over someday, so that's why I'm a business major."

Mom starts in again, but I cut her off.

"We should get going."

She appears a tad put off but recovers. "Did you get a muffin? I made those especially for you. Denver, you're welcome to one as well."

"I would love a muffin, thank you."

I grab one for each of us and rush toward the door.

"Bye, Mom, love you."

"Have a good day, sweetie. Love you too."

As soon as we're on the other side of the door, I start apologizing. "Oh my gosh, I'm so sorry. I don't know what that was about."

He pauses at the bottom of the porch steps. "It's fine, I promise. I like your mom. She's feisty like you."

"What? I'm not feisty."

His eyebrows rise. "Yes you are. You're almost as feisty as you are beautiful. And that's saying a lot."

I roll my eyes. "Now I know you're lying. I barely had time to shower this morning, much less worry about anything else."

"You're beautiful to me."

My face heats at his words. I shove a muffin toward him and start down the driveway. "Here's your muffin."

Denver laughs behind me. "Thanks."

For the first time I notice the vehicle he's in. "Really, Denver? A Porsche?"

"What's wrong with my Porsche?"

I adjust the backpack on my shoulder. "I'm way more inconspicuous in my Jetta. This car screams *look at me.*"

"Are you embarrassed to be seen with me?"

"What? No! I'm not used to being noticed, that's all."

"Jada, you're no wallflower. You have strength and confidence in you, I can sense it."

"I definitely feel stronger when I'm with you. Healthier too. I should have grabbed two muffins."

Denver opens my car door to let me in. "Here, eat mine. I can eat breakfast when I get home."

"Thank you."

I scarf down both muffins in record time. Denver looks over at me and smiles. I'm a little embarrassed in retrospect, but what're ya gonna do?

"I don't know why I ate those so fast. Earlier, I didn't want to think about food. Is that why you picked me up this morning?"

His hand reaches across the seat and covers mine. A warmth and vigor rushes through my veins. "Yes. Dad thought it would be good for both of us if I took you to school and picked you up after. Is that okay? If it's too much, tell me."

"I'd love that." I gaze out the window for a moment. There's so many things I want to say, so many questions, but I don't know where to begin.

"Jada, I know you have questions. I promise we'll get there, okay?"

"Okay."

"So, what are you doing after school? You want to hang out?"

"That would be great."

He pulls in the lot and parks.

Denver nods in the direction of the school. "You ready for this?"

"Not really."

"Just think, in a couple of months, you'll be rid of this place."

I let out a sigh. "It's hard to believe I'm getting ready to graduate. I have no idea what I want to do."

"Did you apply to colleges?"

"Yeah. I've been accepted to several, but I kinda want to stay close to home. Maybe do community college."

"That's not a bad choice. Especially the staying close to home part."

I smile and bite the corner of my lip. "Well, I better get going."

"Hang on, let me get your door."

I try to tell him that isn't necessary, but he's already out and on his way. He opens the door and helps me to my feet. "Thank you."

We stand there staring at each other, not knowing what to do. Denver steps aside and lets me pass. "Have a good day, Jada."

"You too. See you after school."

He winks and then goes back to the driver's side of the car.

Halfway to the building, I turn around. Denver runs his hand through his hair. I swear there's a rope between us being pulled taut as I walk away from him. This is going to be a long day.

I barely make it inside the building before I'm accosted by Grainger.

"Denver driving you to school now?"

I'm so not in the mood. "Yes, Grainger, he is."

"What the hell is up with that?"

A teacher passes us in the hall. "Language, Mr. Nelson."

"Sorry, Mr. Cox."

I stop at my locker to get what I need for my first few classes. I'm hoping if I ignore Grainger he'll go away.

"I don't get you at all, Jada. This is not like you."

"I don't have to explain myself to you." Grainger flinches as if I've slapped him. "I'm sorry. I can't explain it to myself, much less to anyone else. We're hanging out."

"Every single day?"

A sigh escapes my lips. "Grainger, please, I don't want to do this right now."

"Whatever. For the life of me I can't figure out why you're throwing away what we have."

"I'm not. You're the one who's doing that. You're still my best friend." I don't give him time to respond. I slam my locker door and stomp off down the hall.

It's lunch time before I run into Emily.

"Oh my gosh, Jada! You're the top of the gossip chain this morning."

I roll my eyes. "Why?"

"Why? Why, she says. Because you got dropped off by a hottie in a Porsche, why else?"

I can't help but chuckle. "I told him the Porsche was too much."

"Give me the scoop. Are you and Denver dating already?"

"No, he wanted to give me a ride. It's not that big of a deal."

Emily huffs and slaps her leg. "You're kidding me, right?"

"What? A boy brought me to school. Why's everyone freaking out?"

"Wait. Who else is freaking out?"

"Never mind."

Thankfully, the cafeteria lady asks me for money. Once we've paid we take our trays to our normal spot. I attempt to eat my lunch in peace, but Emily is having none of that.

"Jada, who else is freaking out?"

"Grainger."

"I knew it. What did he say?"

I push the food around on my tray. "He broke up with Candy."

"I know. That's going around too. What did he say to you about Denver?"

"He thinks I'm crazy. Or that Denver is drugging me. Or both. He tried to kiss me Saturday."

Emily chokes on her drink. "Grainger or Denver?"

"Grainger."

"No shit?"

"I'm so not kidding. I pushed him away and he got mad. Then he saw Denver dropping me off this morning and got mad again."

"Oh wow. This is primetime stuff. What are you going to do?"

"I wish I could tell you. I can't lose Grainger. But then…"

"But then, Denver shows up and steals your heart. And don't try to deny it. I know you, Jada."

I shove my tray away. "How is that even possible? I barely know him."

"I have no friggin' idea, but the boy has done what no male has ever been able to do before. I never thought there'd be a day you weren't head over heels in love with Grainger Nelson."

"That makes two of us."

"Who's in love with Grainger?"

I jump at the sound of Mitchell's voice. "Hey Mitch...er uh, Mitchell. Sorry."

"It's fine. Denver's the only one that calls me that, but I can make an exception for you. You girls mind if I sit for a second?"

Emily practically swoons, her finger finding purchase in her gold curls. "Sure, go ahead. What's up?"

Mitchell peers at me and then his gaze is back to Emily. "You didn't answer my question. Who's in love with Grainger?" His scrutiny settles on me, and it's unnerving.

Emily laughs. "You only caught the tail end of the conversation. No one is in love with Grainger. Anymore."

He's staring directly at me now. "But you were in love with him?"

Well, this isn't awkward at all. "I guess I thought I was. Or at least the idea of us. It's complicated because we've been best friends since we were like five."

"Right. You know, I really don't want my brother to get hurt."

"I don't want that either."

"Good." His mood shifts from serious to smiling in 0.6 seconds. Emily gets his undivided attention. "I wanted to know if we could talk later, maybe get some dinner?"

Her smile is plumb goofy. "Of course. What time?"

"I'll pick you up at six."

"Sounds perfect."

Mitch studies me and his eyes crinkle in confusion. "That is the weirdest thing."

My shoulders tighten. "I'm sorry, what is weird?"

He shakes his head as if to clear it. "Nothing." The chair scrapes as he pushes from the table. "Catch you later, Jada. See you tonight, beautiful." He takes her hand and kisses the back of it like they do in the movies. Makes me think of his father. Are these guys real?

We act like everything is normal until Mitch is out of sight. I grab Emily's hands and we're both squealing the second he's gone.

"Oh my gosh! I think he's finally going to ask you to be his girlfriend."

"I know! Oh my God, what do I wear?"

"You *would* think of that. Come on, the bell's getting ready to ring, and I need to swing by my locker before English."

Emily starts clapping and jumping up and down while I'm getting out my English book. "Oh my God!"

"What?"

"We can go on double dates and hang out together. I'll be with Mitchell and you'll be with Denver. How awesome is that?"

"That sounds terrible."

She slaps my arm. "Hey!"

"I'm kidding. It sounds wonderful. But for now, we have to go to class."

She lets out a huff. "Fine. But don't think I'm going to be able to concentrate on anything besides my date with Mitchell."

I pull her down the hall. I hate being late to class. "I knew that was coming. You can borrow my notes."

"Thanks."

I THANK the stars above when the last bell of the day rings. I cannot wait to get out of here. Way too much staring and whispering as I walk down the hall. Plus, there's the fact that I want to feast my eyes on Denver. Thinking of him throughout the day has created a longing inside of me for his presence. Somehow I know he's outside waiting for me. Not because he said he would be, but because there's an inkling in my bones.

As soon as I walk out of the building I spot him leaning against the front of his car waiting for me. I swear he gets more gorgeous every day. He's wearing blue jeans and a black T-shirt, which doesn't usually turn heads, but on Denver...I mean good Lord. His chest fills out every inch of fabric in his shirt. His muscular arms are flexed as he leans on them for support and his thighs push the denim to the limit. He's wearing sunglasses, so his eyes are hidden, but I know he's watching me. A small smile plays on his lips.

He stands up as I approach. I don't know why, but I *need* to be near him. It's like I require his physical touch to live. I drop my book bag on the ground and walk right into his arms.

I lay my head against his chest. His shirt is warm from the afternoon sun. "I'm sorry. I know this is hard for you, but I felt like I needed this. Needed you."

"Don't ever be sorry for that again. You hear me?"

"Yes." After a few seconds I pull back. "Are you drugging me?"

His laugh resonates in my soul. "No, silly. I put a spell on you."

I tap the end of his nose. "I knew it was something."

"Come on, let's get out of here." Denver grabs my bag and opens my door.

"Sounds great."

We leave the lot and it hits me I have no idea what we're doing. "What's the plan?"

He shrugs. "Don't have one. Is there anything you need to take care of? Go by your house, homework, anything?"

"Not really. I have some homework, but I can do it when I get home tonight."

"Okay. What would you like to do?"

I play with the hair tie on my wrist. "Honestly? I'd like to go on another motorcycle ride."

"Damn, girl. I think I just fell in love with you."

I gaze out the window for a moment and then return my focus to Denver's handsome profile. His jaw clenches once and releases. "According to your dad, you already have."

He groans. "He's not lying."

"How does that happen exactly? You know, so quickly."

"I don't think either of us are ready to have that conversation."

"How do you know I'm not ready?"

Denver lets out a huff. "Well, then let's say I'm not ready."

"But we will have it?"

He takes my hand and pulls it to his lips, grazing my knuckles with kisses. "Oh, we'll have it. I can promise you that."

I close my eyes and revel in the sweetness of his lips on my skin. I could get used to this. Denver laces his fingers in mine and then places our hands on my leg. We ride in silence for a while, and I'm content to stare out the window at this beautiful spring day. From time to time, he squeezes my hand or runs his fingers over my skin, causing ripples of energy to pulse through me.

"Can I say something weird?"

He chuckles. "I'm pretty good with weird, let me have it."

"Being near you is like drinking an energy drink over and over. That's crazy, right?"

"So not crazy. Being near you is more like an energy drink on steroids for me."

"Does it wear off?"

"Oh my gosh, no. My parents for example, they still act crazy in love after thirty years. It's kinda disgusting to Mitch and me, but it's what we've grown up around, so you get used to it."

I sigh. "I wouldn't know anything about that. My dad's been gone for over thirteen years."

"Jada, I'm so sorry. I didn't know."

"It's okay. You couldn't have known. Anyway, it was hard at first, but I've come to accept it."

"Do you ever see him?"

"No. He came around for a while but slowly pulled away until I didn't hear from him at all. I have no idea where he is."

"That sucks. I could maybe help you find him if you're interested. My dad knows a lot of people."

Do I want to find him? The man who left his wife and daughter for no apparent reason? "I'm not sure I care to locate him after the way he took off. Let me think about it."

"Sure."

"In case you're wondering about Grainger, I'd like to clear the air."

"Okay, I'm curious, to say the least."

"Talking about my dad brings back a lot of memories. Good and bad. Grainger and I grew up together. He lives next door, has my whole life. Anyway, we've played together since we've been old enough to have play dates. He's been by my side through everything with my dad and so much more. We made a lot of promises as kids. Promises I think he's ready to cash in on."

"And what about you? What do you want?"

"Up until a few days ago, I thought I knew."

"And now?"

I search Denver's face and study his handsome features. And he's got plenty. But more than that I sense kindness, purity, inner strength, integrity, intelligence, and a crazy, fierce love that I can't explain. I don't know him well enough to know those things, but again, the awareness of it resonates in the depth of who I am.

I bite my lip. "Now, I think I want you."

"You think?"

"The jury's still out."

"Hmm. How do I influence this jury? I've got money. I'll pay them off if I have to."

"Haven't you heard the saying money can't buy you love?"

"Yes. Yes, I have." He pulls into the garage and kills the engine. "I guess I'll have to win this one the old-fashioned way."

"Oh yeah, and what's that?"

He winks and opens his door. "With my good looks and charm of course."

Lord knows he has both of those down pat. We walk inside and stop in the kitchen. Aurar is sitting at the island.

"Hey you two. How was school, Jada?"

"It was high school. Apparently I was the talk of the hall because a hottie dropped me off in a Porsche."

His mom laughs and it's the sweetest sound. It's light and feminine and perfect, like her. "He is a hottie."

I shrug my shoulders. "I suppose."

"Uh-oh, Denver. You've got your work cut out for you."

He gives me a smile. "You have no idea."

I playfully punch his arm. "Hey."

"Kidding, babe, kidding. Did you want a snack before we go on a ride?"

"Um, sure." I am freaking losing it. Him calling me babe has sent my internal temperature on the rise. I'm sure my face is red.

Denver either doesn't notice or he chooses not to embarrass me, and I'm grateful. "Sit at the bar and I'll fix us something. What time's dinner, Mom?"

"Same as always. Six thirty."

Denver grabs two Cokes and some chips and salsa. Man after my heart for sure. "That gives us plenty of time to take out the bike."

Aurar sits up straight. "You're taking her out on that death trap? You know how much I hate that thing."

"She asked to go. I'm merely carrying out her wishes."

I roll my eyes. "I did ask him to take me, Mrs. Stone."

"Call me Aurar, please." She turns to Denver. "You better be careful with her, Denver."

"I will, Mom. Promise."

After our snack, I follow Denver back to the garage. He rubs the thin material of my T-shirt between his fingers and then walks to a coat rack. He grabs two leather jackets and hands one to me.

"I know it's nice out, but it'll be cool on the bike. You wanna put this on."

"All right. Whose is it, Mitchell's?"

"No, it's my mom's."

"Your mom's? I thought she didn't like motorcycles?"

"Yeah, right. She loves motorcycles. She and my dad ride all the time. What she doesn't like is *me* on motorcycles."

"Gotcha." I zip up the jacket and take the helmet Denver hands me. "Will you help me with this?"

"Yep, but you gotta come a little closer." I take a step in. "Closer." I take another step. "Closer." He's grinning now. I take the last tiny bit of space left between us. Our toes are touching.

"Is this close enough?" I say in a whisper. A couple more inches and our lips would be touching. I put my hand on his firm chest. His heart pounds under my palm.

"I forgot how excruciatingly painful it is for you to be this close."

I don't back away. "You're the one who kept saying to come closer." I consider his full lips. "I forgot how your lips sing to me. Is that part of the spell?"

Denver takes two steps back and swears. "I'm sorry, Jada. I want to be near you, and Lord knows how bad I want to kiss you, but I can't go there yet."

"I can wait, Denver. It's okay."

He pushes out a long breath. "Thank you."

The helmet is still in my hand. "So, can you help me with this or not?" I start to hand it to him but then let it drop by my side. "Maybe we could ride without helmets?"

"My mom would kill me."

I use his weakness to my advantage and step forward. "Please, Denver. I want to experience the freedom of being on the bike and the wind on my face. Please? You can't tell me you don't ride without a helmet."

"Of course I do, but that's different. I don't want anything to happen to you."

I make another advance in his direction. "Please. I know you'll be careful."

"Shit. Okay, hop on. If my mom spots us, I'll never hear the end of this. And I do mean never."

He gets on the bike, and I jump on as fast as I can, not giving him the time to rethink his decision. I scoot in close and close my arms around him.

"Hold on, babe."

Oh, I'm holding. Any chance I get, I'm holding.

We ride all through the country. Most of the time I have no idea where we are and couldn't care less. Denver is cautious in the beginning, but the longer we ride, the more he becomes fluid with the bike. I mold to him and the bike as he takes every curve. I was right about not wearing a helmet. It's a total rush out here on the open road with the wind in my hair. Most of the ride is quiet as we enjoy the scenery and the closeness. We stop a few times to stretch our legs or for Denver to show me something about the area. He points out a waterfall as we pass, and I realize I've lived my whole life in town not knowing what beauty was beyond.

We arrive back at Denver's, and I hate to let go of him, but I do. I slide off the back and wait for him to park.

"What did you think?"

"That was amazing. I could do that all day."

Denver braces his hands behind his head and focuses on the ceiling. He takes a few breaths and then relaxes. His eyes glow as they find mine. "If I were better with words, I could tell you how perfect you are for me. I'd tell you how you complete me in every way. I'd tell you you're more beautiful than any picture I've ever taken at the Boundary Waters. And I'd tell you your soul is the most alluring soul I've ever experienced."

I close my eyes as his waves of emotion wash over me. It's almost overwhelming. My body trembles and I want to lie down and soak him all in. Denver's arms go around me, and his garbled and distant voice rings in my ears.

"Jada?"

I open my eyes and Denver is cradling me like he's going to carry me over a threshold. "What happened?"

"I think you fainted."

"I did?" I have no recollection of that.

"Are you unwell?"

"No, I'm fine. It's just—"

His eyebrows hike in concern. "It's just what?"

"That thing you do." I huff in frustration. "You can put me down."

Denver puts me down but doesn't let go for fear I might fall again. I brush his hands away.

"I'm okay, really."

"We'll pay my dad a quick visit."

There's no time to protest. Denver pulls me through the house until we reach his dad's study.

"Dad, can we come in for a minute? I'd like for you to take a look at Jada."

"Of course, son."

Denver guides me to a chair and I take a seat. "This isn't necessary. I'm fine."

Bolivar goes over to a closet and pulls out a black bag. "What happened, Denver?"

Denver paces beside me. "We were in the garage, standing there talking, and she passed out."

Bolivar pulls out a stethoscope, placing the cool chest-piece against my shirt. "Nice strong heartbeat. Do you have issues with your sugar?"

"No sir."

He continues to examine me. He listens to my lungs and takes my temperature and then my blood pressure. "I can check your sugar if you like."

"Are you a doctor?"

He sits back and smiles. His gray eyes seem full of wisdom, and for whatever reason I know I could trust him with my life.

"I dabble. Why don't you tell me what happened."

I glance at Denver and he nods. Here goes nothing. "All right. It's hard to explain, but I'll try." I play with the rips in my jeans. "Denver was talking. He was saying these lovely things about how he felt, and then..." I hesitate because I'm going to sound insane.

Bolivar reassures me with his smile. "It's okay, Jada. You can tell us anything."

"Okay. So, it's like Denver's emotions roll off of him onto me. It's beautiful and comforting, but also a little overwhelming. Obviously, since I passed out."

Bolivar laughs and begins to repack his bag. "That, my girl, explains everything. We've all been on the receiving end of Denver's emotions."

"You have?"

"You remember I said our family is different?"

"Yes."

"This is one of those ways. We wear our feelings on our sleeve, if you will. We don't hide or mask our emotions. And Denver here, he's an exception to all of us. His soul is so exposed and his affections are so strong, sometimes it's a lot, even for me."

Denver is standing beside me but glaring out the window. Almost...embarrassed. I take his hand in mine. He peeks down at me with eyes full of worry.

He loves me. I don't know how or why, but he loves me. I know it in my core. "It's incredible, and I'm honored to be the one to acquire your affection."

Bolivar replaces his bag and stops before us. He and Denver exchange a glance. "I'll let you two talk. Dinner will be ready shortly."

"We'll be right there." Denver kneels at the corner of my chair. His strong hands hold mine. "I'm sorry."

I'm taken aback by his apology. "I'm not." I pull one hand free and touch the side of his face. He leans into my hand.

"I'm not sorry for being in love with you. I'm sorry that it's causing you pain. I hate that you get weary in my absence and that I make you pass out. I'm sorry that I've disrupted your life and changed your plans."

I take his face in both hands now. "I'm not sorry, for any of it. I've never felt so alive. I've never been on this side of such extravagant love. Only a fool would throw that away for a few inconveniences. I want to be with you, Denver."

His forehead falls to mine. "Oh, Jada. You have no idea how happy you've just made me."

His words resonate within me. His joy becomes my joy. I think I'm falling in love with Denver Stone. "I have a pretty good idea. I could learn to surf on your waves."

He lets out a half breath, half laugh. "Can't hide anything from you, can I?"

I bite my lip and take deep breaths. All of a sudden the craving to be physical with him overcomes me, and I can't see past my pulsing desire. I pull back to create space between us. "Was that you or me?"

"I think it's both. You're starting to associate with the pull. It gets stronger every day."

The door swings open, and Mitch comes in with Emily. Her eyebrows go up as she takes in the scene before her. Mitch is indifferent. "Dad said to come get you guys for dinner."

"Be right there."

Like earlier with his dad, Denver and Mitch exchange a look, and I have a hunch it's deeper than what's on the surface. He pulls me to my feet. "After you, babe."

CHAPTER NINE

JADA

Denver has picked me up all week for school. No Porsche since Monday. My favorite was the ancient Ford truck. He said it had belonged to his grandpa. It's big and orange and rusty, but I love it. It's Friday and he should be here any minute. Emily and Mitchell are officially dating now. I've never seen her so happy.

Grainger avoids me like the plague. This division between us is killing me, but I don't know how to fix it. He swears Denver is holding something over me, and I can't convince him otherwise. My mom seems to like Denver, but there's something she's holding back. She's been weird this week and gets aloof when I ask her about it. Last night she was on her cell in her bedroom for over an hour. She hates talking on the phone. I asked her if she had a boyfriend and she assured me, several times, that she did not. Denver and I have been careful not to be alone together, or not get too close if we are. Hugs and motorcycle rides are our form of closeness.

I got up early this morning so I could take my time with my hair and makeup. I'm wearing a cute outfit as opposed to jeans and a T-shirt. Well, I'm still wearing jeans with holes, but they're white and Emily lent me a sexy swoop neck top that I would never purchase for myself. The four of us are going on a double date after school, so I want to be beautiful.

The aroma of blueberry coffee hits me as I leave my room. My mom and I have to drink the good stuff that you order and grind yourself. I lay my bookbag on the chair and walk over to the coffeemaker.

"This smells so good. I'm glad we decided to try the blueberry."

"That was a good call. I wasn't sure about it at first, but I do love it. You want some scrambled eggs?"

"Sure, be great." My mornings are so much better now that I spend my evenings with Denver. I'm a tad shaky, but as soon as he gets here that will be gone.

Mom plates my eggs and I sit at the bar. I've taken two bites when the doorbell rings.

"Eat your breakfast. I'll let Denver in."

"Thanks."

My mom comes back in the kitchen not with Denver, but with Mitchell.

"How many boyfriends do you have, Jada?"

I roll my eyes. "Hey Mitchell, what are you doing here?"

"Denver had a rough morning, so I offered to pick you up on the way to Emily's."

"Is he okay?"

"He'll be fine. Nothing a good nap won't fix."

My mom clears her throat. "And this is?"

"Oh, right. This is Mitchell, Denver's brother. He's also Emily's boyfriend."

"You boys look so much like your...like each other. I mean I should have guessed because you two favor each other. Anyway, you boys know Jada has a car, right? She can drive herself to school."

"Yes, ma'am, but we're going on a double date after school, so this was easier."

"That's fine. Jada, please be careful."

I shove in the last bite of eggs and get my things. My mom is staring a hole through Mitchell. What is her deal? "Have a good day, Mom. Love you," I say as we head toward the door.

"Love you too, sweetie."

Mitchell opens the back door to his BMW. "Jump in. We'll talk on the way."

I buckle up while he gets in and starts the car. "What's wrong with Denver?"

"He was helping Dad with something and fell off a ladder."

"Oh my God! That sounds serious. Should I go check on him? I can skip school."

"No. It sounds worse than it is. He wasn't at the top of the ladder, and he's just bruised up. I promise he'll be fine. Dad examined him and gave him a pain pill."

"You swear he's okay?"

"Jada, if something was wrong with my brother, you think I'd be going to school?"

I grab the back of my neck to rub out the tension. "Right. Okay."

"He'll be good to go in a few hours. Actually, he said to meet him in the parking lot at lunch. He didn't want you to go all day without seeing him."

"I wondered about that, but him being okay is more important."

"Funny. He said the same thing about you. Dad insisted that he stay home and rest. Denver was not happy."

I smile at the thought of him trying to convince his dad of anything. "I bet."

Emily is waiting on her porch when we arrive. She waves and darts inside to grab her bag. Mitch opens her door, and she spots me in the back seat.

"Hey, Jada. Where's Denver?"

"He's home recovering from a ladder accident. Mitch says he'll be fine, though."

"Oh wow. I'm glad he's okay."

"Me too."

"You're super cute, by the way." Emily winks because I'm wearing her wardrobe.

"Thanks. You're pretty hot yourself."

Mitch decides to jump in on that one. "You are gorgeous, Emily."

"Thank you." She reaches over the console to give him a kiss on the cheek.

No fair! How come she can kiss Mitchell and I can't kiss Denver? I eye Mitch in the rearview mirror. He shrugs. Turkey. He knows something I don't. Heck, he probably knows everything I don't. I sure hope to get some answers soon.

Emily and Mitch are having their own conversation. I stare out the window and worry about Denver. I take out my phone to send him a text, but he's beat me to it.

Denver: Hey babe. It sucks not picking you up this morning. I told dad I was fine, but he said a hard no. Can't wait to see you at lunch. I'm having Jada withdrawals.

Me: I'm so glad you're okay! And I too need a Denver hit.

Denver: Did I mention I'm in love with you?

Me: Once or twice.

Denver: Making sure. What do you want for lunch?

Me: I'll grab a sandwich from the cafeteria. We're already going out for dinner.

Denver: All right. C you soon.

Me: Get some rest.

Emily slaps my knee. "Are you texting Denver?"

"Guilty."

"I could tell by the goofy grin on your face. Where do you guys want to go eat tonight?"

I roll my eyes. "You know I don't like to decide. Whatever everyone wants is fine with me."

Emily runs her fingers down Mitch's arm. "I told you she'd say that. Where do you and Denver want to go?"

"Steak sounds good. What about Texas Roadhouse?"

"Works for me. You good with that, Jada?"

My mouth waters. I've been eating a lot lately. I'm not gaining weight, only muscle. Maybe all that running is finally paying off. "It's perfect."

"Sweet, now that we've settled that, we can talk about the movie."

I let out a groan. "Let's pick the movie after dinner."

Emily sighs. "Fine. We're here anyway."

The three of us walk in together, but I veer off to go by my locker, telling Emily I'll catch her later in class. I'm almost to my locker when Grainger grabs my elbow.

"Can we talk?"

"That depends. Are you going to ask me if I'm on drugs again?"

"No. I want to apologize."

At my locker, I pause to hear him out. "I'm listening."

Grainger leans against the lockers. "I miss you. It sucks not being able to talk to you in the halls at school or come by your house. I hate that Denver monopolizes all your time. Can we hang out or something?"

My eyebrows rise in part frustration, part pity. "That didn't sound like an apology, and now you know how I felt about you and Candy."

He lifts off the locker. "Is that what this is about, payback?"

"No, Grainger. I actually like Denver. I'm not using him to get to you. I know this isn't how we thought things would be between us, but it's how it is. Can you be my friend or not?"

"I'll always be your friend. You should know that." He studies me like a puzzle piece he's not sure where to place.

"Why are you looking at me like that?"

"You've changed. It's like you're you, but different. More confident maybe, I don't know. Shit, now I'm talking crazy."

"No, I agree." I shake my head. "Anyway, you know I'm here for you. You're the best friend I've ever had. Maybe you could hang out with us sometime."

Grainger switches his weight from one foot to the other. "*Us* being you and Denver?"

"Yes. Sometimes we hang out with Emily and Mitch too."

"Sounds awkward to me." He shrugs. "Maybe sometime, I guess."

"That would be awesome. Thank you, Grainger." I reach out and give him a hug.

"What was that for?"

"For trying. For being my friend. I'll always love you."

The bell rings. "All right, well this is too much emotional crap for me. I'm going to class." He takes a few steps and stops. "And Jada, I love you too."

That exchange with Grainger was like a boulder being lifted off my shoulders, leaving me lighter and free. I'm smiling from ear to ear as I enter my first class of the day.

By lunch, I'm sluggish and my brain is full of fog. I'm pretty dang sure I failed a quiz in Spanish last period. I really need to see Denver. My legs are wobbly as I stop by the cafeteria for food. I hurry through the line, grabbing a sandwich and some chips. Emily and Mitch wave as I make my way out of the crowd.

Denver is sitting on a bench in the shade. His back is to the school, but somehow he knows I'm coming and stands up to greet me. "Hey, beautiful."

I set my lunch on the bench and practically jump at him. His arms encircle me and I breathe in his fresh scent. Strength begins to flood my body. A warmth starts in my middle and spreads in both directions, making every part of me whole. I let out a long sigh. "That is so good."

His chest vibrates as he chuckles. He kisses the top of my head, making it tingle. "Yes, it is."

In my eagerness to get my hands on him, I forgot that he was hurt. I jerk back and scan the length of him. "Oh my gosh, I'm so sorry. I forgot about your accident."

He pulls me back to him. "My dad overreacts. I'm fine."

I let him hold me a minute longer, but I'm not done with this conversation. "Tell me what happened."

He stares off in the distance. "Jada, I don't want to lie to you, but I can't tell you the truth either."

"You didn't fall off of a ladder?"

He points to the bench for me to sit. I pick up my sandwich and start to eat. "No. My dad told Mitch to say that, but I don't want our relationship to be built on lies."

"I appreciate that, and I trust you. You can tell me, Denver."

His fists clench and unclench at his sides. "I want to, I do, it's just…"

"Can you show me?"

"Show you?"

"What happened to you. Where are you hurt?"

He hesitates but then starts to lift his shirt. It's the first time I've seen Denver's six pack. It's hard not to stare at the bumps and valleys that make up his abs, but my eyes eventually find the big purple bruise on his right side.

"Denver, oh my God. You're the color of a plum. Are they broken?"

He drops his T-shirt and my hands itch to push it back up. I stare at where his beautiful abs are now hidden.

Denver clears his throat. "Thankfully, I'm only bruised. It barely hurts at all." He stops speaking and laughs. "Hey, you going to look up at me, or are you only interested in my T-shirt?"

His eyes are glowing when my gaze finds his. "It's not your T-shirt that interests me."

The invisible rope between us tightens. I am so attracted to him it hurts. My limbs are tense as I fight the urge to touch him. Denver jumps up, giving me the space I need to relax. I roll my head from side to side to stretch my taut neck and shoulders.

Denver pushes out a short breath. "That was my fault. I didn't think about, you know…"

I laugh. "What, me wanting to attack you after a glimpse of your abs?"

"Yeah, that."

My face burns as the realization sinks in. "I'm not like that. I mean, you make me feel things, and I've never even touched a boy in a sexual way, and not that I want to have sex with you—oh my God, I need to stop talking."

Denver rejoins me on the bench. His finger lifts my chin so that I'm forced to look at him. "I understand. Have I told you I've never had a girlfriend?"

"That's not possible."

"I swear it's the truth. I've never had a girlfriend, I've never kissed anyone, and I've certainly never had sex. I was waiting on the right person to come along. Someone special. I was waiting on you."

I'm breathless as his words wash over me. My heart jumps inside my chest. I'm falling in love with Denver Stone. "What have I done to deserve you?"

He smiles. "I was thinking the same thing."

I stare at his mouth. "I dream of the moment when your lips touch mine."

Denver gently rubs his thumb over my lips. "I dream a lot of things."

He removes his hand from my face and I bite my lip. I'm not sure how much longer we can stay composed if we continue in this line of thinking. I force my mind to focus away from the hunger and channel my thoughts to what started all of this in the first place. Denver's bruise. Right.

"How did you get the bruise? Are you some kind of fighter?"

"In a way, I am. I protect people."

"Is that all I'm going to get for now?"

He nods. "Yeah."

"Then I'll accept that, for now."

"Thank you, Jada, for not pushing."

"You'll tell me when you're ready." I chew the last bite of my sandwich and pick up my trash to take inside. "I better get back. Lunch is almost over."

"All right, babe. And so you know, it's Friday, and I'm driving the Porsche."

I roll my eyes. "At this point you could probably show up in a jet and no one would be surprised."

"Really? My dad has a friend…"

"NO! No jet, I was joking."

"What about a helicopter?"

I glare at Denver. "Don't you dare. I'm going to class now. I'll see you after school, in the Porsche."

His throaty laugh echoes at my back as I walk away.

The hands on the clock in the front of the room are not moving. Not fast enough anyway. This last class has been excruciatingly slow. I want to be done with this school day and move on to my weekend. My weekend spent with Denver. Emily is a walking cheerleader today. She screams and jumps up and down every time I pass her in the hall, with a cheesy big smile on her face. I need to buy her some pompoms. All she's talked about all day is our date.

I know she likes Mitchell, and he likes her, but it's not the same as what is happening between Denver and me. I've spent the last ten minutes of class thinking about how that makes no sense. Emily and Mitchell have known each other longer. They've declared themselves boyfriend and girlfriend, but what Denver and I have seems deeper. Emily hasn't talked about how she perceives her relationship or what connection they have. I don't want her to get hurt.

The final bell rings, relieving my swirling thoughts. I sprint to my locker and throw everything inside. I finished all my work so there would be no homework this weekend to keep me from spending time with Denver.

I spot Emily in the hall and dart over. "Thank goodness that's over. My last class was torture."

She waves at a couple of girls walking by. "I know, right? Are you riding with us, or is Denver picking you up?"

"Denver's picking me up. He threatened to come in a helicopter."

She throws her head back and laughs. "He would do it too. Oh, there's Mitchell. I'll meet you at their place."

I give her a quick hug. "See you soon."

I have to squint in the afternoon sun when I walk out of the building. This last week of March has been perfect. Bright blue skies with wispy clouds, flowers in full bloom, budding trees, warm temps, and a light breeze. Add this gorgeous guy standing in front of his car to all of that, and my heart is on the edge of combustion. He drove the Porsche as promised. He's wearing dark jeans and a short sleeved blue button up that brings out the blue in his eyes. When he pulls down his sunglasses, his eyes have that glow I've come to love. His gaze is full of longing and wonder that tell me I'm treasured and valued.

As soon as I'm close enough, he captures me for a hug. "It's been way too long."

His face is all chiseled jaw and perfect skin. I roll the corner of my lip under and Denver lets out a slight growl. "It's been three hours."

"Like I said, too long." He kisses the top of my head and releases me. "I better let you go before I lose my mind."

I take a step back and smile. "You gonna get me out of here, or what?"

"Absolutely."

We talk about school and weekend plans on the way out to Denver's house. I tell him about Grainger and ask if he could hang out sometime. Denver is completely on board, knowing how important Grainger is to me. We agree on a hike tomorrow once I've finished my chores and run. Hopefully my body will hold out long enough for me to get those things done. When we reach his driveway, he continues past without saying a word.

"What are you up to?"

"Patience."

He drives the ten minutes out to the lake near his home. We stop at the same dock we did the night he brought me here on his motorcycle. Denver helps me out of the car and intertwines our fingers. We stroll lazily out on the dock.

I close my eyes and let the sun warm my skin. Birds sing and frogs croak around us, and the leaves rustle in the wind. Water ripples, a squirrel scurries in the leaves, and a woodpecker taps on the bark of a tree. If I focus, I can identify other sounds as well. Maybe sounds I shouldn't be able to hear? My senses are heightened. As I start to ponder what's happening, Denver breaks the silence.

"This sounds lame, even in my head, but will you be my girlfriend?"

My eyebrows hike. "Why is that lame?"

He releases my hand and paces the end of the dock. He pushes his hand through his already messy blond hair. It sticks up and I have the urge to get my hands tangled in it. I cross my arms around my middle.

"That didn't sound right, I'm sure. It's only lame because the word girlfriend falls way short of what I want from you. If I said what I wanted to say, you'd probably run for the hills, thinking me a madman."

I close the gap between us. "Mmm, I think it's too late to send me running now." He closes his eyes as I reach out my hand to his chest. His heart beats triple-time under my palm. I think of his sculpted abs underneath and my body shivers. "You have to know that I'm falling in lo—"

Denver's eyes snap open. "Jada, wait." He covers my hand on his heart with his. "It's not that I don't want you to say it, but I want you to be sure. If you say you're in love with me and then decide you're not, my heart will shatter in a million pieces."

I lay my head against his shoulder, our hands still pressed between us. I'm in love with him, and whether I say it now, or next week, or next month won't change anything. But I'll wait to say it out loud if he wants me to. I lift my head and say the only words I'm allowed.

"Yes. I will be your girlfriend."

He lays his forehead to mine. "I'm the happiest and luckiest man in the whole world."

"Now that was lame."

Denver laughs as he backs away from me. Like he always does when we've been close for several minutes. "Was not."

I roll my eyes. "Yes it was, but it's okay, I still lo—like you."

Denver starts walking to the car. "Let's go, princess. I've got a date planned for tonight."

We're laughing as we walk in from the garage. Emily and Mitch are sitting at the island having a pop.

Emily has a mischievous grin on her face. "Where'd you two disappear to?"

I stand across from her at the island, and Denver hands me a

Coke. "We stopped by the lake for a few minutes." I turn to Denver. "Thank you."

Mitch and Denver are nodding at each other. Mitch is smiling. I'm trying to watch them, but Emily continues to talk.

"There's a lake?"

"Yeah, it's not that far from here. It's so beautiful. I think I could live out there."

Denver chokes on his drink. "Really?"

I shrug. "Yes, really. It's like a little slice of heaven. So tranquil. Can't you picture a cabin out there in the woods?"

Denver and Mitch exchange yet another look before he pulls me to him. "I've pictured it many times." He kisses my head and lets me go. It's my new favorite thing. Those simple kisses send tiny pulses throughout my entire body. Imagine what a real kiss would do.

Emily thrums her fingers on the bar. "So, boys, what time are we leaving? Us girls need to freshen up a bit."

Mitch shrugs. "What ya think, bro? Maybe in thirty minutes?"

"Yeah, sounds good."

Emily slides off her stool. "Perfect." She waltzes over to me and grabs my hand. "I'm stealing her for a few minutes."

Denver leans on the counter. "A few minutes is all you get."

Emily blows him a kiss as we round the corner. "She was mine first."

We giggle as we walk down the hall toward the bathroom. As soon as we're inside she shuts the door.

"Holy cow, but that boy is in love with you!"

The mirror reflects my reddening face. "I'm in love with him too."

Emily sits on the counter. "No shit. Even a fool would notice. I'm happy for you, I truly am, but don't you think it happened a little fast?"

I shrug and play with the lotion bottle on the counter. There's no good explanation for what's happening between us. At least, not one that I know of. "It did."

She lets out a single laugh. "It sure as hell did. Well, I say go with it. I've known you a long time and I've yet to see you this, I don't know—happy, peaceful, intoxicated?"

"Intoxicated. I like it. It's so accurate."

"That it is, girl, that it is." She throws her bag on the counter. "Well, we better get beautiful for those two hotties waiting in the kitchen."

I let Emily touch up my makeup. She's a master with eyeshadow. When we walk back in the kitchen, the guys are still sitting at the bar drinking beer instead of Coke.

Denver glances up and lets out a whistle. He's on the verge of saying something when his mom comes into the room.

She ruffles both boys' hair as she walks by. "There's my two favorite boys. Hello, Jada and Emily. I understand you have a hot date tonight."

Emily seems petrified by the woman, which makes no sense at all. She practically drips honey, she's so sweet.

"Hey, Aurar. Emily and I do have hot dates, but they haven't arrived yet."

Aurar laughs. "Oh, Jada. I like you more and more every day."

Denver grunts. "Mom, really?"

"What? It's good to be humbled every once in a while." She winks at me and then proceeds to the refrigerator. She pulls out a beer and hands it to Denver to open.

He passes it back. "You drinking beer now?"

She lets out a sigh and gives Denver a long stare before answering. "It's been a long week."

He nods in agreement. I imagine that has something to do with Denver's *accident*, but they don't speak of it. Denver punches Mitchell in the arm. "You ready to go, bro?"

"Ready is my middle name."

"Have a good time tonight. Be careful. Denver, be responsible."

"Yes, ma'am." He kisses her cheek as we pass.

"Bye, Aurar. Have a nice evening," I say as we exit. Emily squeaks out a goodbye.

The boys vote for the BMW, so we pile in and head to the nearest big city. There's a total of four restaurants here in Forrest City. If you don't want a burger, Mexican, pizza, or a sub, you're out of luck.

The lights of Diamond Hill can be seen miles before you enter. It's the total opposite of our small town. We call it our little New York. The streets bustle with life. People of all races and colors walk the sidewalks and hail cabs. There's a bar on every corner. Music blares from all directions, cars and pubs alike. Whatever your interest, you can find it here. I wouldn't want to live here, but it's fun to visit.

Denver rolls down the windows so we can better take it all in. The air smells of car exhaust and mouthwatering food. My stomach growls in response. Denver spies a parking spot by the street and whips in a parallel park faster than I can utter the words parallel park. Emily and I wait on the sidewalk while the guys pay the meter.

Denver puts his arm around my waist. "Here we are. What do you girls want to do first?"

"Eat," I blurt before Emily has time to butt in. "I'm starving."

Denver and Mitch fist bump. "That's my girl," says Denver.

We walk the few blocks to Texas Roadhouse and put our names on the waitlist. We grab a bucket of peanuts and sit outside to enjoy the last of the day's sunshine. Emily and I talk about school and graduation while the boys have their own conversation. They mention names I don't recognize, and I wonder if Denver will introduce me to his friends. They throw around words like patrol and elders. Denver catches me eavesdropping and changes the subject. They don't speak of business again after that.

Emily opts for a salad, but I order a steak like the boys. She'll have to be proper tonight all by herself. I'm so hungry right now I want to eat the table. When the rolls are brought out, I force myself to stop at two.

Denver places his hand on my knee as he talks to Mitchell. I peek under the table, wondering if there are real flames or it's my imagination. Nope, no flames. He absentmindedly rubs his thumb over my knee, touching skin where my jeans have holes. For the second time today, my senses go on high alert. His thumbprint brands my skin.

It's such a tiny movement, but I can't take it anymore. I put my hand over his to stop him from roaming.

Denver jerks up instantly. "Are you okay? Your hand is hot." He reaches up to touch my forehead.

"Hungry, but good."

"Your head is warm."

"I'm fine. Really."

He squints at me with pursed lips, then he pins Mitch with a glare.

"Why do you guys do that?" I bounce my knee under the table, buzzing with energy.

Denver squeezes my knee. "Do what?"

"Look at each other like you're having a silent conversation."

"We're brothers. We are having a silent conversation."

Emily rolls her eyes, but I think he's serious.

Mitch shrugs and throws his arm around Emily's shoulders. Brat. He's not going to say anything.

I glare at Denver. "We're not done talking about that."

He sits up as the waitress approaches. "Hey, our food is here."

"You're lucky I'm willing to let this drop…because this steak is too tempting to ignore."

He hands me a knife. "Don't let me get in your way."

I clean my entire plate. Me, the girl who eats half her food now and saves the rest for later, has all but licked the damn plate. What is wrong with me?

The boys say nothing, but Emily kicks me under the table.

"Hey, Jada, you want to go with me to the bathroom?"

I toss my napkin on the table. "Sure."

Denver lets me out of the booth and I follow her to the back of the restaurant. The door barely shuts before she starts in on me.

"Are you pregnant?"

"I think one has to have sex to be pregnant."

"I'm serious, Jada."

"Seriously? You think I've had sex? With who, Denver? We haven't even kissed."

She paces the floor. "Grainger?"

"Oh my God, no. You know me better than that."

She stops and gets right in my face. "Then what is going on?"

"Why are you so bent out of shape because I ate my dinner? I told everyone I was hungry. I had a tiny PB & J for lunch."

She crosses and uncrosses her arms and begins to pace once more. "It's not only that. You're acting strange, and even Denver said you had a fever earlier."

"Maybe I'm coming down with something. Is the flu going around?"

She twirls her hair with one hand and bites her thumb of the other. "I don't know what it is, but something is off about you."

I huff and throw my hands in the air. "Well, when you figure it out, let me know, cause I've got nothing. Now if you'll excuse me, I actually do have to pee. And it's not because I'm pregnant. It's because I drank two glasses of Coke."

Emily sighs. "Jada, I'm sorry. I shouldn't have attacked you like that. I'm worried is all."

I'm drying my hands when she comes out of her stall. Her cheeks puff up with air before she pushes it from her lips. Neither of us speak as she washes and dries her hands.

We're all but out the door when she spins around. "I really am sorry. I love you."

I throw my arms around her. "I love you too. Everything's fine."

"Promise?"

"I promise."

I'm not a liar by nature. I most likely would tell her what was happening if I knew, but I don't. So there's no reason to worry her with my recent oddities. I suspect Denver and Mitch have an idea, but they're both tight as a vault. Then again, maybe it's me. I suppose I could be getting sick. Who the hell knows. Add *cussing more* to the list.

The guys have paid and are waiting by the door. Denver grabs my hand and squeezes.

"You okay?"

I attempt a smile. "I'm good."

Emily bounces from foot to foot. "What's next?"

Denver holds the door open for our group. The cool night air refreshes me as we exit the restaurant. On the sidewalk, we try to agree on which direction to go. The movie doesn't start for another hour and Emily wants to go by the mall, but I have no desire to go shopping.

"How about this: we split up for an hour and meet at the movie theater at nine?" Leave it to my knight in shining armor to save me.

Mitch slaps Denver on the back. "I like it. Gives me time with my girl." He winks at Emily and any reservation she has melts away.

"Perfect." Denver puts his hand on the small of my back and leads me down the sidewalk.

We stroll down a couple of streets gazing in shop windows. I'm content to hold Denver's hand and be alone with him.

I'm admiring a dress when Denver jerks me from the store front. "Oh my gosh, I forgot this place was here."

Two stores down is an ice cream parlor. He wiggles his eyebrows and it makes me laugh. "You're telling me you want ice cream after all we just ate?"

He cocks his head. "You're telling me you don't?"

"What the heck. I'll run extra tomorrow."

"That's what I'm talking about."

We place our order and sit at a small table for two at the back of the store. Denver gathers my hands in his on top of the table.

"You seemed upset earlier. Did Emily say something?"

I chew my bottom lip. I'm gathering my thoughts when Denver's finger runs over my mouth.

"Hey, you want to take it easy on that lip? I'd prefer it be in one piece when I'm ready to kiss it."

I release my lip and lean across the table. "And when might that be?"

"Jada." Denver grips the edge of the table. "Do you realize how tempting your lips are to me? How tempting you are to me? Imagine a bloody fish being dangled over a shark, and then multiply that by ten."

I lean back in my chair. "Well, that's a first. I can honestly say I've never been compared to a bloody fish."

Denver laughs so hard he doubles over in his seat. His laughter becomes contagious and I join him, laughing until tears are running down my face. The girl brings over our ice cream and looks at us like we're crazy. Maybe we are.

Denver catches his breath but then says something about bloody fish and starts laughing all over again.

I push his ice cream in front of him. "People are staring. They're going to think we're on drugs and call the cops."

He scans the room and shrugs. "Who cares?" After settling down he picks up his spoon. He takes a bite and moans. "That is so good."

"It is pretty amazing. Please don't tell Emily we ate ice cream. She already thinks I'm pregnant because of how much I ate at dinner."

Denver coughs and his eyes get big. "What the heck? Why would she say that?"

"She says she's worried. That I'm acting different. I don't know, but please don't say anything."

"It'll be our secret, my little fish." He starts to laugh again.

"Don't you do it."

"You bloody fish, you."

"Stop it."

He reaches over and wipes ice cream from my lip. "God, I love you."

I don't say anything in return, as requested.

DENVER and I join Mitch and Emily at the theater. The boys beg to watch the newest action film, so that's what we see. While I enjoy it, Emily seems miffed the whole time.

The tension between Emily and me lifts on the ride home. Denver has everyone rolling in laughter at me being his bloody fish. He doesn't share our ice cream secret as promised. His constant contact is calming yet tantalizing at the same time. I'm thankful he's driving and that Mitch and Emily are in the car.

By the time Denver drives me home, it's two o'clock in the morning. I've done nothing, yet I'm exhausted. My limbs are weightless and rubbery. Denver's creased forehead doesn't help settle my anxiety. He assures me it will all be okay. For some reason he needs to talk to his dad, but he says it will all make sense very soon. I'm too tired to press for more. He's picking me up tomorrow at one to take me hiking. He hasn't left my porch, and I already can't wait to see him. We hug for several minutes until it's too much to bear. He leaves me with a kiss on the head.

I barely get my clothes off before climbing in bed. I drift off to sleep with a smile on my face. He won't let me say it, but I love Denver with all that's inside of me. And no amount of time will change that.

CHAPTER TEN

DENVER

What's that knocking sound? The sunlight spills in through the crack in the curtain, causing me to squint. Do I have a hangover? I don't remember drinking last night. Memories of the evening with Jada flood my mind. Okay, so no drinking. More knocking.

"Dude, are you getting up today or what? Mom has breakfast ready and she won't let me eat until you come downstairs."

The door creaks open and Mitch comes in.

I sit up on my elbows. "What time is it?"

"It's after eight."

"Shit."

"Yeah, you look like it too."

I groan and cover my eyes. "You remember that night my senior year I drank way too much?"

"Who doesn't?"

I attempt a hateful glare but can't quite muster the strength. "That's what I feel like."

"Dad figured as much. Here."

"What is that?" I push myself up and take the mug from Mitch.

"Some herb concoction Dad made. He said the demon poison

would kick in this morning. The pills he gave you yesterday will have worn off."

I touch my tender ribs. Damn demon took me by surprise and knocked me into a tree, bending my body in half. Then he had the nerve to bite into my ass. His last mistake. "How does he know all this stuff?" I sniff the liquid and almost gag. "What the hell? Smells like cow poo."

Mitch has the nerve to laugh. "Drink up, brother. I'm starving."

"I hate you." I hold my nose with one hand and down the green slime in one gulp. It's all I can do not to throw up. "How long before it kicks in?"

"I think he said five minutes." Mitch takes the cup and retreats to the hall. "Put some clothes on before you come down. I see you naked enough as it is."

I glance down and realize the covers are pushed to the end of the bed. It's not uncommon for wolves to have hot flashes. And with the demon poison in my system, I'm sure I was burning up. I grab the closest thing I can find and throw it at Mitch. "You're just jealous!"

"Like hell." He tosses my shirt back in the room. "Seriously, dude. I'm hungry."

"Fine. I'll be down in a minute."

By the time I put on some sweatpants, brush my teeth, and throw some water on my face, I'm a new man. My stomach growls, letting me know things are back in order. The bruise on my ribs is faded to a light purple. It'll be gone tomorrow. I pray the poison is gone as well. I can't drink anymore of that seaweed shit.

Dad and Mitch are at the table. Dad is reading the paper, and Mitch has a plate piled high with pancakes and eggs. Mom stands by the stove pouring batter in the pan.

I nab a plate off the counter and kiss her cheek. "Thanks, Mom. Smells delicious."

"You're welcome. How are you?"

"Better now, thanks to Dad's nasty brew of cow poo and green slime."

She ruffles my bedhead hair. "I'm glad. That demon got ahold of you pretty good."

"Only for a minute."

She lets out a sigh. "I'm thankful it was only a minute."

"It's part of the job."

She turns back to the stove to flip the pancake. "I know all too well, but I don't have to like it."

"True." I fill my plate and join the men at the table. I shovel in several bites before speaking.

"Hey, Dad?"

He folds his paper and lays it on the table. "Good to see you up and moving."

"Yeah, thanks for that. I think."

"Pretty nasty stuff. I've had to down it more than once."

I shudder at the idea of having to drink that again. "Nasty is putting it nicely."

He chuckles. "I suppose it is. What did you want to talk about?"

I glance at Mitch. Oddly enough, I don't think he's been in my head this morning. "Did you tell him about Jada?"

"Nah. I figured you'd want to do it."

I nod in appreciation. "I think she's going through the change."

"What symptoms does she have?"

I think over the last few days. "Hot flashes, healthy appetite, her friends think she's moody, and I think she's starting to experience heightened senses. Probably more perceptive and observant. But that last part is obviously speculation."

"I'm sure you're right. You would know more than anyone. Is she talking about it?"

"Not really."

Dad taps his chin. "You'll need to keep a close eye on her. It could be a week or even a month."

"What do you think she is? There's not even a hint of wolf on her mom, and we know nothing about her father. You think she's wolf, shapeshifter, or what?"

"I don't have the facts to determine her origin. Each bloodline has its own variation. The Stones are pure wolf on both sides for genera-tions. Still, there's something special about that Jada of yours. When are you going to tell her about us? About you."

Ugh. Under the current circumstances I need to tell her sooner rather than later. She's going to need my help. She'll need all of us. "Soon, I suppose. It terrifies me, if I'm being honest."

My dad gives me a reassuring grip on the shoulder. "She's stronger than you think."

"I hope you're right."

Mitch and I clean the kitchen in silence. I'm so wrapped up in my own situation, it doesn't hit me until I'm back in my room that Mitch was unusually quiet. And now that I'm giving it consideration, I remember him practically pushing me out of his head earlier. Some-thing is bothering him. I take my shower and dress and walk down the hall to his room.

The door is slightly ajar. Light music plays from his bluetooth speaker. There are clothes all over the floor. I knock on the door.

"Yeah."

"Can I come in?"

"Sure."

Mitch is sitting on his bed texting. His room is an absolute mess. He must be storing up water bottles in case the zombie apocalypse happens.

"Clean much?"

He shrugs. I clean off a spot on his loveseat and sit down. "You texting Emily?"

He tosses his phone on the bed. "Yeah."

"You gonna tell me what's eating at you, or am I going to have to beat the crap out of you first?"

His phone dings, and he pushes it off onto the floor. "I don't know what the hell I'm doing. Am I going to screw this up?"

"I assume we're talking Emily here?"

"Yeah. I kissed her last night."

"Wow. I'm kinda jealous. How was it?"

He opens up to me for the first time today and it all comes

flooding in. "Damn. Must have been pretty good. So what's the problem?"

"What if she's not the one? What if we get in this thing, and I end up hurting her? And yeah, that kiss was amazing, but when I glimpse what you have with Jada—well, let's just say it's some strong shit."

"I'm not trying to be an a-hole here, but I did kinda say that in the beginning."

"I know. I wish I was as strong as you, but I'm not."

"That's bull crap. You're every bit as strong as I am. I can't tell you what to do. Whether you break up with her now or later, you will break up with her if she's not your mate. I can guarantee you that much. Maybe in the long run it's better to do it now, but again, I'm not telling you what to do. You have to decide."

"I hate this. I think I know what I have to do."

I stand up and walk toward the door. "Good luck."

"Same to you, with the whole telling Jada you're a wolf and all."

"Ugh, thanks. I might need reinforcements."

"I've always got your back."

"Ditto."

"And Denver?"

"Hmm?"

"I'm the one that's jealous. When you and Jada do finally kiss, I fear for the lives of anyone standing close, cause it's gonna be like a damn grenade going off."

I laugh as I go out into the hall.

You're next, brother. That big-ass Mack truck will plow you over before you know what hit you.

Thanks, Denver.

Yep.

IT'S sunny and at least seventy-five degrees. I can't waste a day like today driving in a car, so I ride the motorcycle to Jada's. She's sitting on the porch steps when I pull up. Her auburn hair is blowing in the breeze and her brown eyes sparkle in the sunlight. Her eyes remind me of melted chocolate, and I want to march over there and kiss them. She gets more beautiful every day. Her rosy cheeks match the red T-shirt she's wearing. I want to kiss them too. Lord help me. I think my talk with Mitch this morning has me riled up. I walk up the driveway toward her, and her full, pink lips spread into a wide smile. My heart hits turbo speed faster than my Porsche. Come on, man, get ahold of yourself.

I stop a couple of feet shy of where she's standing. I'm scared to get too close at the moment. I seem to be taking a trip on the struggle bus. "Hey, babe."

She licks her lips and rolls her bottom lip under, taking her sweet time in releasing it. Then I swear her smile is seductive in manner as she checks me out. My heart is going to stop. Damn thing is going to lock up, I know it.

"Why are you way over there, handsome?"

I take two long breaths. Mylanta, what was in that crap Dad gave me this morning? Maybe he mixed up the poison relief for some sort of damn love spell.

"I'm staying over here because you are way too hot for me right now. I want to kiss your eyeballs to see if they taste like chocolate." Oh God, did I say that out loud?

"My eyeballs? Is that where you want to kiss me, Denver?"

What is she doing? My lungs can't keep up with the breaths I'm trying to take in. I swallow. "It's one of the places."

She takes a step in my direction. My feet are like lead. I need to move back, but I can't.

"Where else, Denver?"

She's like a magnet. I need to step away, but I move forward instead. She meets me in the middle until there's nowhere left to go. I reach up and touch her soft lips. They part in a sigh.

"Damn it, Jada. I'm about to freaking hyperventilate over here. What are you doing to me?"

She clutches my shirt in her hand. She wets her lips as she leans in a little closer. "Can't we at least try?"

"Where's your mom?"

"Out."

Don't get me wrong. I want to kiss her more than I want to live, but I'm worried about how I'll react, or where it will lead. Not that anything is going to happen on her front lawn. I don't think. That's the problem right there. When she's this close, I can't think. Not with my brain anyway.

"Jada, I—"

"Hey, guys, what's up?"

Jada steps back with a huff. "Hey, Grainger."

I don't know whether to thank him or punch him. "Hey man, what's going on?" I offer him my hand.

"Not much. Ran an errand for my mom and saw you guys out here. Thought I would say hey and um, you know, no hard feelings or whatever."

"Thanks, man, I appreciate it."

"Yeah well, I guess I'll head back in. See you around."

"Hey, my family is having a BBQ in a couple of weeks. You should come. Mitch and some his buddies will be there, and some family friends."

"Sure, sounds good."

"Sweet. Jada can give you the details when it gets closer."

She glances from me to Grainger. "Be glad to. Thanks for coming over." She touches Grainger's arm and for a split second I'm jealous, but her smile toward him is so genuine and full of love, there's no room for my idiotic jealousy.

He smiles in return. There's an exchange between them. Not like what Mitch and I have, but they know each other so well, there's an unspoken flow of gratitude.

Grainger walks away without another word. I'm standing in awe of this woman in front of me. The depth of love I have for her is earth-core level.

I push a stray hair behind her ear. "You love him."

"I do. Not in the same way I love you, but I do love him."

"I understand."

Her head cocks to the side. "What, you're not going to fuss at me for saying I love you?"

"Nope."

"Good. Now where were we?"

"Nope again. Moment is gone. Get your backpack off the porch and plant your beautiful self on my bike."

She grunts as she stomps off to the porch. "You will kiss me, Denver Stone."

I throw my leg over the motorcycle seat. "Get on the damn bike, you bloody fish!"

She tries not to laugh, but to no avail. In the end I get a massive eye roll and a slap on the arm. Her arms wrap around my chest, and we zoom out of town toward my house and a much-needed hike through the woods. Surely nothing can go wrong on a hike.

JADA WALKS THROUGH THE WOODS, her eyes lit up in amazement. I can't be sure to what level she's experiencing the new sights and sounds and smells, but man, it's going to be so awesome when she gets the full measure. Which won't happen until the change. I can't keep my eyes off her. I've tripped several times because I'm not watching my step. We've been a couple of miles, and she hikes like a champ. Must be the runner in her, plus her body and muscles will continue to strengthen for the next several years. I'm glad I get to be on the receiving end of that. We're not too far from the cabin. My cabin.

I almost had a coronary when Jada said she'd love to live in a cabin. Little does she know I own one. I don't live in it because I'm saving that chapter for after I get married. Mitch also has a home a few miles from here. It's part of our inheritance. Another perk of being an umpteenth generation wolf family. I won't show Jada the cabin today. That's a secret I'll hold onto for a while longer.

We're not far from today's destination, a peak with a killer view. The last bit is straight uphill, so I stop at the bottom to take a break.

I lift the backpack off my shoulders and get out two waters. "You want a drink?"

"Yes, thank you." She drains half the bottle. "That is so good." She takes a few more sips and leans against a tree. "Is this not the most beautiful day? I mean is it me, or is there new life stirring in the woods?"

"It's the most beautiful day ever."

Her hand goes to her hip. "Really? And how would you know? You've been staring at me the whole time."

"I know. That's what makes it the most beautiful day ever."

"Don't start what you can't finish." Her eyebrows rise in challenge.

I throw my hands up in the air. "Okay, okay. I give."

Her water bottle flies in my direction. "That's what I figured. So, are we heading to the top?" Her head tilts back as she gazes up at the top of the hill. All that fully exposed neck and collarbone has my insides in knots. The sweat glistening on her skin is intoxicating. We need to keep moving.

"Yep. Let's get a move on."

Jada follows right behind me, never losing step. The breath coming in and out of her lungs makes me crazy. How can everything about her be sexy? I thought for sure a hike would be free from any physical tension, but I was wrong.

We're both breathing hard when we reach the top. I lay down my bag and pull her to me so that her back is to my chest. The sun is high in the sky and the beams shine down on the tops of the trees, whose leaves are full and green. The soothing burble of a creek reaches my wolf ears. Farmers' fields are sprouting knee-high corn with promise of a bountiful fall harvest. The lake glistens as the rays of the sun dance across its surface. "Pretty cool, huh?"

"It's breathtaking." She scans the scenery before her. "Is that your house over there?"

"Yes. All the homes out here are either family or friends of the family."

"Wow. You have a big family."

"I guess I do." I put my chin on her shoulder. I want to tell her she's part of my family. That I want to marry her and spend the rest of my life with her. I want her to have my babies. But of course, I can't say any of that. Add that to the list of things like, by the way, I'm a wolf, my whole family are wolves, you're my mate, oh and I think you're a wolf. Holy mother of pearl, this isn't complicated at all.

Jada shivers beneath me. "Denver, my God. You can't hold me close like this and breathe in my ear and expect me not to notice."

I don't release her, because I can't. "I didn't know I was breathing in your ear."

She spins to face me. "Well, you are."

"I'm sorry."

"No, you're not."

I slide my hands in her windblown hair. "I don't think I'm going to survive this whole dating thing. You're killing me here."

Jada does that sexy thing with her lip. "At least we're on mutual ground."

I let out a huff. "I don't know about that. Every single thing you do turns me on."

Her hand touches the bottom of my T-shirt and then slides underneath. "Really? Everything?"

Holy shit. Her soft fingers on my bare skin are about to send me over the edge. The edge of what, I'm not sure. The edge of life as I know it. "Jada." I pinch my eyes closed.

And that's when I get a whiff of something not good. My eyes spring open and I push Jada back. Ah, hell no. Not now, not like this.

Mitch! Can you hear me?

Loud and clear, bro.

I might need some help. I think Jada and I are going to have company.

Shit. Where are you?

Past the cabin, top of the hill.

Be right there. Did you tell her?

No.

Oh boy.

Dude, hurry up.

"Why did you push me? What's happening?"

"Jada, I need you to listen to me very carefully." I guide her back to a rock between two trees. "I need you to sit right here and don't move. I'm so sorry, Jada. I didn't want it to happen like this."

"You're scaring me."

"I'm so sorry, babe. I'll explain later, but right now I seriously need you to stay here. I won't be able to concentrate if I'm worried about where you are. Promise me you won't leave this spot, no matter what."

"I promise."

The all-too-familiar stench of rotten eggs burns my nostrils. I don't have much time. I take off my shoes and socks and then my T-shirt. Jada is staring at me as if I've lost my mind. This is nothing, I think to myself. I thank the stars above that I put on boxers this morning as I pull down my cargo pants. I wish I had the time to appreciate the way she's admiring me right now, but I don't. I apologize one more time, then I leap away from her and burst into wolf form.

Mitch's paws pound the dirt as he races up the hill. I peek back at Jada, and she's as white as a sheet. She's frozen in place, and I'm thankful for that. Her safety is more important to me than anything else. We'll deal with the rest later. Mitch comes up and stands beside me.

Stinks like rotten skunk. What's the plan?

I'm not sure. Don't know what it is yet.

Maybe it's simply passing through the area.

I doubt it. We're not leaving this hilltop though. I won't leave Jada unprotected.

Got it.

After several seconds, I begin to think Mitch was right. The demon wasn't interested in us but happened to be close by. We pace the perimeter of the peak, watching and waiting. I'm gonna be kinda ticked if I changed in front of Jada for nothing. This is not at all how I wanted this to go down. I glance back, and she hasn't moved a muscle. I'm trying to read her expression when Mitch interrupts my train of thought.

Denver, our guest is here.

A black form hovers at the edge of the cliff with red eyes and a huge mouth, breathing out the rancid stench of death. Claws dangle at its sides waiting for an opportunity to strike. Mitch and I growl and hold our ground. The form begins to shift, and what once seemed ghostlike turns to solid body in the shape of a lion with a dragon head. It lets out a loud screech right before it lunges at Mitch. Jada screams behind me, which tells me she has enough of the sight to see the demon.

While the demon is midair, I jump on its back. My bodyweight forces the demon off course—it misses Mitch by inches and we tumble to the ground. We roll across the dirt and then skid a few feet before coming to a stop. My side screams in pain, but there's no time to worry about that now. We continue to grapple for the upper hand. I'm on top, the demon's putrid breath seeping into my lungs, but I can't keep it still long enough to get my jaws on its neck.

Mitch is standing back waiting for the right opportunity to be of some help.

I have an idea, Denver.

Lay it on me, man. It's too damn strong for me to hold down.

Flip over. Put the demon on top and I'll jump him from behind. He'll be sandwiched between us. Then we'll bite the hell out of his neck.

I like the way you think. I'm flipping in three, two, one...

I roll with the ugly beast, leaving his backside exposed. Mitch pounces before the thing knows what hit him. I grab one side of his neck and Mitch gets the other. A thunderous roar breaks free from the dragon head right before the whole thing explodes. Acrid demon blood sprays over us and the surrounding area.

I hate shapeshifter demons. Now I need another shower, Mitch grumbles as he tries to shake free the demon remains.

Nice work, brother.

Thanks. You too.

A noise from behind causes me to jerk around. Jada is rising to her feet. Her legs wobble as she takes a tentative step toward us.

"Denver, are you okay? You can still understand me, right?"

Well, I'm gonna let you handle this one on your own. I'm heading home for that hot shower.

What happened to you having my back?

Sorry, bro. This is all you.

Mitch takes off down the hill. Jada and I are left alone facing one another. I move closer to her and she doesn't shy away. In fact, she comes to stand in front of me and squats down. She's staring into my eyes.

"This is why your eyes glow." She raises her hand to touch me but pauses. "Is this okay? Can I touch you?"

I lick her hand and she laughs. "I'll take that as a yes." She slides her hands into the fur around my neck. She examines my face next. Her gentle fingers trace every feature. "You're kinda gorgeous. Is that weird that I think you're gorgeous?" When she pulls her hand back, it's covered in demon blood. "You're kinda gross too."

I nuzzle her belly and she falls back on her butt.

"Hey, cut that out." She tries to sound peeved, but the huge smile on her face gives her away.

I want to try and speak to her, but I don't want to freak her out. With her being close to the change and being my mate, the bond should be strong enough.

With Mitch it's like breathing. There's no thought involved. Jada and I will be that way too, but for now, I put all my focus on reaching out to her.

Jada

She gasps and her hand flies to her mouth. "Oh my God, Denver. Say something else."

You are so beautiful.

She bites her lip. "Again."

I'm so in love with you.

A tear slides down her cheek. "I'm in love with you too."

Why are you crying?

"I'm not sure. I'm overwhelmed. I don't understand this deep longing within me to be with you. And I think it's beautiful, what you are, and that you can communicate that way. I guess my cup overflows, if that makes sense."

It makes perfect sense. Being with you fulfills me in every way.

There's a million more things I want to tell her. I have so much more to share, but I think she's had enough for one day.

Stay here for a second. I'm going to change back and put some pants on, okay?

"All right."

I can't help but nuzzle her neck as I pass. She swats at me, but I jump out of the way. I step behind a tree and morph back to my human body. I grab my pants and slide them on before letting Jada see me.

"You can turn around now."

Jada stands and wipes the dirt off her butt. She seems to have rebounded from the sight of the demon earlier. With my T-shirt, I wipe demon blood from my face and chest. Jada comes over to inspect my scrapes.

"You've lost a layer of skin."

"It's not as bad as it looks, plus we heal quickly."

"We being you and Mitch? That was Mitch, right?"

"It was. My parents also. And their parents, etc."

"No way. Your sweet mom?"

I laugh. "She's actually a total badass. Especially if you mess with her boys."

"Now that I believe."

"Come here." Without hesitation she wraps her arms around me. I want to hold her forever. I want to soak her up like a sponge. Breathe her air.

Her head is against my bare chest. Her fingers start to roam up and down my back. She peers up at me and crinkles her nose. "You know, you're kind of sticky and you smell bad."

"You don't have to touch me."

Her hands find their way to my chest and stomach, her fingers drawing tortuous circles over my skin. "Your body is so beautiful. I had no idea the male anatomy could have this many muscles. I've seen guys without their shirts on, but holy crap, Denver."

"So you do want to touch me?"

Her seductive smile has me undone. "I think it's obvious, don't you?"

"Shit." I gaze up toward the sky for someone to save me. Something, anything to save me from myself. I need to be sure I'm in control of my emotions enough to stop at kissing. Wolves find their mate and then they—well, they mate. I will not risk Jada's virtue for a need. Surely I'm strong enough to draw that line.

"Denver, you look like your dog died. Tell me what you're thinking."

I take her face in my hands. "My love for you is so strong it scares me. I want to touch you and kiss you, but I don't want to go too far."

"We can do this together. What if we have a code word, and if one of us needs a breather we say the code word. Or if we think the other person needs a breather, same thing. Or I could knee you in the balls. That might work too."

I laugh and then cringe. "Let's go with the code word. I don't care for the other option."

"I figured. What's our word going to be?"

"Hmm. What about bloody fish?"

"NO."

"Why not? It's perfect."

"Absolutely not. It's bad enough you want to use it as a nickname."

"Okay, what do you suggest?"

Jada traces my tattoo with her finger. "The Boundary Waters, right?"

Where is she going with this? "Yes."

"Boundaries are for our good, for our protection. We want to preserve something beautiful, so therefore we don't want to cross a line."

I reach up and cup her face with my hand. "A beautiful boundary."

"Exactly. So as a safeguard, we need to hold the line."

My thumb caresses her cheek. "Hold the line. Together."

Her tongue sweeps across her full lips. "Yes."

I try to speak but my throat is constricted, closing off my air.

Jada's eyes fall to my mouth, then slowly make their way back to my heated stare. "Denver, please."

I push my hands in her hair and lean in close enough to let her breath caress my face. I want to know what's it's like to be skin to skin, so I rub my cheek against hers. She's so soft and perfect. She wets her lips and it's almost more than I can take, but I don't want to rush this moment. I lay soft kisses across her forehead and nose. I move to her neck and drag my tongue across her throat. A growl grows in my chest and I start to tremble. Jada has goosebumps on her neck and her nails are digging in my back. I stop and put my forehead to hers for a time out. I need a minute, but I may very well die if I don't taste her full, pink lips.

With all the self-control I can muster, I touch my lips to hers. A moan escapes her, and her fingers dig deeper into my flesh. I want to memorize her luscious, soft lips. I kiss each one, giving them equal attention. I'm trying so hard to take it slow, but Jada apparently has other things on her mind. She takes my bottom lip in her teeth and then slides her tongue over my lips. I lose control and kiss her hard. Nothing could have prepared me for this moment. Kissing my mate. A stick of dynamite may as well have exploded in my body. Every part of me sparks to life as the dreams become reality. Her warm breath mixed with mine tastes like caramel popcorn—salty and sweet. Her voluminous lips are wet and pliable but also powerful and passionate. It's enough to bring a man to his knees. I can't get enough of the feel of her tongue inside my mouth. I start to push her back-ward. I don't know why, or where we're going, but there's an urgent need to have her beneath me. A warning bell goes off inside my head. Somehow I manage to pull back.

"Damn." My heartbeat is erratic.

Jada clings to me, her breaths coming in and out almost as fast as mine. "Oh my God. Denver that was—what was that? It sure felt like more than a kiss."

I run my thumb over her swollen lips. "I just became an addict. I'm a Jada Brooks addict. I'll never get enough. I can kiss you forever and it won't satisfy my thirst for you."

She places her hand over my heart. "We'll start with forever and see how it goes."

CHAPTER ELEVEN

JADA

Denver is taking a shower. A much-needed shower. I'm sitting on his bed processing the events of the afternoon. Not that any amount of processing changes the fact that I have a wolf for a boyfriend. A very sexy wolf boyfriend. His body is the stuff dreams are made of. But I can't wrap my brain around what I saw. Wolves and demons. What else exists if those things are real? And that demon, most hideous thing ever. The stuff nightmares are made of. Denver thinks I screamed because I saw the demon, but I cried out because I was concerned for his safety. This is what he does, what he is—a demon slayer.

I loved putting my hands in his thick, smoky-gray fur. And those glowing blue eyes. He was my Denver—yet different. And Mitch. I might not have guessed, but he has the same striking blue eyes as his brother. His fur was a sandy brown opposed to Denver's gray. I wouldn't have believed it had they not been right there before my eyes.

I lie back on his bed and close my eyes. I'm tired and hungry. Mostly hungry. There are changes taking place within me, and I think Denver knows something. But he says I've had enough crazy for one day. He went on and on to his parents about how proud he is of me. He can't get over how well I have accepted and responded to this new revelation. He didn't give me time to talk to his parents but instead whisked me up to his room for a shower. He did stink in all honesty.

Warm lips brush mine and a whisper of a moan breaks free from my mouth. I open my eyes to Denver standing beside the bed in nothing but a towel. I rake over his glorious body, taking in every detail.

"I'm calling a Hold the Line. You have got to put some clothes on right now."

"I have one question first."

I wave my hand for him to speed this along.

"Why in the name of all that is good, did you not call a Hold the Line up on the hill? I was about to push you to the ground, Jada."

I sit up on the bed. How does he expect me to focus? My head is buzzing with provocative speculation. I close my eyes again. "Please put on your clothes."

His steps retreat across the room. Hangers scrape against metal and a drawer opens and closes. I don't dare open my eyes until he's back by the bed. He's in jeans and a T-shirt.

"Better?"

"A little. Memory is a powerful tool. You're wearing clothes, but I'm remembering the version of you in a towel."

"Why didn't you call a Hold the Line on the hill?"

My face heats. "I was lost in you. The feel of you, the taste of you. My body reacted before my brain."

"This code thing won't work if we don't have the right mind to use it."

"I called it with the towel. We can do this."

"I'm telling you now, if it gets too hard, there will be no more testing our limits. Do you understand?"

"I do."

He pushes his hand in his messy, wet hair and lets out a long breath. He surprises me by scooping me up off the bed into his arms. "I friggin' love you so much." He kisses my forehead and puts me down. "I need food. Let's go to the kitchen—or better yet, I'm craving a burger. Can I take you to dinner?"

"Burger sounds perfect, but I need to change out of these hiking clothes."

"Right. You remember where the spare bedroom is?"

"Yes. I'll go freshen up and meet you in the kitchen."

"Okay, babe."

I'VE BEEN SO busy this afternoon that I haven't checked my phone. I find several texts from Emily and a couple from my mom.

Mom: Hey Jada. Hope you're having a good day with Denver. Please check in and let me know what time you'll be home.

Me: I'm good and we are having a great day. Going to dinner shortly. Not sure how late I'll be.

Then I open Emily's texts.

Emily: I tried to call you. Mitch came by this morning to break up with me.

Emily: This sucks so bad. I like him so much. Where are you?

Emily: Did you know?

Emily: I need to talk to my best friend!

Oh my gosh, poor Emily. She must think I'm terrible.

Me: I swear I had no idea. I'm so sorry!! What was his reason?

Me: Do you want to hang out tonight? I can have Denver drop me off after we eat.

Emily: He said it was complicated. I hate when guys say that. Oh, but he likes me. It's him, not me, blah, blah, blah.

Me: There has to be a reason. I'll try to find out from Denver. Can I come over later?

Emily: I would like that.

Me: I'll be there.

My heart hurts for my friend, and I'm kinda miffed at Mitch. Why did he ask her out only to break up with her? Seems like a jerk move to me. Thing is, Mitch is not a jerk. What happened to make him change his mind? Hopefully Denver will fill in some blanks. Although that's not his specialty. Oh crap. Emily doesn't know. Maybe it has something to do with the whole wolf situation. And if that's the case, I won't be able to give her answers either. Ugh.

My freshen up consists of clean clothes and putting my hair in a ponytail. I get all my things together and head to the kitchen to join Denver.

Denver isn't in the kitchen, Aurar is.

"Hey Aurar. Where's Denver?"

"Hey, sweetie. He went to grab his wallet from his room. You guys going for burgers, huh?"

"Yeah. Sounded good."

"You've had a big day. How are you handling this development?"

I set my bag on the floor and perch on a barstool. "Pretty good, I think. It's a lot to take in, but it doesn't change anything. And I think you guys are pretty amazing too."

"Oh, Jada. As far as we're concerned, you're a part of this family. Our home is yours. The guest room is yours. Stay any time you like."

"Thank you. Wow. I don't know what to say."

"Say about what?" Denver strolls in and lays a kiss on my head.

His mom smiles and shrugs her slender shoulders. I wonder to myself what she looks like as a wolf. "Don't you worry about it, Denver. Take this beautiful girl to get some food. Her stomach rumbles louder than your motorcycle."

I bite my lip. "All the excitement from today has made me hungry."

"Same. There's a mega burger and fries calling my name." He hugs his mom as we pass by her on our way to the garage. "Love you."

"You two have fun."

I EXPECT Denver to get on the motorcycle, but he doesn't. He grabs the keys to the Porsche and lets me in. We ride for several minutes in silence. I'm worried about Emily and what to tell her.

Denver rubs the back of my hand. "What's bothering you, babe?"

"Emily texted me while we were hiking. She said Mitch broke up with her. Did you know?"

"I had a good idea. He was super torn this morning and asked my advice."

"Did you tell him to break up with her?"

"No. Not exactly. Well, sort of, but it's comp—"

"Don't say it's complicated. Girls hate that."

"Mitch is a wolf. You tell me what it is."

"It didn't stop you."

"That's different."

"Why is that different? You can date me, but he can't date her?"

"It's comp—right, don't say that. What we have is different."

"You already said that. How is it different? Why did he say he wanted to date her and then break her heart?"

"He shouldn't have done that. I tried to tell him."

"You told him not to date my friend?" I don't know why I'm getting angry, but I am. Why can't he be straight up with me?

He's smiling at me. Why is he smiling? I want to punch him.

"You're sexy when you get mad."

"Denver Stone, don't you try to distract me."

"And feisty too."

"I mean it." I cross my arms over my chest and glare out the window. "Can you please be serious. My best friend is hurting."

"You're right, I'm sorry." His grip tightens on the wheel. "It's just...I don't know if you're ready for what I have to say."

"Try me. You can trust me, Denver."

He starts and stops twice. "Promise me you'll have an open mind and you won't freak out."

"You're acting crazy. What on earth could be more difficult than telling me you're a wolf?"

We pull into Hagerdy's Burger. Denver grabs his keys and wallet and gets out of the car. He walks over to my side and opens the door.

I sit in my seat with my arms crossed. "I'm not going in until you talk to me."

He reaches down and pulls me out of the car. His hand caresses my face. "This is not a car conversation."

There's a small sitting area down the block with a little grassy spot and park benches. An elderly couple sits on one side, so Denver pulls me to sit on the farthest bench from where they are.

He holds both my hands in his. "All right. Here goes." He blows out a breath. "You're not a girlfriend to me. You're my happy ever after, my forever, my lifetime partner, my lover, my mate. Wolves fall in love with one person. You're my person. Mitch hasn't found that yet. He's not old enough. If he finds his mate later on, he'll end up hurting Emily. I thought it might be better to end it now as opposed to waiting until they got more involved and then crushing her later."

His blue eyes are brilliant in the evening sun and pierce my soul. "I'm your mate?"

"Yes, Jada, you are. You're everything to me. Everything. I would marry you tomorrow if I could. I want to spend the rest of my life making you happy."

"What if I say no? What if I don't want the same thing?"

"Then I spend the rest of my life miserable, dreaming of you by my side, but never having you."

Holy shit. This is serious. I get it now why he didn't want to tell me. We barely know each other, yet he's ready to commit the rest of his life to me. I love him. I do. But this is forever. He's talking forever. The thought of not being with him makes my gut hurt, but still, it's a little soon to confess this level of commitment. At least for me it is. He speaks with conviction, and I believe every word. Oh, Emily. I understand now why it was best they not be together.

Denver leans over placing his elbows on his knees. "I knew it was too soon. You're freaked out, aren't you?"

"I mean somewhat, but give me a minute." My knees brush his as I scoot closer. "You've had your whole life to prepare for this. It's normal and natural for you. I, on the other hand, have been thrust into a world I didn't know existed. I need time to work this all out."

"Baby." Denver cradles my head with his hands, pulling our foreheads together. "I'm not asking you to make any sort of decision.

Take all the time you need. The only reason I told you is so you'd know where I'm coming from and why I didn't think Mitch and Emily are a good idea. I don't want to lie to you."

"And I appreciate that, but I don't know what I'm going to tell Emily."

"I'm sorry, Jada. I did warn Mitch that this would happen. He only realized too late that I might be right."

"She's tough. She hurts now, but in the end it's for the best. I told her I'd come over, by the way. After we had dinner. I hope that's okay."

"Of course. You're free to live your life however you want. I will not force anything on you."

"I might not be ready to marry you, but there's no denying the connection, the rope binding us together. I'm not oblivious to the fact that we have something special."

"Jada. Words fail me…"

I push my lips to his. My hand trails up his stomach, and he trembles at my touch. I whisper my love to him as we breathe in each other's air. His chest vibrates with a growl. We're able to kiss tenderly for a moment, but the intensity starts to build and I pull back.

"Hold the Line," I say, almost panting. "Is this physical attraction part of the mating thing?"

Denver has to catch his breath before speaking. "It is. I didn't touch another woman before you. I wanted to experience all my firsts with the one I love. My mate. A wise man once said, *Don't excite love, don't stir it up, until the time is ripe—and you're ready.*"

"Who said that?"

"It's in the *Song of Solomon*."

"Hmm. Very smart man."

The older couple that had been seated across the way walks in our direction. They're holding hands and it's so sweet. The gentleman pauses and places his hand on Denver's shoulder. "You make a wonderful couple. Reminds me of myself and my beautiful Rosa. May you always find happiness in each other."

Denver smiles and nods. "Thank you, sir. That's the plan."

"All right then, carry on." He winks and they walk away.

I run my fingers up Denver's arms. "You heard the man, carry on."

"Not happening." Denver stands.

I put on my best pouty face. "Why not?"

"Two reasons. One, I'm hungry. And two, I've already taken approximately ten cold showers since the day we met."

Heat creeps up my neck and face. "That was both sexy and a little TMI." I hold out my hand for him to pull me up. "Food it is."

AFTER DINNER, Denver drops me off at my house. I attempt a goodbye kiss, but he pushes me out of the car. Says he's trying to keep the cold showers to a two-a-day maximum. I tell him how frustrating he is, and he lets me know how feisty I am. We make our plans for tomorrow, and now I'm in my room packing a bag for Emily's. My brain hurts from wondering what in the world I'll tell her that will make the situation better. I'm shoving in my toothbrush when there's a knock at my door.

"Hey sweetie. You're home early." She takes in my packed bag. "Where are you going?"

"Hey, Mom. Emily needs a girls' night. She and Mitch broke up, so I wanted to keep her company. She's probably into her second ice cream carton by now."

"Poor Emily. He seemed like a nice boy. You and Denver are good, I assume?"

"He is a nice guy, and yes, Denver and I are great."

She tries to hide a smile. "I figured as much. Well, have fun at Emily's. Will you be home in the morning?"

"Yeah, I'll be home to shower around ten. Denver has some sort of family thing tomorrow he wants me to go to. I need to be out at his place around noon."

"You two are spending quite a bit of time together."

Oh geez. How do I respond to that? *Yeah, Mom, Denver wants to marry me and spend the rest of his life with me. I'm leaning toward yes, but you know, I'll give it a few more days.* "I like him a lot."

"You certainly do. How is Grainger dealing with all this?"

"We're working through it. Denver invited him to a BBQ in a couple of weeks, and he said he would come."

"That's good. I know he means a lot to you."

She cracks her knuckles and dances from one foot to the other. My mother is not a Nervous Nelly. Her uneasiness makes me uncomfortable.

"Is there something else? You're acting funny."

"No sweetie. I love you is all." She wraps her arms around me in a bear hug. "I love you so much. I know things are changing, but I don't want you to forget that."

I have the strangest sensation there's more to her anxiety, but I don't press. "I love you too, Mom."

She holds me at arm's length, smiling at me. I think we're having one of those mother-daughter moments. Her eyes become glassy and she clears her throat. "I've held you up long enough. You and Emily have a nice time. I know she appreciates you being there for her."

"She would do the same for me." I gather my things and follow my mom down the hall. She turns for the kitchen, and I head for the front door. I expect her to look back or say something, but she doesn't.

I WAS right on the ice cream. Emily finished off the chocolate and is currently eating chocolate chip cookie dough. She'll be sick if she keeps this up.

I take the ice cream from her tight grip and steal her spoon as well. "You better let me have some of that. I don't want to clean up puke in the middle of the night."

She falls back against the bed frame. "It's not nice to steal from someone who's feeding their suffering."

"It is when you're keeping them from vomiting."

A tear slips down her cheek. "I really liked him."

I shove the ice cream on the nightstand and put my arm around her. "I know. I'm sorry."

"I thought he liked me too."

"He did, he does, but he's not ready for a relationship."

Her pupils darken and her nostrils flare. "Is that what he said? What a jerk face. He shouldn't have asked me out if he didn't want to be in a relationship."

"That was Denver's explanation. I haven't talked to Mitch."

"Whatever. He's still a jerk face."

"I truly am sorry."

"Me too. I've spent my whole senior year pining over this guy and then he dumps me. I wanted him to ask me to prom."

"Oh Lord, prom. I haven't given it much thought."

She sits up in the bed. "Do you think Denver will ask you to go?"

"Why would he? He's not in high school anymore."

"He can still go. All you have to do is fill out the visitor form and he's under 21, so he's eligible. You should ask him."

I roll my eyes. "I'm not asking Denver to the prom."

"Why not?"

"It's weird, okay."

"Jada, we have to go to prom. It's our senior year."

Ugh. Honestly, I couldn't care less, but I'll go for Emily. "Maybe you and Mitch could go as friends. Or I'll be your date. Or..."

"Or what?"

"What about Grainger?"

"Hold the phone. Exactly what are you saying?"

I grab a throw pillow and hug it to my chest. "He's a great guy, Emily. You know he broke up with Candy, so he's not going to have a date either."

"I can't believe I'm hearing this. It's too weird. He is a nice guy, but—no, not gonna happen."

"Fine. It was merely a suggestion." I toss the pillow and snatch the ice cream. "Do you want me to talk to Denver? If you want to go with Mitch as friends, I'll ask him and see if it's a possibility."

She falls back over a mound of pillows. "I don't know. Maybe."

"No pressure. I'll do whatever you want."

Emily continues to stare at the ceiling. "Thank you. What would I do without you?"

"You'd be puking up ice cream."

She laughs. "Truth."

"You wanna watch movies? I can make the popcorn."

"Sure, why not."

I shuffle to the kitchen and pop two bags of popcorn and nab a couple of Cokes. By the time I get back to her room, she's got the pillows stacked up and the covers pulled down. We sit nestled in her bed for hours watching movies until we can't hold our eyes open any longer.

"JADA, WAKE UP."

My eyes have sand in them, I'm sure of it. They burn when I try to push my eyelids open. "I don't want to."

"Okay, but it's ten-thirty, and I'm pretty sure you have a date with a certain hottie today."

I sit straight up in the bed. "Shit. It's ten-thirty already?"

Emily holds her phone up as proof. "Yep."

"Crud. I have an hour to get ready. I don't have time to go home."

"Don't you worry. I've got this. Go jump in the shower, and I'll put together a killer outfit."

"Really?"

"Yes, really. Now go."

"I love you."

I leap off the bed and run to Emily's bathroom. A hot shower never felt so good. I let the spray hit me in the face and run down my body. The only thing I need now is a cup of coffee. Or two. I literally got like five hours of sleep. Not to worry. When I get my hands on Denver, I'll have all the energy I need. My heart squeezes at the thought of being near him. The things he told me yesterday bring light to several unanswered questions. When we're apart, I have this deep longing inside of me only he can fill. His presence saturates my soul. His voice soothes me and his love brings me life. A part of me resonates with his confession of his desire for a lifelong partnership. How would I live without him? Oh my gosh, what am I thinking? I'm an eighteen-year-old girl on the cusp of graduating high school. Shouldn't I be ready to sow my wild oats or some shit like that?

"Jada! Hurry up. I'm gonna need time to do your makeup."

Crap. "I'm coming! Hey, Em, will you do me a favor?"

"Depends."

"Use my phone to text my mom and let her know I overslept and I'm getting ready over here."

"All right."

"You have a text from Denver. He says to hurry the hell up."

"Tell him to chill."

I towel dry my hair and then wrap the towel around me. Emily has eighties music playing from her speaker and is dancing in front of the mirror.

"Bout dang time."

"Sorry. It felt so good." I stop by the bed to glance at the clothes she's laid out. "Emily, you want to tell me where the rest of the material is for these shorts?"

Her hand goes to her hip. "What? That is a perfectly good pair of shorts. You've got killer tan, long legs. We might as well put them to good use. Denver won't be able to keep his hands off you."

"Uh, yeah, we don't have any problem with that."

"What? I need deets. Did you kiss him?"

I stammer to answer her and she starts screaming.

"Holy cow, you did! This is huge, Jada. How was it?"

I reposition my towel and sit on the bed. "Everything I dreamed and more. It was like I lost all coherent thought and control of my body or will. In that moment, there was nothing but him."

Emily fans herself with her hand. "Dang girl, sounds hot. When was this?"

I fiddle with the edge of my towel. "Yesterday."

"Why didn't you tell me?"

"You were upset with you-know-who, so I didn't want to bring it up."

She huffs and rolls her eyes. "You-know-who is still on my crap list, but I'm happy for you. I truly am."

"Thanks."

"Shoot. We need to get you ready." She points to the clothes. "Put those on."

"Yes ma'am." Denver is going to have a conniption. Don't get me wrong, the outfit is super cute. The summer-yellow top is low cut and flowy with daisies on it. She's paired it with the ripped jean shorts and a cute pair of sandals. There's even a white denim jacket if it gets cool later. But oh man, there's a lot of skin. Denver may need an extra cold shower today.

CHAPTER TWELVE

DENVER

Sweat drips down my body. My muscles ache, and I'm tired and hungry, but I beat the crap out of the punching bag in front of me. Mitch and I have been working out and sparring for over two hours. I throw a few more punches and decide to call it quits. Mitch is on his last set of bench presses.

I sit on the bench next to his and wipe sweat from my face with a towel. "Nice workout today, brother."

He pushes up the bar for the last time and sits up. I throw him a clean towel.

"Yeah, well, I did kick your ass in the ring earlier."

"Whatever, dude. If it helps you sleep at night, you keep on telling yourself that."

He pops me with his towel and a welt forms on my thigh. He points toward the ring. "Let's go right now. I'll prove it."

"Ain't nobody got time for that. I need food and a shower before Jada gets here."

Mitch scrunches his face as if I'd punched him. Again. "Did Jada say how Emily is doing?"

"We haven't texted since last night. She said Emily was eating a lot of ice cream." I shrug. "I think that was supposed to be a bad thing."

"I'm such a prick. I hate that I did this to her. I like her. She's fun to be with, and she's smart and hot, and she's kind, and did I mention hot?"

I laugh. "You did. Have you said anything to Dad? He might have some advice. I mean, it's odd that you're drawn to her at all. No one sparked even the tiniest bit of interest in me until Jada showed up. It could be you have some sort of pre-mate premonition. You're almost eighteen."

"You making up crap now to help me feel better?"

"Talk to Dad."

"Yeah, maybe. At this point the deed has been done. The hard part will be keeping my distance. Damn. I don't know why I went and kissed her. It's all I think about."

"I can relate to your pain on that one. And speaking of such matters, I need to shower. I hate you're going through this. I'm here if you need me."

We fist bump as I pass. I would give him a hug, but we're both dripping sweat. Our bond is such that we don't need words to communicate. He knows I would move heaven and earth for him if need be.

AFTER MY SHOWER, I eat a second breakfast and then walk down to Dad's study. He's talking to someone—maybe an elder about the recent demon attack on us yesterday—so I wait in the hall. It was odd for a demon to be out in the woods like that, unless...

The phone call ends and I tap on the door. "Dad can I come in?"

"Yes, Denver, of course."

His desk is a mess. Papers are scattered and spread out in every direction. There's a stack of files to one side and his computer is covered in sticky notes. He leans back in his chair and sips on his coffee.

My dad is always trying to save the world. Fix all the problems. Find all the answers. I love his tenacity and his fierce passion for life, but the worry lines and dark circles tell me he's tired and over-whelmed.

"Did you sleep at all last night?"

"Not much, son. There's so much going on."

"What's happening now?"

He throws his feet up on the desk. "Where to begin." He takes another drink of coffee and puts the cup on the corner of the desk. "Tell me first. How are you and Jada?"

"We're great. She found out we're wolves and she's my mate all in the same day and didn't bolt, so I'd say that's pretty good. She's so strong. Mentally. Incredibly strong. Lord knows how attracted I am to her, but the beauty in her soul makes her that much more irresistible."

"She is certainly special. The more I'm around her, the more I sense it. A light sizzle emanated as I passed her last week. Mitchell experienced something similar at school the other day. Did he share that with you?"

"He did not." I sift through a pile of papers on his desk. "Is that one of the many searches you've got going on here?"

"Yes. It is. But I suppose we'll know more when she changes. Any development on that front?"

"Not yet. Were you talking to an elder?"

He blows out a long breath. "I was. They're concerned about the attack yesterday."

"I figured. Is it possible the demon was after Jada? I've been hiking these woods for years and never encountered a demon. Why now?"

"That appears to be the question of the day. Again, there's something unique in her presence. I have no idea why a demon would be after her though."

"Me either. So weird. Where are we on the demon shift?"

"Something is stirring. Waiting. For what we don't know. The elder also said a fellow wolf spotted a royal in town. So now there's that to add to the mix."

"A royal?"

"I've told you the stories. Wolves of royal blood. Once upon a time I knew a man, a royal, but he and his family have been gone for years."

I wave my hand in the air. "I remember the stories, but why would a royal be here? Could it be your old acquaintance?"

"He was more than an acquaintance, and I would like to think my friendship meant enough that he would pay me a visit if he were in town. Anyway, like I said before, several events transpiring all at once. Don't worry. We'll figure it out."

"I'm not worried, except over the fact that my dad needs some sleep."

He yawns to prove my point. "Maybe I will nap before the gathering today."

I nod. "Solid plan, Dad. Oh hey, I did have one question."

"Regarding Mitchell and Emily. You leaked that one."

"I've got to do a better job of guarding my thoughts around here. Any ideas?"

"You gave him sound advice."

"Aren't his cravings toward her strange?"

"Could be simple infatuation."

I push my hands in my hair. "But what if it's not?"

My dad pushes up from his seat and leans his head from side to side. His neck cracks and pops in both directions. "I'm going to leave that mystery to you. I've got plenty to keep me busy for a while. I want updates on Jada's progress. We'll have to tell her soon."

"Yes sir."

"Tell your mother I've gone to lie down."

"I'm sure she'll be glad to hear it."

My head is spinning as I amble around the house searching for my mother. Jada will be here soon, but I want to let Mom know Dad went to rest. My search indoors comes up empty handed, so I go out on the back deck. The weather has been so warm, Mom's flowers are in full bloom. The scrape of a bucket lets me know she's near. I find her watering the roses.

"Hey, Mom."

She wipes her hand across her face, leaving a smear of dirt. "Hey. I'm surprised you're not waiting out front for that sweet Jada."

I smile and point to her cheek. "You've got a little something…"

She makes another swipe with her hand, doubling the dirt on her face. "Oh well, I'm taking a shower shortly. Did you need something?"

"Dad wanted you to know he's taking a nap before the gathering."

The proud-mom smile takes over her features. "Thank you, Denver."

"You're welcome. I'm gonna go wait on my sweet Jada."

"All right."

I pass through the kitchen and grab a cold beer. It must be near eighty today. Perfect day for a wolf gathering. We attempt to get together with the other wolf families once a month. Not to talk business, but to have fun. There will be tons of food, laughter, and games. I hope Jada is good at cornhole. I don't like to lose. My phone alarm goes off in my pocket. It's noon. The gathering isn't until later this afternoon, but I didn't tell Jada that. I needed her all to myself before the onslaught of introductions and socializing. Before her car is in view, the noisy muffler on her Jetta announces her arrival.

I'm sitting on one of the many porch rockers as she exits her car. I nearly spew beer all over myself. Ah, hell. Is she trying to freaking kill me? Her toned, long legs glitter in the sun. In fact, her entire body from head to toe seems to have been kissed by the sun god himself. She's practically glowing. I shake my head in disbelief. How is it that she's more exquisite every time I see her? I bound down the steps and push her against her car before she knows what's hit her.

I lean into her and sniff her hair. Her vanilla and coconut scent makes me wish we were on a beach somewhere. I want to say something, but all I'm able to croak out is her name. "Jada."

She moans something or other about the way I say her name. Her hands slip under my T-shirt and trail up my back. The contact sends me reeling and I know I'm on the verge of losing my cool. Why did she wear these damn shorts? I hate her and I love her for it.

A growl escapes my throat as I rip myself apart from her. I curse the sun god as I pace the driveway. She doesn't move or speak. When I'm focused enough to make coherent sentences I stop in front of her.

"It's a reoccurring theme here, but I'm sorry. I didn't mean to attack you, but what the hell were you thinking wearing those sexy shorts over here?"

She leans back and crosses her ankles. It's like she taunting me. "So what—I have to wear jeans all summer?"

"Yes, please."

She laughs as she pushes off the car. She strolls right by me and bounds up the porch steps. I trail behind her like a lamb off to the slaughter. Killing me would be easier than this.

Jada pauses at the door waiting for me to catch up. "Could I have a drink?"

I can't resist the urge to kiss her forehead but don't touch her anywhere else. "Sure, babe. Come on. Oh, hang on." What's left of my beer still sits on the table, so I grab it up and take it with me. Dang, but I might need a few more of these today.

Jada sits at what appears to be her seat at the bar. I get her a pop and myself another beer. She eyes me but doesn't say anything.

Mitch comes in while I'm still in the fridge. "Damn brother, what's got you all tied up? Your distress signals are through the roof." I nod in her direction. "What's up, Jada?"

"Hey, Mitch. Apparently I'm not allowed to wear shorts."

Mitch glances around the end of the bar and whistles. "Makes perfect sense."

I slug him in the arm with force. He swears and excuses himself.

Jada bites her lip and smiles. "He was messing with you, Denver."

I lean on the opposite side of the counter to keep some distance between us. "Let's just say he was more appreciative of your legs than he should have been."

Her face turns pink. "Oh."

"In fact, you might as well prepare yourself for more of the same later."

She scrunches her nose and forehead. "What do you mean?"

"This gathering we're going to is a wolf thing. There will be several families and lots of hormonal teenage boys. I'm sure they will appreciate your legs as well."

"Oh Lord. Why didn't you tell me?"

"Would it have mattered? You seem pretty hell bent on torturing me today."

"The truth is, I overslept this morning and Emily picked out my clothes. I didn't have time to go home. But in this heat, I would have opted for shorts over jeans anyway. I can't wear pants all summer, Denver."

I finish off my beer and round the bar. "I know, baby. This is so difficult for me. It's no secret what you do to me, but it's my demon to slay. You can wear what you want."

She jumps off the stool and pushes her body against mine. "You think you're the only one tortured here? Do you even look at yourself? You don't think your perfectly sculpted body screams at me? And those damn lips of yours, so full and sexy, begging to be kissed. You are sadly mistaken if you think you're the only tormented person in this relationship."

She's angry. It's rolling off of her like hot lava. Her wolf, if that's what she is, imploring to come out. I whisper to her through my mind to help calm her down.

Jada. My beautiful Jada.

She gasps but then smiles.

We're such a hot mess.

"Yeah, we are. Does it get any easier?"

I uh, think there's relief once we, you know, but we'll always crave each other. And not only physically. We fulfill each other mentally and emotionally as well.

"Will I be able to speak to you this way?"

Yes.

"When?"

You want to try now?

"Yes!"

The first thing you need to do is detach your body from mine. Please.

"Right. My bad. I got a little ticked off there. Sorry."

I laugh out loud. "It's okay. I like being on the receiving end of your energy. No matter what it is."

My mom and dad enter the kitchen. I'm sure they caught some of the waves leaving this room. Dad is the first to speak.

"You two okay in here?"

I smile at Jada. "Better now." She kicks me in the shin.

My mom holds no punches. "You could cut the sexual tension in here with a knife." She glances at my dad and winks. Yuck.

"We were struggling, but I think we've found something to occupy our time for a while. Jada wants to try working on her telepathy skills."

"That's a great idea. I remember when your dad and I first discovered our bond in that way. It's very special. Why don't you take Jada out on the deck by the pool and I'll bring you some refreshments."

"Thanks, Mom."

I overhear my mother as we exit the room. "You think they're going to make it? Their bond is stronger than any I've seen."

My dad sighs. "I'd marry them right now if I could. They're making me miserable."

Mom's singsong laugh fills the room. Then silence. I don't want to know what they're doing.

Jada and I sit at the edge of the pool with our feet in the water. It's a great day for a swim. I wish I'd thought of it this morning for cardio instead of running. I want to ask Jada if she likes to swim, but the thought of her in a bathing suit makes my heart rate go up.

Jada splashes water in my direction. "You ever go swimming?"

"Yeah. Mitch and I do a lot of laps in the summer. Or sometimes for fun too. Mitch loves to have people out for pool parties. I bet he'll have one for graduation."

"I love to swim and lay out by the pool. You think I could come over and lay out this summer?"

I kiss the back of her hand. "I don't think you understand this whole mate thing. Everything I have is yours. You are a part of this family. My parents love you. You can live here this summer if you want. Or forever would work too."

Jada's lips curl up along with her eyebrows. "Can I drive the Porsche?"

"Well...maybe not everything."

She slaps my arm. "So not cool."

"I'm joking, babe. You know how to drive a stick shift?"

"No, but you can teach me."

"That will be our next project."

Jada peers down at her feet as she swirls them in the water. "Were you serious about me living here?"

"Absolutely."

"Your parents wouldn't care?"

"Not at all. Of course you'd have to stay in the spare bedroom unless you're ready to marry me. I'm gonna go out on a limb and say you're not there yet."

She sucks up the corner of her bottom lip. I want to help her out with that. I know I'm staring at her mouth, but I can't stop. She leans forward, so I lean forward. Her cinnamon breath tickles my lips. I've decided to close the gap when there's a scrape on the table behind us. Jada jerks back and her attention is down at her feet once more.

My mom places a tray of fruit and cheese on the table. "Have you made any progress?"

"We haven't started yet."

Mom's hand goes on her hip. "Uh huh. You were about to start something."

I throw my hands in the air. "We're going to work on it now. Promise."

She walks over and ruffles my hair. "Behave, Denver Stone."

"Lord knows I'm trying."

"JADA, you're trying too hard. You look like you're constipated."

She grunts and leans back in her chair. "What am I doing wrong?"

"Don't force it. It's a natural flow between us. Close your eyes."

She straightens her shoulders and closes her eyes. "Now what?"

"Relax. Take deep breaths and think about somewhere you'd like to be."

"Okay." Her breathing evens out and her tense shoulders release.

"Tell me about where you are."

A faint smile appears on her face. "On a beach. The sun is warm on my skin. There's a slight breeze. Warm sand between my toes. Waves crashing on the shore. You're there too."

Oh my God, I've got to take this woman to the beach. Honeymoon perhaps. Not that she has agreed to marry me. Yet. "That's perfect. Reach out to me with your mind. Tell me something as we sit on the shore together."

A moment of silence passes. I don't press or speak. She continues to take steady breaths and her smile broadens. A single tear slips down her cheek.

I love you.

Holy shit. I was not expecting that. Her words are like tiny, warm, sparks traveling through my bloodstream. I freaking tingle all over.

Her eyes flash open and she stares at me while I try to compose myself. "Did it work?"

I thought I wanted her before. Everything she does pushes me further over the edge. My mom and dad might be right. If I can't get her to marry me soon, we could be in trouble.

"Jada. I love you too."

"You heard me."

"Loud and clear."

"Oh my gosh. That is so amazing. And sensual. The connection is very intimate."

I let out a nervous laugh. "Yeah, it doesn't feel like that when Mitch does it."

"Oh really? How was it?" Her expression is heated as she slides off her chair and flirtatiously strolls in my direction.

I rub my temples. "Jada. I can't—my control is slipping."

She climbs in my lap and straddles me. "My control slipped a long time ago."

Her lips brush mine and a deep growl burns in my chest. My vision blurs as the need for her takes over every part of me. I press my mouth hard against hers, and she parts her lips for me. My tongue explores her and she shows me the same desire. We kiss and lick and bite. I trail down to her neck and she moans her approval as she throws her head back. My hands are tangled in her hair. This primal urge overwhelms me to lay her down and take all of her.

She wraps her legs around me as I stumble to a lounge as we continue to kiss. When she's beneath me, it's the most euphoric thing I've yet to experience. A part of me whispers we need to stop, but the dominant flesh is winning this battle. Her hands are like fire to my skin. The kiss continues to ignite and I fear I'm being too rough, but she matches my every move with the same force. She is my mate. My bones ache at the knowledge of how much I love her and how badly I want her.

Jada pulls back panting. "Denver, we need to Hold the Line."

I slide off of her and plant my butt on the deck beside her. "Shit."

She sits up and scoots to the end of the lounge. Her fingers twist in my hair.

Denver?

I nod in answer.

I do want to marry you.

Time slows down as I process her words. A life with her is what I want more than anything, but I don't want her to make a hasty decision.

"Jada, you don't have to say anything right now. I can wait. I'll wait for as long as you need."

She runs her thumb over my lips. "After graduation then."

"Is that what you want? Are you sure?"

"Denver Stone, I love you and I want to spend the rest of my life with you. I can't explain how, but every fiber of my being knows we belong together. I need you more than food or water. I need you to be by my side forever, or I can't face forever."

"My beautiful Jada." I climb up on the lounge and sit beside her. She curls up into me. "I am yours forever, whether or not we marry or have

sex. I want you to know that. If you want to get married after graduation, I'll be the first one there. If you want to wait, that's fine too."

"I don't need time to…"

"Let me finish. After you graduate high school, I'll give you a
proper proposal. If you accept, then we'll figure out the when and
where. Not before."

"You drive a hard bargain." Her finger caresses my cheek. "It's a
deal."

I lightly kiss her lips. I have to quit there or we'll be in the same
predicament we were earlier. "Thank you for calling a Hold. I needed
that."

"It was difficult. Sometimes I swear it's like something else takes
over when I'm near you."

I know what she means, but we're so not having that discussion
today. "Come on, babe. Let's go see if the fam is ready to head to the
gathering."

MY MOM COOKED enough food for an army. It's a group effort to get
all the dishes and bowls to the car. We all pile in Dad's Cadillac
Escalade and take off to my aunt and uncle's house. They have kids
our age, but Jada won't know them because they homeschool. Most
wolves do, but not all. She should recognize Rieder. Mitch and I
were homeschooled for several years, but we begged to attend public
school. Mom finally gave in.

We've been in the car all of two seconds when Mitch starts in.

Dude, can you try to dial down the make-out sessions?

Jada has a coughing fit beside me so I pat her back. "You okay?"

She attempts to whisper, but it does no good in a vehicle full of
wolves. "How does *he* know?"

Mitch leans forward in his seat. "Wait. You heard that?"

Jada nods.

I glance back and forth between Mitch and Jada. "You heard
Mitch talking to me just now?"

She smirks at me like I'm dumb or something. "Yes."

What the hell. "Dad, are you catching this?"

"I am."

"What do you make of it?"

"I told you our girl is special."

Jada grabs my thigh and squeezes. "What? Did I do something wrong?"

"No, babe. You're advanced is all. It's normal to start with your mate and be able to communicate with them that way, but it usually takes longer to pick up on others." I tap my mom on the shoulder. "Say something to me."

Did you unload the dishwasher?

Oops.

I glance at Jada. "Anything?"

"Sounds like you forgot to unload the dishwasher."

"Holy cow. That's crazy." I grab her face and kiss her full on the lips. "You are amazing."

Her face turns pink as she thanks me. The rest of the ride we attempt to explain the ins and outs of telepathy. Our family is close knit and we don't hide much, but you can block your thoughts if you want to. I roll my eyes as Dad talks about how *loud and strong* I can be. Mitch gives a hearty amen and I slug him. Jada laughs. She becomes mortified as she learns Mitch not only hears but can sometimes feel as I do.

He's been trying to block my recent flow of hormones but can't always make it stop. Hence the reason he knew about our make-out session on the deck. Honestly, Mom and Dad probably know too and were ready to step in if need be, but they don't let on to Jada. She's fascinated and eager to learn. It makes me fall in love with her all over again.

Jada's mouth falls open as we make our way down the tree-lined drive. The mansion is quite impressive, I suppose. I've been coming here my whole life, so it's not a big deal to me.

Jada takes my arm as we walk around to the back of the house.

"This place is breathtaking. It's like stepping into a scene from a movie. I've never seen so many columns before."

"This plantation home belonged to my grandparents, and their parents before them, etc. Now my aunt and uncle live here with my two cousins. It's a very old home, but updated of course."

"You're telling me four people live in this gigantic house?"

I shrug. "Yeah, and the people they hire to cook and clean."

"Wow. I thought your house was big."

"This could have been our home, but Dad wanted to live a simpler life with his family. He's not much on this sort of grandiose thing."

Jada laughs. "Really? You could have fooled me. One of your cars costs as much as my whole house."

I smile. "We do like our cars. Does it bother you that we have money?"

"It would if you were a prick about it, but you're one of the most humble people I know. Your family treats me with kindness and love and respect. So, no."

I pause before we reach the corner and have to dive into full-blown wolf society mode. "This could be a little crazy. Are you ready to meet everyone?"

She lets out a short puff of air. "Lead the way."

I lean in and kiss her soft lips. "I love you."

CHAPTER THIRTEEN

JADA

I'm not good with architecture, but you don't need a degree to know this home is worth millions. The grass is perfectly manicured, not a weed in sight. Pink azaleas and blood-red roses line the front. The landscaping is flawless. The massive white structure has a porch for days, and I've lost count of the Greek-style columns. The upstairs balcony rail is covered in vines, but it gives off an elegant vibe, not one of neglect. I knew Denver and his family were wealthy, but this is extravagant to say the least. I break out in a sweat and force a slow breath in and out of my lungs. How will I ever fit in with these people? As Denver and I approach the backyard, music and laughter fill my ears along with the squeals of children and splashing water. Of course they have a pool. Denver stops before we round the corner and asks if I'm ready. Honestly, I'm not sure, but what choice do I have? He kisses me tenderly and then says he loves me with so much devotion I have the courage to face this head on.

We stop by a table and unload the food we're carrying. I'm overwhelmed by the number of people here. Denver grabs my hand and whispers not to worry. Easy for him to say. I take in the grounds as Denver scans the crowd for his aunt and uncle. He pulls me along the deck housing the pool and tons of seating all around. Colors burst from the potted plants of all shapes and sizes. The deck opens up to a grassy area where a white tent has been set up. Beyond that, more open yard, and then a garden with a fountain in the center. Several cornhole games are underway. A few teens play volleyball, and a game of croquet causes a young man to swear.

We reach the tent, and I spot a gentleman that must be Denver's uncle. He has Bolivar's kind smile and the same bright blue eyes. He stands with his arm around a strawberry-blonde woman. Their faces brighten as we approach, and the man clasps Denver's hand.

"How's my favorite nephew?"

"Never better." Denver hugs the woman. "I want you both to meet Jada. I'm sure Dad has filled you in."

"Jada, this is Dad's brother Alexander and his wife Vashti."

Alexander takes my hand and smiles. "It is our pleasure, Jada. Welcome to the family and to our home."

"Thank you. It's nice to meet you."

Vashti surprises me with a hug. Her smile is genuine and her tone is soft as she speaks. "Anyone who makes our Denver happy is all right with us. Please make yourself at home and let me know if you need anything."

"I will, thank you. Your home is beautiful."

"We're blessed to be here and to be able to share it. Would you like a tour later?"

"I would like that very much."

She pats my arm. "I'll find you after bit and we'll walk and talk. I'd love to hear how Denver swept you off your feet."

I smile at Denver. "He tries."

Her laugh is soft like her voice. "I like her already."

Alexander kisses my cheek. "You are a special girl. Bolivar is right in saying so." He takes his wife's hand. "We need to greet other guests, but we'll have you out soon for dinner so we can get to know Miss Jada better."

"That'd be great. I'm going to introduce Jada to the rest of the gang."

Alexander smiles. "Of course."

As we walk away, Alexander and Vashti are laughing with another couple. "They are so nice."

"What did you expect?"

I shrug. "I don't know. Snobby, rich people."

Denver wraps his arm around my waist. "Not everyone that has wealth is rude and arrogant."

"I'm starting to figure that out."

We walk toward the cornhole boards, which appears to be the hotspot for our age group. I recognize a kid from school coming our way. Denver nods as he approaches.

"What's up, Rie-man?"

"Not much, WP. You in on a game of cornhole?"

"You'll pay for that later. You know Jada from school?"

"Yeah, man. We have a class together. Hey, Jada."

"Hey, Rieder. So what does WP stand for?"

Denver shoves Rieder in the shoulder. "Never mind that. Let's play cornhole."

Rieder winks at me as we walk to an empty set of boards. "I'll tell you at school tomorrow."

"You really are asking for it." Denver picks up the bags and nudges my elbow. "You ever play?"

"Nope, but I'm pretty good at horseshoes. Seems similar."

He hands me the bags. "Here, do a little warm up. Obviously the hole is the best shot, but getting them on the board counts too."

"Okay. Where do I stand?"

"Don't pass the end of your board and you're good."

I throw all eight bags in a row. The first two end up on the ground, but as I get used to the weight of it, two end up in the hole and the rest on the board.

"Nice. So, Rie-man, who's your partner gonna be?"

"He's on his way."

A young male voice pops up in my head.

Damn Denver, your girl is fine.

A younger version of Rieder walks up. He has the same dark hair, emerald green eyes, and muscular build. The biggest difference being where Rieder has scruff, this boy has a smooth, baby face. Both are extremely handsome. He continues to speak to Denver. *If you ever need me to take her off your hands, I'll be glad to get my hands...*

Denver cuts him off. "I wouldn't do that if I were you." He points in my direction.

He scrunches his nose. "There's no way."

"Jada, you want to tell the boy what you heard?"

I bite my lip. This is kinda fun. "Thanks for the compliment, but I'm pretty sure Denver won't be letting *your* hands anywhere near me."

Denver and Rieder are both rolling in laughter as the younger boy tries to apologize.

"Shit, I'm sorry...I didn't know...I mean, I was just messing around—"

Poor kid is dying over here. "It's fine. I'm Jada, and you are?"

"Layne." He points to Rieder. "This dork is my older brother."

Rieder holds his side. "Dude, you calling me a dork? I think we all know who the dork is."

"Whatever. Are we playing or what?"

"Yeah sure. You stay down here with Jada."

Denver kisses my head. "You'll throw against Layne and I'll throw against Rieder. It'll be more even that way."

He and Rieder walk down to the opposite board. Poor Layne, he's embarrassed and stares straight ahead.

"So how do you guys know Denver? You cousins or something?"

"Nah. Denver and Rieder are like best friends. Plus, we patrol together."

"Patrol?"

"Yeah, you know, walk the streets at night, make sure there's no demons causing trouble."

"I wasn't aware, but I'm still learning all this wolf stuff."

"Oh, right. It's pretty awesome. Killing demons that is."

"I bet. So what grade are you in?"

"Freshman."

"Really? You go to the high school?"

"Uh huh."

"Wow. I don't know that I've noticed you before."

"I've definitely noticed you."

His face turns red with his last statement. I don't want to embarrass him further, so I don't respond. It's our turn to throw anyway.

Denver and I squeak out the win over Rieder and his brother. We play two more games with other opponents before it's time to eat. I meet several of Denver's friends and pack members. Everyone is friendly, but Denver is right about the boys—Layne's aren't the only comments. Lots of hormones around here. Briar and Brantley Stone are perfect gentleman like all the Stone men. I also meet a young girl named Kalika and her friend Jovana. There are several others, but their names escape me.

These families sure know how to cook, and they make plenty of it. I guess that's necessary when you're feeding packs of wolves. After dinner, Vashti steals me for the grand tour of the house. We hit it off immediately, and I enjoy her company very much. Afterward, the kids our age get in a best three out of five in volleyball. I haven't had this much fun or felt so accepted in all my life. These people have taken me in, no questions asked. The only thing that would make this more perfect would be sharing it with my two best friends, Grainger and Emily.

The volleyball game leaves me hot and sweaty. And thirsty. Denver excuses himself to get us a drink. He returns shortly with my water and beers for all the boys.

The guys talk demon hunting for a while and then Denver grabs my hand.

"You want to walk through the garden?"

"I thought you'd never ask."

Denver winks to the guys as we walk away. "Catch you later, boys."

The garden resembles a maze with lots of twists and turns. We stroll quietly for a while, enjoying the tranquility it provides. Denver guides me to a bench in a sitting area with a small pond full of goldfish.

I lay my head on his shoulder while watching the fish swim back and forth. "Thank you for today."

Denver kisses the top of my head. "You're welcome. You are a part of this now. And all of this is a part of you. My family is your family. My friends are your friends."

"Because I'm your mate?"

"Yes, but it's more than that. They love *you*. I have seen where a family doesn't instantly connect with someone's mate, but my family loves you. You have felt it, right?"

"Yes. Your family is amazing."

"You're the one who's amazing. You played some kickass cornhole and volleyball today. And won over my family to boot. I don't deserve you, Jada."

I twist so that I can stare into his blue eyes and find his irresistible lips barely a breath away. He smiles and that sexy dimple pops up on his right cheek. "Can we kiss without everyone here knowing about it?"

"My thoughts are locked up tighter than a bank vault."

"Perfect."

Our tender kiss escalates into a blazing fire. My lips tingle and my insides burn with a new zeal. I don't remember Denver pushing me down on the bench, nor do I recall pushing his shirt up. My body is feverish and my pulse points pound out erratic beats. The energy Denver is pushing through me makes me lightheaded and dazed.

I push against Denver's chest and call a Hold.

He sits up, his eyes dilated and wild. "What the hell happened?" Denver bolts up and paces in front of me as I sit up on the bench. He clutches the back of his neck. "I mean, I know what happened, but at the same time, I don't. Shit, now I sound crazy."

I can't answer him because I'm in the same boat.

He kicks the bench leg with a swear and sits on the edge of the seat. "Jada, we can't do this anymore. I thought I could control myself, but apparently I'm not strong enough. When I kiss you, I lose any semblance of integrity."

My stomach is queasy at the thought of him not kissing me. I know he's right, but I don't want to face the music. "Can't we try again? Maybe in a few days when we've had time to cool down."

Denver stands up once more and pushes his hand in his hair. "That's the problem. We don't cool down; we continue to heat up. It's like every kiss builds on the last. I swear on my honor as a Stone I will not kiss you again until you become my wife."

That sounds like freaking agony. "No kissing at all?"

"Not on the lips. I can't, Jada. If we went too far I could never forgive myself."

I moan in defeat. "I understand. It sucks, but I understand."

He holds out his hand to pull me up. "Come here."

I fall into his arms. Now that my head's had time to clear, I love him even more for caring enough to value the choice we made to save ourselves for marriage. Not too many guys out there give a rat's butt about purity. Most of them are hell bent on making sure you don't have any left to give.

"I love you, Denver Stone, and I can't wait to marry you. Are you busy tomorrow?"

He kisses my forehead. "I love you too. *If* you agree to marry me after graduation, we can look at some dates for this fall."

"This fall? Why not in the summer?"

His laugh vibrates in my chest. "Someone flipped a switch somewhere. I thought I was the one in a hurry to get married, not you."

"Well, that's before you said you wouldn't be kissing me anymore. Now, I'm in a hurry."

"My little bloody fish. What am I going to do with you? Like I said, we'll discuss it after graduation."

"Ugh. Fine."

Denver slips his hand in mine. "We better be heading back. My family will be worried with me having shut them out. They know how hard this is for us."

I roll my eyes even though we've started walking and Denver can't see me. "Tell them not to worry because you've sworn off my lips until further notice."

"Jada Brooks, are you salty?"

"A little."

"You'll get over it."

"You better hope so."

THE PARTY IS BREAKING up by the time we return. We make our rounds saying goodbye and then load up in the car. Once we're home, Denver, Mitch, and I help clean up dishes and put things away in the kitchen. Bolivar and Aurar kiss us goodnight and retreat to their room. Denver nods at his brother and smiles.

"What are you guys thinking?"

"Ice cream," they say in unison.

"I'm in. What kind do you have?"

Denver lists off several different flavors.

I sit at the bar and kick off my sandals. "Chocolate."

The boys divvy out ice cream, and we sit at the bar together. For a moment, the only sound is the ticking of a clock and the scrapes of our spoons.

Mitch breaks the silence. "Hey, Jada?"

"Yeah?"

He clears his throat. "I wanted to say I'm sorry about Emily. I know she's your friend. And for the record, I really like her."

"I get it now that Denver explained the situation. I hate it for her, though. She really likes you too. And not to be mean or anything, but she's been crushing on you all year and she was hoping you would ask her to prom."

"Dang. I figured as much. I can still take her. What do you think, Denver?"

"I guess that would be okay. As friends of course. Why don't we all go together? Will you go to prom with me, Jada?"

I take my last bite of ice cream and shove my bowl to the side. "Wow. That was the most unromantic promposal ever."

Mitch laughs beside me. "She's right, Denver. That was crap, man."

"That was terrible. Forget I said anything. Don't repeat any of this to Emily. Mitch and I will come up with a promposal that neither of you will be able to refuse."

I act like I'm zipping my lip, lock it, and then toss the key. "Don't take too long. She may get another offer. And we still have to go dress shopping."

"Shoot, okay. We'll make it happen." He holds out his fist to Mitch and they fist bump.

They start talking prom plans and restaurants and tux rentals and flowers and cars and forget I'm in the room. I slide off my stool, rinse the bowls and put them in the dishwasher, then excuse myself to the bathroom. They haven't moved or stopped talking when I return. My gosh, they're worse than two girls.

"I hate to interrupt, but I'm asking for a friend: Will there be kissing on prom night?"

Denver cocks his head to the side. He bites his lip to hide his smile. "Tell your friend there will be no kissing on prom night."

Mitch glances between us, his eyebrows scrunched together. "Why the hell not?"

"For one, you and Emily are going as friends, and Jada and I are no longer kissing."

"Why the hell not?"

Denver lets out an exasperated sigh. I can't help but laugh.

"Which part don't you understand?"

"Any of it. Emily and I have already kissed. I think it would be rude not to kiss her on prom night. Don't you agree, Jada?"

I lean across the counter from Denver. "I do."

"Seriously. You're in cahoots with my brother now?"

"If it gets me a kiss, then yes."

Mitch taps his fingers on the counter. "I missed something here. Why aren't you guys kissing?"

"Because it's too damn hard. We spiral out of control faster than the Porsche picks up speed."

"That's rough. It sucks to be you."

"No shit."

Mitch isn't ready to give up yet. "But maybe on prom night you could make an exception?"

"I think prom night should definitely be an exception to the rule," I say as I fist bump with Mitch.

"This alliance is not a good thing." He glares over at his brother. "Technically, I can't tell you who to kiss, but you know where I stand. And you—you're like a hit of heroin. You know how difficult it is for me to restrain myself."

Denver's glower turns on me, his blue eyes blazing.

Mitch decides to bow out. "I'm going to my room. See you at school tomorrow, Jada."

"Bye, Mitch."

I reach over the bar top and grab Denver's hand. "I'm sorry. I was having a bit of fun with your brother. But truthfully, it would be nice to have at least one kiss to look forward to between now and our wedding."

"After my reaction today, the best I can do is say I'll think about it."

"That's fair." I pull my hand back and grip the bar. Will you walk me out?"

"Of course."

We stop by my car and Denver wraps me in his arms. "I love you. So much, Jada."

"I love you too. I'm sorry for giving you a hard time. It's fine if we wait."

"I'll pick you up in the morning." He kisses my head and releases me.

As soon as I'm out of sight, tears slide down my face. I wouldn't say we had a fight, but it's unsettling the way we left things. I shouldn't have pushed so hard. He's trying to do what's right and I'm tempting him to do otherwise. I'll text another apology when I get home. I always thought prom was lame, but now I'm excited to go. Denver has that effect on me. Changing my mind about the way I view things. He's turned my whole world inside out. Maybe Emily was right. The universe has shifted.

Lights are coming up fast in my rearview mirror. I flip the mirror to keep the brights out of my eyes. My phone vibrates in the seat between my legs. I figure it's my mom, but it's Denver.

"Hey. Miss me already?"

"Pull over."

"What?"

"I'm right behind you. Pull over."

"Okay, hold on."

I hang up the phone. There's no room on the side of the road here, but on the outskirts of town is a small gas station. I turn on my signal and pull in the parking lot. Denver is hot on my heels.

I'm barely out of the car when Denver crushes me to him.

He kisses my head. "I shouldn't have let you leave like that. I'm not upset with you, I'm mad at myself."

For a couple of minutes we stand there holding each other in the gas station lot. I don't want to move. Ever. Life is so much better when I'm being held by Denver.

I have to extricate myself from Denver's arms to see his face. "I said it's okay if we wait. There's no need to be angry with yourself, or anyone else for that matter. We'll manage, Denver. I love you."

He pulls me close again and sighs in my hair. "Thank you."

"I'm glad you chased me down."

"Me too."

"Are you sure you can't marry me tomorrow?"

"Oh, Jada. Always tempting me, my little bloody fish."

"Ugh. Can't you come up with a better nickname?"

"Hmm. What about catnip?"

"Um, no."

His upper body shakes with his laugh. "How about smack or dope?"

"Never mind. You're going downhill with this thing."

"Bloody fish it is."

I stand on my tiptoes to kiss his cheek. "Good night."

"Love you, babe."

I smile and bite my lip. "Now that one I like. Love you too."

He walks backward to his car, never taking his eyes off of me. I roll my eyes as I climb in the Jetta. At the last second, I remember something I wanted to ask him and jump out of the seat. Denver is opening his door.

"Hang on, I meant to ask you."

He leans his arm on the car door. "What is it?"

"What does WP stand for?"

"It's nothing. Rieder is a dork."

"Tell me."

Even at a distance I hear him groan. "Whipped Puppy."

I turn my head to the side trying to hide my smile. So not working. When I look up, Denver is glaring.

"Don't even think about it."

"Goodnight, WP." With that, I jump in my car and speed out of the lot. If he can call me Bloody Fish, I sure as hell can call him WP.

CHAPTER FOURTEEN

DENVER

On the drive home, I contemplate our kiss from this afternoon. I have never felt so utterly powerless to my body's desires. Jada can't possibly understand. When I kiss her, my mind is blanketed into a deep fog. All intelligence is stripped and every atom of my being focuses on the primal need to have her. It will be a battle every day not to touch those soft lips, but I cannot put her in that position again. I won't.

I would marry her tonight. She has to know that. I want her to experience what's left of her senior year without people wondering why she jumped into a marriage with a guy she just met. Her classmates would probably assume, like Emily did, that Jada is pregnant. And who knows how her mom would react. I can't put her through that. Plus, these last couple of months should be fun. The pinnacle of high school should be prom and graduation, not a rushed wedding.

I'm gripping the back of my neck as I come in the back door. My thoughts swirl and spin until I'm dizzy. Knots bulge on my neck and shoulders. I either need to find a distraction or drink enough wine to put me to sleep. And I don't like wine.

The refrigerator holds no answers as I stand there with the door open. Beer or water?

"There's quite a bit of tension coming from this room."

I spin around with beer in hand. "I'm a little stressed."

Dad's eyebrows are drawn together, his lips in a tight line. "I have a job for you. You won't be able to drink that."

I trade the beer for a bottle of water. "What you got?"

"I need a couple of guys to patrol a certain neighborhood tonight. Jada's neighborhood."

My knots double in size. "Is she in danger?"

"I don't think so, but the elders want to be sure. That random demon attack in the woods has them nervous. Plus the ripple in the sky moves about like a baby in the womb. Whatever is holding them back won't keep them at bay much longer." He waves his hand as if to dismiss the rest of his thoughts. "Anyway, I'm offering the job to you since you have precious cargo in the area."

"Yes. Absolutely yes. Should I get Mitch?"

"No need, brother." Mitch strolls in with our duffle over his shoulder.

Dad shrugs. "I knew you'd say yes." He hands me a paper sack. "Your mom made you boys sandwiches to eat on the way."

"Tell her thank you."

"There's not been much activity, but be careful all the same."

Mitch and I both agree to do so before heading out. Mitch wants to drive, and I have no qualms with it this evening. Hopefully his head is clearer than mine at the moment. Although, being on patrol gives me something to do with my time and helps me focus on something other than Jada's lips. We eat our sandwiches and chat very little on the way.

Mitch pulls off the side of the road in a secluded, dark area near an empty field. There are no houses on this end of the street, so it's a perfect spot to go unnoticed. The sky churns above the field as we exit the car. To the normal eye, nothing is amiss, but to me it swirls like a tornado brewing in the clouds. The purple and black colors make the sky appear bruised. I've never witnessed anything like it.

A shoulder brushes mine. "That is some freaky shit."

We stand in awe or terror—or a bit of both—at the heavens. "No kidding. This explains why Dad is so worked up."

A shiver runs through me as I consider what's coming, but there's no time to be afraid. We strip down and discuss the plan for patrol. Since it's a smaller area than we're used to, we split up and agree to meet every hour at the edge of Jada's yard. There's a pine tree grove next to her house that's great for cover.

OTHER THAN JUMPING up several cats and a couple of raccoons, not a single thing has happened all night. I'm waiting in the pines for Mitch to do a final check and then we'll go back to the car to change and go home. I stare at Jada's window, wishing I could sneak up and take a peek at her sleeping. That's not creepy at all.

The rustle of pine needles lets me know Mitch is approaching.

I was attacked by a crazy cat. Damn thing actually lunged at me.

What were you doing, eating its cat food?

Hell no. That's disgusting.

Mitch sits beside me as I continue to stare at Jada's house. *Her scent is stronger.*

I agree, but I'm surprised he noticed. *Sniff test, brother. What you got?*

Mmm, something sweet like cinnamon rolls, but mixed with a metal, like gold.

That's her blood. What else? Dig deeper.

Mitch sticks his nose to the air. *Vanilla and coconut.*

Good. Anything else?

A fresh air, earthy scent.

Nice work.

Thanks, but if we're done smelling Jada, I'm ready to go home. You know, school and all that fun stuff.

Yeah, I guess we better.

A branch snaps close by. A few seconds later, a rather large wolf comes into view. We know all the wolves in the area, and this guy is definitely new. Mitch lowers down into a pounce position, but he won't move without my order.

An air of haughtiness crackles around our intruder. He's as black as night, and his yellow eyes bore into mine. His presence is intimidating, yet I don't feel threatened. There's a familiarity in his scent.

I attempt to find out if our guest is friend or foe. *Who are you?*

His deep laugh rolls like thunder. *Question is boy, who are you?*

I am the oldest son of Bolivar Stone, Denver. This is my brother Mitchell. We are patrolling the area assigned to us by my father, the pack leader.

Ah yes. Bolivar did have two boys. Your father and I patrolled together back in the day. He was a good man.

He still is. Might I ask again who you are?

I am Roland Kingston the third.

The royal?

That is correct.

Forgive me, sir, for being so rude. I had no idea.

It's fine, son. You want to call off your brother?

Mitch rises up from his attack position. We stand side by side.

Roland sits and he's still a head above us in height. *Tell your father I would like an audience.*

Of course, sir. Is there a time you prefer, or will you be in touch?

I'll make time later today. Have him expect me at one o'clock.

Yes, sir. If there's nothing else, we should be getting home.

I will make your father aware, but there's no need for you boys to patrol this area. I assure you it is well protected.

I understand, sir, but I'm invested for personal reasons.

As am I. My one and only daughter lives here.

Oh shit. *By here, do you mean at this particular house or here in the vicinity?*

This is my house. Jadaline Kingston is my daughter.

I fall back on my haunches. Jada is a royal? *To be clear, Jada Brooks is your daughter?*

You know my Jadaline?

Yes sir. Well, sir, Jada is my mate.

Roland laughs. *I already knew that, son. My wife keeps me informed of what's happening with Jada. You were starting to shake in your fur.*

I choke out a half laugh. *Yes, sir, I was. Wait. Does Jada know you're—*

She will today. It's almost daylight and we all need to get out of sight, but you're welcome to join your dad and me later. I have many questions for you both. As I'm sure you have questions for me as well.

Yes, sir. I'll be there.

Very good.

With that, his black body disappears deeper in the pines. Mitch and I sprint to the car. We rush to get dressed before daylight and speed all the way home. I must speak to Dad before I pick Jada up for school. Oh God, Jada. How on earth will she react to seeing her dad after so many years with no contact? I'm sure he had his reasons, but I can't think of any good enough to make me leave my family behind and let my daughter think I didn't love her.

I run in the kitchen from the garage yelling for Dad. He's sitting at the table with his coffee. Mom is making breakfast.

"I'm not deaf, son. Get you some food and sit down."

I forgo the food and dash to the table. "You're not going to believe who I spoke to."

"Considering I was up all night connecting some dots, I'm going with Kingston."

"How did you know?"

He pushes his chair back. "I need more coffee." Mitch sits across from me with a heaping amount of bacon and eggs. My stomach growls, so I move about the kitchen as we talk.

"All this time something was niggling at the back of my mind concerning Jada. Her scent was strange yet familiar. I don't know why I didn't put it all together before now."

"She's a royal, Dad. That kinda freaks me out."

"It changes nothing. Neither your love for her nor hers for you."

"That's true enough." The four of us sit at the table together. Mitch has all but cleaned his plate. "So tell me what you know. Oh and before I forget, Roland wants to meet with us today at one."

"That's wonderful. My gosh, it's been ages. It will be good to catch up." He laughs and glances at my mother. "Dear, do you remember that time we all went to the bar in Diamond Hill and—"

"Honey, I don't believe it's necessary to go into any of that at the moment."

Dad clears his throat. "You're quite right."

"I've got to pick Jada up soon. Can we get back to the dots?"

"Kingston and I used to be good friends. In high school we ran around together, and as we got older patrolled together. He was with me the night I found your mother. And soon after, he met Lisa. They lived with his parents until Lisa found out she was pregnant, then they moved to town. Where Jada lives now. We both began our families and drifted apart. I'm sure none of you remember, but you played together a few times as children. Anyway, being a royal has complications. Kingston was getting threats. His parents had decided to move back to their hometown in Charleston, leaving them with no family. Not long after that, Kingston told me they were also moving to Charleston. I may have run into him a couple of times beyond that day. As far as I knew, he and his family were gone. He never made contact, and I didn't go digging him up."

"You didn't recognize Jada?"

"She was probably two the last time I saw her. And I knew her as Jadaline Kingston, not Jada Brooks."

"So he changed her name to hide her?"

"Apparently."

"Wow. That's kinda messed up. I mean why would he leave his family?"

"I cannot answer that. I imagine he deemed it necessary."

I rub my temples. "What made you think Jada might be Kingston's daughter?"

"Like I said, her scent had me baffled. I knew it but couldn't place it. She's the right age, similar name, and in the same house. Then the reports of a royal being spotted around town. Up until you ran in here this morning, it was mere speculation."

Mitch excuses himself to get ready for school. Mom is cleaning up the dishes. I have a massive headache. Dad studies me with squinted eyes like I might fall apart.

I might.

"He plans to meet with Jada today. I don't know what that means exactly, but I'm worried about her."

"Be her rock today, she'll be yours tomorrow. When one is weak, the other one carries them until they are ready to stand once more. And vice versa. You'll spend the rest of your lives caring for one another. Love without strings and expectations is what makes a marriage great. Love because you choose to, not because you want something in return. This will be your chance to carry her."

"And I will, for as long as she needs."

Dad comes around the table and grips my shoulder. "I have no doubt, son."

I slide my chair back and stretch. "I need a hot shower. When I get back from town, I have homework to do and then I hope to slip in a nap. I'll see you at one."

"We'll meet in the study."

THERE'S A STEAMING cup of liquid on my desk when I come out of the shower. A note in my mother's handwriting reads *For your headache.* Mint and lemon fill the air. To give the concoction time to cool, I wander to my closet for clothes. I don't think Jada's dad will pop in this morning, so I opt for my regular jeans and T-shirt.

I pick up the tea. There's no time for enjoyment here, so I down it in a few swigs. I grab my wallet and walk swiftly to the garage.

Jada is waiting on the porch when I pull up. Her smile is carefree as she bounds down the steps toward the car. I jump out to open her door.

My lips brush her hair in a soft kiss. Her smile falters when she notices my wrinkled brow.

"Are you okay?"

"I'm tired. Hop in and we'll talk on the way. Sorry I'm running late."

When we're both belted, I shoot out of her driveway.

Jada's brows pinch together. "Expand on why you're so tired."

"We haven't talked much about what I do, but I was on patrol last night."

"Layne mentioned that on Saturday. What does that mean? Is it dangerous?"

"It can be. Basically it's like being a cop in wolf form, but we're hunting demons, not criminals."

"And why do you do that exactly?"

"Well for one, it's been done for generations by my family. It's what we're born to do. We start learning and training at a very young age. That's why most wolves are homeschooled. But we also do it to protect our loved ones and the community. Demons are pure evil. Their only purpose is to steal, kill, and destroy. Nothing good comes from letting a demon run free."

Jada stares out the window deep in thought for a moment. "What made your family want to hunt demons?"

"My dad says that one of the original Stone wolves lost his wife to a demon attack. Legend has it that the young man went crazy with grief and spent the rest of his life killing demons. He taught his sons to kill demons, and it has been a way of life ever since. If you are a Stone, or in the pack of a Stone leader, it's what you do."

"Huh. What do other wolves do?"

"There are other packs that also hunt demons. Some find the need to rid the world of vampires or fairy folk. Some wolves choose to live a life of normalcy, like every other human. Except they're not. They only change for fun or sport. I've heard of underground wolf fights, but there's nothing like that around here."

"I'm sorry, did you say vampires and fairies?"

I chuckle. "Yes. I'm surprised you didn't already ask."

"I guess I was still trying to process the whole wolf thing. So, did you fight any demons last night?"

The school lot is close to full when we arrive. "No. I guess I'm tired from being up all night. I try to sneak in a nap before I pick you up, but there was no time today."

"Denver, you don't have to take me to school every day. I'm healthy and full of energy since we've been spending so much time together. I'm sure I can manage a couple of mornings."

I reach over and stroke the smooth skin on her hand. "I want to do it. I swear I'm fine. Thankfully wolves don't require much sleep."

"Was Mitch with you last night?"

"Yes. We always patrol together."

"How does he do it?"

I laugh. "He drinks a lot of coffee."

Jada stares out the windshield. Her fingers fiddle with the hem of her shirt. "I don't want to go to school. I have so many questions. Can we go somewhere and talk?"

"I'd love nothing more than to spend the day with you. Unfortunately, I have homework due today and a meeting at one o'clock."

"Oh, okay." She reaches for the handle and pauses, her hand falls back in her lap. "I have to ask—"

I knew this was coming. "Go ahead."

"Are there vampires in Forrest City? In my school?"

"A few, but we're not at odds with each other here. They are welcome to live in peace as long as they don't kill people."

"Oh my gosh. This is too weird. I'll be checking out all my classmates now trying to figure out who drinks blood."

"Gross. It's so much cooler to be a wolf." I push open my door. "Wait there, I'll come around."

I step out in the warm morning breeze. It's a gorgeous spring day. Rain is in the forecast for tomorrow, but for today, the sun shines in all its glory. I open Jada's door and assist her out of the car. I can't help but pull her close and breathe her in. Her vanilla shampoo centers me. Reluctantly, I let her go.

"I love you."

She kisses my cheek. "Love you too."

Jada turns around before entering the building and waves. I wave back. I never leave until she's safely inside. I catch movement out of the corner of my eye. Sure enough, there's a man standing by his car at the far end of the lot. A large man. In a very expensive car.

Jada's dad. He nods at me once and gets in his vehicle. I guess he likes to make sure Jada gets to school safely too. Or he's watching me.

MY ALARM GOES off at twelve thirty. I shuffle like a zombie to the bathroom and splash water on my face. My homework took longer than expected, so I didn't get much rest. I hurriedly shove on some nice jeans and a polo shirt. I need food and caffeine.

Mom and Dad are in the kitchen. There's a sub piled high with meat and a drink on the counter. Mom winks as I approach. "Thought you might be hungry."

"This is amazing. Thank you."

I've barely finished eating when the doorbell rings. I enter the living room at the same time my dad opens the door.

"By the heaven's above, it is you." My dad extends his hand. Roland firmly takes it and then the men laugh and hug, patting each other on the back.

"Boli, old boy, you haven't changed a bit."

Both men are in excellent shape. Roland is a head taller and a bit thicker than my dad. He has Jada's brown hair, but his eyes are a golden yellow. Neither of the men appear their age. A perk of being a wolf.

They continue catching up, talking of the aches and pains of getting older. I clear my throat to remind the men I'm in the room.

"Kingston, you've met my oldest, Denver."

I walk over and shake hands with Jada's father. "It's nice to meet you, formally."

"You as well. It's obvious why Jada is smitten. You're a very handsome young man."

"Thank you, sir."

My dad squeezes my shoulder, a broad smile on his face. "I'm proud to say both of my boys live up to the Stone name."

"That's wonderful news, considering he wants to be with my daughter." Roland relaxes his shoulders. "Honestly, I couldn't have picked a better mate for her. I don't know of a more honorable family than this one."

My dad chuckles. "You getting sentimental in your old age?"

Roland's eyes widen. "I'll show you sentimental. I'm sure I can still kick your—"

"Boys, boys, have we not outgrown the silly competition stage?" my mother says as she approaches Roland.

"My God, Aurar, you get more beautiful with age."

They hug and then she moves to my father's side. This is all a little weird for me. I get it, they're friends, but it's been years since they've seen each other. And he left, letting them believe he took his family with him. Not having any connection with this man makes it hard for me like him. I'll have to try for Jada's sake, but right now, I'm not digging it.

Eventually the men make their way to the study, so I follow behind. My mom makes excuses to disappear. Her expression is that of relief and I wonder what that's about. My dad sits in his executive chair behind the desk and Roland lights in the wingback across from him. I sit to the side on the loveseat.

Dad shifts from friend to business. "So what brings you back to town, Kingston?"

Roland steeples his fingers. "Same reason I left. Jada."

"You want to fill us in? All these years I believed you left with your family. It's quite a shock to find out they were here the whole time."

"As you well know, Lisa and I have had a different relationship."

My dad nods. "Because she's fully human."

No wonder I wasn't able to pick up a scent. I'm a little surprised at this revelation but say nothing.

Roland leans forward slightly in his chair. "As well as other complications."

"Roland, I thought you worked through all this. You and Lisa seemed happy."

It's not lost on me that my dad went from calling him Kingston to Roland.

"We were to an extent. Not the Bolivar and Aurar kind of happy."

My dad tenses. "That was your choice. I knew you hadn't mated with Lisa, yet you tried to convince us all. Did you ever find her, your true mate?"

Roland glances out the window. "I saw her from afar once. I was traveling through Charleston on business shortly after I moved there. She walked down the other side of the street into a coffee shop. My heart leapt out of my chest and I couldn't breathe. I actually fell to my knees in anguish at the sight of her. Of course I could do nothing because I had already made a vow to Lisa, and I stood by that vow. But I was a miserable wretch for years. Longing for something that would never be mine. I traveled all over the world after that, trying to get her out of my head."

"Roland, I'm sorry."

Roland shakes his head and lets out a sigh. "As you pointed out, I made my choice, so I have to live with it."

I can't keep quiet any longer. "Where does Jada fit into all of this?" I need to know why this man is here and why he wants to upset Jada after all this time.

He sits back in his chair, his face solemn. His expression then switches to confusion. He turns to my father. "What in the hell is that?"

My dad smiles. "That, my old friend, is what it's like to be loved by your mate. You're experiencing his intense emotions. He loves Jada more than anything in this world. His goal is to protect her and make sure she's happy. I'd say he thinks your presence will upset her."

"I fear you're right, but I've come to make amends and to be here for the battle."

"What battle?" My dad and I say simultaneously.

Roland stands and begins pacing the room. "Every royal at some time in their life will battle a greater demon. This particular type of greater demon has one purpose. To wipe us from the face of the earth. Royals are becoming extinct, if you will. I felt my battle was drawing nigh, so I left here to protect Jada and her mother. I gathered wolves from my hometown and we defeated the demon, but we lost several in the fight. I had many injuries that took considerable time to heal. This all took months. By the time I came back to be with my family, Lisa had decided she didn't love me anymore. I went back home to lick my wounds, and that's when I saw my mate. I had refused Lisa a divorce but told her I would let live her life as she pleased. We're still married to this day and I have never cheated on her."

This man has lived a life of pure hell. I can't wrap my brain around forcing a relationship and then seeing Jada for the first time. I almost feel sorry for him. But right now, there are more pressing matters at hand.

Roland sits back down, giving me the floor to pace. "So you're telling me this greater demon that's been looming over town wants Jada?"

"I believe so, yes."

"She hasn't even turned. She's defenseless against a demon."

Dad taps his fingers on the desk. "Maybe that's what it's waiting for. Jada to come into her wolf form. It would explain how it hovers but doesn't strike."

I push my hands in my hair. "We've got to pull a team together. We need to prepare and strategize. I'll let Mitch know. We'll train extra hard with our group. Dad, can you call the elders and find out if we can get help from out of town? And could you do some investigating on this sort of demon? It would help to know if it has any weaknesses. And…"

"Denver," my dad says with force. "Please calm down. Your stress levels are extremely high. I can hardly breathe, the air is so tense."

I collapse on the loveseat. My head falls between my hands. He's right. I'm so stressed out I'm queasy.

"Damn, that boy is something. Has Jada experienced this?"

"Yes. She passed out once because of it."

"I believe it. Tell me, Bolivar, how much does Jada know?"

"Denver, can you answer?"

I sit up and take a deep breath. "Yes, sir." I turn toward Roland.

"She knows we're wolves. All of us. She met the pack, along with some family and friends at the last gathering. They all love her, by the way. Um, what else. She's aware she's my mate. We've touched on patrolling. She asked this morning about other things that go bump in the night, but we didn't have time to discuss it. Oh, and she has seen a demon. Mitch and I took one out the other day while Jada watched. Not by choice, mind you, it happened upon us. Well, maybe."

Roland wipes his hands on his thighs. I find it odd for this big man to be nervous.

"Do you think she knows or suspects anything about herself?"

"She hasn't shared it with me if she does. We weren't one hundred percent sure ourselves, not knowing her background, but she has shown a few early signs."

"That's why her mother called me. Lisa was worried Jada would change and she wouldn't know how to help her. I gave her some signs to watch for. I can't begin to tell you how grateful I am to all of you for your love and support to my Jada."

The hair on the back of my neck bristles every time the man says *my Jada*. I hate to tell him, but she's *my* Jada now.

Roland laughs. "You know you can't hide much when you throw out your feelings like that. And I suppose you're right, she is your Jada. Hell, I've been such a crappy father, she may not want to have anything to do with me."

"No disrespect, sir, but it is possible."

Dad gets up from his chair and comes to stand by his friend. "I imagine it will be a shock, but there's always hope for redemption. You must give it time."

Roland attempts a smile. "I have never deserved your friendship. Not then and definitely not now. But I will need it. I'll need all of you to help save Jada from this demon. And then I want to win back the affection of my wife and have a relationship with my daughter."

Dad looks at me and then back to Roland. "We'll do everything we can."

CHAPTER FIFTEEN

DENVER

My father and Roland begin preparations for the battle to come, but I need fresh air. Dad is calling the elders as I leave the room. He promises to fill me in later and suggests I go for a walk. I'm in no walking mood. I sit down on the leather seat of my Ducati and close my eyes. I smile thinking about Jada commenting on how much we like our cars. I'm glad she doesn't ask how much they cost. There's over a million dollars in this garage. As I reach up to hit the start button I realize I'm wearing a pink polo shirt. Not cool. I run upstairs and throw on some ripped jeans and a black T-shirt. Much better.

High speeds and miles on the open road bring some relief to my burdens. My tires screech as I rush into the lot and park under a tree. There's a good ten minutes before the bell, so I get off the bike and stretch my legs. A vibration in my pocket signals a text. I dig out my phone to check the message. It's from Jada.

Jada: I don't know what's wrong, but I'm burning up and shaky. Are you here?

Shit.

Me: Yes, where are you?

Jada: In the bathroom.

Me: Which one?

Jada: Near the band room.

Me: I'll be right there.

I run across the grass and enter a side door propped open by the gym. I'll have to get down the hall unnoticed to make it to the bathroom. If I get caught, I could always say I'm here to visit my brother. I walk down the hall with purpose. There's no one about because classes are in session. Thankfully, I've not been grabbed up by the collar.

I tap on the door. "Jada, you in here?"

"Yes, you can come in."

Jada is standing in front of a sink. Her head is down as she grips the edge with both hands. I rush up behind her for support.

She lifts her head and a faint smile passes her lips. Her cheeks are red. I don't know if it's from embarrassment or fever. "I'm sorry you came in here. It's passing now."

I let out a sigh of relief. "Baby, don't be sorry. I'll always come to your rescue."

She turns around and places her forehead on my chest. She's hot. Fever hot.

"Why does this keep happening to me?"

"Where is your backpack?"

"I left it in the classroom. I thought I was going to be sick, so I ran out."

"Are you well enough to get your things? There's maybe two minutes until the bell."

"Yes."

I want to get her out of here before the chaos hits, but that's not going to happen. I follow her out of the bathroom and she stops three doors down.

"I need to talk to my teacher. I didn't ask to leave the room."

"I'll be right here."

The bell rings while I'm waiting, and the hall quickly fills with students. I've been gone a couple of years, so I don't recognize any faces until Rieder spots me.

"Hey, man. What are you doing here? Is Mitch okay?"

"Yeah, he's good. I ran in to check on Jada. She was having a moment."

"Oh shit, is she…"

"Hey, Rieder."

"Hey, Jada. Well, I'll let you two get out of here. Call me, Denver."

"Yeah, I will. I've got some updates for ya."

"Cool," Rieder says before he slips into the hallway traffic.

Jada goes in the other direction, so I follow close behind. She stops by her locker and exchanges some books. Emily runs over with a huge smile on her face.

"Hey guys. Mitchell asked me if I could meet him on Thursday. Said we were all doing something together? He was very vague. Do you know what it is?"

The girl is practically dancing on the balls of her feet. Jada and I both swear we don't know, and I can honestly say I'm telling the truth. I suppose it has to do with our promposal, but we don't have a plan together yet. I've had other things to occupy my mind. She squeals in excitement, but for what I don't know. I want to roll my eyes but refrain. I'm so thankful for Jada's even temperament. I like Emily fine, but Lord, the drama.

Emily skips away all smiles. I shake my head as she bounds down the hall. Jada laughs beside me, pulling my attention to her beautiful face. Her cheeks are now a light pink.

"I think we've created a monster," Jada says.

"You might be right. I hope this prom thing is a good idea." I can't get Roland's story out of my head. I do not want that for my brother. And speaking of my brother—

"Hey, bro. Why are you here?"

"Jada was puny and needed my help. Hey, I might need your car."

"Why?"

"I rode my bike. I don't know if Jada should ride today."

She throws her backpack over her shoulder. "I'm fine now, promise. I want to ride the motorcycle."

"You sure?"

"Yes. It will be nice, truthfully."

I shrug. "Okay then, never mind. So I'll catch you later. Oh, and you need to fill me in on your grand scheme for Thursday."

Mitch smirks as he backs away. "Don't you worry your little head about Thursday. I'm cooking up something delicious."

"This can't be good."

Jada grabs my hand. "Come on, let's bust this joint."

I realize, now that we're by the bike, I left without helmets. I was in such a hurry to get away it didn't cross my mind. Of course, my little rebel Jada couldn't care less. She slides in close, pressing her chest to the contours of my back. I sigh in pure ecstasy. She whispers something in my ear, but all I can focus on is her breath caressing my ear and her hair tickling my neck. Time to go. I'm learning my limits, and when Jada's this close, I better find a distraction quick.

I weave in and out of every back road possible out to my house. Jada loves to ride and she's much more relaxed now than the first time I took her. The downside: she doesn't hold on as tight and her hands tend to roam over my chest and stomach. It's a high I can't explain. My response is to drive faster, and she then cinches her arms around me. Seriously, I could do this all day, but I have other plans for Jada today.

Jada sits at the bar while I rummage for a snack. I lean on the bar across from her while we share chips and salsa with a veggie tray. Her hair is windblown from the ride and her cheeks are a rosy pink. Her deep brown eyes captivate me, but not as much as her full lips. As I stare, her tongue makes a sweep over her lips and I find myself groaning.

I slam my hand on the counter. "Damn it. Who made up this stupid no kissing rule?"

She bites her lower lip. "That was you, actually."

"Well, I hate it."

Her eyebrows rise as she speaks. "Really? How much do you hate it? How whipped are you, Denver Stone?"

"Not enough to go back on my word."

"Ugh. You're so stubborn." A chip flies by my head.

"You two throwing food in here?" Dad says as he walks to the fridge.

Jada tries to hide her smile with her hand. "Sorry, Bolivar. Your son is so darn frustrating."

He twists the lid off of his water and takes a drink. "Son, I thought I taught you better than that."

"Now hold up, Dad. You're siding with Jada before you know the facts."

"Tell me then, so I can make an accurate judgement."

Jada cuts me off. "Your son has sworn off kissing me until we're married. The problem is, I really like kissing your son. Sorry if that's weird."

Dad smiles. "Well now. That would be very frustrating."

"Really, Dad? Not helping."

"I didn't say you were wrong, I merely agreed it would be frustrating."

I lean back on the counter and cross my arms. "We can fix this right now. Dad, go get your black book. Marry us, and we can kiss all we want."

Jada immediately perks up. "He can do that?" She looks to my dad. "You can marry us?"

"I can. I will, if that's what you both want."

I push off the counter. "I was kidding."

"Why would you do that? That's not funny. We could be married and not have to torture ourselves."

Okay, this is not going down the way I imagined it. "I only said it because I thought you would say I was crazy."

"So you don't want to marry me?"

"Baby, you know I do."

"Then what's the problem?"

"I want more for you than a kitchen wedding. What about your mom? You'd strip her of the joy of planning her only daughter's special day. You haven't graduated yet. We haven't even been to prom. Help me out here, Dad!"

"I think Denver is right on this one."

My bloody fish continues to plead her case. "We don't have to tell anyone. We can get married now and have a wedding later. No one will be the wiser."

"Jada, you're killing me. There's nothing I want more than to be married to you. But, I'm not convinced this is the right way to do it."

Jada slides off her stool, her pleading eyes on my dad. "Bolivar, I respect your opinion. What do you think?"

"I think you two put me in a very tight spot. And I think it's for the two of you to decide and agree upon. I'll marry you today, and I'll marry you in the future. I love you both and you have my blessing."

I round the end of the bar and slide my hands in Jada's hair. Her kissable lips are so close it's painful for me not to do something about it. Out of the corner of my eye, I notice my dad slip out of the room. He sends a quick message, guarded for my ears only.

It's here.

"I propose a compromise."

Jada grumbles. "I'm not getting married any time soon, am I?"

"Hear me out." Her nod prods me to proceed. "As much as it pains me, I'll revoke the no kissing rule if you'll give me the honor of properly proposing to you and giving you the wedding of your dreams."

Jada grazes her lips against mine. "It's a small victory, but I'll take it."

My limbs melt like soft butter with that one graze. "Jada, we still have to be careful."

Her hands cling to the front of my shirt. "We will. Now will you hurry up and kiss me already."

Damn it. I'm pretty sure she got what she wanted all along. All I know to do is pray for the willpower not to ravage this woman before our wedding night.

Our lips collide and I can't help but moan. We kiss hungrily like two lovers that have been apart for weeks. I pick her up and set her on the counter, but that's where it ends.

"Well, that no kissing thing didn't last long. I'm glad you're feeling better, Jada."

"I was coerced," I say as Jada takes one last bite at my bottom lip.

Jada leans back on the counter. "Hey, Mitch."

"I'm sure it was damn hard to force your hand." Mitch douses a carrot in ranch.

"Shut up. It was either this or marriage."

"Marriage has its advantages, brother."

Jada points to Mitch. "See. He agrees."

I pull Jada off the counter. "I'm not letting you guys gang up on me again. Come on, babe. I have a surprise for you."

"Ooh, I like surprises."

Jada is hot on my heels as I pad out to the garage. I purposefully parked near the door when we got here, but now I stroll to the very end of our six-car garage. Hiding behind Dad's SUV is a brand-new, candy-apple-red Jetta GLI. Dad put a big bow on top.

I dangle the key in front of her. "What do you think? Do you like it?"

"Oh my..." Her voice cracks as she speaks. "Denver, no. I can't."

"I'm pretty sure it's okay to buy my future wife a gift. Plus, it was Dad's idea. Well, he wanted to buy you a BMW, but I talked him into the Jetta."

A tear escapes and she wipes it with the back of her hand. "It's beautiful. I don't know what to say. It's too much."

"Nonsense. Say you love it."

Jada almost knocks me to the ground when she jumps into my arms. Her legs wrap around my waist and she presses her lips to mine. I can taste the salt from the tears sliding down her cheeks.

"I love it."

I back against the hood for support. Anytime Jada's body is pressed to mine I struggle with the right thing to do. Her moans and roaming hands draw out a growl from within me. It vibrates in my chest with every breath. Jada finally takes a breather and my head clears with the slight distance. I peel her off of me and stand up.

"I should have said yes to your kitchen proposal."

"How about a garage proposal?"

"That's even worse. Let's check out your new car."

She holds her ground in front of me. "A little FYI, it's so, so sexy when you growl like that."

"Stop baiting me, my little bloody fish, and get in the damn car."

She smiles but steps aside. "Can we go for a drive?"

"Not yet. It's a stick shift, so I'll have to teach you to drive it."

"Teach me now."

"I have found your one flaw. You have no patience. I'm going to teach you, but not in your car. You can practice in the Porsche."

Her hands go to her hips. "I don't know a ton about cars, but I know your Porsche is worth more than the Jetta."

"That is true, but we don't want to take the chance of denting up a new car. *If* something were to happen to the Porsche, it would give me an excuse to get a new one."

"Oh my gosh. You are ate up."

Jada and I sit in her car, and I explain all the bells and whistles. She has to touch, push, and try everything. The sunroof gets a good workout. Her smile makes me want to buy her a dozen cars. May have to upgrade the three-car garage at the cabin, which is fine by me. After the twenty-minute tutorial in her car, we hop in the Porsche and I take her to the end of a dead-end street. The only thing she could hit out here would be a tree. We trade spots and I attempt to explain the relationship between the clutch and the gas.

The engine has been killed at least a dozen times and I have whiplash. Jada throws her hands in the air with an exaggerated *ugh*.

"I give up! This is too hard."

"Babe, you can do this. You're letting the clutch up too fast. Be easy with it. There's a sweet spot that you can only find if you go nice and slow."

Jada glares at me and I have no idea what I've done. "Are you messing with me?"

"What? No."

"Your word choice was very sensual. I thought you were trying to get my mind off driving."

"Oh my God, Jada. Why? Why do you torment me? I'm being serious. About driving. Kiesha has a sweet spot…" I burst out laughing. "I'll never be able to drive this car the same again."

"Should I be jealous?"

"Maybe. Kiesha and I do have a good thing going."

She rolls her eyes. "Whatever. I think I'm done for today."

"No way. I taught Mitch, and I can teach you too."

"Was he as bad as me?"

"Worse. So much worse."

"Who taught you?"

"Dad. And yes, I killed the engine too."

"Why didn't your dad teach Mitch, if he taught you?"

"He said he didn't want to spend more money on chiropractor bills. He claimed my neck was younger and could handle it."

Jada's smile has returned. "Okay, fine. I'll go again."

"That's my girl."

After half an hour, her shift out of first gear is flawless. An hour later and she's flying up and down the road. I talk her into driving us home and her shifting is as smooth as silk. I'm beaming with pride by the time she parks in the garage.

Jada tries to walk by me, but I grab her wrist and spin her around. I back her into a work table and plant my hands on either side of her. "A little FYI, it's so, so sexy when you drive like that." She thinks I'm going to kiss her, but I turn around and walk toward the door.

"I hate you."

I open the door to the kitchen and wait for her to go in. "If you say so."

The aroma of garlic and basil hits me as soon as I get inside the door. It makes my mouth water. My parents and Mitch are in the kitchen setting up for dinner.

Jada runs up to my dad and gives him a big hug.

"Thank you. Those are inadequate words, but I don't know what else to say."

"You're very welcome. You're a part of our family. There's nothing we wouldn't do for you."

Jada's misty eyes bounce between my mom and dad. "I love you all so much. I wish there was something I could do to show you."

Mom glides over to Jada and embraces her. "You love our Denver. That's how you show us love every single day."

Mitch makes a noise from the dining table. "Can we continue this love fest later? I'm hungry."

Jada laughs and waltzes over to Mitch. She wraps her arms around him as he stands there frozen. "I love you too, Mitch."

Mitch glances at me and I make sure to convey with my eyes if he touches her, he's dead. He shakes free and rolls his eyes. "Okay, whatever. Everybody loves everybody. Let's eat."

We all laugh at his awkwardness. He goes back to setting the table as if nothing happened. Jada helps him with the plates.

I kiss Mom on the cheek. "What can I do?"

"Help your dad put the salads on the table."

"On it."

Once everything is set to Mom's specifications, we sit at the table and hold hands while Dad prays. Mitch and I have our nightly contest to see who can get the most on their plate. I'm definitely winning tonight. Dinner conversation is light and fun. No one brings up anything concerning wolf business, demon business, or Roland business. Wondering if he'll be there when I take Jada home makes me nauseous, but I keep eating.

When dinner is said and done, and all the clean-up is cleaned up, I can't think of a reason to stall any longer.

"You ready for me to take you home?"

Jada slips her phone from her pocket. "It's a little early."

"I know, but it's been a full day and it's a school night."

She groans. "I do have some homework to do."

Jada tells everyone goodnight and I drive her home. My nerves are shot to hell by time we get to her neighborhood. Jada keeps glancing at me suspiciously, but I ignore her unease and continue to talk about school, music, movies, and anything else I can think of. My fear becomes reality as we near her home and I spot Roland's car in the driveway. Jada does a double take at the sight of an unfamiliar vehicle there.

"Oh boy. My mom has finally brought her *friend* home. This should be interesting. You coming in for a minute?"

"Of course." There's no way I'm letting her face this alone. My stomach seizes at the thought of her reaction, and now I'm wishing I hadn't eaten so much.

Jada walks in the front door and throws her bag on the floor. Roland's and Lisa's voices drift from the kitchen. He wants them to try and work things out. Before entering the room, Jada stops short to listen to the conversation. I wince knowing this is going to hurt her.

"Come on, Lisa. Not once have I betrayed my vows to you, and you obviously haven't moved on. Let's give us another try."

"I asked you to come for Jada's sake, not mine."

"Are you sure that's the only reason?"

Lisa doesn't answer right away and I guess Jada's heard enough. She storms into the room with clenched fists. "What in the hell is going on here?"

Roland and Lisa must have been pretty cozy, because Lisa jumps back at the sound of Jada's voice.

"Jada. I didn't know you were here."

"Well that's pretty obvious." Her back stiffens and her jaw goes rigid. "Why are *you* here?" She spits out the words in pure hatred. Damn, this is going to be worse than I thought.

Roland makes a step forward with his hands out like he's been caught in the act of something illegal. "Jada, please let me explain."

Jada is shaking. She takes a step back and bumps into me like she forgot I was here. "Don't you come near me."

"I only want to talk."

"I have nothing to say to you. You lost your right to speak to me when you walked out of my life like I meant nothing to you."

Roland retreats at her words. "That's not how it was. I love you, Jada. I always have."

She laughs and it's not a nice laugh. I'm starting to fear for the man's life. "You've got a shitty way of showing it."

The color drains from Lisa's face as she leans on the counter for support. I don't think she expected this much anger. But how could she not? One of the people Jada should have been able to count on the most abandoned her. Shit. I'm not sure what to do.

Lisa finds her voice albeit a shaky one. "Jada. Your dad wants to— no, he needs to talk to you. There are some things you must know, and I prefer you learn them from him."

I wrap my arm around Jada to let her know I'm here. She leans on me heavily, making me worry she's about to collapse.

Jada straightens, her fists balled up at her sides. "This is who you sneak off with? This is who you talk to on your phone at night?" Jada's voice escalates. "You two have had some secret thing going while I was left to believe he wanted nothing to do with us? I hate you both!"

Lisa begins to cry. "Jada, please don't say that. It's not like that, if you'll let me ex—"

Jada is screaming now. "Don't talk to me! I'm done with your lame excuses."

Roland attempts to placate Jada. "It's not your mother's fault. Let's all cool down for a minute."

"I can't stand to look at either of you right now. I'm leaving."

She starts to leave the room and Roland calls out to me. She stops. It didn't hit me until now how mad Jada would be at *me* for knowing her father was here.

"Denver, can you please make her understand how important it is that we talk?"

Jada spins on me, and I never want to experience the disappointment on her face again.

"How does he know your name?"

"Well, we uh…"

"You knew he was here? Is this why we left early?"

Shit. "I thought he might be. I swear I've never laid eyes on the man before this morning."

Jada is shaking again. All this anger is not good. It could cause an early change, which is way more painful than if it takes place more naturally.

"So you've known all day and didn't think that was something you should tell me?"

"It wasn't my place."

A tear slides down her face. My heart breaks in two. I've hurt her.

Jada has gone from screaming to barely a whisper. "You say I'm your mate and you want to marry me, yet you hold back information that you know will crush me and lead me right into the lion's den?"

Oh God what do I say? She's right. I should have told her. I'm such an idiot.

"Baby, please."

Jada doesn't let me finish. She storms down the hall and slams her door shut. I give Roland a glare that I hope he understands. If he comes anywhere near me right now, I'm going to lose my shit.

I go to her door and turn the knob. It's locked. She's crying, and what was left of my broken heart shatters into a million pieces. I may be sick.

I tap on the door. "Jada, open the door."

Something slams against the wall. "Go away."

"I'm not leaving and if you don't open this door, I swear to you I'll break it down."

"I said go away!"

"And I said I'm not leaving."

"You can sit out in the damn hall and rot for all I care!"

I lean my forehead on the frame. "You don't mean that. Please open the door. Please."

She says nothing in return.

"Jada. You're absolutely right. I should have told you. I'm a jackass. But this jackass loves you, and I need to hold you right now. We don't have to talk, just please let me hold you. Please let me in."

The bed squeaks as her weight lifts. She sniffles as her steps shuffle to the door. The lock clicks as she releases it, but she doesn't turn the handle. Her socks scoot across the floor as she goes back to her bed and lies down. I try the handle, and sure enough she has given me entrance to her room. I slip inside and lock the door behind me for privacy. I need this time with her. I say nothing as I climb on her bed. She's lying on her side with her back to me, so I scoot up behind her and pull her as close as I possibly can. When my arms are tight around her, she breaks, and I break right along with her.

JADA CRIED HERSELF TO SLEEP. She's been out for a few hours. My arm is numb, but I refuse to release her. I have failed her so miserably I don't know if I can forgive myself. When she wakes up I'm going to tell her everything I know. I don't give a shit what Roland thinks.

I must have dozed off. Something stirs beside me and then my mouth is met with warm, soft lips. My heart does a roller coaster loop in my chest when I open my eyes to Jada lying next to me. Our bodies are pressed together in all the right places. Her hungry eyes are so dark they appear black. Her breathing is quick and loud. Mine is catching up quick. She kisses me again, but with a fierce urgency. She's doesn't realize she's getting stronger and her kisses become more powerful in more ways than one. She radiates her hunger for me and it's so freaking good I want to scream. Warning bells go off in my mind, but I don't stop her. She pulls my shirt over my head and kisses my chest. I cram my hands in her hair all but begging for more. It's not until she straddles me on the bed and starts to remove her shirt that I snap out of it.

I grab her hands to keep her from undressing herself and pinch my eyes closed. "Jada, don't."

"Denver, please. I need this. I need you."

"This is the last thing you need. You're hurt and you're angry, and as good as this will be, now is not the right time."

Jada jerks her hands from mine and climbs off the bed. Thank God. She's pissed but that's okay. I sit up on the side of the bed and try to catch my breath. Jada stares out the window into the night. Rain taps lightly on her window.

She turns to face me. "I'm sorry. You're right, I just—" A tear rolls down her face.

I rush over to her and pull her to me. "Don't apologize. You've been to hell and back tonight. I get it."

Jada steps back and glances around the room. "What time is it? You know what, it doesn't matter what time it is. I don't want to stay here. I don't want to face them in the morning. Can we please go to your house?"

"Of course. Pack a bag and we'll go."

She thanks me and then rushes around the room gathering some clothes. She disappears in the bathroom next and comes out with another small bag. After rummaging through some drawers that I believe hold lacy things, she goes to her desk and gets some papers and books.

"Oh crap."

"What is it?"

"I left my bookbag by the door."

"I'll get it."

The hall is dark and quiet. I tiptoe toward the living room trying not to wake anyone. I spot Jada's bag and grab it off the floor. Light spills out from the kitchen along with the sound of ice clinking against glass. Great. Someone is awake. I'd bet my money on Roland. I take Jada her bag and ask her to wait there for a minute. As much as it pains me to speak to the man, I make my way to the kitchen.

Roland is standing—barely—by the counter. He has a scotch glass in one hand and a bottle in the other. When he spots me, he raises his glass toward me.

"Look who it is, the man of the jour."

Jour, really? Dude is toast. "I have two things to say to you. One is, I won't tell Jada how shit-faced you are, and second, she's going home with me. When she's ready to talk to you I'll let you know. Do not show up at my house."

"Densher, wait."

Ain't nobody got time for that. I rush back to Jada's room and pray she's ready to go.

"You ready, babe?"

"Yes. Thank you, Denver."

"Listen, I have so much to tell you, and now's not a good time, but you have to know how sorry I am. I failed you and I am gutted over it. I don't expect your forgiveness, but I'm sorry."

"Denver—"

"No. Don't you dare say anything. Especially if you're going to say it's all right. Because it's not all right. And I'll spend the rest of my life making it up to you, I promise."

I grab her hand and practically drag her down the hall and out the front door. I don't want to give Roland the chance to say or do anything stupid.

By the time we get to my house, the rain is coming down in freaking torrents. The thunder sounds off at the same time the lightning splits the sky in two. We barely make it in the garage before pea-size hail pings off the roof. Kiesha was saved from that pounding at least. Normally I like storms, but tonight it reminds me of the unsettling storm raging around my heart. I'm sick over the fact that Jada is hurting and even more frustrated that I had a hand in it.

I'm surprised my mom is seated at the bar when we walk through the kitchen. It's nearly two a.m. She's holding a mug with both hands.

"Mom, you okay?"

Her smile is strained. "I was worried about you two. I knew it would be a rough night. How are you, Jada, honey?"

Somehow she still has tears left to shed. "Tired and angry."

Mom nods. "To be expected. Denver, after you tuck Jada in, will you come speak with me for a minute?"

"Yes, ma'am."

I walk Jada to the spare room, and she decides to take a hot shower. At the mention of Jada and shower, I get out quick but promise to check back in.

Mom hasn't moved. I go over to the bar and lean on it for support. I can't remember the last time I felt this drained.

"It will get better," she says as she ruffles my hair.

A whiff of strong liqueur invades my nose. "What you got in that cup and are you sharing?"

She laughs. "Don't tell your dad, but I found his stash of whiskey."

"It will be our secret, I swear."

"All right, one glass. It's behind the Raisin Bran."

I shake my head and laugh. "Nice job, Dad. No one in their right mind eats Raisin Bran." I shuffle to the cabinet for a glass and then pull out the whiskey. "Holy cow, Mom, this is the good stuff."

"Yes it is, so don't get much. And then come sit down so I can get something off my chest."

I groan. "I don't like the sound of that, and I'm already spent in every way."

"I know baby, it won't take long, but I need to explain something."

She waits for me to replace the whiskey and sit by her at the bar.

I nudge her shoulder. "This have something to do with Roland?"

"You're too perceptive for your own good."

"He's already on my shit list, so anything negative you have to say will only add to it."

"Denver, maybe he's trying to change. I hope for Jada's sake that he is. Time will tell, if he sticks around that long." She takes a sip of her drink and blows out a breath. "Your dad is a very forgiving man. And I too have forgiven, but Roland makes me uncomfortable. I didn't meet your dad first; I met Roland first. I was at a bar with some friends, and Roland was there with his buddies. I was a lot like you. I wasn't interested in dating anyone that wasn't my mate, so I ignored them. Roland kept hitting on me and by the end of the night he was drunk and tried to kiss me. I slapped him. Hard. It felt good actually. Anyway, my friends and I left, and I hoped to never lay eyes on him again. But fate had other plans.

"Roland seemed to be everywhere I went for three weeks. I was sick of running into him, but it turned out to be the best thing that ever happened to me. I met your father because of Roland. One glimpse across that bar and we knew. Roland was not happy, but eventually he came to accept the fact that your father and I were mated and there was nothing he could do about it. Shortly after that, Roland met Lisa and tried to tell us she was his mate. We knew he was lying, but you can't tell Roland anything. He thinks his royal blood makes him irresistible and superior."

I rub my temples. "I need to punch something. If he tried to touch you…"

"He'd have to get through your father first. Roland has never been inappropriate since the night he tried to kiss me, but the way he used to ogle me still gives me the creeps. But a man can change. Like I said, hopefully he's come to make things right."

"He did tell Lisa he wanted to work things out. He says he's never been with anyone else, but who knows. I don't trust him. Not yet anyway."

"That's probably wise. He'll have to earn it the hard way. With all of us. Watch out for Jada."

I down what's left of my whiskey. "That's one thing you won't have to worry about." I take my glass to the sink. "Hey, Mom."

"Yes?"

"Do you think you could call the school tomorrow for Jada? We have a lot to talk about and she's had a long night."

"I'd be glad to."

"And if I don't make it to my room—"

"Denver, I trust you to do the right thing."

"Thank you."

Jada is curled up in the covers, her wet hair splayed out over the pillows. I climb on the top of the bed beside her and kiss her cheek. Her eyes flutter open and she smiles.

"Will you stay with me?"

"Always."

Her eyes close and reopen slowly. She's beyond exhausted. "I don't want to go to school tomorrow."

"Shh. Close your eyes. Don't worry about that, baby, get some sleep."

I run my hands through her hair and massage her scalp. She's out within minutes. I watch her sleep until my eyes burn and my body is lead. I kiss her one last time before I too succumb to the sleep my body craves.

CHAPTER SIXTEEN

JADA

Someone is beating me upside the head with a hammer. Has to be. There's no other reasonable explanation for the pounding. And my mouth is as dry as the desert. I attempt to force my eyelids open but they're weighted and puffy. It's several minutes before I'm successful in keeping them open. I'm at Denver's. The curtain is drawn, but it appears to be dark out. Maybe even raining. I slept here because—crap, I remember why I slept here. I stayed here because I hate my family. I stayed here because my father thought it would be a good time to waltz back in my life like he never left. And my mom. Her betrayal is worse by far. How could she do this to me? She's lied to me for only God knows how long. She's been talking to him, I know she has. My head hurts so bad.

I scoot up in the bed and find a note on the nightstand.

Hey beautiful. Text me when you wake up. No need to get out of bed, I'll bring you whatever you need. Love, Denver

Oh my gosh. I'm seriously going to marry this man. He even left my phone right by the bed. And a glass of water. I gulp down half the water and then grab my phone. Dear Lord! It's eleven o'clock.

Me: Morning. I'm awake. I can get it, if you'll please let me know where to find something for a headache.

Denver: I'll be right there.

Two minutes later, Denver walks in with a tray. "Good morning, sleepyhead."

"Yeah, I didn't mean to sleep so late."

He sets the tray on the nightstand and leans down to kiss my head. "You needed the rest."

"Did you sleep?"

"Like the dead. I haven't slept that many hours in a long time. Waking up to your beautiful face will be the highlight of my day, though."

"Hmm. You mean to tell me we slept together and I don't remember?"

"Damn girl, you know how to hurt a man's pride."

Denver can make me smile even on the crappiest of days. "We can always try again. Maybe it will be more memorable next time."

"All right, smart ass. You're awfully feisty for somebody with a headache."

I rub my neck at the mention of the word. "I really do. Did you bring me something?"

"Mom's miracle drug."

He hands me a mug, and I lift my other hand expecting some sort of pills. "Is this it?"

"Trust me on this one." He motions for me to slide over to give him room, so I do. He sits on top of the covers beside me. "I also brought fruit, toast, and more water. Mom said you'd be dehydrated."

"I'm as dry as a good red wine."

"And you're as fine as one too."

I roll my eyes. "Whatever. I know I'm atrocious."

"Baby, you're so far from it, I'm going to sit on my hands so I don't attack you."

He actually puts his hands under his butt.

I take another sip of tea and realize my headache is starting to recede. "What is this miracle tea? You could bottle and sell this stuff."

Denver shrugs. "I have no idea. Mom makes it. You want some fruit?"

"Please."

He grins as he pulls his hands out. "I'm not responsible for what happens next."

"Just pass me the tray. And you call me a smart ass."

Denver kisses my forehead and slides off the bed. "I'll be back in a few. You need anything else?"

I can't stop my bottom lip as it pokes out in a pout. I want him to stay here with me. "Where are you going?"

"I'll be right back, I promise."

"Fine. Oh, wait a second. School?"

"No worries. Mom called you in sick."

"Tell her thank you."

"Yep. Be right back."

I lay my head against the headboard. I've done nothing to deserve this amazing family. Nothing. Yet they love me like their own. My brain cannot wrap around that kind of love. It's so selfless and honest and pure. They make me want to be the best version of myself. Their love makes me confident and strong. And my Lord, Denver. The pull between us is so undeniable, it might as well be a law of physics. I used to think I loved Grainger that way. Boy, was I wrong. I do love him, but not like this. Denver is my center. My home. Thinking about him now makes me ache. I want to be so close to him, I'd crawl inside of him if I could.

I raise my head and shake it back and forth. Okay, that was a weird train of thought. My body breaks out in a sweat as a hot flash overtakes me. I'm shaking as I reach for the water and accidentally knock what's left of my tea on the floor. Shit. I try to get out of bed to clean up the mess, but the world gets a little fuzzy.

"Denver!"

His heavy steps precede him into the room. I cinch my eyes closed because everything is spinning.

"Baby, what's wrong?"

He lays his hand on my forehead and says several choice words. After laying me back in the bed he rushes off to get a cool washcloth. "It will pass shortly." He continues to fuss over me, placing the cool cloth on my head and playing with my hair. The episode subsides, and I open my eyes to Denver's pinched expression.

I reach for his hand and kiss his palm. "Thank you."

"Don't try and get up. Give it a couple of minutes."

"The tea. I knocked it over."

"I'll get it. Promise me you won't move."

"Promise."

He's gone only a minute and returns with a vase full of gorgeous wildflowers. It's bursting with color like a bag of skittles. "Don't tell Mom, but I picked these from her flower garden."

"Denver, it's beautiful. Will she be upset?"

He sits on the edge of the bed. "I'm kidding. It was my idea, but Mom put it together. How are you?"

"Weak, but better. Everything went gray for a second there. Denver, what is happening? You know something, right?"

"We're going to cover everything here in a few minutes. I swear to you, I'll not keep anything from you ever again. It crushed me last night when I realized I had let you down. I'm so sorry."

I slowly push myself up to a sitting position. We're face to face. Denver's hard jaw has a couple days' stubble, and his blond hair is a sexy mess. The blue waters of the Caribbean float in his eyes, but it's the full lips that have me mesmerized. I rub my thumb over them. He shivers.

"I do wish you had told me, but it's over now. I know your heart was in the right place. Let's move on, okay? I forgive you."

He lets out a sigh of relief. "Thank you."

I'm a raging hormonal maniac lately, but I can't help myself when he's this close. I inch forward until our lips are barely touching. He must have recently brushed his teeth. The mint lingers on his lips and breath. I swallow hard. Denver hasn't moved a muscle but I can hear his heartbeat racing like a wild animal after prey. We're not kissing yet and I tingle all over. The blood in my veins burns. What the hell?

I fall back against the pillows. Denver is smiling from ear to ear.

My voice is raspy when I speak. "Why do my insides fizzle like they're going to explode? It's painful to be near you. It's embarrassing how bad I want you."

"Welcome to my world, Jada Brooks."

"What does that mean?"

"You're getting a taste of what's it like for me to be near you, and it gets worse. Or better, depending on how you view the situation. I'm not going to sugar coat this because we're running out of time." Denver pulls in a long breath and takes both my hands in his. "Jada, your dad is a wolf. *You* are a wolf."

"That's not possible." I shake my head in disbelief. "No. You're mistaken."

"Baby, I saw your dad yesterday in all his wolf glory. He's huge. Mitch saw him too. We already suspected something but had nothing to go on. Your mom is fully human, and we had no idea who your dad was before yesterday. You are a wolf and you're going through the change. It won't be long now. Days at the most."

My hands tremble and my stomach churns. Not so much at the fact that I'm a wolf—it could be cool to experience Denver's world and truly be a part of his family, but then again… Holy shit, I'm a *wolf*?

Denver yells for his mom and dad. Dots on the ceiling. Why am I sweating, but cold?

Everything goes black.

An angel calls my name. Her voice is musical and soothing. I want to answer her and tell her I'm all right, but the world is still dark. She strokes my hair and face. My body feels like it's being pulled through the mud, but to less murkier water. The angel speaks again. The water is almost clear now.

"Jada, can you hear me?"

My angel is actually Aurar. She's smiling at me. The world comes back into focus in short bursts until finally I can observe in real time.

"Aurar?"

"Hey sweetheart. My lands, you had me worried."

"What happened? Where's Denver?"

"You went into shock and blacked out. Denver was going mad

with worry, so Bolivar sent him outside to cool off."

"Huh, okay. How long was I out?"

She pushes my hair behind my ear. "Several minutes longer than I wanted you to be. Do you think you could sit up a bit? A little sugary Coke might help."

"I think so." I attempt to push myself up, but my arms are like rubber. "Then again, maybe not."

"It's fine. No hurry."

"Aurar, what's it like?"

"Being a wolf?"

I nod.

"It's amazing, Jada. The entire world changes and you experience things from a new perspective. You become a part of nature, and your senses are heightened to the sounds and smells of the earth. There's a closeness that occurs to the creator of the universe and you're more centered. You mature in who you are—your identity is more clear. It's a very powerful and sexy mystery. And you'll love the running. There's nothing more freeing."

"Wow. Not sure I was expecting that. Does it hurt?"

"The first few times can be uncomfortable, but I wouldn't say painful. You're going to do great."

"I'm scared."

"Oh sweetie. That's to be expected, but we're here for you. I do think you'll love it. And the boys will never tell you this, but make sure you have on a bra and panties, or you'll be as naked as a jaybird when you change back. Only the clothing closest to your skin survives the transformation."

"Mom, you weren't supposed to tell her that."

She winks at me. "Told you. I'm going to fix you some lunch. You need to eat something."

Denver takes his mom's spot at the edge of the bed. He leans over me, placing his forehead to mine. "Jada."

I reach up to his face and push my hands in his damp hair. "Is it still raining?"

"A little. Baby, are you all right? You scared me to death."

"I guess your news was a tad bit shocking. Maybe some sugar would have been good."

He chuckles. "Ya think? At least I know how to tell my next girl-friend she's a wolf."

Denver grunts with the blow he receives to the gut. "That is not even funny. Help me sit up, I'd like some Coke."

"Yes, ma'am."

I'm sipping on my drink when Aurar and Bolivar come into the room. She's fixed up a yummy lunch spread.

Bolivar kisses my cheek. "Your color is back. I checked your vitals earlier and everything was fine. I'd say you're much improved."

"Thank you for everything. And the food looks amazing. I'm starving."

He smiles. "That's a good sign. I'll keep a check on you today. Denver has some other things to share with you, but if you're not up for it, please say so."

"There's more?"

"You're over the biggest hurdle, if that helps."

"I suppose it does. Thank you for everything. You all have been so good to me."

Bolivar speaks as he steps back to give his wife room to deliver the tray. "Your family, Jada. We love you."

Aurar sounds on the verge of tears but composes herself. "Yes we do, and here's your lunch and you better eat every bite."

"I will, thank you."

Denver is watching from across the room. His back is to the wall, his muscular arms over his chest and his feet crossed at the ankle. He's so damn beautiful in that moment my lungs spasm, along with every other organ for that matter. My breath catches in my throat, and then I cough and choke on my own saliva. Of course everyone rushes over and are once again fussing over me. I'm trying to catch my breath and calm my nerves that have suddenly decided to spark like live wires. My entire body, inside and out, has let me in on a secret.

Aurar is patting my back. "Bolivar, do something."

I hold up my hand with one finger letting them know I need a minute. The coughing fit has caused my eyes to water, but that's not the only thing making my eyes leak.

"I'm okay." I start to laugh and I must seem mad.

"Are you sure, sweetie?"

"Yes. Yes, I'm better than okay. Denver is my mate."

Denver pushes between his parents to my side. "Baby, I think we've already established that."

Aurar smiles and pulls Bolivar toward the door. "We'll leave you alone for a minute."

I pat the other side of the bed. "Come sit by me."

He walks around the end of the bed, takes off his shoes, and sits beside me. I set the tray aside for the moment because I don't want anything between us.

"What's been established is that I was your mate." I sit up to be closer. I don't want him to miss this. "I'm saying, you're *my* forever, *my* happy ever after, *my* lifelong partner. You. Are. *My*. Mate."

The revelation hits him hard. His hands fly in my hair as he pulls me close and buries his face against my neck. Hot tears fall on my collarbone, and his body trembles next to mine. When he's finally ready to meet my gaze, the passion in his eyes fills my entire being. Every atom, every cell, every drop of blood, every piece of my heart and soul has been claimed by Denver Stone. There's no going back for me now.

"It's in your eyes, Jada—the trust, the bond, the peace of mind, the finality." His fingers make a burning trail down my face and neck. "I love you so much."

His touch is different. Even the lightest graze of his finger creates a hunger I've never known. My skin stings, yet it yearns for more. The innermost part of my being needs to be connected to my mate. I cram my hands into the comforter and hold on for dear life. He must realize my situation because he jumps off the bed.

"Shit. This is not good. This is not good at all."

Denver paces the floor while I get my bearings. The distance helps. "Stay over there for a minute."

"At this point I'll need to be in another country. Shit. I can barely hang on as it is. Or was. But now. God, your desire roars over me like an avalanche. The other was bearable, but this. I can't do this."

"What do we do?"

"I'm not sure."

After several deep breaths, I'm gaining control. Denver, not so much.

"Denver, it's okay. You can come back."

"Yeah, that's a negative." He continues to pace with his hands shoved in his hair.

Mitch yells from the kitchen, "Denver, what the hell?" And then from the hall, "Dude, your sexual frustration is hitting me like a damn freight train." And now he's in my room. "Oh hey, Jada. Sorry."

"Hey, Mitch. It seems we've hit a new milestone."

"Do I want to know?"

I laugh. "Our mating equation is no longer one sided."

"Great. I could hardly stand him before. Way to go, Jada."

"Hey! It wasn't on purpose."

Mitch grunts. "Denver, go take a cold shower, or go on a run, or something. I'll keep Jada company."

He stops pacing and lets out a long breath. "You mind, Jada?"

"Of course not. Go ahead."

We both watch him leave the room. Mitch whistles. "He is all sorts of messed up. I say we marry you guys right up and end this hellish torture. For all of us."

"I've tried. He won't budge."

"Hmm. Try again. I'm telling you, dude is about to break."

"Thanks for the intel." I point to the bed. "You might as well sit down."

He plops down and puts his hands behind his head. "Don't mind if I do. Some of us had to go to school today."

"How is Emily?"

He shrugs. "Good I guess. I'm trying to be friendly but also keep my distance. Denver kinda freaked me out this morning with the whole Roland story."

"What Roland story?"

Mitch pops out of his relaxed position and sits up. "Shit. I thought he was going to tell you."

"Yeah well, we've had a few interruptions. Namely me. I had some sort of episode this morning, and then Denver told me I was a wolf, which sent me into shock, and then I woke up and realized Denver was my mate. You've missed quite a bit of excitement."

"I knew I should have stayed home. So how are you with the whole wolf thing?"

"I guess I'm still getting used to the idea. Denver says it won't be long."

"It's so awesome. I can't wait until you're out there kicking some demon butt. You're gonna be a total badass."

"Mitchel Dean."

He mouths *oops* and then turns to Aurar. "Hey, Mom."

"What have I told you about swearing in my house?"

"Denver does it too."

"We're not talking about Denver, are we?"

"No, ma'am. Sorry."

She notices my half-eaten lunch and tsks. "You have food to finish, young lady."

"Yes, ma'am."

"All right, well see that you do. Is Mitch bothering you?"

I smile. "No he's keeping me company while Denver cools down."

"You'll let me know if you need anything?"

"Of course."

She turns on her heel and walks out. Mitch and I laugh.

"You're in trouble now. She's gone full-blown mother hen on ya."

"I noticed. She's pretty great."

"That she is." Mitch's expression grows serious. "You're Emily's friend. How do you think I should handle our situation?"

"Honestly, my answer may have been different an hour ago, but mating with Denver has changed everything. I love Emily, but I don't think you should settle for anything less than your true mate."

"You sound like my brother. So, prom?"

"Can you go as her friend?"

"I think so. I'm drawn to her and find it hard to stay away, but it's one night. I can do one night."

"Is it possible she's your mate?"

He throws his head back and stares at the ceiling. "Shit if I know. Generally wolves find their mate between eighteen and twenty-one."

"When's your birthday?"

"The day after prom."

"That's next month. It's so close." I play with the edge of the pillow. "I don't want to give you false hope. It's best not to pursue her for the time being. Just in case."

"You're probably right."

I stretch out my legs and realize I'm stiff from sitting all day. Other than a potty break, my butt has been in bed. And I stink. "I think I'll take a shower. Will you let Denver know to give me about thirty minutes?"

"You got it." He scoots off the bed and heads toward the door. "Hey, uh, I wanna say you're gonna be a pretty cool sister."

I take a deep breath to let my heart expand a little bit more. "I always did want a little brother."

He rolls his eyes. "We're practically the same age."

"Twin brother?"

His smile crinkles his eyes. "I like it."

Sometimes a shower is more than a shower. I'm a brand-new girl as I pad to the kitchen. I take my unfinished lunch to the bar and get a fresh Coke out of the fridge. I've taken the last bite of my sandwich when Denver comes through the garage door. He's soaking wet. His shirt and running shorts cling to his body. I have to glance away to keep my cool. After counting back from ten I'm able to give him my attention. He's smiling at me from across the room.

"Hey, baby. I'm sorry I took off like that, but I needed to clear my head."

I bite my lip. "It's okay. Were you running?"

He reaches in the fridge for a water and takes a long drink. "Yeah. I normally hate running, but it was good therapy today. The physical strain was enough to get my mind off *things* and help me focus." He shakes his head. "My bloody fish. What am I going to do with you?"

"You could always marry me."

"Are you up for a walk? The rain has moved out."

"That sounds great, actually."

"I'll go clean up and be back in ten." He walks toward the hall, making a wide arc to avoid getting too close.

I put away my dishes and go back to the bedroom to get my shoes. The room is a mess, so I take a minute to make the bed and put some of my clothes in the dresser. In all of the craziness this afternoon, not one person bothered to clean up my spilled tea. They were more worried about me than they were the stain in the carpet. God, I love this family. I go back to the kitchen in search of something to clean it up with. Aurar is filling the coffee pot with water.

"Hey sweetie. What can I get for you?"

"I need something to clean up the tea stain in the bedroom."

She waves her hand in the air. "Don't worry about that. I'll put some spray on it for now. Brandy will be here tomorrow to clean. She's always complaining that my house is too clean for her to come once a week anyway."

"I hate to tell you, but your house is always clean."

Aurar winks at me. "Brandy needs the money and I like her company. It's a win-win."

Denver walks up behind me and wraps me in his arms. "You ready?"

"Where are you two going?"

"On a walk—we won't be too long." He releases me and walks in the opposite direction of the garage. I shrug and follow him out.

We step out onto the deck. The fresh air fills my lungs with the scent of flowers in full bloom. I haven't changed to a wolf yet, but every scent and sound is amplified. Aurar is right. It's amazing. Denver doesn't recognize I'm having a moment, and he pulls me through the garden and past the pool. He barrels past the gate and down to the end of the yard where a path leads into the woods.

I tug on Denver's hand, and he pauses to let me speak. "Are we in a hurry? You're practically dragging me."

He pushes his hair off of his forehead. "Sorry, babe. I'm excited to show you something. I'll slow down."

I intertwine our fingers together. "We've got the rest of our lives."

He touches his lips to mine but doesn't give me the kiss I'm hoping for. He turns and continues to drag me through the woods. He does slow down, but not by much. We continue down this tiny path carved through the lush trees. The ground is wet from the rain, but all other traces are gone. The sun has come out to play, warming my face as I gaze up to the sky. Most of the path is shaded, but every once in a while the sun's rays peek through. After ten or so minutes Denver stops. There's a clearing in the path up ahead.

"Are we there?"

Denver rubs the back of his neck. He's nervous, but I have no idea why. His throat bobs as he swallows.

I love you, Jada.

I reach up to touch his clean-shaven face. He leans his head into my hand.

I love you too, babe.

He sucks in a breath and pushes it out. He pulls my hand to his mouth and kisses my fingers. My eyes flutter closed at the headiness of his lips and tongue on my skin. Sadly, it's short lived, because like his kiss earlier he breaks the contact before I'm ready. He smiles and tugs on my hand.

When we reach the edge of the path, Denver steps aside to give me a full view of the clearing. There, in the middle of a perfectly manicured lawn, sits a cabin with a porch that wraps around to the other side. There are two rocking chairs and a swing visible past a beautiful red door. The hostas along the front are full and deep green.

"My God, Denver, it's beautiful. Is this your parents'? Who lives here?"

He's quiet as he digs a key out of his pocket. He pushes the door open and gestures for me to go inside. We pause in the spacious living area and I spin around in a circle, trying to take it all in. A massive rock fireplace is the focal point of the room with a thick, raw-cut, wooden mantel above. The walls are a rich, red wood and I breathe deep the scent of oak and cedar. My fingers skim the soft fabric of the sectional as I walk further into the cabin. Sunlight fills the space from several large windows and the greenery and pops of white give it a splash of color.

"What is this place? Do your parents rent it or something?"

Denver still doesn't answer me. We walk through every room as he explains the way it was put together and how some of the logs are from the 1800s. His face lights up every time I ohh and ahh. From the outside it didn't appear that big, but now that we're inside, I discover three bedrooms, two bathrooms, and a loft. I love Denver's parents' home, but this is like a dream. I could live in the master bedroom, never leaving the king-size four-poster bed. When the tour is over, Denver leads me back to the living room.

"Jada…" He hesitates and pushes his hand in his hair. "This seemed a lot easier when I was out running earlier." He paces for a few seconds and stops in front of me. "Don't misunderstand me here, there's absolutely no hesitation on my part." Denver goes down on one knee and takes my hand. "I love you with everything that I am. I'm ready to spend the rest of my life with you, but I didn't want to rush you or push you. Without a doubt, you are the most important thing in my life. I will spend the rest of my days making you happy if you'll let me."

He reaches in his back pocket and pulls out a silver band covered in diamonds. My hands fly to my face as warm tears run down my cheeks. I don't stop them. I wish I could convey to him the fact that I have no reservations whatsoever. He's my forever. My heightened senses allow me to hear his heartbeat keeping time with mine.

"Jada Brooks, will you marry me?"

I drop to my knees and crush my mouth to his. He lets me kiss him with all the passion I can muster and I never want to stop. Our hungry bodies need no instruction. Hands are everywhere and I'm practically panting when Denver pulls back.

"Damn it, woman. We're not married yet. So is that a yes?"

"Yes. Yes, Denver, yes! There's nothing I want more than to be with you always."

He stands to his feet, pulling me up with him.

"Hold out your hand."

I hold out my left hand for him to put the ring on my finger.

"I didn't have time to buy you a ring. This was my grandmother's, and Mom said I could give it to you."

The delicate band fits my small finger like it was made for me. "It's perfect," I choke out as more tears slide down my face.

Denver lifts my chin, taking my eyes from the ring to him. "Welcome home, baby."

I shake my head in disbelief. "This is your house?"

"No, it's our house."

I FLOAT BACK to Denver's house. I've never taken drugs, but this is what I imagine that high to be like. My mind is consumed with the when and where. I hope and pray Denver doesn't want to wait long. It will kill me if he's still planning on waiting until after graduation. We're hand in hand and all smiles when we come through the back door. I follow Denver to the kitchen where his parents and Mitch are waiting on us to return.

His mom rushes to me and throws her arms around me. "I finally get a daughter. Congratulations, Jada."

Mitch is right behind her. "Congrats, sis."

"You guys knew?"

Bolivar laughs. "Denver has a hard time keeping things to himself. After his run today, he sought me out to ask my advice. With your declaration today, there's no reason in my mind for you two to wait. Aurar of course, agrees. This is who we are and we make no apologies for our ways. But Jada, there are people that won't understand. Your friends cannot and will not grasp what you're going through. They don't know the bond created between mates, and honestly may think you're crazy."

"I get that, but I don't care. True friends will support me no matter what. This is my choice to make, and I'm not going to worry about what people think. What about my parents? They should be good, right?"

"Your father will be fine. It could be a struggle for your mother, but she knows what's going on even if she's never experienced it herself."

"I don't get that. Why did they get married?" I glance over to Mitch. "Is this part of the Roland story?"

Denver glares at his brother. "What did you say?"

"Nothing, man. I only brought it up because I thought you guys were gonna talk it all out today."

"That was the plan, but plans change. Dad, maybe we could have a family meeting and fill in the gaps for Jada?"

"I think that's a great idea."

WE SIT around the study and each family member takes turns updating me on my family history and of the things to come. I'm still mad at my parents, but the comprehension of the *why* is more clear. I get why he fled to protect me, but I wish he had tried harder to pursue my mom when he returned. It was another shock to learn I have a greater demon wanting to kill me. They assured me I won't be alone and a plan is coming together within the wolf community. We'll fight together, side by side. The big question is: When will I change and unleash this beast in the sky?

I stop Bolivar mid-sentence. "I don't get this whole royal thing. Why do you call Roland a 'royal'?"

"Wolves used to be under royal rule. We had kings and queens. The only way to be a royal is to be of the royal bloodline. It's not only a title, but in your blood. It has been said that those of royal blood have heightened abilities, greater strength, or even supernatural powers. Your father is the only royal I've ever had the privilege to know, until now, of course. It's a gift, Jada. But also a curse. As long as there have been royals, there have been demons out to get them.

Greater demons abhor anyone in power—whether human or wolf. All demons are evil to the core and oppose anyone who stands for good. Unfortunately for you, they view royals as an extra threat and have been trying to eradicate them for centuries. There aren't many royals left, from what I'm told."

"I don't even know how to process all of that."

Denver senses my overload and wraps his arms around me. "I think she's had enough for one day."

Bolivar agrees. "I tell you what. Why don't we order pizza, get out the cards and beer, and call it a day."

Mitch pumps his fist in the air. "Hell yeah!"

Aurar glares but then smiles. "I'll let that one slide. Jada, what kind of pizza do you like?"

"Anything except anchovies."

"All right then, I'll go take care of the pizza order."

She leaves the room, taking Mitch with her to help get everything set out.

Bolivar sits behind his desk with his chin in his hand. "All right, kids. How are we going to do this?"

Denver darts his eyes in my direction. "Jada?"

I grab his hand and place it on my heart. "The sooner the better."

Bolivar laughs. "I thought you might say that. Talk it out and let me know."

"Yes sir." Denver says, never taking his eyes off of me.

AFTER A FUN EVENING of beer and pizza, I'm exhausted. We all hug goodnight, and I go to my bedroom to change into something more comfortable. Denver has gone upstairs to do the same and suggests that I call my mom. She answers on the first ring.

"Jada, thank God. Are you okay? I'm so sorry, Jada. I should have told you."

"Yes, you should have. I'm still pretty pissed. I called to let you know I'm staying at Denver's for a while, but I'm fine, and I'm safe."

She sniffles, and Roland speaks in the background. "Your father says he's sorry too, and he loves you."

"Will you get back together?"

"I don't know. We're going to try. Neither of us have been able to move on."

"I want you to be happy."

"I'll be happy if you forgive me."

A heavy sigh leaves my tired body. "I'm working on it."

"I love you, Jada. So much. You've been my whole life and brought me so much joy. I could not be more proud of the young lady that you have become."

Tears slide down my face. You'd think I'd be dry by now. "Mom, I'm marrying Denver. And soon. We haven't worked out the details, but I want you to be here. Roland too."

A sob breaks from her and she's unable to speak for a moment. I can hear Roland asking her what's wrong. He genuinely sounds concerned. When my mom tells him what I've said, he laughs and says something about "been expecting that." She gathers herself enough to speak once more.

"Oh baby, you know we want to be there. It would kill me if you got married without me there to fuss over your hair and makeup, and all the other annoying things moms do."

"I love you, Mom. We'll talk soon, okay?"

"Okay, baby. Goodnight."

"Can I speak to Roland for a second?"

She sounds surprised. I'm a little surprised myself. "Sure, hang on."

His voice is unsure. "Jada?"

"Hey, uh, I guess I wanted to tell you I know everything now. I have questions, but I'm not ready to meet yet. I've had a lot to digest in the last few days, but I'm working on trying to understand and forgive. But I will try."

He breathes hard into the phone. If I had to guess, I'd say he's working hard on keeping his emotions in check. "Thank you, Jada. I can't ask for anything more."

"All right, well, I'll be in touch."

"Goodnight, my baby girl."

My chest convulses at his words. I remember. He used to call me his baby girl. God, I loved him so much and thought the man hung the damn moon in the sky.

"Goodnight, Roland."

I hang up and push down the emotions that are wanting to gush out like a volcano. The hole he left in my heart is so gaping big, I don't know if there's enough forgiveness in the world to fill it. I said I would try, and I will.

My attention and thoughts are overtaken the second Denver comes into my room. He's in a T-shirt and cotton shorts. I really, really want to jerk that shirt over his head. He's holding a blanket.

"I said I would stay with you, but I'm not sleeping under the covers."

"Okay."

I slip down in the bed and he climbs up beside me, covering up with his blanket.

"How did it go with your parents?"

"Not too bad, I guess. I told them about us."

His eyebrows go up. "And?"

"My mom got pretty emotional, but she responded better than I thought she would. Roland acted like it was inevitable."

"He's not wrong."

I lean forward and kiss his cheek. "No, he's not. I love you."

"I love you too, babe."

"What are the chances we can drop the bloody fish nickname after we get married?"

He gently traces my face with his finger. "I don't think there will ever be a day when you're not bait for this shark."

"I was afraid you'd say that." I lay my head on his chest and listen to the cadence of his heart.

Right before I drift off to sleep, Denver whispers in my ear. "No one deserves to be this happy."

CHAPTER SEVENTEEN

JADA

The next week is a blur. Between school, homework, planning a small wedding, Denver's nights on patrol, meetings with his dad, more episodes of the change to come, and convincing Emily I'm not mad for getting married, Denver and I barely have time to be alone together. Which is probably a good thing. He sleeps with me every night but always above the covers. I haven't had a sit-down yet with my parents. Every time I pick up the phone to call, I back out. Denver is patient, but I know he wants me to take that step toward healing.

Grainger hasn't spoken to me since he saw the ring on my finger. We were at school, and he walked away swearing and punching everything in sight. His anger surprised me. I had kinda thought he understood how serious I was about being with Denver. Apparently not. Anytime I attempt to say hey, he runs to the other side of the hall to dodge me. I'm getting tired of his pissy mood.

On Thursday, Emily and I discover how outrageous our boys can be. As school is letting out, half the student population is buzzing about a helicopter on the football field. Of course, Emily and I have to go check it out. I die a thousand deaths when Denver jumps out and strides over to me. He kisses my hand and pulls me toward the windy beast. Emily yelps, and I turn to witness Mitch carrying her over his shoulder. We all file in and the copter lifts off the ground. We fly over Forrest City and Diamond Hill, taking in the landscape from above. It's quite exhilarating to say the least. Emily squeals a lot. On our last pass through Diamond Hill, the chopper flies over a tall building with a billboard on top. Emily shocks me with a scream, almost giving me a heart attack. I follow her line of sight to our names on the billboard. The boys are asking us to prom and it's plastered on the top of a building for all the world to see. Emily is beside herself the rest of the ride. She talks poor Mitch's head off, but he doesn't seem to mind. Denver nudges my neck with his nose and lips, and I grip his thigh to tell him he better knock it off. He holds me in his arms the rest of the ride, and that's by far my favorite part. Denver knows that pomp and circumstance aren't my style. All I need is him.

By the following Monday, I've decided I'm going to talk to Grainger whether he likes it or not. As soon as the bell rings, I run outside to wait by his car. He pauses for a moment when he spots me hovering by his vehicle. His shoulders slump, and then he continues to lumber my way.

He tosses his backpack in the back seat and shuts the door. My mouth is dry, and I stammer for what to say.

"Jada, I have somewhere to be."

He reaches for the door handle, and the fact that he can't even face me is like a knife piercing my heart.

I grab his wrist and hold on tight. "Grainger, please talk to me."

He jerks his hand away like it's on fire. "Damn it, Jada. I don't know what you want me to say. I'm happy for you?"

"Yes, for starters."

He swears and his eyes grow dark and angry. "I can't do that. You know I'm in love with you. I've always loved you, Jada."

I stumble back. The knife twists and turns at his words, at the hurt written all over his face. "Grainger, I'm sorry. I guess I thought—"

He takes a step toward me. "You thought what, Jada? You thought I was fine with you being with another guy? You thought I could just turn off my feelings for you? You thought years of waiting meant nothing to me?" He steps closer. "I love you."

Insert knife number two. The tears have started. "I love you too, but not like that." I try to touch him but he flinches. "What can I do to make this right?"

He grimaces as he backs away. "Stay the hell away from me."

Insert knife number three. I'm bawling now. Grainger gets in his car, and I stand there like an idiot letting tears fall freely down my face. He zooms out of his spot without giving me a second glance.

A familiar voice calls my name. Arms hug me.

"Jada, what the hell is wrong with you? Are you hurt?"

It's Mitch. All I can do is nod and cry into his shirt.

"Do I need to kick someone's ass? Are you sick?"

Emily's hand grabs hold of mine. "Oh, Jada. I'm sorry. He'll come around."

Mitch is so clueless. "Who will come around?"

"No, he won't. He hates me. He told me to stay the hell away."

Emily pushes Mitch aside and holds me while I cry in the school parking lot. "He didn't mean it."

"So much anger in his face. He meant every word. I've lost him."

"God, will someone tell me what's going on here?"

Emily huffs. "Grainger. Her best friend since birth."

"Shit. I'm sorry, Jada. You want me to talk to him?"

I straighten my spine and take a deep breath. "It won't do any good. Can we go home?"

Mitch puts his arm around me and walks me to the BMW. "Come on, sis, let's go."

Emily waves goodbye and says to call her if I need anything. She's the only one who understands the relationship Grainger and I share.

I've been riding with Mitch to school. It took some convincing with Denver, but he realized there was no point in him driving me when Mitch is already going. Most days we roll down the windows and listen to loud music or cut up with each other, but today it's quiet. I sniffle as the last of the tears dry up.

We're almost home when Mitch bangs his fist on the steering wheel. "Let me talk to him. I hate seeing you like this."

I continue to stare out the window. "I don't know if that's a good idea." No one knows Grainger like I do, and he was angry. As in, I need to murder something kind of angry. "I think he needs some time."

"I'll give him a damn day. Dude is gonna hear me out."

"Mitch—"

"Don't worry about me. I can take care of myself."

There's no talking him out of it. Mitch is Mitch. "All right."

As soon as I'm in his presence, Denver knows something is wrong. "Baby, what happened?"

Mitch storms by us mumbling under his breath. Denver watches him go. "And what's eating at him?"

A chuckle escapes me and my gosh but it's good to laugh. "He's playing the protective brother. He's quite good at it."

"Damn right he is," Denver says as his mother enters the room.

"Denver Stone."

"Sorry, Mom, but I have to give praise where praise is due. No one has my back like Mitch."

She ruffles his hair. "You boys wear me out." She commences to making their afternoon pot of coffee. "Jada, I want you to know that I taught these boys better than that, but they don't listen to me."

Denver rolls his eyes. If his greatest offense is a few swear words, I think I'll be okay.

With his mom's back to us, I kiss Denver softly on the lips. He searches my face for answers.

"You gonna tell me what happened, or are you avoiding the subject?"

Aurar turns to me. "Do you two need some privacy?"

"No. I had a run-in with Grainger after school, and he said some pretty hurtful things. But I guess hurting people say hurtful things. And I've hurt him."

I sit at the bar and put my head down.

Denver places a cold drink in my hand and I lift my head up. "He's still in love with you, isn't he?"

"Yes."

"I figured as much. It's not like he can shut down his feelings because you've moved on."

"It's killing me. What do I do?"

"There's nothing you can do. He needs time and space to get over you. I think he'll come around when he realizes how happy you are."

"I wanted him to come to our wedding."

He kisses my head. "I know, baby."

"Unfortunately, Denver is right. Not much heals a broken heart other than time. Although, he has a choice. A very tough choice, but he has choice."

"What choice is that?"

"To put your happiness before his own. His anger will subside, and he'll be faced with the hard truth of what your friendship really means to him. That's when the rubber meets the road. A friendship is easy when everything goes your way. The real test is when everything goes wrong. That goes for marriage as well."

"Wow, Mom, that's deep."

She leans on the counter. "Your dad's not the only wise one in this family."

Denver smiles. "I never thought he was."

The coffee pot beeps, announcing its job is done. Aurar pours two cups and leaves us alone in the kitchen.

"What would you like to do tonight?"

"No patrol? No meetings?"

"Nope."

"Hmm. I can think of a few things I'd like to do." I grab his shirt and pull him closer.

"Baby, stop baiting me."

"Then hurry up and marry me."

"We've been round and round this bush. There's too much going on to throw something together."

"Says who? I'm fine with us standing on the deck with our family, repeating our vows, you carrying me to our house, and throwing me on the bed, and—"

His mouth shuts me up. We've been super busy, but when we have time to kiss, it's fatal. There were a couple of moments the lines got smudged a bit. Denver swears a lot. And paces a lot. And he's picked up running these last several days.

He's usually pulled away by now, but he continues to spur me on and drive me crazy. My hands sneak up to find his tight abs. He growls low in his throat as I trace every muscle. His hands are pressed hard on my back, pulling me as close as possible. My head falls back as he explores every piece of exposed skin with his tongue. When he finds my mouth again, I'm over the top. I shove him against the counter and pull up his shirt.

"Shit, Jada. I'm sorry. I let that go too far." He holds both my hands in his to keep me from undressing him. His breaths are erratic, and his neck pulses in time with his accelerated heart rate.

I lay my forehead on his chest in defeat. He's cutting us off. Which he should.

"Can I let go of your hands?"

"I'm okay."

He gives them a squeeze and releases. "My God, Jada, that is so good, can you imagine…"

I gaze up into his beautiful face. "Oh I imagine, Denver. Believe me, I imagine." I place my hands on either side of his face. "And you know what else, I'm not ashamed of the fact that I want you. You're going to be my husband, and I can't wait to fulfill your every desire in the bedroom."

I watch him fight the urge to ravish me all over again. "Baby, I've not laid a finger on another woman while I waited for you. I promise you, you have me heart, soul, and body. And when I get you in my bed—God help us because I won't hold back any longer."

"I'll be mad if you do."

"Damn, baby, we gotta get married."

I roll my eyes. "Seriously, Denver? You're the one that says everything has to be perfect."

"When you say I do, it will be perfect. No matter what."

"You need to stop being so sexy right now. I need a distraction."

"Name it."

"Hmm. How about bowling?"

He chuckles. "You want to go bowling?"

"Yes. Let's take Mitch too. He's been pretty darn great."

"Bowling it is."

MITCH IS MORE than pumped about going bowling. He wants to take a fourth person, so Denver calls Rieder. I would have liked Emily to come, but I know that's a tricky situation for Mitch, so I don't bring her up. Denver drives the BMW and we run over to Rieder's place to pick him up. The guys make me laugh so hard that my side is cramping by the time we get there. It's true what they say about laughter being good for the soul.

The place is packed for a Monday. The guy at the counter explains it's league night, but he does have one lane on the end. We get situated at our lane and the guys order wings and a pitcher of beer. I ask Denver how they get away with that. He says his dad knows a lot of people.

After the first game, even with a score of 144, I'm in last place. Denver bowls over two hundred.

"Geez, Denver. You didn't tell me you were professionals."

Rieder sits beside me at the table while we take a break between games. "Denver is good at everything. He's one of those annoying people like that."

Denver taps the table. "I am not."

"Bullshit. You have to be better at everything. You remember the first time we went skiing?"

Denver laughs and shakes his head. "That was not my fault."

"I'll blame you for the rest of my life."

"I'm dying here, what happened?"

Mitch is back from the bathroom and sits down. "I love this story."

Denver slugs Mitch on the arm. "Shut up."

Rieder leans forward to fill me in. "So Denver was twelve, Mitch and I were ten, and Layne was probably seven. None of us have ever been skiing, so we don't know what the hell we're doing. Denver being Denver picks it up right away and starts going down some of the bigger slopes. The rest of us losers are still on the kiddie ones. By late afternoon, Denver is showing off. I had graduated to the blue hill but was still struggling. You have to understand at that age, I thought Denver was a god. So when he asked me to go with him down the black hill, I agreed."

"Oh no, this doesn't end well, does it?"

Denver is twisting in his chair. "Shouldn't we start a new game?"

"Hold your horses there, WP."

I laugh and Rieder glances from me to Denver. "You told her?"

Denver shrugs.

"Damn, it's worse than I thought. So anyway, we get to the top of this enormous hill and I am petrified. I'm about to chicken out, but Denver gives me the peer pressure, ya know?"

Denver snorts. "I did not peer pressure you."

"Hey, I'm telling this story. Denver zooms off down the hill and I'm gonna be a chicken shit if I don't go, so I bite the bullet and shove off. I'm okay for a minute or two, but you pick up some crazy speed on these hills, and I'm not ready for all that. About a quarter of the way down, I get all tangled and twisted up, and next thing I know I'm rolling and tossing around like a sack of potatoes. Somewhere in all that rolling, my knee popped and I knew I was in trouble. By the time I stopped, I didn't know where any of my poles or skis were. Some other dudes on the hill called the medic, and they took me down the rest of the way on a gurney. My knee was toast. I wore a brace for three weeks."

Denver sits back in his chair. "You act like I pushed you down that hill."

"You might as well have."

"Whatever. I felt really crappy that you messed up your knee."

Rieder laughs. "I know, man. Your dad told me you cried."

"What the hell? He told you how upset I was and you still tell that stupid story?"

"Dude, you're so damn perfect, I gotta have something to hold over your head."

"That's messed up, man." Denver gets up and heads toward the bar. "I need a beer."

When Denver is out of earshot, Rieder continues, "I give him a hard time about that, and my knee was jacked up, but it would have been worse and taken longer to heal if I hadn't been a wolf. I like to give him hell, but I look up to Denver to this day. Don't you dare tell him I said that."

"I would never." I love these guys more every day.

"So what's the hold up with you? Everyone kinda thought you'd have your first change by now."

Mitch chokes on his beer. "Dude, that's inappropriate."

I laugh. "It's okay, Mitch. I don't really know. Some days I think it's close, and other days, nothing at all."

"Well, we're stoked. Nothing exciting has happened around here for a while. I know you're going to be the bomb, and don't you worry about that demon. Every wolf in Forrest City is more than happy to defend one of its own."

I reach over and place my hand over Rieder's. "Thank you. That means a lot."

Denver walks up and pops Rieder on the back of the head. "Dude, you groping my girl?"

"Nah man, she can't keep her hands off me."

"That's it. Outside."

Rieder jumps up from his chair. "I'm not in the mood for an ass whooping. Let's bowl."

Denver points toward the lane. "Get to it then."

I walk over to Denver and whisper against his neck. "Be nice."

He squints in Rieder's direction. "That was nice, and he knows it."

We bowl two more games and I officially suck. These guys are too good for me. But I have fun. Denver settles up our tab and we stroll out into the night air. The temperature this spring has been warmer than usual and tonight is no exception. I love it. There's a big full moon hanging low in the sky. A ball of creamy orange. It reminds me of a dreamsicle. Denver places an arm around me as we walk to the car.

"Why do people think wolves only come out on a full moon?" I wonder out loud.

All three boys answer at the same time. "Movies."

"Yeah, I guess that's where I got the idea. This is still so crazy to me. You guys have had your whole life to prepare for what you are. I've had days."

Denver squeezes my side. "You're gonna be awesome. Honestly, it's kinda hot, and I can't wait to witness your first time."

I stop walking. He's not told me that before. Now that I think about it, his opinion had me worried.

"Really?"

He pushes me against the car. "Are you serious? Everything about you drives me crazy, but knowing we'll be able to share this turns me on even more—if that's possible."

Mitch makes a gagging sound. He and Rieder are waiting for us to finish our moment. "Dude, you see what I have to put up with?"

Rieder grumbles while kicking a rock on the pavement. "I hate him so much right now."

Denver pushes off the car. "I heard that."

Rieder punches him in the arm. "I know you did, idiot. Hey, man, are we good?"

"Yeah. We're good. But if you so much as touch her…"

Rieder throws up his hands. "Damn, bro, you know I would never do that."

Denver opens my door to let me in. He and Rieder fist bump their agreement and all is forgotten as we ride home, laughing and joking.

By the time we crawl in bed later, my body is done. So much has changed in the last few weeks. My world has been flipped upside down and sometimes I'm not sure which way is up. All I do know is I love this sexy guy beside me, and the fact that he's all mine makes me giddy inside.

Denver pushes my hair behind my ear. "I know that face. What are you thinking about?"

"Everything."

"That narrows it down. Thanks."

"I'm being serious. I have so much running through my mind it's dizzying."

"It has been a whirlwind for sure. I know you've been over-whelmed. I'm so proud of you for the way you're handling everything."

I roll my eyes. "Yeah, passing out is so cool."

He chuckles. "That was a big deal, and my delivery could have used some finesse. Sorry about that."

"You're forgiven."

"Speaking of forgiven..."

I sigh. "I know. I need to talk to my parents. Can you go with me tomorrow after school?"

He leans over me, pressing his chest to mine. The heat and weight of his body shoots electricity through my nervous system. His hand fumbles around on the nightstand beside me, but all I can do is stare at his face an inch from mine. My breath picks up and Denver real-izes his mistake.

He lies back on his side of the bed and pushes my cell in my hand.

"Text your mom. Let her know we're coming tomorrow."

I'm motionless as I try to settle on one single emotion. "God, Denver, don't ever lay on top of me again unless you plan on doing something about it."

"Don't start with me, woman. Text your mom."

"Ugh. You're the most frustrating person on this planet." I send my mom a text and throw the phone on the bed. "Happy now?"

He taps his finger on my nose. "I've been happy since the night you walked out on our deck and rocked my world."

"I know what you're trying to do."

"Is it working?"

"No, I'm still mad. But I love you."

"I love you too."

GRAINGER SKIPS SCHOOL the next day. He's avoiding me and it makes me sad. Emily's focus is prom. A part of me is excited, but at the same time, prom pales in comparison to my wedding to Denver. The fact that we haven't been able to set a date irritates me. He's so worried it won't be all I've dreamed, blah, blah, blah. All I want is to marry the man. He's right about one thing; we have a lot going on. Everyone holds their breath in anticipation of my first change, including me. There's a demon waiting to take me out. Prom and graduation. If Denver would listen to me, we'd already be married. A simple ceremony on the deck with our families. Then have a small wedding later. The man drives me insane.

Speaking of my hottie, he's waiting by his motorcycle when I walk out of the building. Sometimes all I have to do is look at him and my temperature goes up. Denver says the attraction between mates is unlike anything else. He doesn't have to convince me. My traitorous body tells me every damn day.

He shakes his head as I approach him. "I can feel that, you know?"

"You're not going to do anything about it."

He growls and grabs my face, planting a much-needed kiss on my lips. "You do realize I'm about to buckle, right?"

"I'll believe it when it happens."

"Put your helmet on. Let's go meet your parents."

I do as I'm told and throw my leg over the seat of the bike. I slide in as close as I can and wrap my arms around him. I love the bike because I can grope his chest and abs and there's nothing he can do about it. When we pull up to my house, my mood immediately shifts. I am so dreading this. Denver is still reeling from me torturing him and jumps off the bike swearing. He storms up and down the driveway while I brace myself for what's to come.

He marches up to me ready to pick a fight until he notices the stress etched on my face. He takes three long breaths and pushes them out slowly.

"Baby, come here. It's going to be okay."

I let him hold me and it gives me the strength and encouragement I need to face the moment. Backing out of his embrace, I stare at the home I grew up in. There's a separation that takes place in my heart. So many wonderful memories flash in my mind. A few not so wonderful flashbacks as well. Everything that's happened up until now has helped shape me into the person I am today. But it's now my decision to choose what I'm going to do with it. I'm not happy with the way my parents handled things. They screwed up. We all do. I can spend the rest of my life letting the bitterness poison me, or I can forgive and live in peace. This is no longer my home. Denver is. No point in making two people suffer when they were trying to do what they thought was right.

I put my hand in Denver's and squeeze. We walk up to the door, and oddly enough I don't know whether or not to knock. In the end, I push the door open. Roland is sitting on the edge of the coffee table. My mom is folded up on the couch holding a tissue. She's been crying. It wrecks me to see her in such a state. This woman has given everything to raise me. Her sacrifices have been endless. Her love, extravagant.

She lurches from the sofa as we approach, and I rush over, throwing my arms around her. She shakes as sobs escape her. We hold each other, crying for all the things we can't say in this moment.

Several minutes later, she holds me at arm's length. "I'm so sorry. For everything. I love you so much and I hope you can find it in your heart to forgive me." She glances at Roland. "Forgive us."

"I do forgive you, and I love you too."

Her shoulders lift and fall with the breath she takes. A heavy burden being released. A spark lights in her eyes. "You two sit down. I'll go get a snack." She disappears into the kitchen, leaving us with Roland.

Denver extends his hand. "Roland. Good to see you again."

Roland takes Denver's hand in both of his. "Thank you, Denver. I know you've been taking good care of Jada. We have much to discuss, but for now, tell me, when is this wedding?" He smiles and my heart makes a tiny space for the man who is my father.

"We haven't set a date. I would like to wait until after graduation, but Jada, well she's pushing for something sooner."

Roland throws back his head and laughs. It surprises me. "I take it you've both mated then?"

"Yes, sir."

"That's great news. I know you'll be happy and have a wonderful life together, like your parents."

Denver squeezes my hand. "Yes, we will."

My mom scurries back in the room with a tray full of hors d'oeuvres. "What did I miss?"

Roland puts his arm around her, and she leans on his shoulder. "These two have officially mated."

She jerks away from him and squints at Denver. "What does that mean exactly? Are you having..." She can't even say it.

"Mom, no. We're not having sex. It means that we belong to each other and no one else. For life. I told you we're getting married."

"Thank God."

She sinks back into Roland's arms as the rest of us laugh at her reaction.

We learn through conversation that Roland never shared a lot of his wolf heritage and what that entails with my mother. It's part of the reason she never understood who he was. They're working hard to make amends and have a relationship built on truth and trust. I'm truly happy for them. We talk for well over an hour, from our current situation to Roland's family history. It's still hard to believe I'm of royal blood. My mom listens intently as we share different aspects of wolf life. The more the guys share, the more excited I get about my own change.

The last time I left in a hurry, scrambling to get what I needed. This time, my mother helps me pack a suitcase while gushing over the upcoming wedding. As much as I hate to admit Denver was right, he was right. I can't rob my mom of being a part of my special day.

Graduation isn't that far away. But once graduation is out of the way, I will be getting married. And soon.

THE WEEK ROLLS on with no changes. I'm starting to get flustered and think something is wrong with me. Could it be possible I'm some sort of fluke? Maybe because my mother is human, I'm not going to experience wolf life. Denver says I'm too stressed and I need to relax.

It's Friday night and we're cuddled up on the couch watching a movie, some action film that Denver picked out. Mitch is in the chair, half watching, half on his phone. He doesn't talk about Emily much, but I know they text each other. I hate this situation for them both. How sucky would it be to want to be close to someone and know you can't do anything about it? Prom is in two weeks, so that will be interesting. Emily and I are going dress shopping tomorrow. Who knows what we'll find this late in the game, but it should be fun. I haven't had a girl's date in a while.

I'm all but asleep on Denver's shoulder when I'm jostled awake by loud knocking. Denver and Mitch glance at each other and Mitch gets up to answer the door. The person is shouting angrily. Denver bristles beside me, and I sit up in case he needs to assist Mitch with the situation at the door.

The second Mitch opens the door, I recognize the slurred voice. "Where is she?"

Mitch swears while trying to keep Grainger outside the house. Denver and I jump up at the same time.

Grainger is unsteady on his feet. He has his finger poked at Mitch's chest, and he's angrier than a hornet. "I said, where is Shada?"

"Dude, you are three sheets to the wind. And get your hand off me."

I force my way in beside Mitch. He still has Grainger outside the door.

"Grainger! What in the world? You're drunk."

He sways, and Mitch grabs him by the arm. "I'm shorry. I love you, Shada."

Oh dear Lord. I give Denver an apologetic smile. "We can't let him leave. He shouldn't be driving."

Denver nods. He and Mitch each take an arm and bring him inside. They start to the kitchen, so I shut the door and follow along.

"Okay, buddy. Let's attempt to get you sobered up a bit." Denver starts some coffee and makes him some toast.

Mitch holds Grainger up since he can't sit on his stool without falling over. "Damn, dude, can you sit still?" Mitch looks over at me. "You know he's going to be puking his guts up later, right? I'm not holding him then. Just saying."

Denver brings over a slice of toast and pushes it toward Grainger. "Try to eat some of this." He then grabs a bottle of water and sets it on the counter as well. "The coffee is almost done."

"What are we going to do? I can't take him home like this. His mom would have a conniption. He's never been this drunk, and I feel responsible."

"He can stay here. In the other spare bedroom down the hall from yours."

"Thank you."

Grainger scrunches his face and hits the counter with his fist. "Hell, no. I'm not sheeping here wif him." He points at Denver and then burps.

Denver sighs. "It's going to be a long night."

Grainger lays his head on the counter and shuts his eyes. He grumbles but nothing he says makes sense.

"I'm so sorry," I say, but to who I'm not sure. "I better go get my phone and text his mom."

My hands tremble as I walk down the hall, and I shake my arms to get rid of the stress. I can't believe Grainger showed up here completely inebriated. By the time I text Mindy to let her know Grainger is with me, I'm shaking all over. Sweat beads up on my forehead. Oh great. Now is not the time for one of my episodes. My body heats up and my insides are twisting. All of a sudden it's extremely stifling in the bedroom and I itch all over. I need fresh air and now.

The hall needs to stop moving. I can't walk straight. I hate to pull Denver from Grainger duty, but I need his help. I yell for him and he's immediately beside me.

"You're okay, baby. Let's get you outside." He picks me up and carries me in his arms.

We pass through the kitchen on our way to the door.

A huge smile breaks out on Mitch's face. "Hell yeah! Is it time?"

Denver smiles as well. "I think it is."

Grainger stumbles from his stool. "What's wong with Shada?"

"Nothing that concerns you. Drink your coffee." Mitch tries to convince Grainger to sit back down and a scuffle is followed by the crash of a chair as we go out the garage door.

Denver carries me to the end of the yard near the woods. The night air helps to cool the sweat beading on my skin. He sets me down on my butt and steps back. I close my eyes and try to breathe through the waves of energy pulsing in my system. My organs twist and shift and there's a dull ache in my bones. A commotion coming from the yard causes me to open my eyes. Mitch and Grainger are headed this way.

Denver yells at his brother. "What the hell, Mitch? He shouldn't be here!"

"Dude, short of physically strapping him down, there was nothing I could do. Maybe it'll help him cope with things."

"Shit. I don't know. What if he tells someone?"

"He would have to remember first. He's pretty wasted."

Grainger sees me on the ground and tries to rush over. "Shada!" Both Denver and Mitch hold him back.

Denver pushes his free hand in his hair. "Jada, it's up to you."

After all we've been through, I actually want Grainger to be a part of my new world. "He can stay."

Denver shoots Grainger a glare of warning. "Stay back or I will have no problem knocking you on your ass."

A fresh wave of inner turmoil causes me to suck in air between my teeth.

Denver squats beside me. "You're close now. How much do you like these clothes, cause they won't make the change?"

Damn it. These are my favorite jeans. I remember Aurar saying to be sure and have on underwear. Oh great. What if I'm wearing a thong.

My cheeks go warm. "Save the clothes."

He grins. "Okay. Stand up." He holds out his hand and pulls me to my feet. "I know this is awkward, but trust me when I say it gets easier. Mitch and I patrol with girls and they have no problem stripping in front of us."

My eyebrows pinch together. "I don't think I like the sound of that."

"Baby, it's not like that. Although, they're not *you*, and this will be damn hard now that I think about it."

I groan as another wave rolls over me. "Do it."

Denver yanks my shirt over my head and helps me out of my jeans. Grainger is swearing and trying to figure out what is going on.

The last thing I recall is Denver saying he'll never be able to look at me the same again.

CHAPTER EIGHTEEN

DENVER

An angel has fallen out of the sky. A star, celestial being, goddess—hell, I don't know, but Jada is the most beautiful creature I've ever laid eyes on.

Mitch curses behind me and Grainger falls to the ground, but I can't take my eyes off of her. Her chocolate-brown pupils now have a golden-yellow ring around them. For her petite human frame, she's a big wolf. Her stance is bold and confident, and something inside of me wants to bow to her. But it's her coat that has me mesmerized. I've seen every color of wolf except white. There's not a spot or blemish on her. She's as white as freshly fallen snow. The air around her crackles and I remember that same sensation when we met Roland, but Jada's is stronger. Damn. Her presence is so heavenly I momentarily avert my gaze. She takes my breath away.

Mitch interrupts my reverent thoughts.

Wow. I mean, just, wow.

Yeah, I was thinking the same thing. How's Grainger?

He's good. Fell back on his ass, but he didn't pass out. He's been stunned into silence, thank God.

Jada has been taking in the sights around her but settles on me. *What is it? Why are you guys gawking at me like that? Am I ugly or something?*

Mitch and I laugh. She's the furthest thing from ugly.

What? Am I not even a wolf?

Baby, you're without a doubt the most incredible wolf I've ever witnessed. So, what do you think?

It's amazing. Unbelievable. Transforming. Free. Restless. Like I need to run. What do I look like?"

Mitch nudges me in the shoulder. "You should take her to the lake."

"The water. Good idea." I pull my shirt over my head then unbutton my jeans. Shit. "Uh, Jada, you might want to turn around. I'm not wearing underwear."

Well, that painted a nice image in my brain. Fine.

She turns towards the woods and I finish undressing. Grainger has found his voice and sounds as if he's not as drunk as before.

"What the hell? Dude, I really could have gone without seeing you naked."

I ignore him and immediately shift to my wolf form. Grainger swears some more. Mitch is laughing. I walk up next to Jada and nuzzle her neck with my nose.

You ready for a run?

Lead the way.

We weave in and out of the trees, run alongside the rushing water of the creek, and up and over every hill. We could have gone straight to the lake, but what's the fun in that? No words are necessary. The wonder of her transformation emanates from her. Our paws hit the dirt hard as we run faster. Jada is matching my speed stride for stride. Neither of us are panting, so I push her harder. She is unaffected by the change in pace. We're near a full sprint when we reach the lake.

That was awesome! I believe I could run all night.

You could.

Wow. This is exceptional. So much better than I imagined.

I told you you'd love it.

We sit near the edge and stare across the lake. It's not a full moon, but it's close. The moonlight shines like a flashlight across the water.

Jada inches closer to the edge and peers over. I join her there, gazing in awe at her reflection.

I'm white. Wasn't expecting that.

You're insanely beautiful. Like a rare diamond.

I think you exaggerate.

Actually, I'm not. I'll have to ask my dad, but as far as I know, there's not one solid white wolf around here. I suppose it could be the royal gene. Your dad is solid black. That too is rare, but there have been a couple of those.

Huh. She continues to stare at herself, then studies me. *I'm almost as big as you.*

I noticed that too. I think you could kick my ass if you wanted to. Your energy sizzles like bacon in hot grease.

Let's wrestle and find out.

Um, no thanks. I'm used to being the strongest guy around. I don't want to lose my badass reputation to a girl. Besides, we should head back. There's Grainger to deal with and I know my parents are waiting to congratulate you. Plus, I really, really want to kiss you right now.

Jada licks me in the face and laughs.

Yeah, that's not gonna cut it.

God, you're right. That was not near as satisfying as licking your sexy, full lips.

Jada, please stop. My adrenaline is through the roof. Running with you was like a new high. I may devour you when we get back and I can feel you next to me again.

She growls, and it's not a girly sound, but a throaty, sexy, lusty sound.

I get what you mean about the growling thing. I may have to move out until our wedding.

Her laugh resonates in my soul. Every moment with her makes our bond stronger. I'm gonna have to run like hell all the way home to shake me out of the state I'm in. And I'm not sure that's going to work. But one can hope.

. . .

THE RUNNING DOESN'T HELP. In fact, I'm more infatuated with her than before. Jada is fast. Her royal blood must give her an advantage over typical wolves. I had to come into my strength. I continually work out and train to be the best I can be. It's natural to Jada. She's more sexy to me right now than she's ever been. Honestly, I'm not sure how that's possible, but it's true.

We reach the backyard in less than half the time it took to go out to the lake. Jada follows me to the garage, and I discover Mitch was decent enough to fold our clothes and leave them there. This is where it gets tricky. On any given day it's no big deal to change back, but this is different. I swallow hard recalling helping Jada out of her clothes earlier. My body is tighter than a guitar string. I'm on the edge of losing control, like the day Jada said she had mated with me. I'm going to need help.

I turn to examine Jada still in her wolf form. She's radiant. *Baby, I'm struggling right now. I may need some extra time to cool down. Do you mind?*

I think that would be best. What do I do?

Mom, can you come out to the garage and help Jada? I need a time out.

Yes! Oh my gosh, yes. I'll be right there.

Thank you.

Jada ambles up beside me. She nuzzles my neck and I growl. *Denver, I love you more than my life. Some days I think I can wait to marry you, and other days the anticipation is pure agony. Then some days, like now, I wish we were already married. Most days I wish we were already married. How can you love a person this much? Not only my body, but my soul is tortured, longing to be one with you.*

Baby, please...you're killing me. When is graduation?

May thirty-first.

June seventh. Our date is June seventh. I can't wait any longer than that.

Seriously! Oh my gosh, I can't wait to tell everyone!

The garage door swings open and my mother rushes out. She gasps and her hand flies to her mouth. "Jada. Mitch was right, you are extraordinary! Bolivar, hurry up."

Dad bursts through the door then. "Sorry, I was helping with Grainger." Not much surprises my dad, but his eyes grow huge at the sight her. "What a beauty. I knew I called you princess for a reason." He clears his throat and continues. "I know this is hard for you both. The tension is apparent. This experience only fortifies your love for each other. You haven't shared your plans. Have you made a decision?"

I'll let Jada tell you. I'll be back in an hour.

He nods his understanding. "All right then, I'll let you girls get situated out here."

I leave Jada with my mother, knowing she's in good hands. For the next hour I run. I run as hard and as fast as I can. My paws tear at the earth as I exert all my energies in and through my muscles. I'm actually tired by the time I return.

I get dressed in the garage and walk through the kitchen. No one is around. I grab a beer and go down the hall. Jada isn't in her room, but the sweet sound of her voice carries from the other bedroom. I walk to the door and watch her. She doesn't notice me because her attention is on a puking Grainger. She comforts him as he leans over the bed throwing up into a trash can. He apologizes and she wipes his face with a wet cloth. I find I'm not the least bit jealous. We're so in tune, I sense her compassion and concern for him, but nothing else. She loves him, but as a friend. There's no hint of anything more.

Grainger lies back down, and she moves to clean up the mess.

"Can I get you anything? I'm not good with puke, but I'll help if you need me to."

She grins and bites her lip. My heart does a damn bungee jump to my toes. All that running shot to hell.

"I think I can handle it." She glances at Grainger. "He should rest for a while. I'll be in the bed shortly."

"All right."

I relax on my side of the bed and finish my beer. Six weeks. Six long weeks before Jada will be my wife. In a natural setting, six weeks isn't that long, but one day more might as well be an eternity. Like Jada said earlier, I wish we were already married, but I've tried to do what's right by her. I want her to finish high school. Initially I thought I was strong enough to wait longer. Give her the chance to make up her own mind about her future, but now that she's mated with me, I can't do it. I'm selfish, and I need her, and I'm too weak to hold out longer than the promised six weeks. It will be the longest six weeks of my life.

Jada comes in and flops on the bed next to me. "Wow. He is so sick. Please don't ever let me drink that much."

"You got it." I nestle into her side. "He's lucky to have you to take care of him. Did you tell everyone the news?"

"Your parents are ecstatic, especially your mom. I'm pretty sure she'll be up all night planning. I called my mom as well. She's happy for me, but I think she struggles with me getting married so young. I also called Emily. She cried because I asked her to be my maid of honor. So yes, we are a go for June seventh." She sighs. "Why does that seem so far away?"

I twist a strand of her hair. "Because you can't wait to get your hands on me."

She sits up and pushes her lips to mine. It's not gentle. So not gentle. I never want her to kiss me any other way again. I shove my hands in her hair and moan into her mouth. All of the adrenaline of the evening is rushing back and I know we're in trouble. I can't tell who wants who more. Jada is straddling me now and we become a tornado of hands and lips and hisses and moans. I try to avoid touching her bare skin, but my fingers find their way up her stomach. I'm at the base of her bra, torn with indecision. That's when Grainger saves me. Damn it, but I'm going to owe him one. He starts to puke in the other room, and Jada comes to her senses.

Her face is pink and her lips are red and swollen. She peeks at me apologetically. "I should go check on him."

I grunt, unable to make my voice work. She slides off the bed and starts to leave the room. I hate to do this, but it's for my sanity.

"Jada?" She stops and turns. "I think I'll sleep in my bed tonight."

She's disappointed. Her shoulders slump and my stomach pains me as if someone stuck me with a screwdriver.

"And the night after that?"

Shit. I don't know. She has me all sorts of confused. It's so hard to be near her. "Maybe."

She lays her head on the doorframe. Grainger continues to get sick in the other room. "Okay."

Then she's gone down the hall. My stomach is twisted inside out too, Grainger.

GRAINGER SHUFFLES to the kitchen the next morning looking like death. I'm sitting at the bar drinking a Coke and playing Fortnite on my phone.

"Hey. Can I get you some coffee?"

"That would be great."

We trade places. He sits at the bar, and I get up to start some coffee. Once the coffee maker is going I lean on the counter to wait. "How about some toast?"

He starts to shake his head and then groans. "I don't know if can eat. I'm sorry to be a pain in the ass. I know you probably don't even want me here."

"It's a little weird, but I'm not doing it for you, I'm doing it for Jada. I know she cares about you."

He winces at the sound of her name. "You really love her, don't you?"

"More than you could ever know."

"I've loved her longer. I thought she would marry me some day. Had it all planned out. Then you came along."

"It's not a competition. And you can't really understand the complexity of what Jada and I have. But if it makes you feel any better, if I were in your shoes, I'd hate me too."

"Sometimes I seriously do hate you. Murder has popped into my head once or twice."

I chuckle at his honesty. "I'll keep that in mind when you're around."

A beep beside me lets me know the coffee is done. I pour a cup and pass it to Grainger. Black is all he gets. I don't like him enough to ask if he wants cream or sugar. He sips it slowly and rubs his temples. Damn. I'm gonna have to be nice again.

"You need something for that headache?"

"Yes. I swear I'll get out of your hair once I get woke up. Where is Jada, by the way?"

I open the ibuprofen and pass him three pills. He's not getting my mom's special tea.

"She went to visit her mom, and then she and Emily are going prom dress shopping."

"Oh, okay. Will you thank her for taking care of me last night?"

"Sure."

He downs the pills with his coffee. He lifts off the stool and then sits back down. His fingers tap nervously on the counter. I watch his mouth open and close twice.

"You want to know about last night?" I can't deal with his fidgeting any longer.

"Did you do that to her?"

What the hell. Breathe, Denver. Breathe. "Did I do what to her?"

"Hell, I don't know. Make her some sort of beast?"

Count to ten, Denver. He's ignorant to our ways. Shit, this dude is making me talk to myself. Think of Jada. He's her friend.

I push out a breath, but my jaw clenches as I speak. "Jada is what she was born to be. I had nothing to do with it. And I think if you want more than that, you'll have to ask her. I'm not really in the mood to share my life story with you."

"Sorry. Obviously I've offended you. I mean all I know about this sort of thing is what you see in movies. This morning I tried to tell myself it was all a dream, but I know what I saw. At the same time, I don't know what in the hell I saw. I've known Jada her whole life and I'm pretty sure I would have known if she was a—"

"Wolf. Jada is a wolf. As am I. Last night was her first time, but we've known it was coming for a while. Look, man, talk to her. It will be easier coming from her."

"You're right."

Grainger stands up and takes his cup to the sink. His deathly pale face has a hint of color, but he's still got the bedhead going on. Okay, last time today I'm being nice to this guy.

"You're welcome to take a shower before you go. There's towels and stuff in your bathroom. You'll have to show yourself out, though. I'm leaving with Mitch to go check out tuxes."

"Thanks. For everything. You could have thrown me out on my ass last night."

"Thought about it."

He turns to leave, shaking his head. His faint chuckle drifts down the hall after him. I could possibly like the guy if he weren't in love with my future wife.

MITCH and I haven't hung out in a while. It's good to chill with him and not be concerned with wolf business. We used to do everything together, but of course, Jada is my everything now. We order our tuxes without much fuss. There's no debate because we both agree that a classic black tux can't be beat. The lady at the counter tries to talk us out of the most expensive one, but we assure her it's what we want. She has nothing else to say when I pay her in cash. The order will make it just in time for prom.

Jada has sent me several pictures of her and Emily in dresses. She asks my opinion, but she's beautiful in every single one.

Jada: You are impossible. I need help here. Pass the phone to Mitch.

Me: Why? I don't want him drooling over you.

Jada: OMG. Show him the pics.

Me: You decide. I'm going to love you in whatever you wear.

Jada: Ugh. Fine.

Me: Use the card I gave you. Don't worry about the price.

Jada: Price? What's that?

Me: Lol

I shove my phone back in my pocket. There's no way I'm showing Mitch those pictures. He's my brother, but he's still a male.

"Dude, what are you grumbling about?"

"Nothing. Where do you want to eat?"

"Burger sounds good."

We grab a late lunch and then head home. Mitch laughs hysterically as I tell him about my talk with Grainger. This is one of those times when I want to punch him in the face. The more I say it's not funny, the more he laughs. Why does everyone want to push my buttons today? God, I'm grumpy. I need some Jada time. I need to touch her. I didn't sleep by her last night, and we barely had time to say hello this morning. I'm pathetic, and I know I'm pathetic, but I need a hit.

Jada walks in an hour after Mitch and I return. She's carrying several bags and I jump up to help her. The dress she chose is in a garment bag, so I can't tell which one it is. We take everything to her room and put it in the closet.

She flops down in the desk chair. "I hope it's okay, but I got shoes too. And a couple of other things."

I pull her to her feet and she grunts, so I sweep her in my arms and carry her to the bed. "Baby, I don't care what you buy." I lay her down and scoot in beside her, inhaling the scent of vanilla in her hair.

Her body relaxes and she sighs. "I missed you too." She rolls on her side to face me. "I thought of something today we haven't discussed."

"What's that?"

"A honeymoon."

"Hmm. I like the sound of that. Where do you want to go?"

She traces my lips with her finger. It makes me shiver. "What are my options?"

"Anywhere. You name it and I'll make it happen."

"Somewhere warm. I picture you and me on a beach, holding a drink, with our toes in the sand. I'm in a string bikini, you're in a speedo—"

"Hold up. You want me to wear a speedo while laying out with you in a string bikini? I don't think that's wise."

"Oh geez, Denver. Okay, forget the speedo."

I run my fingers through her silky brown hair. "There's lots of beaches, baby. You got to give me more than that."

She hesitates, probably thinking about the money.

"Jada Brooks. Tell me where you want to go."

"Hawaii?"

"Done. That wasn't so hard was it?"

She starts kicking and screaming. "Really? Oh my gosh, Hawaii! This is like a dream."

"I tell myself that every day."

Jada's eyes gloss over in lust, and I know we better abort before things get out of hand. Again. I brush her lips lightly and slide off the bed.

"I also thought of something today that we haven't discussed."

She sits up on her elbows. "Oh yeah, what might that be?"

"You need some training. Mitch has agreed to help me teach you some fighting skills."

"Right. I kinda forget there's a demon wanting to destroy me."

"We won't let that happen, but you need to know how to defend yourself."

"How much time do you think we have?"

"I have no idea. My dad has the area covered twenty-four seven. So far, there's no change. In fact, there's been very little demon activity at all. I suppose they're waiting for the final battle."

"Wow. You sure know how to kill a girl's libido."

"Six more weeks, baby. Six more weeks." I pull her to her feet. "Come on, let's go get sweaty."

JADA'S never seen the gym where Mitch and I train. It's always been our bonding place, so I made sure earlier today he was okay with bringing Jada here. He surprised me with his enthusiasm to train Jada.

We change clothes and I tell her to meet me in the garage. She walks in wearing running shorts and a tank top. I'm glad I'm not wearing a speedo right now. Mitch stumbles out of the kitchen door behind her.

He starts dancing around Jada like a boxer. "You ready to do this?"

She rolls her eyes at him and laughs. I love how close they've become. "In here?"

Mitch takes Jada by the arm. "Oh no, not in here." He walks to the end of the garage and pushes open the only door Jada's never been behind. "In here. Welcome to the man cave."

Jada strolls across the room, running her hand over the equipment. She makes a full circle, then stops in front of me with squinted eyes. "I'm trying not to be pissed at you for holding out on me. This is awesome."

I hold my hands up in mock surrender. "Baby, it's the man cave."

"Whatever. So, where do we start?"

Mitch and I work Jada over for the next two hours. We start with cardio and lifting, and then put her in the ring with Mitch. I go over basic stances, punches, and kicks, while Mitch demonstrates and then Jada practices each move. Like with the running, she's stronger than you think. She and Mitch do some light sparring at the end, and it's impressive how much she's learned in the last hour. I can't help but laugh my ass off when she sneaks in a left hook that connects with Mitch's jaw. He swears, rubbing his jaw line.

Jada rushes over to Mitch. "Oh my God! I'm so sorry."

Mitch starts laughing. "Damn girl, remind me to not piss you off."

Jada leans against the rope and grunts. "I'm exhausted and hungry. Can we call it a day?"

I hold open the rope for her and Mitch to climb out. "I think we'd better. I'll be brotherless if we continue."

"Shut the hell up." Mitch grumbles as he pushes past me.

I turn out the lights and catch up to Jada as she jokes with Mitch about his hit to the face. It's hard not to stare at her toned legs. It reminds me of the first night she showed up here in a dress. I recall her discomfort. Today she exudes pure confidence. It's sexy as hell.

Jada spins around. "Are you checking me out, Denver Stone?"

Either she was in my head or she felt it, but I'm busted. "Guilty as charged."

She lets out a breath. "Six more weeks."

IN THE EVENING, Dad cooks steaks on the grill and they are frigging mouthwatering. We sit around the table eating, talking, and laughing. My heart is so full, I may combust. This is my life. Jada is going to marry me. My family loves her. She's my heartbeat. I'll get to wake up to her every morning in our cabin. We'll start a family of our own. My insides constrict at the thought of the beautiful baby Jada and I will make.

The conversation pulls me back to the present. Mom and Jada get sidetracked with wedding details and us boys talk demon fighting. Every once in a while I glance at the woman who has me captivated. My bloody fish. She smiles and bites her lip. I groan. It's our cycle.

I slide onto the bed by Jada. Last night was hell being apart from her. We don't get carried away by lust. Jada barely has the strength to change clothes after the workout we gave her earlier. I think I've figured out how to survive the next six weeks. Kick Jada's butt in training. Every damn day.

CHAPTER NINETEEN

JADA

Denver is trying to kill me. My entire body aches. It hurts to sit on the toilet or climb stairs. There are muscles in my body I didn't know existed. I fall in bed every night depleted of any and all energy. I realized a couple of days ago that's been his plan all along. He all but admitted he's keeping me busy to keep me from attacking him. I would be mad, but I'm too tired for that too.

It's been two weeks since we started training. I love it. The instinct to fight runs in my veins. Mitch and I spar quite often and it's getting easier to keep up with him. Denver refuses to get in the ring with me. He does run with me though. After the first few changes to my wolf form, it's easier to switch back and forth. Denver and Mitch take me exploring, and every time, some new sight, sound, or smell fills me with wonder. Denver was reluctant to let me join them on patrol, but I can be persuasive when I want to be.

The entire drive to the warehouse, Denver bombards me with his ridiculous rules.

"I'm serious, Jada. If we're engaged in any sort of skirmish, I want you to stay back."

"I might as well hole up in the car. Maybe take a nap or scroll social media. Mitch, be sure to send me a Snap."

"Sure thing, Jada. With filter or without?"

Denver's grip tightens on the steering wheel. "You two are hilarious."

The warehouse was not what I expected. I had envisioned dust, crates, concrete floors, and oddly enough, cages. Don't ask. Instead the place is more like an office building. Denver tosses some maps on a conference room table and begins to mark each one in colored ink. While he's engrossed in his work, I venture out into the hall. I pass several meeting rooms and offices before I'm faced with a left or right decision. I go right. Light spills out from a room near the end. Curiosity gets the best of me, so I creep along the dimly lit hall approaching the space. A nice breakroom catches my eye, but I continue on.

A lamp light shadows Mitch's frame. He's bent over a desk, riffling through a drawer. Rows of TV screens line the wall behind him.

"You can come in, Jada."

So much for stealthy. Mitch slams one drawer and searches another. I gawk at the technology as I brush past him.

"What is this?"

"Dad's office. He runs his security business from here."

"I assumed when you guys spoke of the 'security business,' you meant the whole wolf patrol thing."

"That's part of it." He tugs on the last drawer. "Found it." He palms a ledger book in his hand. "Dad asked me to grab his logbook."

"So your dad actually runs a legit security business? Is there anything he can't do?"

"He's terrible with cars. He can buy them, but not fix them."

"Too funny. Do we have time for a quick tour of the rest of the place?"

"Super quick. Denver gets irritable if you're late for instructions."

Once Denver doles out assignments, he allows fifteen minutes for gabbing and a restroom break. Observing him in this leadership role creates a brand-new respect within me. He's organized, self-assured and thorough, but he's also kind and approachable. He and Rieder razz each other while I chat with the girls. When break is over, everyone makes their way to the locker room.

I strip down with the females of the group and it's not nearly as awkward as I thought it would be. Basically it's like wearing a bathing suit. As soon as we step outside the building, we transform to wolves and meet the boys on the other side of a partition.

Denver, Mitch, and I have the territory on the west side of town and then the woods beyond. I trot alongside the boys as we make a sweep through the city, sticking to dark alleys and side streets. A barrage of unpleasant odors invades my snout—rotten food, animal feces, urine, trash bins that smell like vomit, carcasses, and alcohol— it's enough to make you gag. I'm unable to shake free of the deluge of stink until we hit the residential stretch of our patrol. This is much more enjoyable, I think to myself, right before a large, angry cat jumps out of the bushes and lunges at me. I don't know why I jump, but I do. I could eat this guy for a snack.

Mitch cackles as I gain my composure and bare my teeth at the cat, scaring it away. The next hour is more of the same. Dogs, cats, rats, and every other critter object to our presence. I'm getting a complex.

The forest is another world entirely. My pupils adjust to the dark as we enter the trees. A soft, warm wind tickles my fur and the ground is mossy and cool beneath my paws. The strong scent of honeysuckle wafts by, followed by pine needles and moist dirt. We zigzag in and out of trees as we dart over roots and dodge briars. It's invigorating to say the least.

But the excitement happens on our third circuit in town outside a makeshift bar. I know something is amiss the second Denver bristles beside me. His lifts his muzzle to the sky and snaps out a sharp bark. Mitch hunkers down on my other side, ready to pounce. I'm utterly confused when four men strut in our direction out of the recesses of the alley.

Get behind me, Jada. Those are not men, Denver says as he sidesteps in front of me.

The evidence is apparent in their black, soulless eyes, but I can't get past the fact that they appear as people. I've retreated several steps before I realize it, but Denver and Mitch have advanced, keeping themselves between the demons and me. One single flinch from the demon side and the fight is on. I wonder how this could be a fair match when one of the demon men opens and stretches his mouth into a cavernous hole full of teeth. The hideous creature bends over Denver and I yelp. An unfazed Denver strikes his attacker with his paw, knocking it to the ground. He then bounds on top of the demon and separates its head from the body, while simultaneously kicking the demon behind him with his back legs. Mitch has his foe backed against the dumpster where he shoves back the head and rips out his throat. My preoccupied mind is jarred to the present when teeth snap—nearby. I freeze, torn between fight and flight, but the wolf in me decides her own course. I spring for my enemy. My advance is short lived as Denver attacks from behind, ripping the demon's back open, his guts spilling out right before he implodes. A spray of demon blood hits me in the face.

Jada, are you all right? Denver rushes to my side.

The only thing hurting is my pride. I can't believe I backed away like that.

Mitch strolls up licking his fur. *Don't sweat it, Jada. I freaked the first time I saw a demon morphed as a man too.*

Besides, baby, when it came down to it, you were willing to defend yourself.

I suppose.

There'll be plenty more chances for combat. Be grateful today wasn't that day. Come on you two, let's skim the perimeter and then join the others at the warehouse.

I LIE in bed contemplating the night and my response to the demons. I'm not thrilled with the way I handled things, but Denver is totally right. My time is coming to fight. The sky above the field rumbles and groans with birth pains. Any moment the heavens will split and a flock of demons will attack us. Attack me. The thought makes me shiver. Courage is the key. In spite of the fear, I'll do what is necessary to defend my loved ones.

A few hours later Denver greets me with smiles and sass, the night before all but forgotten.

"You're awake. I brought you some coffee."

"Mmm. Thank you." I take the mug from him, and he lights on the edge of the bed.

"Today's the big day. What time are you going to Emily's?"

It's prom night. Not *the* big day. That big day is still four weeks away. My mind automatically strays to me walking down the aisle toward Denver. Our wedding night. Our honeymoon.

Denver is snapping his fingers. "Where'd you go?"

I shake my head, but it has no effect on the state my body is in. "Uh, sorry. Somehow I went from prom to wedding night. I'm supposed to be at Emily's at one. Our hair appointment is at two, then we'll go back to her place to do makeup and get dressed."

"I can't wait to see you in your dress."

My eyebrows rise with my smile. "Which one?"

Denver growls deep in his chest. "Damn, woman. All I wanted was to say good morning, not be tortured."

I melt when he looks at me the way he's looking at me now. So full of need and desire. "How quickly we fall. All I wanted was to drink my coffee. You didn't answer my question."

"Both. I know you'll be ravishing tonight and on our wedding day. More the latter, but for now, I'll settle for the prom dress."

"Same. Except I hope you're wearing a tux and not a dress."

"No worries there." He laughs. "Mom made breakfast if you're hungry."

My stomach growls at the mere prospect of food. "All I do is eat with you working me over every day. I'll be out in a minute."

He leans in to kiss my nose. "We'll take a break today."

I shuffle to the bathroom to splash water on my face and brush my teeth. I stare at my reflection in the mirror. It's me, but it's not. The physical differences are easy to find. I'm healthier, tan, and toned. My muscles aren't bulging, but there's definition. My cheeks are pink from running in the sun and lying by the pool. But it's what's beneath the surface that makes me smile. When my dad left, it crushed me. I felt abandoned and insecure. Unloved even. That girl is long gone. Partly because my dad and I have made amends, partly because of Denver's love, but also because I know who I am. My identity doesn't come from my father or Denver, but from having purpose and believing in myself. It comes from being who I was created to be and being in touch with the creator. I can now be bold and confident in who I am. There's a hell of a lot of freedom in that.

My stomach growls again. I pull on some shorts and go down to the kitchen. Denver has a place set for me at the bar with a plate full of bacon and eggs. I sit down beside him and push up his sleeve to kiss his tattoo.

I shove a bite of eggs in my mouth. "You should get more tattoos. It's so sexy on you."

He twists my hair around his finger. "Really? I've actually considered it, but didn't know if you'd like the idea."

"Yes. My answer is yes. Do you know what you want?"

"I have a few ideas. Once we're married, I want to get a band on my finger. And somewhere on my body I want your name. I've also always wanted to do a wolf on my arm. What about you? You ever wanted a tattoo?"

My fork is midway to my mouth. Why does everything that comes out of his mouth make me go warm all over? The eggs don't make it, but go back on my plate instead.

"I do now. I want your name too. Is that cheesy?"

"Hell no, it's not cheesy. My name on your skin for life is so not cheesy."

"Okay, so let's do it."

Denver chuckles. "Slow down. It's permanent, you need to be sure."

I roll my eyes. "Sometimes you're too grown-up for your own good. Be spontaneous. Get a tattoo with me."

He leaps off his stool and grabs my shoulders. "Next weekend. I'll set it up. You better decide where you want my name on this luscious body of yours." Then he crushes me with a hot kiss that ends too quickly. "I need to shower. Mitch and I have things to do. We have a very important date tonight."

I'm dizzy from his fierce lips. "I swear sometimes I hate you. In a non-hate kind of way."

"Ditto."

The morning is painfully long. No one is in the house, so by noon, I'm more than ready to leave. I throw my stuff in the Jetta and take off.

Emily greets me in her underwear. "Oh my gosh! I'm so excited. Have the boys told you anything at all?"

"Of course not. Those two are like Fort Knox. Denver only said it would be nice, but simple. Whatever that means." I flop across the bed.

She pulls a shirt over her head. "It's going to be amazing no matter what. Does Mitch talk about me?"

I hate when she brings this up. "You don't want to wear that shirt."

"Why not?"

"You need a button up so you don't mess up your hair taking it off."

She shucks that shirt on the floor and goes into her closet. She returns in a flannel. "Good call. So, does he?"

Dang it. I stare up at her ceiling so I don't have to make eye contact. Sometimes I wish she knew about us. "He still wants to be friends."

Her sigh carries a sad tune. "I wish I knew what I did to push him away."

"You didn't do anything. I promise you that much."

"Whatever. I'm glad we're going to prom, but I'm kinda getting over this Mitch crush that's had a hold on me."

This shocks me. I sit up on the bed to better read her face. She's serious. "Wow, Emily, I'm proud of you. Mitch is a great guy, but I think there's someone better for you out there."

She curls up beside me on the bed, laying her head on my shoulder. "You inspired me. I want what you have with Denver, and I don't think Mitch likes me that way."

He could someday, but for some reason my gut tells me Emily is not his mate. I throw my arms around her. "You'll find it, probably when you least expect it."

"Hopefully. So how are things between you and Grainger?"

"Oh, um, not that good. We've hardly spoken since the night he came over drunk." Since the night he saw me turn into a wolf.

Emily slides off the bed and starts to pick clothes up off the floor. "Rumor is he found a date for prom. Some junior named Rachel."

Interesting. "I'm glad he's going. You know, Grainger's a great guy too."

Emily snaps her head up. "That would be too weird." She drops the pile of clothes at the end of her bed. Then she picks them up again and moves them to a basket outside of her closet.

What the crap is she doing? She's nervous, but why?

I walk up to her and grab her shoulders, forcing her to look at me. "Emily, it's okay. If you like Grainger, I'm totally fine with it. We're friends. I love Denver."

"Oh, God, I don't know what's happening." She slumps to the floor, so I join her. "We've been texting a lot because he needed someone to talk to, and he's so sweet, and he probably doesn't care for me at all, but I find myself thinking about him. Why do I always fall for the wrong guy?"

"You don't know if he's the wrong guy. You haven't given him a chance to be the right or wrong guy."

"He's in love with you, so there's that."

Her point is valid but also moot. "Grainger and I were in love with the idea of us together. We were so dependent on each other growing up and I let him fill a void that my father left, but I don't think what we had was ever meant for more than friendship. I needed to figure out who I was, and so does he."

"Yeah, maybe."

"Take it slow. Be his friend and get to know each other. If it's meant to happen, it will."

"Thank you, Jada. I love you and I would never do anything to hurt you."

"I love you too. And if my two best friends get together, that will only bring me joy."

Emily jumps up. "Geez, we need to get going or we'll be late for our appointment."

We rush around the room, gathering our phones and wallets. "Let's get beautiful. It's going to be a fun day and there's no one I'd rather spend it with."

"Heck with beautiful, we'll be smoking hot. Denver won't be able to keep his hands off you."

I laugh because she has no idea how hard he tries to keep his hands off me on a daily basis.

IT'S ALMOST SIX, and we are *hot*. I'm in a long, red A-line satin number with a slit up the front. The V-neckline reveals a hint of cleavage. A girl has to leave some to the imagination. Emily is wearing a gorgeous, powder blue two-piece that shows off her abs. The slender skirt hugs her curves.

We stand in front of her mirror making last-minute makeup touch ups. Our parents are waiting in the living room to take pictures, but the boys aren't here yet.

Emily stares at me in the mirror. "You've changed you know?"

"I do know. Can you believe it's prom night, and we graduate in a few short weeks? Where has the time gone?" I'm emotional all of a sudden and I don't want to cry.

"I know right? It's crazy. And then you're getting married. Married!"

My insides flutter with anticipation. A huge smile erupts on my face. "I can't wait to be Mrs. Stone."

"I thought you were insane at first, but it's obvious how much you love each other. I know you guys will be so happy together."

The doorbell rings announcing the arrival of our dates. I hold out my elbow for Emily. "Shall we?"

The living room is a cacophony of sound as we approach. Our parents are chatting and laughing and fussing over their handsome boys. When Emily and I reach the room, everyone falls silent. Then our parents rush at us, saying how beautiful we are and pushing us toward the fireplace for pictures. I want a dang minute to appreciate how delicious Denver is in his tux.

He walks toward me grinning. *Jada, you are extraordinary. How am I supposed to be near you all night?*

It's going to be a rough night for both of us. You are downright dreamy. Don't be in my head if you don't want to know what I'm really thinking.

Too late. He kisses my head and then says, "You are breathtaking, Jada."

I take his hand and squeeze it. "Thank you."

The boys have flowers for our wrists and boutonnieres for themselves. It's a trick for me to pin Denver's on his jacket without sticking him. We take so many pictures, my cheeks hurt from smiling. My parents and Denver's hug us several times before we're able to get away.

We walk out in the warm evening air to a black stretch limo. Of course Emily screams. The limo ride is a blast. The guys take us to an expensive five-star Italian place in Diamond Hill for dinner. From the dimly lit, secluded table to the cloth linens, the roses, sparkling wine, and soothing music, we are completely enthralled. By the time we get back to Forrest City for prom, I've already had a fabulous evening.

The limo drops us off at the front door of the prom venue. The trees are covered in twinkling lights, and the path to the door has a Hollywood-style red carpet. Photographers line the path taking pictures like paparazzi. We stop at the booth inside the door for formal pictures then make our way to the ballroom. All along the walls are different movies scenes where you can take fun pics. The dance floor is lined with palm trees wrapped in lights, and people line up for requests at the DJ table on the other end. Students are crowded on the dance floor, seated on the sides, and gathered at small tables eating cake.

Mitch and Emily go immediately to the dance floor. Denver gets us some punch and pulls a chair next to mine at a table. We sit and people watch for a few minutes. Emily and Mitch seem comfortable with the friend status tonight, sometimes dancing with other people. Denver notices as well.

"Emily is having fun."

"She shared with me earlier that she may *like* Grainger. Don't you dare say anything."

"No way. That's kinda cool, actually. I saw him with a redhead when we came in."

"If I had to guess, I'd say he's miserable." I point to the other side of the room, where Grainger sits with his date.

"Dang, poor guy needs an escape. Why don't you go save him?"

"I'm not sure he wants to be saved by me."

A slow song comes on and Denver winks at me. "He's your best friend, of course he does. I'll take the next one."

I'm nervous as I make my way around the dance floor. Grainger is holding his punch with both hands. Neither he nor Rachel seem the least bit interested in each other. They both stare blankly across the room. As I approach, Grainger sits back and crosses his arms over his chest. Will he refuse to dance with me?

Rachel gives me the stink eye when I stop by Grainger.

"Hey Rachel, my name is Jada. If you don't mind, I'd like to steal your date for a few minutes. He's my best friend in the whole world, and I'll be severely disappointed if we don't get in a dance."

"Oh sure, of course. I'll go sit with some of my friends." She practically runs over to a group of other junior girls.

Grainger hasn't moved, so I hold out my hand. "Grainger?"

"Yeah, sorry." He leads me to the dance floor. "Thank you, by the way. You didn't have to do that."

I put my hands on his shoulders as we sway to the music. "I wanted to."

"Did you mean what you said? You know, about me being your best friend."

"I'm sad that you have to ask. Yes, Grainger, I meant what I said."

He lets out a nervous breath. "I'm so, so sorry for the other night. I was such an idiot. I don't know what possessed me to drink that much."

I laugh at the memory of him wobbling about. "You were so wasted. And equally sick."

"I *never* want to do that again. Thank you for taking care of me. I asked Denver to tell you, but I don't know if he did."

"He did, and you're welcome." My throat gets tight with emotion. "Grainger, are we going to be okay?"

Grainger glances over to where Denver is sitting and back at me. "I've been thinking a lot these last couple of weeks, and I always come up with the same damn conclusion—you're happy. What kind of friend would I be if I stood in the way of your happiness? Not a very good one, and I'm sorry I didn't come to my senses sooner."

Tears sting my eyes. Emily will kill me if I ruin my makeup. I take a long deep breath. "I want to ask you something."

"Shoot."

"Maybe it's asking too much, but I hoped maybe you would walk me down the aisle at my wedding."

Grainger stops moving. "I know your dad is back in town. Why aren't you asking him?"

As hard as I try not to cry, a tear slides down my face. "Because he left and you didn't. Every time he should have been there, you were. All the things he should have taught me, you did. All the talks I should have had with him, I had with you. The hole he left in my heart, you filled. I'm the person I am today because of you, not because of him."

Grainger's jaw clenches as his eyes pool with tears. He crushes me in a bear hug. "I love you so much, Jada. I'd be honored to give you away."

"I love you too." I pull out of his embrace and hold out my pinky. "I still promise to be by your side forever. I know it's not in the way we originally planned it to be, but I hope you accept my offer of life-long friendship."

He takes my pinky with his. "Pinky swear?"

"Pinky swear."

A hand goes around my waist. Denver's sexy voice vibrates in my chest. "Should I be worried here?"

"Grainger agreed to give me away at our wedding."

Denver pats Grainger on the shoulder. "Thank you, Grainger. I know how much it means to Jada."

Grainger holds out his hand to Denver. "As much as I hate to admit it, you're an all-right guy."

They laugh as they shake hands. "So are you. Now, if you don't mind, I'm going to take this little lady off your hands."

Grainger backs up a step. "Sure, man."

She's going to kill me, but I can't help myself. "You should ask Emily to dance, I know she would like that."

He scans the room and spots Emily sitting at our table. "Really? Um, okay."

We watch him make his way to Emily. Her smile says it all as they slip onto the dance floor.

My attention is quickly averted from Emily when Denver pulls me close. The heat radiates through the silk of my dress everywhere we touch. Even in a crowded room, I want to do things I can't.

"Denver, what are you doing?"

We're barely moving to the music. "Dancing with you."

His waves of lust and love start to wash over me, making my legs go wobbly. I'm dizzy and lightheaded and know from experience I may possibly pass out. I want to merge our bodies into one and never come apart.

"Denver, I'm going to be on the floor if you don't pull back."

His emotions begin to slightly recede. He lips brush the side of my neck and I moan. "Red was a very appropriate color, my little bloody fish. You're irresistible to me on a normal day, but damn baby, this dress…"

My body is a limp noodle. My heart rate has accelerated to a full-on sprint. I'm dying to touch his skin and thoughts of yanking up his shirt have consumed my mind. I need his mouth on mine, but we're in the middle of a school function. I'm seriously about to push him out into the hall, bathroom, something, anything—

A new set of arms grabs me away. "I think I better cut in. You guys can't go two damn minutes."

I laugh as Mitch saves our sorry butts. "Thank you."

He rolls his eyes. "Yeah, yeah."

Denver strolls out the front door for air.

Mitch spins me around, and I smile. "It's almost your birthday, so happy birthday."

"I guess it is. Thanks."

"You're welcome. So, what's the plan? Party or what?"

"Nah. Just hang with the fam. We'll probably go get some dinner."

"Am I invited?"

"Hell no."

I pinch the back of his arm. "Hey, that's not nice."

"Ouch! I was kidding. Of course you're invited, ya ding dong."

"I know. I wanted to inflict a little pain. Pay back for all the times you punched me in the ring."

"For that, I may be extra hard on you tomorrow."

"Tomorrow? Ugh, can't we take another day off?"

"You know good and well Denver will have us back at it."

Mitch twirls me out and pulls me in, then lays me back for a dip. I laugh as he raises me up. "You're a pretty good dancer."

"Taught by the best."

"Your dad?"

"Nope, Denver."

The slow song ends and Denver has not returned. Mitch grabs my hand. "Come on, let's find Emily and get this party started."

Emily and Grainger are already dancing with a group to a hip hop song that the DJ has mixed in. Mitch and I join them and not long after, Rieder and some of his buddies jump in as well. A few minutes later, Denver joins the group. We dance and sweat and jump and laugh and grind the night away. The chaperones have to push us out the door at midnight.

Once we're outside the building we decide on an impromptu

after-prom slash birthday party for Mitch, so several new bodies climb in the back of the limo with us, Grainger being one of them. He sits next to Emily, and it makes me smile. Denver nudges me with his knee. I couldn't be happier right now if I tried. I take that back. Four more weeks.

WHEN WE GET BACK to the house, we all run inside to change clothes. Denver called his parents, and they've ordered pizza and put coolers out by the pool. Emily has to borrow a swimsuit, so we rush back to my room. We're the only girls.

I lay out several suits on the bed. "Which one do you want?"

She's already out of her dress. "You know Grainger best, which one would he like?"

I jump up and down and then run over and hug her. "Oh my God! You really do like him. I'm so excited."

"He makes me nervous and unsure of myself. Mitch never made me nervous. It's kinda scary."

"Oh Em, he's one of the sweetest people I know. His heart is gold, I promise."

"But what if he doesn't like me back?"

"I think he's interested. Give him time." I study the swimsuits on the bed and hand her the black string bikini. "Here, wear this one."

We both change and throw on a T-shirt before heading to the pool. I wear my red bikini to stick with my color scheme for the day. I'm not sure how this is going to go because Denver doesn't usually come out here when I'm sunbathing. He says it's too hard to see me in such little clothing.

The boys are already in the water. Rieder splashes us with a cannonball off the diving board. Emily and I sit on the edge of the pool with beers in our hands and our feet in the water, and watch the boys try and drown each other. Emily takes off her shirt, but I don't.

"It must be awesome to live here."

"It's nice, but I can't wait to show you the cabin."

"I forgot you have your own house now. That is so crazy. When can you show me?"

"Whenever you want. Drive out one afternoon and we'll walk over there."

"Sweet. I'll come by one day after school." Emily bumps me with her shoulder. "So, sex in four more weeks. Are you nervous?"

Heat radiates from my core. Denver winks from across the pool, and I know he's eavesdropping on our conversation. "Not in the slightest."

"I'm envious that your first time will be so special. Not many people get that."

"Emily, have you…I mean I thought you were still a virgin?"

"Geez, Jada, I would tell you if I had sex. That's pretty monumental. But…I don't know if I'll wait until I get married."

"I get that, but you won't be sorry if you do. It's incredible knowing no one else has experienced this most intimate act with Denver. He's all mine. And I'm all his."

"It sounds amazing, but let's face it, there's not many virgins left out there."

It's my turn to bump her with my shoulder. "Grainger is."

She watches Grainger do a front flip off the diving board. "Wow. Are you sure?"

"Positive." We made a pact to save ourselves for each other, and Grainger is a man of his word.

We finish our beer and decide it's time to join in on the fun. I sense Denver's eyes on me as I slide my shirt over my head. When I turn around, he's staring at me shaking his head no. I ignore him and get in the pool. Every time I try to get near him, he swims away. It's starting to piss me off.

Emily and I climb out of the pool to dive off the board. Denver is in the shallow end talking to Rieder, giving me an opportunity for a sneak attack. When I dive off, I swim under water straight to an unsuspecting Denver. I come up right behind him and wrap my arms around his chest. What I don't expect is our reaction to the skin-to-skin contact.

I don't remember Denver turning me around and pushing me to the side of the pool. He's got me pinned with his body and his mouth is on mine. The growl deep in his throat drives me mad. Nothing else matters. The others fade away as I lean into Denver, encouraging him. His hands are tangled in my hair, and I rake his back with my nails.

Someone is pulling Denver's arm. "Shit. Help me, Rieder. Damn it, you two."

Denver fights at first. He doesn't want to let me go. There's more cursing as Denver is yanked back. "What the hell, Jada." Mitch is yelling at me. Why is he yelling at me?

Denver's eyes are wild. He's struggling against Rieder and Mitch as they hold him back. Oh God, what have I done?

Mitch is speaking to me. His voice is distant and muddy to my fuzzy brain. "Jada, get out of the pool. Now."

I do as I'm told. I grab a towel and walk straight into the house. I stumble to the bedroom and strip down to get in the shower. It's several minutes before I can think clearly. I don't know why, but I start to cry. I didn't mean to light a match to gasoline, but damn it, I should have known. I'm embarrassed. Mitch and Rieder will under-stand, but I hate Emily and Grainger had to witness that. For the next twenty minutes I let the hot water wash away my tears.

I'm depleted of energy by the time I exit the bathroom. I put on one of Denver's T-shirts and a pair of shorts and slip in the covers. It's two o'clock in the morning. My heart hurts because I'm pretty sure Denver won't be coming in later to sleep by me. I'm surprised Emily hasn't come check on me, but then again, Mitch probably made sure I got the privacy I needed. Poor Mitch. I hate I did this to him, and on his birthday. He probably hates me. Denver too. It's not until the pillow is wet with tears that I fall asleep.

CHAPTER TWENTY

JADA

Rays of sun are trying to trick me into thinking it's going to be a beautiful day, but I know better. Denver never showed up last night, and Mitch is probably mad at me as well. Who knows what impression our incident left on Emily and Grainger. At least Grainger has a clue, but Emily probably thinks I'm horrible. I scream in my pillow. I don't want to face anyone ever. I want to hide in this room and never come out.

I make a trip to the bathroom and then climb back in bed. Coffee sounds so good, but I can't go out there. I glance at the nightstand for a note from Denver. No note. I pick up my phone to find I have a text from my mom, and one from Emily. No text from Denver.

Mom: Hey, sweetheart. How was prom? I know you know this, but your wedding is in four weeks. When are we going dress shopping???

Emily: Are you okay? What the hell happened last night? I tried to come talk to you, but Mitch wouldn't let me.

I scream a second time into my pillow. How do I answer either of them?

Me to Mom: Prom was great. I do realize the wedding is in four weeks. I'll speak to Aurar and let you know about dress shopping. Love you

Me to Emily: I'm okay, thanks for checking. Mitch was right, I needed to be alone. I'll try and call later, not ready to talk about it. Sorry

I hate this pity party I'm having. I wish so badly Denver would come in here and talk to me. Assure me everything is okay.

A knock at the door causes me to jump. "Jada, it's Mitch. You awake?"

Time to face the music. "Come in."

He strolls in with two cups of coffee, not hesitating to sit by me on the bed. "I brought you coffee. I was bored sitting in the kitchen by myself."

I take a sip and let the liquid gold warm my insides. "Thank you."

Mitch crosses his legs at the ankles, perfectly at ease. "What's your plan for today?"

"Um, I don't know. Aren't you mad at me?"

"Why in the hell would I be mad at you?"

Wait, what? "Because of the scene in the pool? Because I ruined your birthday party?"

Mitch laughs. "Seriously? I'm going to be laughing my ass off about that for a long time. I thought you guys were going to go at it right there in front of all of us. The only reason I broke you two apart is because I know it's important to you to wait until your wedding day. And the fact that you had spectators."

I groan and close my eyes. "I'm so embarrassed."

"Jada, don't sweat it. Really. I couldn't care less."

"Okay, so you're not mad at me, but what about Denver? He hasn't spoken to me since. And what do I tell Emily?"

"The only person Denver is mad at is Denver. He blames himself. I tried to talk to him, but he pretty much brushed me off. He's out running. He'll be better when he comes back. As far as Emily goes, maybe tell her the truth. I mean Grainger knows, so why not tell her too?"

"I should have known he'd blame himself."

Mitch passes me his cup to put on the nightstand and then crosses his arms behind his head. "Dude did lose his shit."

I huff out of frustration. "Only because I pushed my half naked body on his. It's my fault."

Mitch glares at me, his nose wrinkled and his eyes serious. "Jada, if you're wanting me to be a part of your wallowing fit, you're barking up the wrong tree. You guys got carried away, get over it. This is who we are. I've been watching my parents make out for as long as I can remember. The people we love, we love with intensity and devotion and passion. Honestly, you and Denver inspire me. I don't want to settle for anything short of what you have."

"He's right." Denver is standing in the doorway. His cheeks are pink and he's sweaty from his run. He pulls his earbuds out of his ears and sticks them in his pocket.

Mitch scoots off the bed. "Time to make my exit."

"Thank you, Mitch."

He smiles before facing Denver. They nod at each other and Denver steps in to let Mitch pass. He slowly walks in the room, stopping short of the bed.

I pat the bed beside me. "Please?" He hesitates but sits on the bed.

Several seconds pass before he speaks. "I've been beating myself up all morning. I came down here to apologize and beg for your forgiveness. Then I hear my younger brother spewing words of wisdom that pierce me to my core. Truth is, I'm not sorry for loving you the way I do. I'm not sorry that I want to make love to you and to spend the rest of my life with you. I'm not sorry that you make me crazy and want to rip your clothes off. I'm not sorry that you're everything to me. I'm not sorry for being zealous for your love and affection. I'm not sorry for any of it. I guess I'm saying I'm sorry...for not being sorry."

Somehow more tears sneak down my face. My voice is a shaky whisper when I'm able to speak. "Denver, that was the most beautiful non-apology I've ever heard. I love you so much." I shrug and bite my lip. "I'm harboring some guilt for pushing you over your limit, but if you're taking the sorry-not-sorry approach, then I guess I can too."

He slides closer and takes my hand. "Baby, it's okay. It's over, let's forget about it. Shit, who am I kidding? I'll never forget that moment.

I don't want to. It was amazing and a small taste of what's to come. This will be the longest four weeks of my life."

There's nothing I can say to let him know how much I agree, so I leap forward and devour his mouth. He doesn't fight me, in fact, he's matching my intensity and pushing the kiss further. After a couple of minutes I call a Hold the Line.

Denver puts his forehead to mine, both of us trying to calm down. "Thank you for that. Can I make one request?" he says as he pulls back.

"Anything."

"No more bikinis. At least until our honeymoon."

I chuckle but agree to his request. Leaning back on the headboard, I pick up my coffee once more. "Speaking of honeymoon, my mom wants to know when we're going dress shopping, and I'd like to get a few things for our trip."

"Absolutely. Get whatever you need. I take that back, it doesn't have to be a need. Get whatever you want."

"I want your mom to go too. And Emily."

"Sounds like a girls' day. Make it happen."

"Thank you." I lean forward and kiss his cheek. "I was thinking we could go this Tuesday. I know it's a school day, but it's senior skip day, so most of the seniors won't be there anyway."

"Mom would love that. You want me to go let her know?"

My coffee cup becomes my focus as I turn it in my hands. "I have one more question."

Denver lifts my chin with his finger. "Baby, you can ask me anything."

"Can I tell Emily about us? It would make things so much easier if she knew what was going on. Plus, I hate keeping secrets from her."

"I think that would be okay. There's no rule that says humans can't know about us, but we don't go shouting it from the rooftops either. All of my close friends are wolves, so I never had to deal with this situation. You trust her, right?"

"Yes, I trust her."

"Then tell her." Denver kisses my forehead and jumps off the bed.

"You need to get ready, we're leaving soon." He starts for the door with no explanation.

"Where are we going?"

He grins and leaves the room. What is he up to?

Before I get ready I text my mother and Emily.

Me to Mom: Dress shopping Tuesday. Aurar and Emily are going with. Be ready at eight.

Me to Emily: We need to talk soon. Dress shopping on Tuesday for senior skip day!

Emily: Yes to both!!!

Me to Emily: Denver says we're going out, but I'll let you know when I can meet.

Emily: Perf

Denver didn't say how to dress, so I go with shorts, a cute top, and sandals. I arrive in the kitchen the same time he does, wearing khaki shorts and a T-shirt. His hair is wet and he looks so good, my heart skips a beat. His muscles stretch the fabric of his shirt. I stare.

He leans on the counter smiling. "You want breakfast before we go?"

"Are you breakfast?"

Denver pushes off the counter and strolls toward me. His eyes are glowing and I know I've hit a nerve. "Why, Jada?" His hand goes to the back of my head, and he pulls me to him with force. His lips brush mine, but it's a tease. He drags his tongue down my neck and I gasp.

"Oh hell no. You guys have got to cut that shit out. It's my birthday and I don't want to deal with this all day."

I laugh and kiss Denver's nose. "Fine." I step back and take a deep breath. "So what are we doing anyway?"

"You didn't tell her?" Mitch says while shoving his wallet in his pocket.

Denver shrugs. "She told me to be spontaneous."

"Cool. We better get going. I want to stop for food. I'm starving."

. . .

WE PICK up breakfast at a drive-through, and I devour my food without shame. I can eat almost as much as the boys. Almost. Mitch is driving today, so I let him and Denver sit in the front. He drives across town past all the normal stops. I wonder where we're going as we pass the city limit sign and continue driving. I'm bouncing in my seat with anticipation.

Five minutes out of town, Mitch pulls into the dirt parking lot of a little hole-in-the-wall building. It's a little shady in my opinion. There's an orange Open sign in the window, and right below it in bright red, glowing letters, another sign reads Tattoo.

I take off my seatbelt and lean forward. "We're getting a tattoo? Today?"

Denver glances back, smiling. "Mitch is eighteen. He's been waiting two years to do this. I'm getting one too. You can, but you don't have to."

"I think I'll watch first." I was so sure the other day, but now that we're here, I'm a bit nervous.

A burly man with a full beard stands behind the counter. He's covered in tattoos. If it weren't for his kind eyes, he would be frightening. He spots the boys and his face lights up.

"Look what the cat drug in, a couple of Stone boys." He gives me a full body scan, finally landing on my face. "Who's your gorgeous friend?"

Denver walks up to the counter and shakes the man's hand. "Watch it, Snake. That's my mate and fiancée you're ogling."

"Well, damn. Like father, like son. You always get the good ones."

"Hell yeah, and I'm next." Mitch also exchanges a handshake with Snake.

"So beautiful, what's your name?"

I take a step closer, but not close enough to make contact. "Jada."

"Damn, Denver. How do you do it? Her name and her voice are as sexy as she is."

"It's a hell of a job, but somebody's gotta do it." He wraps his arm around my waist and kisses the side of my head.

Now I *really* don't know if I want a tattoo. This Snake guy has to touch my body in order for that to happen, and I'm thinking hell no. Denver is at ease, so maybe he's harmless.

"Let's head to the back, we've got a lot of work to do."

We leave the tiny foyer and go into a spacious, clean room that reminds me of a nail salon. There are two tattoo stations, so I wonder if Snake has a partner or another employee. One wall is full of pictures that I assume are past clients. I browse the photos while Snake and Mitch talk business. They're studying Denver's tattoo, so he's occupied as well.

These tattoos are crazy good. They are truly works of art. Some are so delicate, it's hard to believe they're real. And they do everything. Any kind of animal or scenery, flower, bird, writing, faces, seriously anything you could dream up. Some are a mixture of lines, shapes, and swirls. I've definitely misjudged. Snake has a real talent.

I walk over to the boys. Mitch is in a dentist-type chair talking to Denver. Snake is preparing to begin his work.

I point to the other dentist chair. "Is it okay if I sit here?"

Snake glances up and smiles. "Of course, darlin'."

"Did you do all the tattoos on the wall?"

He continues to set up and clean Mitch's shoulder. "Probably a good eighty percent. I have an apprentice named Todd. He'll be here shortly. He did some of those up there. I'm damn pleased with his work. Hopefully he'll take over some day. He's a young guy, a little older than Denver here. Handsome too. The girls love him."

"Is he going to do mine?"

Snake laughs and it's a belly laugh, like I would imagine coming from Santa Claus. "Uh-oh, Denver. You could be in trouble."

My face turns red. "I didn't mean it like that. I was just asking."

"Sure, darlin'. I get it. If I were you, I'd pick the handsome young guy over this old man too."

Denver's eyebrows are so high as they can go. "Snake can do yours, after Mitch."

Snake laughs again but says nothing. I keep quiet as well. No need to insert my foot further in my big, fat mouth.

"All right young Stone, here we go. We'll work on the outline for a bit and then take a break."

"Sounds good."

The needle buzzes in his hand. He touches it to Mitch's skin to give him a preview of what's to come. Mitch nods, so he proceeds. Other than an occasional flinch, Mitch doesn't complain. He says it stings more than anything and eventually goes numb. He's getting a fairly big tattoo like Denver's. Mine will be simple and hopefully quick.

Thirty minutes into the appointment, Todd strolls in. Snake wasn't kidding. He is some kind of gorgeous. In his polo shirt and khakis, he's more the country club type, not tattoo parlor. Speaking of tattoos, there's no visible ink on his skin. Interesting.

I start to get out of his chair, but he motions for me to sit back down. "You're fine. I don't have a scheduled appointment for a couple of hours. Snake asked me to come early and help out with you guys."

"Okay. I'm Jada, by the way."

He smiles and it's swoon worthy. Don't get me wrong, he's not in the same ballpark as Denver, but my gosh I'd have to be blind not to notice him.

"I'm Todd, it's nice to meet you."

"You too."

Denver walks over to stake his claim. His arm goes around my shoulders, and I lean over and kiss his hand, trying to reassure him there's no need to worry. "Hey man, I'm Denver. That's my brother, Mitchell."

"Todd. Nice to meet you guys. So who's going first?"

I start to volunteer, but Denver cuts me off. "I will."

"All right. Let me finish setting up and go wash my hands. You'll need to give up your seat, Jada."

"Not a problem."

When Todd walks to the sinks, I start to slide out of the chair. Denver blocks me in.

He leans over me, inches from my face. "So, you think Todd's hot?"

I lick my lips. "He's not hard to look at."

Denver lowers his body. He's not touching me anywhere, but God, I feel him anyway. "Is that so?" He bites at my bottom lip, and I squirm in the chair. I reach up to touch him, but he holds my hands down on the armrests. I try to lean forward to kiss him, and he leans back far enough that I can't get to him.

I'm about to lose my mind. "Denver, what are you doing?" I try to wiggle out of his grasp, but he's too strong. I need him to kiss me.

He traces my lips with his tongue and I moan. Before pushing away, he whispers in my ear. "Making sure you remember whose you are."

Todd walks out of the bathroom, and now I have to stand on rubber legs. Great. I do my best to get out of the chair gracefully.

I give Denver my best mean face. "I hate you."

Snake is laughing yet again. "Damn boy. I seriously don't know how you do it. That's some serious tension you've got going there."

Mitch pipes in with his annoying opinion. "That was nothing. You should see them at home."

Todd peers around the room in confusion. "What did I miss?"

Snake points to Todd's station. "I suggest you get to work. And any thoughts you had toward beauty queen need to die, and quick. I'm telling you now, boy, you got no chance in hell."

Todd shrugs and walks to his chair. "Understood."

DENVER'S TATTOO is close to being done. He's getting my name on the inside of his wrist. Snake has us highly entertained. Apparently he knows the Stone family well. He tells stories of Bolivar as a boy and how they used to get into trouble. Then he tells a few stories of Denver and Mitch when they were younger. I would have met him at the last wolf gathering, but he couldn't make it. I don't think Todd is a wolf, but by his response to the conversation, he knows. Every once in a while, Denver catches Todd staring at me. He clears his throat to steer Todd back to the job at hand. I can't help but smile. Denver's kind of hot when he's jealous.

Snake and Mitch take a break. All of the outlining is finished. Mitch is getting a similar tattoo to Denver's but with some slight changes. The biggest difference is Mitch is adding a wolf to his scene. After the break, Snake begins the shading and it's really coming together. I'm in awe of the process and his ability. It's all totally freehand.

Todd wipes Denver's finished tattoo clean before the bandage. My name is in bold letters across his wrist. At the end, in bright red, is a drop of blood.

I bite my lip and smile. "Really babe?"

He stands up to stretch. "I told you, you'll always be shark bait."

I sit in the chair and wait my turn. Todd sanitizes his area and gets out sterile equipment. When he's ready, I lay my arm on the armrest and hold my breath. I'm getting "Denver" on my wrist with the outline of a shark underneath. My script isn't as bold as the one he got, and Todd assures me it won't take him long.

I squeeze my eyes closed and give him the okay to begin. He touches my skin with the needle, and I suck in a quick breath. He stops, so I open my eyes.

"You okay?"

"Yeah, sorry. Go ahead."

It's not all-out painful to get a tattoo, but it's not comfortable either. The constant needle prick stings and certain spots are more sensitive, causing me to suck in air through my teeth. It's beyond me how Mitch has endured it for so long. I must be a candy.

Todd's "not long" and mine are not the same. But oh my gosh, when he's finished I almost cry. It's perfect. Denver comes over to inspect the final product.

"Baby, that is so hot." He nods at Todd, encouraging him to get me bandaged. As soon as he's done, Denver jerks me out of the chair and pulls me out the front door.

"What on earth, Denver?"

He pushes me against the side of the building and cages me in with his arms. His forehead meets mine, but he's yet to say anything. His breathing is labored like he ran a marathon.

I place my hands on his chest as the tension builds.

Denver slightly shakes his head. "Hang on, babe. My name on your skin turned me on way more than it should have. I don't think I can kiss you yet."

I say nothing and I don't dare move. I learned my lesson. We stand there until his breathing begins to slow. He blows out a long breath and his shoulders relax. Then he kisses me. And it's so good I want to slide down the side of the wall and puddle at his feet. As powerful as it is, he's strong enough to pull back.

"Wow. How were you able to stop like that?"

Denver chuckles. "Mitch was in my head, singing."

"Seriously? What was he singing?"

"Itsy Bitsy Spider."

"Okay, that's weird."

"I hate spiders. He knew it would be a good distraction."

"You guys are crazy." I turn my wrist to gander at my new tattoo. It appears distorted through the wrap. "I can't wait to see it again without this stuff over it."

"Me too. The shark was a nice touch."

"Thanks. What should we get next?"

Denver kisses my nose before stepping back. "I don't know, but I'll make sure Todd's not working that day."

I grab his shirt in my fist and pull him back. "You should rethink that. You being jealous is so, so sexy."

He pushes back from the wall once more. "Let's go check on Mitch before I make babies with you in this parking lot."

"I hate you so much."

"Uh huh."

MITCH'S TATTOO takes four hours. It's a masterful work of art. We stop at Hagerdy's for burgers, and it's four in the afternoon when we get back home. Denver needs to meet with his dad about his patrol tonight, so I go to my room to get homework done. Sadly, I have school tomorrow.

Emily and I text back and forth for the next hour while I finish Econ and Finite. She helps me with some of the math when I get stuck. She's ticked I got a tattoo without her, so I send her a picture of the cling-wrap covering. She inquires on Grainger's likes and dislikes. I give her all the dirt, and I've got plenty.

Funny, my two best friends don't really know each other. Hopefully that will change. Emily agrees to meet me for milkshakes after school tomorrow. I need to fill her in on my new secret life. I hope she takes it well. Maybe I should have Grainger join us. The more I think on it, the more I like the idea.

Me: Hey. I'm wondering if you'll do me a favor?

Grainger: Sure, what is it?

Me: I want to tell Emily about the wolf stuff. I was hoping you would join us. Back me up.

Grainger: I mean, I can. Is Denver not going to be there?

Me: I'm sure he will, but it could be good to have back up. You did witness firsthand.

Grainger: I still question my sanity. I was drunk.

Me: You don't have to. It's okay.

Grainger: Don't jump to conclusions. When and where?

Me: Tomorrow after school. Milkshakes at Hagerdy's.

Grainger: All right.

Me: Thank you. You never asked me about it. I kinda thought you might.

Grainger: Not gonna lie, it freaked me out. Mitch grabbed me at school one day and answered a lot of my questions. I'm sorry I didn't ask you.

Me: As long as we're friends, I don't care.

Grainger: We are. Friends forever.

Me: Pinky swear?

Grainger: Pinky swear. TTYL

. . .

"WHAT ARE YOU SMILING ABOUT?" Denver leans on the doorframe watching me.

"Can't a girl be happy?"

"Absolutely. Who are you texting?" He comes to sit on the bed. His fingers make lazy trails up and down my arm.

"Grainger."

His finger stops momentarily. "Grainger, huh?"

"Jealous?"

"Nah. He's not gonna want you now that my name is tattooed on your wrist."

I slap his thigh. "You're terrible." Speaking of tattoo, Denver's is no longer wrapped in film. "Hey, you took off your saran wrap."

"It's not saran wrap. But yeah, that stuff drives me crazy."

"No kidding! Cut mine off too. It's itchy."

"I'll be right back."

While he's getting the scissors, I put my books in my bag and lay out some clothes for school. I'm having serious senioritis. Four more weeks.

Denver returns and cuts off my wrap. The relief from the itching is instant. He hands me an ointment his mom made to keep it from getting dry. I stare at Denver's name on my wrist, turning my arm to admire the beautiful script.

Denver gently takes my arm in his grip and kisses my wrist. "I hate to admit Todd did a great job."

"You have absolutely nothing to worry about."

He smiles. "I know, but the thought of you looking at someone else..."

"There's no one else for me. Only you."

His kisses have moved from my wrist and up my arm. By the time he reaches my shoulder I'm on fire. He realizes I'm having a moment and pulls back.

"Sorry. I didn't mean to start something. You're so damn irresistible."

I sit on the edge of the bed. "Give me a second."

"So why were you texting Grainger?"

"Oh, I want him to meet Emily and me after school tomorrow. I'm going to tell her, well, you know."

"I hope it goes okay."

"Me too. I'm kinda nervous."

Denver caresses the back of my hand. "She's a good friend. I'm sure after the shock factor wears off, she'll be fine." He shuffles his bare feet on the carpet. "Why did you ask Grainger to come?"

He's so cute right now, staring down at his feet. Where in the world is all this jealousy coming from? He should know he has no need to worry. I climb over him and straddle his lap, forcing him to face me.

"I can only endure so much hotness in one day. I want to kiss you so hard and fierce that you'll never give another second of your life worrying about my love and devotion to you. You have all of me, Denver. Now and forever. No one can compete with you. They're not even in the same universe as you. You got it?"

A growl grows deep in his chest. He grips my shoulders like a strong wind might blow me away. After several long breaths he relaxes.

"I trust you, and I know Grainger is your best friend."

"Baby, you go beyond best friend. There's no one I'd rather spend my time with than you. Grainger was there for me growing up and I needed him. But you are the whole package. I need you like I need air, food, and water. And if you must know, one of the reasons I invited Grainger is because I'm trying to play matchmaker."

Denver's lips brush mine. He sucks my bottom lip in his teeth and I whimper. "You're everything to me, Jada. Everything. Before you, I had a good life, but now that I have you, I know I was only existing. Life was black and white, and I wasn't fully living. Life with you is vivid color, exploding fireworks, active volcanoes, bungee jumping, heart-stopping life. I love you. With all that I am. I. Love. You."

His declaration of love has me higher than a kite. I rip his shirt over his head and push him back on the bed. Our mouths fuse with such hunger, it would take a mountain lion to rip us apart. His hands go under my shirt and explore the skin on my back. The more phys-

ical we get, the harder it is to stop. The more we push our boundaries, the more I want. The ring on my finger is a reminder that we'll
be together, and I tell myself it's okay to go further because we're
getting married. My body takes over my brain once again, and I've
lost control. Denver is no better off than I am. He rolls us over and is
on top of me. We need help and fast. I reach out to Mitch with my
mind asking him for intervention before we get to the point of no
return.

Mitch barrels into the room yelling. "What the hell? You two are
freaking wearing me out! Get married already."

Denver groans and rolls aside. "Shit. I don't know if I can make it
four more weeks."

I sit up, repositioning my shirt. "Me either."

Mitch sounds annoyed. "What are you waiting for? Damn it, put
us all out of misery here, I beg you."

Denver sits up swearing. "No. We can do it. That was not my
brain talking."

Mitch and I both swear.

Mitch sighs. "You might as well come eat cake. Mom is putting
the candles on my birthday cake as we speak. And stay the hell away
from each other."

I laugh as Mitch leaves the room. "Poor guy. It sucks always dragging him into this, but I didn't know what else to do."

Denver gets off the bed and puts his shirt back on. He holds out
his hand to assist me up. "He'll survive. Some day, we may have to
return the favor."

"True." I smile at the thought of Mitch finding his mate. "I can't
wait for him to experience this."

"I'm going to give him hell when he does. And laugh. A lot. Especially when he can't control himself. Payback's a bitch."

"You're so mean."

Denver kisses my nose. "Come on, let's go eat cake."

After cake and presents, Denver slips on top of the covers beside
me. "Love you, babe. Mitch and I are getting ready to go on patrol."
He kisses my forehead and nose.

As close as Denver and I have come to going too far sexually, we've never actually discussed protection or children. I have on repeat in my brain his words from earlier about making babies. Lord knows I want to have the man's children, but not for a while.

Denver is studying my face. "What's wrong?"

"Nothing, I…" My palms begin to sweat.

"You what?"

"I'm on the pill."

"Okay?"

"I guess I thought you might want to know. You know, so we don't have to use condoms, but also because I don't want to get pregnant."

He sits up on his elbow. "Ever?"

"No, just not right away. I want to have children."

"Good, me too. But not right away, because I want you all to myself. At least three years' worth of nothing but you and me. And I'm glad we don't have to bother with condoms because I don't want anything between you and me when it's just you and me."

I let out a sigh of relief. "That's perfect."

"Now that we've got that settled, I need to go patrol."

"I love you. Be careful."

He softly kisses my lips. "Love you, too."

I fall asleep with a smile on my face. Denver is right. No one deserves to be this happy.

CHAPTER TWENTY-ONE

DENVER

The horizon reveals a bright peach line as the sun makes its entrance for the day. I'm trying to appreciate the beauty of the burst of color against the dark sky, but last night was hell. Mitch doesn't say a word all the way home. Our minds and bodies are weary from a full night of demon fighting. We're both covered in cuts and bruises. You'd think we'd been in a car wreck or met up with a momma bear. Most of the damage will fade soon, but there are a couple of gouges that will take a little longer to heal. Mitch held his own and had my back. As a leader, I take the front line and the brunt of the blows. Rieder and his brother and a couple of others will also be sore today.

I pull into the garage and kill the engine. With no energy to move, I lay my head back against the headrest. Mitch groans beside me.

"That sucked. I don't know if I can go to school."

Can't blame him there. Other than Jada, there's no one that I love more than my little brother. And I'm damn proud of the fight he put up last night. I told him so when we left the warehouse.

"I'm sure Dad will let you stay home."

"I have a test today. Maybe I'll take a short nap and go in late."

"Sounds like a good plan. I need a shower."

"Yeah, no shit, I'm slimy and gross. Are you going to tell Jada?"

"I have to. She needs to be aware of the danger. I'm guessing those demons were only the beginning of the trouble brewing in the sky. Honestly, it's going to kill me to let her out of my sight."

"At least at school you know I'll be there. So will Rieder and Layne."

"True enough."

We exit the truck and make our way to the kitchen. My muscles scream in protest with every step I take. Dad stands at the bar holding his mug of freshly brewed coffee.

"Hey boys. Heard it was a rough night."

Mitch grumbles something and keeps right on moving.

"It was pretty bad," I answer.

"How are you holding up?"

"Tired. Sore. Sticky. The usual."

"How many do you think you took out?"

I think I shrug, but I'm not sure. My numb limbs hint at a bit of demon poison. "Probably twenty."

His eyebrows rise as he weighs my answer with the evidence of my body. "Twenty? You exhibit the wounds of a much greater number."

"These didn't fight fair."

"I'd say. Well, go get your shower, we'll talk later. I know you want to rest."

"Yes, sir."

Instead of taking the stairs to my room, I turn left and head down the hall to Jada's room. Watching her sleep so peacefully steals the breath from my lungs. Her soft, brown hair falls in waves over the pillow. If I weren't so gross, I'd crawl in beside her.

I don't normally shower in her bathroom, but I'm too worn out to go upstairs. Besides, her alarm for school shouldn't go off for another half hour.

The hot stream is like heaven to my aches and pains. I stand directly under the shower head and place my hands on the wall. Demon blood, mixed with my own dried blood, swirls down the drain. A tinge of nausea hits me and I close my eyes. I'm sure of it now. Damn demon poison. I'm going to need Mom to fix me up a little something. Or Dad. Whoever concocts the magic drink that cures the effects of poison. I lather up and scrub clean and turn off the water.

I'm still in the process of wrapping a towel around my waist when Jada comes into the bathroom unannounced. I suppose it is her bathroom.

Her initial reaction is a gasp and her eyes fill with lust, but as soon as she notices my injuries her expression changes to worry.

"Denver, what happened?"

"Bad night."

She approaches me slowly, asking permission with her eyes to touch me. I nod. Her delicate fingers inspect every cut, and she kisses every bruise. I've completely forgotten what day, time, or year it is.

A shudder rocks my entire body. "Jada, if you kiss me one more time, we will not be virgins on our wedding day."

I can't see her face. She's been circling me and is now at my back. I know she means well, but my God, I'm standing here in a towel for Pete's sake. I might be wounded, but I'm still a man. Her lips don't meet my skin, but she drags her hands down my back, lingering at the edge of the towel.

I shake my head. "Jada."

Her finger runs along the skin of my waist as she saunters around to the front of me. "I was kissing your ouchies away."

"Mission accomplished. I forgot I had ouchies."

She sucks in her bottom lip and lets it go. It's so full and pink, and I want to repeat the action of sucking up her lip into my own mouth. Sweet Jesus, I've got to get out of this room.

Jada takes a step back and smiles. "Get the hell out of my bathroom. You're way too sexy in that towel and I need to get ready for school."

I tuck tail and run. No need for repeat instructions.

Once I've thrown on a T-shirt and some cotton shorts, I drag my butt to the kitchen. Mitch is at the bar sipping from a coffee cup and points to the seat beside him. There's a steaming mug with my name on it. My mother is a godsend. I slouch on the bar and drink without second guessing what it is. It smells like dirty socks, so I down it as fast as I can. Mitch has done the same and is getting coffee. I follow him to the coffee pot. I'm so ready to collapse into bed, but I need to speak to Jada first.

I'm using the counter for support as I sip on Mom's pecan-flavored coffee. Mitch holds up two slices of bread.

"You want some toast?"

"Sure, why not." He adds two more slices and pushes down the lever. I realize Mitch is wearing nice clothes. Not clothes you go back to bed in. "I thought you were gonna take a nap?"

He grunts. "I was, but figured I'd tough it out since I'm staying home tomorrow for senior skip day."

"Oh right. Jada mentioned that. I think she's going dress shopping. You want to do something, just the two of us?"

"That'd be cool. What ya got in mind?"

"Don't know. We could ride our bikes to Diamond Hill, or head the other direction and go to the mountains, hiking or something. It's your skip day, what do you want to do?"

The toast pops up so Mitch grabs the bread and slathers butter on them. He passes me two slices and takes his to the bar.

Mitch inhales his toast, but I take my time. He still hasn't answered my question about tomorrow. "So? What did you want to do for skip day?"

"First of all, I'm sleeping late. Then, I don't know. A hike in the mountains sounds good or taking the boat to the lake? Let me think on it."

"No problem, let me know."

"Yep." Mitch rinses his cup in the sink.

"Have you seen Mom?" I ask.

"Yeah, she said to tell you she's sorry about breakfast, but she has a charity board meeting or some shit. She whipped up that yummy brew we drank and then went to get dressed."

"Gotcha. That stuff is nasty, but it works. I can already tell a difference."

"Me too. Well, I'm gonna run upstairs and brush my teeth."

"Yeah, okay. Have a good day. And keep an eye on Jada."

He rolls his eyes. "Like you have to ask." He punches my arm as he passes.

Jada strolls in and goes straight to the coffee maker. Her movements around the kitchen are fluid and graceful like my mother's. Her hair is down today, and she's wearing a yellow sundress. Her luscious, tan legs taunt me.

She spins around and glares at me. "Denver, cut it out."

Shoot. Busted. Again. "Sorry babe. If you weren't so hot I wouldn't want you so bad."

"I don't even want to hear it. All I can think about is you in that towel. Now go sit behind the bar so I can concentrate on breakfast."

"Yes, ma'am." Jada makes her coffee and gets out some fruit. "Is that all you're eating?"

"I'm watching my figure, I've got a wedding coming up."

My eyebrows hike up. "Seriously? I'm watching your figure too, and it looks pretty damn good to me."

She laughs. "This is to hold me over. Emily texted and said she's bringing doughnuts to school."

"As long as you're eating. We need to get back on schedule with our workouts today."

"It will have to be this evening. Don't forget we're meeting Emily and Grainger after school."

"Crap. I don't like that idea."

She pops a blueberry in her mouth. "We discussed this. You said it was okay?"

"That's not what I mean. Mitch and I got our butts kicked last night fighting off maybe twenty or so demons. They're starting to emerge from the swirl over the field. These were no ordinary demons. I don't like you driving around by yourself."

Her knees buckle, but she grabs hold of the counter. "Oh no. How long do I have?"

"I don't know." I rush over to pull her into my arms. "If anything happens to you, I'll die. And I'll die trying to protect you. I can't protect you if you're out by yourself."

"Okay. So what? I'm under house arrest? I'm supposed to go shopping tomorrow."

I let out a frustrated breath. "I know you still have to go out, but I prefer to be close. Or at least know someone in my family is close. You should be fine to go shopping tomorrow. My mom will be there, and you'll be around lots of people. But you shouldn't be out alone."

"I understand your worry, but what's going to happen while I'm driving through town in my car?"

"You'd be surprised. If a greater demon wants to push you off the road, he can."

"Oh. I hate this looming over our heads. A part of me wishes the demon would show himself so we can get it over with."

I hold her tighter. No one wants to watch their loved ones face their demons. In whatever form that takes. This will be a fight to the finish. Someone has to die—Jada or the demon. And that scares me to death. I can't lose her. I haven't shared with Jada all that I've learned from Dad, but this demon has Jada's name on it. It's his personal assignment to kill her. His purpose. We can help her, but she has to be engaged in the fight. The whole thing makes me sick to my stomach.

"It will be here soon enough. We'll take it one day at a time."

The disconnect is palpable as she pulls out of my arms. "So how do we handle today?"

"Ride with Mitch to school. I'll pick you up after, instead of meeting you at Hagerdy's."

"All right."

Her lips meet mine in a soft kiss. I'm ready to expand on that sweet kiss until Mitch comes barreling through.

"You ready, Jada?"

"Yeah. Let me grab my bag."

She leaves the room and I run my hands through my hair. Anger wells up inside me and my fist meets the counter with a slam. "Damn it!"

"It's going to be okay," Mitch says to reassure me, but it doesn't.

"We don't know that." I lean over the counter and hang my head. "We don't know."

Mitch shoves me, forcing me to look at him. "You're right, we don't know, but we're all going to do everything we can to make sure she gets through this. We love her too."

"I can't live without her."

"Then we make sure she lives."

I don't know what else to say, so I grab Mitch and hug him. We break apart when Jada returns with her backpack.

Mitch and Jada head off to school, and I stumble down the hall to her bed, crawl in her covers, and fall asleep breathing in her vanilla and coconut scent.

THREE HOURS LATER, I wake up in the exact spot I lay down in. I never moved a muscle. And speaking of muscles, mine are sore. After a good stretch, I slide out of Jada's bed and go upstairs to finish my course work for the day. I do a light workout in the gym, eat lunch, and then take another shower. All this mundane activity does nothing to ease my mind over Jada's impending fight. My nerves are frazzled and my limbs are jittery like I've had a couple of energy drinks.

I make my way to Dad's study and tap on the door. "Dad, can I come in?"

"Of course."

Dad is behind his desk, glaring at his computer. I've never seen his desk so messy. These last weeks, papers continue to pile up and spill over each other. A tinge of worry tugs at my insides.

"Dad, you need to take a break."

He peers at me over the rim of his readers. "Son, as soon as this greater demon business is behind us, I'm whisking your mom away for a week vacation."

"Maybe you should make it two weeks."

He smiles. "I've got a wedding coming up." He pulls off his glasses and sets them down. His smile turns to worry. "How are you holding up?"

"Not well."

"I don't know why I asked. I can tell. I would be in the same boat if it were your mother. But we love Jada, and every wolf within fighting age is ready to stand beside her. We'll do all we can. If we only knew the when. That would help."

"I have a thought on that."

Dad sits back in his chair. "Enlighten me."

I sit across from him on the edge of the seat. My leg bounces with nervous energy. "Jada said something this morning that got me thinking. She said she wished we could get it over with. As much as I hate the idea of her in this at all, it's going to happen. So what if, instead of waiting on pins and needles for their attack, we take the fight to them?"

Dad turns his chair to face the window. He gazes out over the yard, his forehead lined with wrinkles as his finger taps his lips. After a couple of minutes, he turns back to face me.

"What are you proposing exactly?"

"I have no idea if it will work, but maybe Jada's presence would entice him to come out. What if the five of us go out in the field and get his attention? We could have the other wolves waiting in the fringe. Then there's no surprise attack, except on our part."

"You may have something here, son. Let me call the elders and inform them of this possible scenario."

"Yes sir." I stand to leave but sit back down. "Dad. I'm scared."

"Oh, Denver, we all are. I certainly wish I could promise that everything will be okay, but I don't have that power. I'm not God. All we can do is trust and pray, and then fight the good fight. And fight we will."

A tear pools in my eye and escapes before I can hold it in. My raw and exposed heart is on the verge of shattering. My Jada.

Dad comes around his desk and I rise to meet him. His strong arms engulf me in a tight hug and I cry. Neither of us say anything else. Sometimes words fail us. They fall short of what's really in our heart. Actions speak louder than words, and when my dad says he'll fight to the finish, he means it.

I leave the room in no better shape than when I went in. I won't be able to breathe again until Jada is free from this demon that wants to take her life. And if he takes hers, he takes mine with it.

I'M WAITING for Jada in the lot when she walks out of the school, smiling and talking to Emily. They stop and turn around. Grainger walks fast to catch up. They all laugh at something he says. I could listen in, but I won't. A part of me is thankful Jada is happy in spite of what's coming, and another part of me wants to scream at the world to stop spinning and take notice of our situation. How dare they laugh when my whole world could come tumbling down.

Jada spots me and smiles. I don't pick her up as often as I used to, and I love the way she saunters toward me with a seductive grin.

Her bag falls to the ground. "Hey gorgeous." She plants a kiss on my lips before stepping into my arms.

I hold on tight without completely crushing her. Sometimes she's in my arms and it's still not close enough. "How was your day? Did you ace the test?"

She pulls back enough to study my face. Her body is pressed to mine. "I appreciate the attempt at small talk, but you can't hide your stress from me."

I kiss the top of her head. "I'm sorry. I don't mean to burden you with my emotions."

"You're worried about me, but you're sorry. Whatever am I going to do with you?"

"Love me forever."

"I want nothing more."

She pushes her lips to mine and it's such a hungry kiss my legs wobble. Now is not a good time to get carried away. The administration would not be pleased with our public displays of affection.

"All right, my bloody fish, that's enough. I don't want you to get suspended for making out in the parking lot."

"Fine, but we will continue that kiss later."

"You're killing me. Let's go talk to Emily."

THE FOUR OF us sit in a corner booth at Hagerdy's. Jada and I are on one side, Emily and Grainger on the other. The waitress has taken our order and let us be for now. Luckily there's no one sitting too close. I'm not sure how this is going to go.

They talk about school and upcoming graduation for a while before Emily speaks her mind.

"As much as I love this, are you going to tell me what happened the other night? Why you two lost it in the pool?"

Jada glances at me and I squeeze her thigh.

With sugar or without?

Without. She seems like a straight shooter to me.

Jada taps her fingers on the table. She opens her mouth to speak, but the waitress brings our milkshakes and fries.

"Can I get you guys anything else?"

"No, thank you," I say for the table.

The waitress waddles off, looking a good eight months pregnant, and we resume our conversation.

"So, Denver and I have a special bond that goes beyond the normal relationship. We know we're forever because we're mates."

Emily shoves a fry in ketchup and then, with equal gusto, into her mouth. "Mates? What does that mean?"

"We're resolved to be together, sort of bound. And our emotions and senses are heightened, making it hard to maintain boundaries."

"Sounds like an excuse to have sex."

Jada chokes on her milkshake. "Geez, Emily. We're not having sex."

"Then I don't get this whole mate thing."

I clear my throat. "That's because she's skirting around the truth. You want me to do it?"

"No, I can do it." Jada inhales and exhales a long breath. "Okay, so here it is. The truth. Denver and I are...wolves."

Now it's Emily's turn to get choked up. "What the hell? Is this some kind of joke?"

"What? No. You're one of my best friends, and I want you to know what I am. What we are."

Emily turns to Grainger. The shock she's expecting to find on his face isn't there. "Wait, you knew? How is this possible?"

He shifts in his seat. "I don't know how it's possible, but I know because I was there."

"Like, you were *there*, there? You saw Jada turn into a wolf?"

"Accidentally, but yes. It was the night I was drunk. Mitch tried to keep me from going outside, but I went anyway. After it happened I tried to tell myself that it was the alcohol, but there's no way I dreamed that up. It was too real."

Emily huffs and tosses the fry she'd been holding back on her plate. "This is nuts. Are you guys punking me or something?"

No one speaks. Jada tries to reach out to touch Emily's hand, but she jerks it back.

We let her process for minute, all the while her face turning white. I'm worried she's going to pull a Jada and pass out.

She glares up at Jada and then me. "Mitch?"

I nod. "Mitch too."

Emily pushes at Grainger to let her out of the booth. "This is too much. I have to go."

Grainger lets her out, and she bolts for the door. Jada tries to get past me, but Grainger holds out his hand.

"Let me talk to her. I understand where she's coming from."

"All right. Please call me later."

He agrees and runs for the door. Jada and I sit in the booth stunned. Well, she's stunned. It's what I expected. Maybe better than what I expected. I'm fairly certain she'll come around.

Jada leans into my shoulder. "My gosh, that was terrible."

"Look at the bright side: you wanted Emily and Grainger to bond. Now they have something in common."

"The fact that they're wolf widows?"

I can't help but chuckle at her method of thinking. "No, I meant, they both have a best friend that's a wolf."

"Oh. That too, I suppose."

"Finish your fries. I'm going to pay so we can go home."

LATER THAT EVENING, Dad calls us all to the study. Jada has been sulking ever since her talk with Emily. She hasn't heard from either of them, and it's driving her crazy. I try to help her forget by pushing her hard during our workout. It helps temporarily. She's gotten so much stronger and faster. Her ability to spar with Mitch amazes me, but that doesn't compare to a demon that wants to kill her. I'm constantly worried, tense, and agitated.

Dad glances around at each of us. He's holding back his thoughts and I can't read his expression. It's not like him to close himself off. "After speaking with Denver this morning, I've called all the elders and pack leaders. Every single one is in agreement that we should initiate the fight. As you boys both know, there have already been demons making an entrance, and they continue to do so. I don't foresee that getting any better. Only worse. Therefore, they want to move rather quickly. They've asked if we would be willing to move forward as early as this Thursday."

Jada gasps beside me. I jump out of my chair. "Thursday! We're not ready. Jada's not ready."

Dad's voice is calm and even. "Denver, we'll never be ready."

I pace the floor, both hands in my hair. "I realize that, but I thought we'd have more than a few days. It's too soon."

"This is hard for all of us. The situation is personal to our family because Jada is a part of us now. But I also have to keep in mind the welfare of our fellow wolves and the people of this town. If we continue to fight the demons spilling out day after day, we'll be worn out and not fit for fighting an epic battle. Which may be their intention. I don't like it any more than you, but it's necessary."

Jada takes a moment to consider his words. "How are the people in Forrest City in danger?"

"We won't be able to hold the demons to the field forever. Eventually, they will make their way to the streets of town and begin to torment the people. The very thing our ancestors have worked so hard to prevent. Do demons slip through? Of course, but we do our damndest to keep our city free of evil."

I fall down in the seat next to Jada. My hands tremble as I take her hand. "Babe, what do you think? We don't have to do it."

"Bolivar is right. I don't want to keep putting others in danger. What's one life compared to a whole town? I say we agree to what they're asking."

"Very well, I will make all the arrangements. The elders request that we be in the field Thursday at sundown."

I slide to the floor, my head between my knees. This can't be happening. If I lose her, I'll die. We haven't had the chance to say our vows, go on our honeymoon, experience life in the cabin, have children, or even wake up in each other's arms.

Jada curls up beside me. The others leave the room. If she says it's going to be okay, I will punch something. This is not okay. I'm grateful when she says nothing at all. She holds me as I struggle to keep my mind from an endless downward spiral. A life without Jada is no life at all. I play Mitch's words from earlier over and over in my head—*we make sure she lives.*

Eventually the mantra gives me a spark of hope, and I lift up my head. I hold Jada's face between my hands. "We make sure you live. The alternative is too painful."

She gives a slight nod as I hold her tight. Then I crush my mouth to hers and kiss her like it's the last time I might get to taste her sweet lips.

CHAPTER TWENTY-TWO

JADA

I've never considered death an immediate concern. I'm supposed to have my whole life ahead of me. I'm supposed to be wild and carefree and living in the moment. Young, dumb, and broke. That's what the song says. I've always lived for the next big thing. I can't wait to drive, can't wait to graduate, can't wait to go to college, can't wait to get married, etc. There's no room for death. Only life. That is, until death is a very real possibility in your near future. Then it's hard not to overthink death. What's it like? Is there a heaven? A hell? Where will I go? Have I been the best person I can be?

I've been trying to make the most of my life over the last couple of days, in case I die. Don't get me wrong, I want to live. But just in case, I've made sure everyone I love knows I love them. I've made amends with my father and mother, and given them my blessing. Emily and I have worked through her questions, and are as good as new. Same with Grainger. I hug Mitch, Bolivar, and Aurar every time I pass them, and tell them how much I love them, and how grateful I am to call them family. Last night, I spent time with Alexander and Vashti. Then there's Denver, who doesn't leave my side unless I'm at school or in the bathroom.

I bought a wedding dress. It's beautiful. Denver insisted that we follow through with our plans on Tuesday. He got angry when I suggested waiting until after Thursday.

I rub the white satin between my fingers. There's no lace. No beads. No sequins. It's plain, yet elegant. Similar to my prom dress, there's a long slit up the front. The neckline is more daring than I would normally wear, and the back also reveals a lot of skin. The moment I slid it on, I knew it was the one. I say a prayer that I will wear the dress three weeks from now, and then push it back in the closet.

Denver comes in my room with damp hair from his shower. "Mom has dinner ready."

"I'm not hungry."

His strong arms envelop me, giving me a short reprieve from my nerves. He kisses my face, neck, and lips. You'd think these last few days we would have called Hold the Line a million times, but that's not the case. Our time alone, even our kisses, are tender. It's more about connection and love, and less about sex. Mostly he holds me.

"Babe, none of us are hungry. This meal is for strength if anything. Mom also made a hot tea to help with healing. It lacks in taste, but it works."

"All right."

At dinner, the mood is somber. Even Mitch. The boys discuss battle tactics and possible scenarios, but other than that, it's quiet. I clean my plate out of pure nervous eating, though I can't taste it. Then I drain the cup of tea. Denver's right, it tastes like pond scum.

Out of habit, we clean dishes and wipe the kitchen until it sparkles. At one point Aurar starts to cry, so I hug her and we cry together.

Bolivar wants to know if we should go over the plan one more time. I decline. We've spent hours discussing tonight, and it will never be enough to prepare me for what's ahead. Anyway, my role is to stay as close to the family as possible. Fight if I have to. Hide if I can.

My mom and dad show up after dinner. All the men go to the study for final preparations. Roland has provided invaluable insight to fighting a greater demon. He seems pleased with our numbers and says we have a chance at walking away without casualties. My stomach plummets to my toes at the word casualties.

I sit with my mom and Aurar in the living room.

"It's horrible being so useless," my mom says. "I've not once envied the wolf life until now. I want to help."

She's one less person I'll have to worry about on the battle field. Along with Emily and Grainger. "I'm thankful a few of the people I love aren't having to risk their lives for mine."

"Well, I hate it. I'm your mother. I'm supposed to risk my life for yours. Someone better call me as soon as it's over."

Aurar places her hand over my mother's. "We will. I promise."

I zone out as the women share stories of motherhood. A few minutes later the doorbell rings, so I offer to get the door.

I'm surprised to find Emily and Grainger standing on the other side of the threshold.

"What are you guys doing here?"

Emily jumps at me, squishing me with her bear hug. "Denver said we should come."

I hold my right arm out to Grainger, inviting him to join in on the hug. "I love you guys so much."

Emily starts to speak but breaks down in tears. I cry again. Grainger, my rock, wipes a tear from his cheek.

A few minutes later, we're all convened in the living room. Somehow, laughter finds its way into the conversation. Denver wraps his arm around me as we talk about anything but the fight ahead. The people in this room are the reason I'm loved and blessed. There's not a single thing that could make me more content than I am in this moment. I've already had a lifetime of love. If I do die tonight, I can die happy.

I insist on a small drink of champagne before everyone leaves. As crazy as it sounds, I already have victory. Denver, who would normally balk at my immature idea, jumps up to help.

When we raise our glasses, Denver winks at Mitch and says, "We make sure she lives."

. . .

WE PARK DOWN the street from the field. It's eerily quiet in the woods. No birds sing, no frogs croak, no crickets chirp, no owls hoot —only stillness. The moon is coming up, a huge, bright ball in the sky. There's a distant crack of thunder as we gather under the trees.

I should be more nervous. That's what I'm thinking as we form a circle. I'm shaking, but not all of this emotion is fear. I'm angry. I'm angry that this demon and his minions want to take out my loved ones. I hate that their lives are on the line because of me. And I'm furious that this greater demon wants to strip me of life and purpose when I've barely begun to discover who I am. My blood boils with rage. I give it permission to build. I'll do everything in my power to protect the people I love.

We hold hands as Bolivar says a prayer. Denver is squeezing the bones together in my fingers. His waves of anger roll out like the ocean.

No one cries. No one speaks. We're here to fight, determination on each face. The only contact includes my father patting my shoulder, and Denver's lips on mine. Then we shift to wolf form and walk to the field.

When we reach the edge of the field, I understand the silence of the forest. Nature is holding her breath. The air reeks of hatred. Its foul stench like rot and sulfur. My nostrils burn and it taints my insides as I breathe it in.

There's already a battle on the field as the wolves on patrol combat demons one after the other. They spill out of the sky, giving no reprieve to the weary wolves. They're scratched and bloody but continue to fight.

For a moment, everything stops as we step out into the field. Our formation is solid; Bolivar and Roland in front, Denver and me in the middle, and Mitch and Aurar in the back. Wolf and demon alike pause for our entrance. Some wolves bow slightly in honor of royal blood, and then the demons pull back up into the sky.

Bolivar thanks the wolves on patrol and sends them home to rest and heal. We take their places in the middle of the field. We are six in the clearing, but the growls of the others rumble in my chest. They are hidden for now on the outskirts, waiting to join us.

There's this moment of peace as the sky turns purple and green, shifting and writhing. Ominous clouds cover the moon and shut out its light. Lightning streaks across the sky with thunder booming on its heels. Screeches that pierce the ears reach us in deafening tones. And then silence. No movement, no sound comes from the heavens.

The anger multiplies inside of me. A growl begins in my lower belly and builds like a crescendo until it's released in a mighty howl. Those around me follow suit, and our war cries invade the silence.

And then it begins. Lesser demons shoot out of the sky with their own battle shout. High-pitched screams bellow from hideous faces. Demons of different shapes and sizes descend on the field. Some of them land and take on animal shapes, and others fly above. Each is grotesque in its own way. And each one has a body part meant to harm—teeth, talons, claws, barbs, blades, or stingers. But it's the eyes that freak me out. No matter the color, the eyes are empty of soul but full of death.

Denver is constantly in my head, yelling for me to stay behind him. The group tries to keep me surrounded as long as they can. It's a good plan in theory. But eventually we spread out as more and more demons spill from the sky. Everyone is engaged in a personal battle and are no longer able to shield me.

Sharp teeth sink into my back leg, and I cry out in pain. I whip around to face off with a black, oily, scraggly coyote creature. His rows of shark teeth drip with my blood. We circle each other, and he licks my blood off his lips. For a split second, something akin to agony crosses his features. I don't have time to think on what that might mean because in the next second he lunges at me.

He's fast, but I'm faster. He's strong, but I'm stronger. He gets in a couple of bites, but it's not long before I sink my teeth in his throat and rip it out.

In the struggle, I lose sight of Aurar, Mitch, and Bolivar. Denver and Roland are close, but both face challengers at the moment.

The field is in chaos. Yelps and wails fill my ears. Demons scream before returning to the pit of hell. Blood—demon and wolf—covers the ground. Shaking with rage, I howl at the top of my lungs. This is my family. I can't take it anymore. The pain of my loved ones is too much to bear.

I run.

Denver calls my name, but I don't stop. Unless I start ripping something apart, I'm going to go crazy. Any demon stupid enough to get in my path, I tear to shreds. Power burns in my veins, so I unleash it.

I lose track of the demons I kill. My fur is covered in demon blood. Cuts, gouges, bruises, and bites cover my body. Demons continue to flow out of the rip in the sky, and my muscles are weakened with fatigue. How do we end this? Must every demon die? We won't make it that long. Keep fighting, I tell myself. But the demon poison in my body clouds my judgement. I shake my head to clear it.

In my moment of weakness, the ground quakes and the earth splits. I leap aside to avoid being swallowed up by the chasm. A roar rises deep from the belly of the earth, followed by a sinister laugh. Before it materializes, it speaks to me.

Jadaline Kingston of royal blood, today you will die. You have no worth, no purpose. You are not loved. Abandoned by your father. You are nothing. You are weak and insecure. You are of no value to this world. You have no peace, hope, or joy. Nothing can save you. You deserve death, and death is what you will get. You will reside with me in the depths of hell, tortured for all time.

A dark film of depression covers my mind and I cry out. His words spread like a disease, eating me away from the inside. I'm emptied out of all that is good. I know I am worthless and life has no meaning.

The greater demon surges out of the open earth. His red eyes sear my soul. He laughs and another quake rumbles the soil. His alligator-skinned, gorilla-shaped body is three times larger than any demon I've fought today. He clacks his razor-sharp teeth and snaps at my neck. Somehow in my state of despair, I manage to have the instinct to move out of the way.

He stalks toward me, and I flounder back. Flies spew from his mouth as he paints my mind in darkness. His form changes from gorilla to man with the same hideous reptilian skin. I'm facing Goliath with no stones.

For a split second, I wonder where my help is. My family. But there's no one. A deep fog has covered the field. There are no voices. No Denver. I'm alone.

The demon uses my fear against me.

Where are they, Jada? Those that say they love you. They feed you lies and you eat them like candy. How stupid can you be? There is no love, only hate. They never cared for you. You mean nothing to them. Nothing. No one loves you. And they never will. Love is a lie.

He continues to spout darkness over me. I'm on the ground, whimpering. I've almost given in completely to the evil when a tiny spark ignites in my heart. I'm enthralled by the bright light in contrast to the black all around. I focus on it, and it calls to me. A whisper. A still, quiet voice beckons me to recognize the truth. To believe in the light. I want to, I tell it. I want to so badly. The light grows and warms my heart. It tells me I'm beautiful and wonderful. It tells me it loves me. It tells me I am loved and cherished, and I have purpose. The more I zero in on the light, the stronger I become. The stronger I become, the more I believe. The more I believe, the more I know. I am not who this demon says I am. His lies have been revealed and his darkness has been dispelled.

I stand up strong in body and spirit and scream at the greater demon through my mind.

Shut up! You are full of lies and I will listen no longer! You don't get to tell me who I am! Go back to the pit of hell where you belong!

His ominous laugh booms in the air. *Oh Jadaline, if only it were that simple. If I can't break your spirit, then I will break your body. We fight to the death.*

In life and in death, I have victory. So bring it on.

The demon sweeps my front feet out from under me and I land

on my chin. I jump up and sprint a short distance away to get my bearings. The fog has been lifted from the field, and every wolf is fighting for his or her life. I have to end this.

Denver's voice has returned. He's frantic, thinking I'm already dead. I tell him I love him and then I tune him out. I won't be able to do what I need to do if he's calling out to me.

The demon encroaches upon me, changing form until only his hollowed-out red eyes remain. He's no longer a man or animal. The monstrous, scaly beast oozes pus from the sores covering its bony arms. It reeks of decay, and razor-sharp canines protrude from his snakelike face, dripping venom.

He extends his arms, and with gorilla strength knocks me a good twenty feet. I slam into the ground, my breath stolen from my lungs. By the time I hoist myself up, another blow to the kidneys sends me skidding on my side. My raw, exposed skin is set ablaze like a lit match to dry grass. I have to move faster.

I roll over twice and jump to my feet. The demon strikes, but I duck beneath his blow.

While his momentum is still in his swing, I pounce on his back. My teeth cut through his thick skin and I use all the power in my jaws to take a chunk out of his neck. In one swift motion, he tosses me off, barely fazed. We continue to circle and thrash at one another while I wait for an opportunity to get at his throat.

I'm bleeding and fatigued, but I can't quit. The others aren't safe until one of us dies. I'd prefer that be him, but I don't know how to defeat him. I take too long to contemplate my next move. He clamps down on my front leg, and I scream in pain. The venom has imme-diate effects on my body. Nausea overwhelms me and spots dance before my eyes. He has me in a death grip, but for some reason releases me. I watch as his face contorts and a violent shudder racks his body. What caused him to let me go? The other demons I fought had similar responses. My blood drips from his face.

My blood. Oh my gosh, he can't stand my blood. But what do I do with this knowledge? If he continues to gnaw on me, he might kill me before he gets enough to bring him harm. I've inflicted plenty of wounds on the demon as well. How do I get the amount of blood in him needed to finish him off? How do I drown him in my blood?

Drown. The lake. I need to get him to the lake. I'm bleeding all over. If I get him to the lake, maybe, just maybe, my blood can seep into his open wounds and kill him. I've got nothing else, I have to try.

I sprint off in the direction of the lake. The greater demon laughs. He thinks it's a game.

You can't outrun me, you stupid girl.

I run faster.

Twice before we reach the lake he grabs my hindquarters. Both times he releases me because he can't stand my blood, but the damage is done. My legs are going numb, my thoughts are hazy, and I'm so nauseous I gag. I stop at the dam of the lake. My life is slipping away. I don't have much left.

I allow Denver in one last time, long enough to express my love and to tell him where to find my body. The way he screams my name causes me more pain than this demon ever could.

The demon lunges at me, and this time I don't move out of the way. I let him bite down deep into my neck and then I fall backward off the dam. At the same time, I change from wolf to girl. The demon tries to release me, but I wrap my arms around his neck and force him to drink my blood.

He writhes beneath me as we break through the water. My blood spreads out across the top of the lake. The demon jerks and seizes for only a moment and then goes limp. A smile forms on my face with the knowledge my loved ones are safe. I dream of kissing Denver's lips, and then the world goes black.

CHAPTER TWENTY-THREE

DENVER

Jada! Jada! Whatever you're thinking, don't do it! Why are you at the lake? Jada! Answer me!

Damn it! She's cut me off again. I've got to go to the lake. Another demon flies down at me, and with pure adrenaline, I take him out in one swipe of my paw. I'm running on empty, like everyone else on this field. There's so much poison in my system I might throw up any minute. I've never witnessed anything like the horror before me. I don't think we've lost anyone, but every wolf is wounded and bleeding. The grass is covered in a swirl of black and red, demon and wolf blood. The sight of this field will forever haunt me.

Dad! Jada is at the lake. She didn't say why, and she's not answering me. I need to get to her.

Go, son!

I turn to run toward the lake, only to get attacked from behind. One minute he has a hold of my leg, and the next…

It's quiet. No fighting. No shouting. No demon screeching. Nothing but wolves, gazing around in shock and wonder as the sky closes up, and the demons left behind are swallowed up by a crack in the earth. As soon as the last demon has descended, the earth pulls back together.

Now I run. With energy and strength I don't have, I run. My primal need to reach Jada pushes me onward. I swallow the bile rising in my throat and urge my weary legs to carry me to my destination. Why would the fight be over? The greater demon never appeared, did he? Unless, in that deep fog, Jada was fighting for her life and we didn't have a clue. The groans of the battlefield fade away, replaced by the pounding of my paws on the hard dirt and my labored breaths. I call to Jada, but she doesn't respond.

Jada! I scream her name over and over. Then I pray. Begging God to let her live.

When I reach the lake, I scan the calm surface. No Jada. It's not until I stand at the top of the dam that I spot her bloody body at the edge of the water. She's lying on her side, curled up like she's asleep.

I change to human form and stumble down the hill. With all the poison in my system, the conversion leaves me lightheaded and dizzy. My stomach rolls, and flashes of silver light dance before my eyes. God help me, please.

I slump beside her and fumble for a pulse. Her body is cold. If she has a pulse, it's so faint, I can't find it. I lay my cheek above her mouth and pray that her breath caresses my face. There may have been a light tickle, but I can't be sure if it's actually there, or it's my hopeful imagination. I long to pull her in my lap, but she's so damaged, I'm afraid to move her. And her neck. Oh my God, her neck. The right side of her neck is chewed up like a dog toy.

"Denver! Is she alive?"

My dad slides down the hill. Warm tears stream down my face. "I don't know."

I step to the side so my dad can have the spot next to Jada. He checks the pulse points on her wrist and neck then looks at me with heavy concern in his eyes. "We don't have much time. She's hanging on by a thread."

I fold over in pain and puke my guts up. My whole body shudders so hard my teeth chatter. I try desperately to hang on, but bright spots shimmer in my peripheral vision. I turn back to my father and there's two of him on the ground by Jada.

"Denver, sit down, you're swaying. Help is on the way."

Too much. It's all too much. Jada. Demon poison. Too much. A siren shrieks in the distance, seconds before I give in to the venom in my body.

Random voices whisper over me and my body is jostled about. A bee stings my arm. Then my leg and butt. I don't recall stepping on a bee's nest. Maybe I'm hungover. No. That doesn't seem right either. Everything hurts. My stomach twists and I puke. At least I think I puke. My thoughts fade in and out of reality and my head spins like a merry-go-round.

For a second there's clarity and I cry out for Jada. Someone pushes the hair off my face.

"I know baby, I know. Hang in there."

"Jada?"

"No sweetie, it's Mom. Jada is in an ambulance with your dad. We're almost home."

"Mitch?"

"He's in the same shape as you."

My eyes are heavy and swollen, but I manage to get one open. Mom sits by me in the back of an ambulance. There's an IV in my arm. She's bruised and bloody, yet she's taking care of me.

"You need stitches." I point to the blood running down her forehead.

"I know. Your dad has a team of his classmates from college waiting for us at the house. He transformed the basement into an infirmary of sorts. He really thought of everything."

I mean to tell her how amazing they both are, but the black drags me under.

THIS IS NOT MY BED. This is not my room. I attempt to lift my head to further investigate, but a grenade goes off in my brain. I moan in agony. Footsteps approach followed by an unfamiliar voice.

"Give him another dose of morphine for the pain. Is he still getting sick?"

"Yes. Every thirty minutes or so."

"All right. I'll let Bolivar know he could use more anti-venom as well."

"Morphine is going in now."

IN THE DARKNESS, an electronic device beeps by my head. Something grips my arm and I bolt upright only to find a blood pressure cuff squeezing the life from the limb. I push my other hand through my hair and try to remember where I am and what's happened. I wince at the sting of the IV in my arm.

What the hell? I know something is very wrong, but for the life of me I can't remember. I'm startled by a groan beside me. I was under the impression I was alone. The moans grow louder, and I identify the sound.

"Mitch, is that you?"

"Yeah."

His voice sounds like he's been eating gravel. Come to think of it, my throat is raw too. I could really use a drink of water.

"Where are we?" I don't know if Mitch will answer or if he knows any more than I do. All I get is another groan.

A curtain slides open, letting in some light that reveals a makeshift hospital room. A woman walks in with a stethoscope around her neck.

"Oh good, you're awake. And not puking. Let's get you checked out, shall we?"

"What's going on here? Who are you?"

"My name is Mary, and I'm a friend of your father's. We went to college together. I'm a doctor up in Diamond Hill."

"What hospital is this?"

She smiles. "It's your basement. Your father is quite the mastermind."

"Where is he?"

"He's tending to…"

Mary repositions her stethoscope and then turns her back on me to fidget with the buttons on my IV pole. What am I missing here?

Oh my God. Jada. He's with Jada.

Mary spins around as I rip off the Velcro from the blood pressure cuff.

"Hold on. You're in no shape to leave."

"Believe me when I say you can't stop me. Where is she?"

"Your dad said you'd be like this. Let me at least take out your IV."

I jerk the needle from my wrist. "Where is she?"

"In her room."

I leap from the bed, but my knees buckle, sending me to the floor. Mary takes me by the arm and helps me to my feet. She shakes her head as she throws my arm over her shoulder and leads me out into the hall.

Our unfinished basement is now a hospital. There are partitioned rooms, set apart by curtains like a triage area in the emergency room. Doctors and nurses move about from room to room. Who are these people? And when did my dad do all of this?

Mary waves to a tall man with salt-and-pepper hair. "Dr. Williams, will you please assist Denver upstairs? I need to check on his brother."

"Of course."

Mary and Dr. Williams trade places. I'm thankful for his strength and stature. I was afraid to put all my weight on Mary. This guy can handle it. He guides me through several turns until we're at the bottom of the stairs.

"Nice and slow."

"Yep." The short walk down the hall has me wiped. By the time we make it to the top, I'm sweating. When we turn the corner to Jada's room, my body is done. The doctor drops me in a chair by her bed.

"He's on the verge of passing out."

My dad and his doctor friend pull me to my feet long enough to get me in the bed with Jada. She lies on her back, her eyes closed. I notice the rise and fall of her chest—that has to be a good thing, right? *Stay with me, Jada.* I muster the energy to kiss her cheek, and then I fall asleep holding her hand tightly in mine.

MY MOUTH TASTES LIKE SKUNK. I rub the sleep from my eyes and stretch my arms and legs. My muscles ache with the movement, but it's an improvement from the last time I came to. I sit up on my elbows and stare at my beautiful Jada. I don't know how long I've been out, but she hasn't moved. Her once-pasty cheeks are a rosy pink and other than a few purple bruises, several cuts and scrapes, she appears to be healing. Her neck is covered in gauze. I tenderly stroke her cheek.

A throat clears from across the room. Emily rests in a chair by the window. "You okay?"

"Yeah. How long have you been here?"

"The whole time. I've been helping out as much as I can. Your mom can be rather bossy."

I chuckle and pain throbs in my chest. I must have broken a rib. "That she can. So, what day is it?"

"It's Saturday. You've been in and out for over twenty-four hours."

"Damn. How is Jada? Do you know what's going on?"

"Your dad said she's in a coma. He's done all he can. It's up to her now."

A coma. I push out a long breath, trying not to hyperventilate. "Hey, Emily, can I have a minute?"

"Sure, I'll go get your mom. She wanted to know when you were awake."

"Thanks." She's almost out the door when I stop her. "Emily. Thank you for helping out. I'm sure it wasn't easy."

A faint smile touches her lips. "I wanted to do it. Grainger helped too. I think he's still downstairs."

"I'll thank him later."

Emily slips out of the room. I turn my attention to Jada, who appears to be peacefully sleeping. I wish I could kiss her awake, but this is no fairytale. I kiss her anyway, ever so lightly on her face and lips. As I run my hands through her hair, a wave of sorrow overtakes me, and if Jada weren't so close, I'd punch the hell out of this headboard.

"Jada, you've got to come back to me. I can't make it without you. Do you hear me, Jada Brooks? I need you to come back to me. Please come back." I collapse beside her and weep into her neck.

My mother's soothing voice brings me back to the present.

"Denver, you need to shower and eat."

"I don't want to leave her."

"I know, son, but we need to change the sheets and check all her dressings. Go clean up, check on your brother, and then come back."

"Fine."

"Stop by the kitchen and eat some homemade chicken soup. Oh, and take your medicine. Your father left some antibiotics on the counter. There's pain pills too, if you need them."

I slip out of bed and a cool breeze hits my bare butt. Nice, Dad. Oh well, nothing my mom hasn't seen before. Emily on the other hand...

I grab the material and hold it closed. "Where is Dad?"

"He's finally resting."

"Okay. I'll be back shortly."

I want to take the quickest shower in the history of quick showers, but there's dried blood in every hidden part of my body. While the water rinses away the grime, I inspect my frame for leftover damage. Most everything is healed, but there are a few remaining scrapes and bruises. Some of the bite marks are still puffy and red, but other than that I'm in pretty good shape. My side is tender to the touch, so I have to assume that I did indeed have at least one broken bone. Jada's body will be doing the same for her—healing and mending and putting her back together. But the question remains, once she's healed, will she wake up? I decide we're going to have a conversation, Jada and I.

After being so crusty and drafty, it's nice to be clean and have on sweats and a T-shirt. I make my way to the basement, where I take in the transformation. I'm in awe of the man I call Father. Why did he not tell me he was putting all this together?

I pass several empty beds—most everyone has been able to go home by this point. There are a couple of doctors still milling about. Surprised I remember the way, I walk to where Mitch is holed up next to the bed I woke up in. He's flirting with someone in the room.

Pushing the curtain aside, I stroll in. A cute blonde is attempting to change a dressing on his leg. She's probably a good five or six years older than he is, but he rattles on telling her how hot she is.

"Give the nice lady a break, bro."

Mitch leans forward and pats her backside. Okay, he's high. Has to be.

"Exactly how much morphine has he had?"

"He's been cut off." She glares over at Mitch. "Haven't you, sweetheart?"

"Yeah, baby. Whatever you say."

I cough to try to cover my laugh. "Geez, I'm sorry. So why is he still here? Is it the leg?"

"Damn shark tried to take my leg off, brother."

I roll my eyes at Mitch and tell him to chill while I talk to the nurse.

"He's not far off actually. The teeth of the demon were very shark-like, and he could have lost his leg. If not for the healing capabilities of his system, he probably would have. He'll be fine in a few days."

She finishes up the dressing on his calf and pulls a blanket up to his waist.

"How did you get involved in all of this?"

"Mary is my mother. She went to school with your dad." She leans back against the counter after tossing her gloves in the trash. "I don't think she wanted to tell me at first, I mean, with you guys being wolves and all, but I can be very persistent."

"Well, I'm very thankful for your help. Truly, I am." I extend my hand, realizing I never introduced myself. "I'm Denver, by the way."

"I know who you are. My mother doesn't shut up about the handsome Bolivar and his boys. I think she's had a crush on him for years. Oh God, I don't know why I said that. She's happily married. My mother. Please don't say anything."

I'm not sure how to take this girl. Is she flirting with me? "I won't say anything. And I still didn't catch your name."

She rubs her hands down her leg and finally accepts my handshake. "Sorry. It's Taylor."

"So we're clear here, I'm engaged."

She smiles and glances at Mitch. "I know that too. Your brother on the other hand, well, he thinks we're an item. When he woke up for the first time yesterday, he started yelling that I was his mate."

"What? He used the word mate?"

She bites on her thumbnail. "Yes. I talked to my mom, and I know what that means. And I'm not a wolf, so it's weird, but then maybe it's the morphine talking. I suppose time will tell." She tries to busy herself by checking his vitals. Mitch has dozed off.

I've heard drugs do funny things to people, but my gut tells me that's not the cause of his actions. I've never seen Mitch so forward before, not even with Emily. Shit. Could she really be his mate? "How old are you, Taylor?"

"Twenty-two."

I can't help but laugh. It would be like Mitch to not only mate with an older woman, but a human as well. Sounds right up his alley. If I'm reading her correctly, she doesn't mind the idea. She's drawn to him already.

"It was nice to meet you, Taylor. It's obvious that Mitch is in good hands, so I'm going to go spend time with my bride to be."

"She's beautiful. Jada. I helped clean her up yesterday."

"She certainly is." I take a few steps and pause at the curtain. "You seem like a nice girl, and grounded. Mitch could use someone like you in his life. He's spunky but has a good heart."

Taylor picks another nail to bite on this time. "Thanks, and I'll keep that in mind."

I shrug. "For whatever it's worth, I don't think it was the morphine."

. . .

ON MY WAY to the kitchen I run into Lisa.

"Were you with Jada?"

She swipes a tear on her cheek. "Yes. No change. It's awful. My baby girl lying there so lifeless."

"She's in there and I'm going to convince her to come back to us."

Lisa reaches out to pat my arm. I don't think she's ever touched me before. "If anyone can make her come back, it's you."

"How's Roland?"

"Rather well. I'm taking him home soon. I'll be back, but please notify me if there's any change."

"Of course. It's none of my business, but are you guys going to work out your marriage?"

A smile replaces the sorrow on her face. "We are. I never stopped loving him. I was hurt and angry when he left. I didn't understand all of this." She waves her hand in the air. "I wish he had handled his wolf business differently and let me in." She shrugs. "Anyway, water under the bridge, as they say."

"Jada will be so happy."

Her smile falters. She's not sure Jada is coming back to us. That's okay. I have enough faith for the both of us.

I stop in the kitchen to grab a bowl of soup and something to drink. I throw my antibiotics on the tray and head back to Jada's room. It's been over thirty minutes, so Mom should be ready for me to return.

"Knock, knock."

"Come in, Denver. She's all done."

I push the door open with my foot and take my tray to the bed. I scoot up beside Jada and kiss her forehead.

"Hey, my love."

I situate the tray in my lap so I can eat. "Thanks for the soup. I'm famished."

"That's a definite improvement. From what I gather, the doctor had to constantly pump anti-venom in your IV. And you still puked for hours."

"Yuck. I'm glad I don't remember." I take a few bites of soup while Mom goes in the bathroom. She and Emily emerge with a load of dirty sheets and towels. "Jada's nice and clean. Did you guys give her a bath?"

Mom rolls her eyes and Emily huffs. I glance back and forth between the two. "What?"

Emily leaves with the laundry, so my mother answers my question. "We gave her a bath yesterday, but *someone* slept with her and got her all dirty again. As well as the sheets."

"Oh, sorry."

"It's fine. I knew you'd be here as soon as you figured out what was happening. I was hoping to get you in the shower first, but you barely made it to the bed."

I point to the cut on her forehead. "How are you holding up? Have you had any rest?"

"Your father all but forced me to get some sleep last night. I'm well rested and my forehead is closing up nicely."

"Thank you, Mom, for everything."

She leans over and ruffles my hair. "Silly boy, you don't have to thank me. I love you."

"Love you too, Mom."

"I've got rounds to make. I'll come back by before bedtime to check in."

"All right. Hey, send Dad this way when he wakes up."

"I'm sure it will be his first stop. Your father has singlehandedly taken care of Jada."

The room becomes blurry as my eyes fill with tears. Will the man never cease to amaze me? If I can be half the man he is, I'll be a damn good person and pack leader.

I inhale my lunch and shove the tray to the nightstand. I lie on my side next to Jada.

"I thought they'd never leave us alone. Your room has a revolving door."

My fingers itch to touch her. I cup her face with my hand, running my thumb over her soft lips. "I have so much to tell you, and so many questions. Where to begin." I pause to gather my thoughts. "I'm so proud of you, Jada. For the life of me, I can't figure out how you took out a greater demon by yourself, but you did. I'm a tad angry that you took off on your own, but damn if I wouldn't have done the same thing. I know you were protecting us. Everyone is doing well, healing, and resting. I haven't heard otherwise, so I think it's safe to say we all made it. Some of us were getting our asses kicked, but the second you took out that demon, the battle ended. You're my hero, Jada. I love you so much. You didn't have to give up your life for us, but that's what you were willing to do." I take a deep breath. "My dad, too. Damn. He's amazing. You're not going to believe the basement. He's got a whole flipping hospital down there. He and Roland have been busy. Your dad is doing well, by the way. Your mom said she was taking him home today. She's worried about you. Emily has been here too, and Grainger, although I've yet to bump into him. Of course, I've been a little out of it."

I trace the outline of her face and play with her hair. "Our wedding is in two weeks. Can you believe it? You need to hurry and wake up or my mom will have everything planned without you. You know how she is. You're going to be stunning. It makes my heart do funny things thinking about you walking down the aisle in your dress. Oh and don't forget about Hawaii. You and me, on the beach, drinking something cold with our toes in the sand. You in a bikini. Me in a speedo. Just kidding. I think we both know what happens to me when you're in a bikini. Anyway, next time it won't matter, cause we'll be married."

I lean over and kiss her face, head, and neck. "Sorry, but it's hard not to kiss you while talking about our honeymoon. So, what else? You've got graduation coming up. That's a big deal." I stop to plant more kisses down her arm. I laugh thinking back on my interaction with Taylor. "Oh, Jada, you're going to love this. Mitch may have found his mate. He's pretty doped up on morphine at the moment, but I think it's legit. She's perfect for him though. I think you'll like her. The crazy part is, she's not a wolf, and she's like four years older than he is. I mean, doesn't that sound like Mitch? I'm excited for him. I mean if nothing else, you need to come back so we can give him a hard time."

I've been holding it together, but a tidal wave of uncertainty crashes over me. "That's bullshit and we both know it. I need you to come back for *me*. Baby, I'm selfish. If you're in some beautiful place right now trying to decide whether to move on or come back—please come back. I know that's probably a terrible thing to say, but I need you. We have so much life to live. I have so much to give. I want to make you happy. I want to grow old with you. Please, baby, please, if you have the choice—come home."

A KNOCK at the door wakes me.

"Come in." I adjust myself to a sitting position as Grainger comes in the room. He plops in a chair next to my side of the bed. "You look like shit, dude."

"I know. I've been awake for forty-eight hours, living off of energy drinks."

"Are you leaving?"

"Yeah, I'm taking Emily home too, so we can both get some sleep. We'll be back in the morning to check on Jada."

"I appreciate all your help. Jada has two really great friends."

Grainger checks the door and then leans forward. "I'm going to ask Emily out. We were talking a little before this, but watching her work her ass off these last couple of days—I don't know, she's pretty cool."

"You hear that, baby? Your matchmaking skills have paid off."

"What do you mean?"

"She's been plotting to get the two of you together."

"No way."

"Yes way."

"Huh. So you think Emily will say yes?"

"I'm damn sure of it."

"Wow, cool. Okay, well, I'm heading out to crash until further notice."

"I promise to call when she wakes up."

A slight smile passes his lips as he gets to his feet. "I like your attitude. When and not if. She loves you too much not to."

"Thanks, man."

THE REST of the evening and the next day are more of the same. Jada's room has a constant flow of visitors. All of her bandages have come off and her neck is ninety percent healed. She'll have a scar, but it will be tiny in size compared to the massive sacrifice she made to get it. I talk to her. A lot. I'm getting ready to find a show on television when Mitch comes in without knocking.

"How's my sister?"

I jump off the bed to hug him. "It's about time your lazy ass got out of bed. How's the leg?"

He turns to show me his left calf. "Almost good as new. Gotta couple of nice scars."

"Is that all you got, brother?" Mitch is radiating lust.

"Shit, you know?"

I motion for Mitch to sit with me on the bed. I take Jada's hand and bring it to my mouth for a kiss, then hold her hand in mine. I turn my attention back to my brother. His face turns pale. We both start to speak at the same time, and I nod for him to go ahead.

"What the hell happened? Is she gonna be okay?"

"No one knows for sure what happened. Apparently when we were covered in fog, Jada was taking on the greater demon by herself. I don't know why she went to the lake. It's a mystery until Jada wakes up to tell us. And she will wake up."

"Damn straight. You holding up okay?"

"Yeah, ya know, chilling with my baby. Sooo, I met Taylor yesterday."

He groans and closes his eyes. "Apparently I was a little frisky while under the influence. Who knows what she must think of me."

His expression is that of a man in pain. "God, Denver, I freaking love her. I'm falling apart on the inside, and I don't know what to do."

I understand all too well. "I get it, brother, I do. Is she still here?"

"No, and that's what sucks so bad. She went back to her apartment in Diamond Hill to get some sleep. She's attending DHU for nursing so it's not like she'll be around. Short of moving up there, I don't know how I'll get to be close to her."

"That does suck. But hey, you're getting ready to graduate. You can move up there in a few weeks and attend DHU. Didn't you apply there?"

"I did and I got in, but I never really wanted to go. I was hoping to hang around here like you did. This is our home. I love it here."

"You can always come back. Think of it as an extended vacation."

Mitch rubs his temples. "Shit. I'm so confused."

I grip his shoulder. "It'll be okay. Talk to her. You did get her number right?"

"Duh. I'm not that dumb."

"You're not dumb at all. I know you better than anyone, and I see how hard you work at your grades. You could probably go into your first year of college as a sophomore with all the college credits you have."

"No shit, that's why I took all those courses, to get out of college earlier. I don't know, maybe we could work something out going back and forth. Diamond Hill's not that far."

"You'll have to decide how to handle all of this, but I don't think you'll be able to stay apart for days at a time. Jada and I can barely go hours."

He laughs. "You guys are highly combustible, that's for sure. I honestly believe you and Jada got an extra dose of the love bug."

"Maybe. Even if that's true, your attraction to her will only grow stronger, and it will be painful to be apart. At the very least, I'd have Dad reach out to some contacts on an apartment near campus."

Mitch rolls his eyes. "He already is. You're all trying to ship me off to college."

I punch him in the arm. "You stupid shit, you know I'll miss you like crazy. Like you said, Diamond Hill isn't that far, you can come home any time you want. Or Jada and I can come visit you."

"Yeah, I guess." Mitch slides off the bed and goes over to Jada. "Hurry up and wake up, sis. I need your help." He kisses her cheek and backs away. "I'm gonna go find some food. You need anything?"

"Nah, Mom brings my meals in here so I don't have to leave."

"Gotcha. I'll come by in the morning. I may go to school tomorrow."

"Oh right, tomorrow is Monday. Will you pick up Jada's school-work for her?"

"Sure thing."

Mitch leaves the room and Mom comes in. Then Dad. Then Roland and Lisa. Grainger and Emily stop by, as well as Uncle Alexander and Aunt Vashti. Everyone wants to know how Jada is doing. Damn revolving door. A part of me wants to lock it to keep them all out, but it's selfish of me to even want that. It's ten o'clock Sunday night before I get her all to myself.

I brush her hair from her face. "Hey, baby. You're a popular lady. Lots of people are anxiously waiting for you to pull through. No one more than me. Mitch might be a close second. He wants your advice on this Taylor situation. Poor guy is a mess. I thought I would give him hell, but I actually feel bad for the guy. On a side note, Emily and Grainger were holding hands when they came in. I know that makes you happy. And your parents, Lord, they can't stop touching each other. Kinda weirded me out, but I thought you would want to know." I stop talking to leave a trail of kisses down her neck. "I miss you. So much. I'm not going anywhere, so if this is some ploy to get rid of me, it won't work. You're stuck with me, Jada Brooks. Soon to be Jada Stone. God, I love the sound of that. Jada Stone. Less than two weeks now. And it's the last week of school. You need to wake up, baby, you've got lots to do. Places to go. Babies to make." Shit. I try to talk to her without crying, but it's next to impossible. Tears stream down my face. "You see what you've done to me? I'm a blub-bering hot mess. If I didn't love you so much, it wouldn't hurt so much. You need to come back and make me whole again because I'm a shell of the man I was without you. You want that on your conscience? You know if you leave me here, I'll die too. So get your ass up and make me the happiest man in the whole damn world."

Guilt-tripping might not be the right approach, but I'll try anything. Anything at all.

I pick up the remote and settle in beside Jada. "What do you want to watch?" I glance at her and then back at the television. "I'll pick this time, but the next one is all you."

At 2:00 a.m. I call it a night. I kiss Jada's sweet lips and curl in beside her, saying a prayer that today will be the day she wakes up. It's only been three days, and she went through the depths of Hades and back, but I need her. Could I live without her? Technically, yes, I could. Do I want to live without her? Hell. No.

CHAPTER TWENTY-FOUR

JADA

I run my hands along the walls of a narrow tunnel. I can't shake the notion that I've left something beautiful behind, but a faint light beckons me forward—out of the darkness. I'm not afraid as I take the necessary steps toward the shimmering door. In fact, I have perfect peace and a clarity of mind about the things to come.

Life is like a vapor or sand slipping through your fingers. There is no promise of tomorrow, or even your next breath. Make the most of the time you're given.

These are the thoughts swirling around me as I approach the door. Somehow I have the knowledge that I've stared death in the face and come out on the other side. This opportunity is precious.

I reach out and grab the doorknob. It twists easily beneath my fingers.

This is my time. It won't be easy street, all rainbows and ponies. Sometimes life is hard, but this girl is going to make the most of the time I've been given. I'm going to live life to the fullest. Will I screw it up and take things for granted? Of course. But I'll pick back up, brush off, and keep moving forward. Until my last breath, I'm going to run a damn good race. *And that race starts today,* I think to myself as I pry my eyes open.

Birds are singing their early morning songs and a tree branch scratches at the window in the breeze. Moonlight spills in the dark room, fighting for the right to stay, but the gray horizon tells a different story. A new day is dawning. I reach for my phone on the nightstand to check the time and get tangled up on tubes coming from my hand. I turn the other way to find Denver sleeping beside me. In this moment his face is the most wonderful, gorgeous, powerful, sexy thing I've ever laid eyes on. He's almost too peaceful to stir awake. Almost.

With my free hand, I gently stroke his stubble-covered jaw. He stirs slightly as I trace his lips.

"Denver."

"Hmm." He wiggles in closer, still in la-la land.

"Denver, wake up."

His eyes blink several times and then he rubs his hand down the scruff of his jaw. When his eyes meet mine, they become bright and full.

"Jada?"

"Hey."

He sits up in the bed and grabs my face. "Jada. Oh my God, Jada. You're awake. Shit. Am I awake? Please tell me I'm not dreaming."

I place my hand on the back of his neck and pull his lips to mine for a quick kiss. "You're not dreaming. I'm here."

He plasters kisses all over my face. "Baby, I love you so much."

I giggle as he kisses my neck and collarbone, confessing his love over and over.

"I love you too." He's yet to give me a real kiss. I point to my lips. "Denver, I'm not broken, you can kiss me."

"Are you sure?"

I growl in response.

"Damn, baby, I missed you." His lips are hungry yet tender. His hands slide up my arms and grip my shoulders, securing me in place. A trail of fire scorches my skin as he leaves my lips to venture down to my neck. I ride the euphoric wave of his want that rushes me without abandon. I'm delirious when he pushes away.

Denver's chest rises and falls in quick succession. "Shit."

I rest on my side and kiss his shoulder. "No kidding.

"I can't wait to marry you, Jada Brooks."

"I could make time in my schedule for later today."

He turns to face me, kissing my forehead. "Still my bloody fish. I will marry you and it's going to be damn good—but not today. And you won't be in a hospital gown with an IV in your arm."

"How long is that exactly? I don't know what day it is."

"Less than two weeks. It's Monday. Graduation is this weekend."

"Oh wow. I was out for three days?"

"Yep. Three long, torturous days."

"I could hear you, you know? Talking to me."

"Was it the guilt trip that brought you back?'

"No. Just you."

He closes his eyes and takes a deep breath. When his eyes flash open his gaze pierces my soul. "I'm going to love you forever."

"I know."

Denver kisses my nose and rolls off the bed. He pulls on a shirt and pushes his hand through his hair. "I better wake up the crew. They'll be pissed if I don't let them know. Especially Mitch. It will be a busy day."

"It's okay. I'm ready."

Denver nods and leaves the room. His voice booms throughout the house as he yells for everyone to get out of bed. Mitch is the first to arrive.

"Jada! Hell yeah!" He pounces on the bed, causing me to popcorn up and down. "I knew you wouldn't leave me hanging. How the heck are ya?"

"Pretty great, actually. How about you? Were you badly hurt?"

"Nothing I can't handle. Anyway, thanks to you, I met my mate."

"Oh yeah? Then you're welcome. What's she like?"

He falls back on the pillow next to mine. "Amazing. Hot. Kind. Compassionate. Smart. So damn smart. I don't know how in the hell I'm going to win her over. She's out of my league."

"I'm not buying it. She's lucky to have you, and I won't mind telling her so."

"This is why I love you. I seriously need your help with all this."

"Mitch, I love you too, and I'm always here for you."

"Jada!" Aurar comes running in with Bolivar hot on her heels. "Oh, Jada. You're awake."

Tears stream down her face as she squats by the bed. "You look wonderful. Doesn't she look great, Bolivar?"

"Beautiful as ever. But how are you really?"

"Happy. Healthy. Blessed. And hungry."

Aurar laughs. "That's my girl. I'm going to go make the biggest breakfast ever, with lots of coffee."

"That sounds perfect. Thank you." Aurar rushes off with her mission face on. I glance up at Bolivar. "What are the chances of getting rid of these?" I hold up my arm full of tubes.

He drops down, taking up the place Aurar vacated. "Jada, I am so proud of you." His gaze falls on Mitch, and then over to Denver who's now standing in the doorway. "When you're up to it, we all want to know what happened out there. Later, not right now. Not many people take on a greater demon and live to tell about it."

"I wasn't sure I *would* live, but I did what I had to do to protect my family."

Bolivar laughs. "We thought we were protecting you. You are an amazing young lady, Jada."

I take his hand between mine. "You all would have done the same for me. I'm happy to get another day. Another chance to live. Another chance to love."

Bolivar kisses the back of my hand. "My sweet princess." He chokes out the last words, trying to keep his composure. After a few seconds, he stands. "Let's check your vitals and get you out of these darn lines."

Mitch kisses my cheek. "That's my cue to go take a shower."

"All right."

Bolivar waves Denver forward. "Son, you want to give me a hand?"

"Yes sir."

Bolivar examines me from head to toe. He listens to my heart, lungs, and other organs. He checks all my limbs, takes my temperature, my blood pressure, and my sugar. He then inspects my neck and deems me healthy.

When he slides out the needle, I rub my arm.

"Thank you. So, can I go to school?"

Bolivar chuckles as he replaces his equipment into his bag. "I don't know if it's the best idea. I'd like to keep an eye on you today."

"I promise I'm fine. It's the last week of school, and I have a lot of tests and exams. Plus graduation practice and other senior stuff. Please?"

He locks eyes with Denver, who shrugs. "Don't look at me, you're the doctor."

"All right, fine. But if it gets to be too much, you text Denver right away."

"I will, promise."

Before exiting the room, Bolivar kisses my check. "I'll leave you to get ready."

"Thank you for taking care of me."

"It was my pleasure, Jada."

Denver sits on the edge of the bed beside me. "You sure you want to go to school?"

"Positive. There's so much to do this week. Today is the senior picnic."

"Will you allow me drive you and pick you up?"

"Mitch can take me."

He leans in until his breath tickles my lips. "I'm well aware of that." He teases me with light kisses on my upper and bottom lip. I try to close in, but he keeps enough distance that I'm unable to reach his mouth. "*I* want to take you to school."

I don't know whether to push him away or grab his shirt and pull him to me. I decide it's best to not start something we can't finish. I lay my hand on his chest and push him back. "Okay, okay. You can take me to school."

"I knew you'd see it my way."

"I hate you."

"You keep telling yourself that." He scoots off the bed and stretches.

I catch a glimpse of his abs as he raises his arms. "Get out of my room, you big tease, or I'll make it very difficult for you to leave."

Denver holds his hands out in front of him as he backs out of my room. "Yes ma'am." He's smiling as he backs out completely and clicks the door closed.

I woke everyone up so early, I have plenty of time to shower and get ready. Before dressing, I inspect my body for injuries. The only lingering evidence of the battle is the scar on my neck, some light bruising, and a few tender muscles. The three-day transformation is incomprehensible. I take the time to dry my hair and straighten it, letting it cascade down my back. I apply a light amount of makeup to my sun-kissed face and then get dressed for school.

Laughter greets my ears as I make my way to the kitchen. The sound of joy squeezes my heart. I round the corner and bump into Denver's solid chest.

Heat fills his bright blue eyes as they trail over my body without a hint of apology. "Damn."

He's also had a shower and is wearing khaki shorts and a blue polo. "I was thinking the same thing."

He pushes me back toward the hall trying to keep me hidden from his family. "Marry me. Right now."

There's absolutely nothing wrong with my heart. It's racing a hundred miles an hour. I swallow hard and lick my lips. "Don't you know better than to poke a tiger?"

"Jada, is that you?"

My eyebrows go up at my mom's voice.

"I called your mom."

I lean into Denver and whisper in his ear. "You remember all those times I wanted you to marry me? You know what they say about payback."

Denver groans as I slide my body across his to escape him. I leave him in the hall to cool down.

"Hey, Mom."

"Jada!" She runs at me and grabs me for a hug. "Thank God."

Roland joins us, wrapping us both in his strong arms. We stand in the kitchen in a group hug, no one wanting to make the move to end it. Finally, Roland releases his hold.

Mom holds me at arm's length. "You're absolutely gorgeous!" She starts to cry and pulls me back in her arms. "I thought I'd lost you."

There's nothing I can say, so I give her the time she needs. After a couple of minutes, she composes herself. "I can't believe you're going to school. You should rest today."

"Ugh. Not you too. I'm totally fine." I spin in a circle for her inspection. "See? Good as new."

Everyone discusses my health as we fix our plates and sit at the table to partake in the breakfast feast Aurar has made. They fuss over whether or not I should attend school, so I ignore them and focus on my food.

The last meal I ate felt like—my last meal. This meal is a new beginning. Every bite explodes with flavor on my tongue.

I don't realize I'm moaning until Denver squeezes my leg under the table.

He leans over to whisper in my ear. "Cut that shit out."

"I'm sorry, it's so good."

He rolls his eyes but laughs as he goes back to his breakfast.

The doorbell rings and I glance at Denver. "Probably Grainger and Emily."

My chair scrapes the wood floor and almost tips over at my haste to answer the door.

They rush in. More group hugging. But long after Emily sets me free, Grainger holds on. I lay my head on my best friend's chest and breathe him in. Pine. So many memories come flooding in, it's all I can do not to lose it. These arms have held me together so many times, I've lost count.

He releases me and steps back next to Emily. He grabs her hand, and they lace their fingers together.

"You guys look good together."

Emily blushes, which speaks volumes in and of itself. "Thanks.

We're so glad you're okay, Jada. Grainger was about to lose his mind worrying about you. We all were."

"Seems it wasn't my time to go." I point to the kitchen. "You guys want some breakfast?"

We get halfway through the living room when Grainger grabs my elbow. The three of us stop simultaneously, curious as to what he's going to say.

"Uh, Emily, do you mind if I talk to Jada for a second?"

"Sure. I'll say hey to everyone."

Grainger walks to the couch and sits on the edge. I follow suit. He shuffles his feet on the carpet and moves around a vase on the coffee table. He looks up with a tight smile, his fingers going up to the scar on his forehead.

"You remember the day I got this scar?"

"Of course I do. I was frantic to hear from you or your mom. I thought you might die or something. All that blood pouring from your head freaked me out."

"You know what I remember?"

"What?"

"You kissed me on the cheek that night when we came by to show you my stitches."

I smile at the memory. "Yeah, I guess I did. I was so glad you were okay. You were my glue, Grainger. My rock. I didn't want to lose you."

He grabs my hand and brings it to his chest. He swallows and glances out the window. "I'm sorry. I don't know exactly what I wanted to say." His eyes light on me once more. "I needed you too, just in a different way. You always made me feel like a superhero. A better version of who I actually was. You gave me confidence because you always believed in me. When you were in a coma..."

A tear slips down his cheek. Then mine. "Grainger—"

"No, let me finish." I motion for him to continue. "I love you, Jada, and I always will. Honestly, I'm still getting over you and the future I had planned out in my mind of us together. But I'm okay with it because watching Denver these last few days has left me no doubt you're with the person you're meant to be with. It's bizarre the way his love for you radiates from his very soul. I know he's going to take good care of you, and you're happy, and that's what matters to me the most. And I like Emily. A lot. I'm excited to explore this thing between us. I know we were okay, but I want to say I'm really okay. And I wanted to say thank you for allowing me the privilege of being your friend."

I punch him in the arm. "That's for ruining my makeup." I swipe a tear from my face. Then I wrap both arms around his neck and kiss his cheek. "And that's for being one of the best people I've ever known. I love you, Grainger Nelson."

He jumps to his feet, and the sudden movement takes me by surprise. "Enough of that." Grainger blows out a long breath and holds out his hand to pull me up. "Come on, it's almost time to leave for school."

Denver scoops me into his side when I get back to the table. I'm with the man I love and all of my favorite people are in this room. The demon battle is behind us, I'm close to graduating, and my wedding is in twelve days. It doesn't get any better than this.

THE NEXT SEVERAL days fly by. Senior year has come and gone. Mitch and I are in cap and gown, headed to the school gymnasium for the ceremony. He's decided to take the college plunge and attend Diamond Hill University. I'm staying home with Denver and taking online courses. Life clicks along. Time waits for no one. She paces herself, steady and sure. Seconds become minutes, become hours, become days, become months, and then become years. Even though you know the truth, the perception of time is not always the same. Like now. Don't get me wrong, I'm excited to walk across that stage and get my diploma, but I'm even more excited to become Mrs. Stone. This next week may be the longest of my life.

"You're quiet. What are you thinking about?" Mitch interrupts my evaluation of time.

"I'm going to miss you."

"Shit, Jada." He reaches over and grabs my hand for a squeeze. "I'm gonna miss you too. If it weren't for Taylor, I'd be staying home. She shot my original plan all to hell."

"I think you'll like college once you get there and get settled."

"Maybe. I didn't know I was a homebody until it was time to make a final decision. I love it here. My family is everything. Denver…" He chokes out his name.

"You can come home anytime you want. Every weekend works for me."

Mitch blows out a frustrated breath. "I guess that will depend on Taylor. I'm not sure we want the same things. She's difficult. Independent. Stubborn. Hell, I don't even know if she's into me or not."

"I'm sorry, who are you, and what have you done with Mitchell Stone? The Mitch I know wouldn't back down from a challenge. The Mitch I know is confident, strong, and sure of himself. Cocky even. Where's that guy?"

"He met a girl that turned his world upside down, and she scares him to death."

"Be yourself. Trust me when I say she won't be able to resist."

He glances at me with a smirk. "Are you secretly crushing on me, Jada?"

"There he is. The Mitch I know and love. And eww, no. You're my twin brother."

Mitch laughs but then pinches his lips in a straight line. "I wish you were going to DHU with me."

"Grainger and Emily will be there. And isn't that where Rieder is going?"

"Yeah he is. I guess you're right. It'll be fine." He pulls into the almost-full lot and parks the car. "Let's do this thing."

His smile doesn't reach his eyes, and it makes my insides hurt. I want him to be happy. He's been thrust into an unfamiliar journey, and he'll have to figure out how to make the best of it. Sadly, I can't do it for him.

I put my arm in his as we walk to the gym. Ending one chapter and starting another. Like I said, time marches on.

CHAPTER TWENTY-FIVE

DENVER

I can't sleep. My alarm is set for six, but I turn it off and throw on some running clothes. Grabbing my earbuds, I ease down the stairs hoping not to wake anyone. The aroma of coffee greets me as I round the corner toward the kitchen. My mom is staring out the window, mug in hand, lost in thought.

"Couldn't sleep either?" I lean over to tighten my shoelace.

"It's not every day my son gets married."

I cross the room and kiss her cheek. "No, I suppose not."

"What will I do with my boys gone?"

"Mom. I'll be a five-minute walk from here."

"It's not the same. And Mitch is running off to college to pursue his mate. Next thing you know, he'll be getting married too."

"Did you want us to become monks and live at home forever?"

"Yes."

I snatch a water bottle from the fridge and take several long gulps. "If that were true, you wouldn't have raised such fine, strong, outstanding young men."

"Stop being so grown-up and right."

She ruffles my hair like she has since I was a boy. I lean into a lunge to stretch my legs. "So what time are you girls leaving for your appointment? You've made it very clear I'm not to see Jada today, so I'm wondering how we manage that all being in the same house?"

"Oh, right." She walks over to the bar and shuffles through a stack of papers. "Here's your schedule."

My eyebrows knit together. "I have a schedule? What the heck, Mom? This thing tells me what time to go to the bathroom."

"You want to get your butt whooped on your wedding day?"

"No ma'am."

"Then stick to the schedule."

"Yes ma'am." After a few more stretches I head for the door. "I guess it's okay to squeeze in a run since my schedule doesn't officially start until eight?"

If eyes had daggers. Note to self. Do not cross your mother on your wedding day.

Starting at a steady pace, I jog down the path toward the cabin. I'm dragging Mitch down later to prepare the place for my wedding night. The mere thought of it raises my body temperature. After today, Jada and I will be living in our new home. Together. Married. No restrictions or boundaries keeping us from loving each other fully—mind, soul, and body. We will be one.

Shit. I push myself harder, trying to leave some of this pent-up testosterone and longing behind. For now, anyway. It won't last long, the woman drives me mad.

The crazy thing is, it's not all about the sex. Obviously, I want to make love to my wife, but the sex is only a tiny portion of the life I dream of with Jada. There's so much for us to experience together. So many things I want to do, so many places to visit. Life with my best friend, exploring and navigating this wonderful union called marriage. And kids. I know Jada will be an amazing mother. Can the world handle a mini me running around? My mother would say no.

Sweat drips from my forehead. I strip off my shirt and use it to wipe my face. Several miles of running hasn't done a damn thing to settle my nerves or make this day go any faster. By nerves, I mean excitement. There's not a nervous cell in my body, no apprehension whatsoever, at making Jada my bride.

I slip in the garage and pry open the back door just a sliver. It's only seven in the morning, but Jada could be awake. The kitchen is quiet, but I yell out hello anyway. No one responds. My mother will hang me from the gallows if I screw this up. I jump inside, grab another water and a banana, and run upstairs.

I stop outside Mitch's door and tap lightly.

"Mom, I'm still naked."

I push open the door and close it with my foot. "Like she would care."

"No shit. She's already been in here twice." Mitch slides up to a sitting position. He reaches over for a sheet of paper on his desk. "Here. You left your holy schedule in the kitchen."

"Oh right. Is there a breakfast time on this thing? I'm starving." I take the schedule and sit on the bed beside Mitch.

"Dude, get off my sheets, you're a sweaty mess."

"Shut up." I skim my finger down the length of the itinerary. "Sweet. Breakfast for the boys is in the study at eight."

Mitch grumbles something about no peace and gets out of bed. He strolls to his bathroom and is in fact naked. Not that either of us care. When you grow up changing back and forth from human to wolf, you're going to catch a glimpse of each other's junk.

I finish my banana and glance over the time slots for the next few hours. Mitch shuffles to his dresser and pulls out a pair of shorts.

"Don't get dressed on my account. I like your cute butt."

"I've heard that one before." He shoves his feet into his shorts and drops back on the bed.

"You wish."

"Yeah, yeah. Whatever. You're cocky cause you know you're getting laid tonight."

"Hell yeah, I am. And I waited longer than most. I'll be twenty-one soon. You've found your mate and you're still eighteen, so don't cry on my shoulder."

"Still. Shit, dude, you're going to have sex. Tonight."

"God, shut up. I came in here for a distraction, not to talk about sex."

Mitch stands up on the bed and starts grinding his hips and singing. "Let's talk about sex, baby, let's talk about you and me—"

I shove him down with a pillow to the face.

"Oh, hell no. Big mistake, brother."

"Bring it."

Mitch snags a pillow and the fight is on. And like all our pillow fights, it ends when somebody gets hurt.

I rub the back of my head as I sit up from the floor. "I have a headache."

He shrugs. "You wanted a distraction."

"Speaking of distraction, what time will Taylor be here?"

"She has a lab this morning, so she said she'd be here around two."

"How's it going with you two?"

"Terrible. This long-distance shit is for the birds. On top of that, I don't think she likes me very much."

"What? No way."

"I'm serious. Our chemistry is nothing like what you and Jada have. Hell, I had more of an effect on Emily."

"That can't be. Surely you're reading her wrong."

"I don't think so."

"You're sure she's your mate?"

Mitch stands and extends a hand to help me up. "We better go eat breakfast. It's eight o'clock."

"Not until you answer my question." I cross my arms over my bare chest.

"If it were my life or hers, I'd pick hers every time. I'd let a train run me over to protect her. I envision our future together. Our unborn children. My heart aches to be near her, and my fingers long to touch her. I want to rip her clothes—"

"Damn. Okay, I get it. She's your mate."

"Don't look at me like that. We're not worried about my shit today, it's your wedding day. Do I need to remind you you're getting laid tonight?"

I shove him in the hall. We're both in shorts and nothing else.

Mom's schedule didn't say we had to be dressed for breakfast. "You're such a prick."

"You love me."

"Yeah, I do."

OTHER THAN DAD'S snarky comment about us showing up half naked, breakfast is a good diversion. Roland and Grainger join us since they're both part of the wedding. Roland is helping Dad with the ceremony, and Grainger is walking Jada down the aisle. Mitch will stand with me and Emily with Jada. Our wedding will be short, sweet, simple, and perfect.

All the guys are meeting at one for pictures, so Mitch and I have plenty of time to chuck Mom's schedule and decorate the cabin. I bought enough candles to burn down a city and enough roses to start a flower shop. Her favorite Andy Grammer CD is on repeat in the bedroom, and our fluffy navy-blue robes hang by the jet tub. I've put up several pictures of us in the last few days that Jada hasn't seen, trying to make this a home. There's a spot above the bed for a canvas wedding photo, yet to be taken. A bottle of champagne is on ice and a fruit tray is in the fridge, complete with chocolate-covered strawberries. My girl is worth this and so much more.

After lunch, we get dressed and go downstairs for pictures. I smile, click after click, until my cheeks hurt and my mom is satisfied the photographer has gotten every possible angle. It's gonna suck for the girls as I'm sure their photo session will take longer than ours.

The deck is bustling with energy and chaos. The DJ is setting up at the far end, past what would normally be our pool. Dad paid a pretty penny to have a special decking made to cover the pool. It is now the dance floor. Beyond the deck, the caterer is barking orders under the massive white tent. People scurry about carrying dishes and flowers. The transformation is unbelievable. Mom has truly outdone herself. And Jada, of course.

I'm trying to take it all in when Mitch pulls me by the arm.

"Dude, I'm starting to sweat. We need to go inside, it's almost time for the girls' photoshoot."

"What's next on our schedule?"

Mitch pulls the list from his pocket. "Beer in the study."

"Now, that's what I'm talking about."

Once again, the men are bound to the study. At least this time, we have a couple of cold beers to keep us busy. Dad rolls his eyes when Mitch and I throw off our jackets and shirts. I assure him it's to benefit all. I'm thankful that the sun will be on the other side of the house by the time the wedding starts.

When the girls are tucked safely away in Jada's room, Mitch and I go upstairs to wipe our pits. I'm straightening his tie when there's a knock at the door.

"If you're a guy, come in."

"Do dads count as guys?"

"Last time I checked."

"You boys are handsome."

"Thanks, Dad. You clean up pretty good yourself."

Mitch walks to the door. "Taylor got held up at school, but she's finally here. I'm going to run down and say hello. I also need to kiss my sister-to-be before the wedding."

"No fair," I whine.

"Mitch, don't be long. We're to be in our places in half an hour." Dad says in his don't-screw-this-up tone.

He pats his pocket. "No worries, Dad. My trusty schedule is right next to my heart." Mitch darts out before Dad can respond.

"He'll be late." Dad says, laughing. "It will be good for him to go off to college. He needs to grow up a little."

"Maybe so, but I'm going to miss him."

"I know you will. You boys have been stuck together at the hip since Mitch was old enough to walk. Of course, you'll have other things now to occupy your time." He wiggles his eyebrows at me, and I wince.

"You didn't come in here to give me a sex talk, did you?"

"Relax, Denver. There's nothing else I can tell you that we didn't cover when you were twelve. Trust me, you'll figure it out."

"Ugh. Can we change the subject?"

He chuckles and points to the bed. "Have a seat."

I do as I'm told and sit on the edge of the bed.

"I was going to ask how you're holding up, but I can tell you have peace."

"I've never been more sure of anything in my life. I probably would have married Jada the day we met."

"Yet you denied her when she asked because you were concerned for her best interests."

"Exactly. I wanted to put her needs before my own."

"And that, my son, is what makes a marriage great. Prefer her above all else. Treat her like the queen that she is. Love her like there's no tomorrow."

"I will, Dad, I swear."

"I have no doubt you two will be happy. It brings your mom and me such joy to watch you succeed in all areas of life. We're proud of you, son. One day, you and Jada will lead the Forrest City pack, and I can honestly say you'll be a fine leader."

"Thank you, Dad. Your faith in me has pushed me to be the person I am today. I love you."

"I love you too, son."

This hug feels significant. Different. Like all the hugs before were man to boy, and this one is man to man.

"So, you ready to get married?"

"You better believe it."

We start toward the door when Mitch comes barreling through. "Told you. Not late. What did I miss? Did you have a heart to heart?"

Dad winks as he grips my shoulder. "Nah. We just talked about him getting laid tonight."

"What the...no, we didn't." I punch Mitch in the arm. "Did you tell him to say that?"

They both laugh. Mitch swears he never said a word. Such a liar.

． ． ．

DAD AND ROLAND stand behind the lattice archway. I wait anxiously on Jada in front of the arch. Mitch seats Mom and Aunt Vashti and then vanishes down the aisle. Mom's flower garden makes a perfect pathway for the bride. Every color possible explodes from both sides. The fountain trickles to my left. Mitch and Grainger roll out a white carpet and leave again. The song changes and a minute later, Mitch brings Emily down the aisle, arm in arm. Emily is gorgeous. They split at the front going to their assigned spots. Mitch is right beside me. A young girl from the pack, Lauren, is the flower girl. Her sweet smile never leaves her face as she tosses red rose petals down the walkway. Lauren takes her place beside Emily.

I know what's coming next. My heart beats triple speed in my chest, making it hard to breathe. Mitch clasps my shoulder and gives it a squeeze. The second Jada appears, my knees go weak and tears sting my eyes. She's perfection. A goddess that I don't deserve.

She and Grainger pause at the back of the aisle for the photographer. She stares straight at me and our eyes lock, causing everything else to vanish. A burst of heat and electricity blooms in my stomach that I can only compare to the glimmer and flicker of the Northern Lights. My eyes have never beheld such beauty. My soul has never felt so full.

There's so much passion inside of me it can't be contained. I push a wave toward her and she stops midway to close her eyes and soak me in. The guests gasp in surprise. Smaller waves leave my body, calling out to Jada. I need her so desperately and I love her so deeply, my bones ache within me. It's a euphoric ride, like a man on drugs. The highest high rides in my veins.

The closer she gets, the more I fall apart. My skin is the only thing holding me together. She walks with confidence, her hips swaying with the satin material. Every other step her dress splits, showing off a tan thigh, and the neckline reveals her soft curves.

But her face is radiant. She's standing in front of me now. I want to drown in her deep chocolate-brown eyes. Jada is glowing. I thought she was an angel the first time I saw her shift, and that's nothing compared to this. Heaven opened and dropped her here. It's the only explanation.

Jada. You are magnificent. Heavenly. Delectable. Beautiful beyond words. And mine. All mine.

I'm yours forever, Denver Stone. From this day forward, we are one.

Roland and my father lead us through the vows and rings. Jada is shocked when Mitch produces a nice-sized diamond from his pocket. I slide it on her finger to go with the band she's already wearing. Dad reads the final benediction and pronounces us husband and wife. Then he says those precious words: You may kiss your bride.

I slide a hand behind her neck and place the other behind her back. I forcefully pull her to me and she gasps. Jada doesn't know this, but it's wolf tradition to practically make out for the kiss. I have to kiss her senseless until the crowd hoots and hollers, or the wedding is a dud as far as my family is concerned. No worries. I've got this.

With a firm grip on her neck, I lower my mouth to hers. I lick her lips and bite until she's begging to be kissed. She hisses my name and I give in to her demand. Her lips open and I invade her delicious mouth with my tongue. I lose all sense of time or reasoning. People are shouting, but I don't stop kissing her until a deep voice speaks directly in my ear.

"All right, son. The pack is pleased, no need to burn a hole in the deck."

I loosen my grip on Jada and try to shake the fog from my head. My dad laughs as he turns us to face the family.

"I present to you Mr. and Mrs. Denver Stone."

THE NEXT HOURS are filled with love and laughter. From pictures to eating, to dancing, to cake cutting, to hugging and congratulating, to more dancing, it has been a wonderful evening. My favorite by far was going after the garter. Jada's smooth skin drove me to all kinds of crazy and back.

Jada and I sway to a slow song. I've lost my jacket and dress shirt.

Her hands slide up under my T-shirt and her nails rake over my skin. I shudder down to my toes.

She kisses my neck, and I growl. "Denver, how much longer do we have to stay here? It's almost eleven. If you don't make love to me soon, it won't be our wedding day any longer."

My forehead drops to hers. "I don't know, but I can't take it anymore. All I can think about is getting you home and touching every part of your body."

"Only touching?"

"Lots of touching and kissing, and then a beautiful boundary to cross over."

She pushes her body to mine. "How many times do you think we can cross the line?"

"Shit. Let's go."

We hug our parents and I get a fist bump from Mitch. The party goes on, but Mom and Dad shoo us away, telling us they'll take care of everything. Jada and I sneak off into the night to our cabin in the woods. She takes off her heels and walks part of the way, but when we get close, I scoop her up and carry her across the threshold.

"Welcome home, Mrs. Stone."

When I put her down she spins around in a circle. "Someone's been busy. It's beautiful."

I walk around and light several candles while she roams the room, skimming the pictures I've hung. I follow her like an animal stalking prey as she saunters to the bedroom. She pauses to breathe in the sweet scent of the roses, and I light more candles. I toss the lighter on the nightstand and turn back around to find Jada a breath away.

She tugs up my shirt so I help her take it over my head. "You're wearing way too many clothes."

My tongue is stuck to the roof of my mouth, but I try to speak. "Jada, I—"

She puts her hand over my mouth. "Denver. I know you love me. I want you to show me. No more talking. Please."

. . .

I WISH I could say we took our time, but it was much later in the night before we were able to slow down and enjoy each other. Every time we make love, it's better than the last. Who in the hell needs sleep? Thank God for wolf blood and stamina.

The exotic pleasure of being with my wife is more than I ever imagined. And I have a damn good imagination. Her body and mine were made to fit perfectly together. We complete each other. God wasn't kidding when he took that rib from Adam and made woman and said "It is good." So. Damn. Good.

SOMEONE other than myself wets my lips. A naked body is pressed against mine.

"Good morning, husband."

"Woman, you are trying to kill me."

"Mmhm." She nibbles my neck.

"We have a plane to catch."

"Mmhm." Runs her tongue down my chest.

"I need to pack."

"Mmhm." Her hands. Oh God her hands. My eyes roll in the back of my head.

"Ah hell. I'll pack fast."

An hour and a half later, we're running to the house. My parents say nothing as we dart through the kitchen half dressed with wild hair and I-had-sex-all-night grins on our faces.

Jada runs to her room and I run to mine. We'll need to move our stuff when we get back from Maui. Jada said she was packed but needed to clean up. I on the other hand have not packed a thing. I yell for Mitch to give me a hand.

He throws open the door and runs in. "What's your deal?"

"Shit. I need a shower and I haven't packed, and I need our passports, and I'm freaking starving cause my wife depleted me of all my damn energy."

He laughs and sits on the bed. "Brother, chill."

"I can't chill. I don't have time to chill."

Mitch stands up and walks to my closet. He comes out holding a packed suitcase. "I packed your bag last night. Your passports are in the front pocket. Mom has breakfast downstairs. Go take a damn shower and chill. I got you, bro."

"Oh my God, I love you."

"Yeah, yeah. I'll see you downstairs."

"Hey Mitch?"

He stops and turns halfway. "Yeah?"

"Sex is some seriously good shit."

"Shut the hell up."

I laugh as I run to the bathroom to take a long hot shower. Now that I have time.

I drag my suitcase down the steps and head to the kitchen. Jada stands at the bar talking to Mitch. I walk up behind her and press against her backside. She tries to ignore me, but I lean in and kiss her neck. She arches her back into me with a moan.

"Oh hell. Didn't you get enough last night?"

"Mitchell Dean." Mom gives him *the look*.

"I know, I know. Stop swearing. Seriously though. You guys can't wait a few hours?"

"I guess I can try." I push away from the counter and get some food.

We have a nice breakfast with my parents and Mitch. We talk about the wedding and how everything went off without a hitch. It was a perfect day. I hate leaving them with a boatload of work to do, but they are more than happy to clean up. I'm sure they'll make good use of Mitch's muscles. They push us out the door with hugs and kisses, telling us to have a good time.

I load our bags in the trunk and jump in the Porsche with my gorgeous bride.

"Twelve days. Me and you with nothing but sun, sand, a fruity drink, food, and all the time in the world to do whatever we want."

Jada licks her lips. "I can think of a lot of things I want to do with you."

"My bloody fish, don't start with me or we'll never make it to the airport."

"Drive fast, baby. Drive fast."

I growl at her choice of words as I back out of the garage and spin out of the driveway. Dad will give me hell for that when I get home. But if I don't leave now, the plane to Maui will have two empty seats. The thought of getting my baby on the beach in that red bikini keeps me going.

This shark has plans for that red bikini. Funny thing is—they all end up the same—with that red bikini on the floor.

TWO WEEKS LATER
JADA

Denver is still sleeping. Our flight coming in from Hawaii last night was delayed, so instead of arriving at midnight, we didn't get in until three in the morning. His mom has texted me twice, asking when we'll be over for breakfast. Our honeymoon was the best two weeks of my life, but I'm so glad to be home.

I lean over Denver to kiss him. My wet hair slides along my neck and lands on his chest. "Time to wake up, sleepy head."

I squeal when he grabs me and yanks me down on top of him. His sleepy eyes open, and he runs his fingers through my hair. "You took a shower without me?"

"You looked so peaceful I didn't have the heart to wake you. Plus, we don't have time for fooling around. Your family is waiting on us."

"Oh shoot. Let me throw on some clothes."

I kiss his nose and climb off the bed. We rush around getting ready and are out the door in ten minutes.

I'm barely in the back door before Aurar wraps me in her arms. "I've missed you two like crazy!"

"We missed you too."

She releases me and holds me at arm's length. "You're positively glowing. Honeymoon was good, I take it?"

Heat creeps up my neck. Bolivar laughs as he steals me from Aurar. "We want to hear all about it."

"What?"

Now they're both laughing. Bolivar kisses my cheek. "Not the sex. The other stuff."

"Oh. Right."

Denver leans on the counter smiling. *A little help here, husband.*

Mitch chooses that moment to round the corner. He stops by Denver for a fist bump, but then grabs me off the floor and spins me around.

"Bout time you get home!"

"Mitch, oh my gosh, I missed you. How's Taylor? When are you moving?"

He puts me on my feet and steps back. His smile slips only for a second, but I notice. "You're not getting off that easy. Honeymoon first. Sex and all."

I none too gingerly punch his arm. "Shut up! You are such a stinker."

"I think we've embarrassed Jada enough. Breakfast will be cold if we don't eat." Aurar winks at me and I send out a thank you only she can hear.

Our plates are clean and pushed to the side. Denver and I have been regaling the family with our honeymoon adventures.

Aurar gasps. "I can't believe you were lost in the State Park!"

"I was so sure the wild pigs were going to eat us."

Denver rolls his eyes. "Babe, it wasn't that bad. We ventured off the trail a bit."

I lean forward. "It was almost dark. We had no idea where we were. There were wild boar trails running in every direction, and not another person in sight. It was a little freaky."

"We never saw a wild boar."

"We could have."

Denver's eyebrows go up in mischief. "You're the one who had to see the redwood trees."

"You're the one who said it wouldn't matter if we got off the hiking trail."

Denver slides his hand up my thigh. "You're the one who distracted me in the middle of the woods."

Mitch grunts. "Can you get to the part where you find your way out?"

I laugh and sit back in my chair. "It's not that exciting. I pulled my phone from my pocket and typed in the name of the park in my GPS and it led us right back to the parking lot."

"Dang. That was a letdown. What else did you do?"

"Whale watching, boat rides, snorkeling, hiking, and some days we simply stayed on the beach all day. It was wonderful."

"Aurar and I have certainly enjoyed our trips to Maui. I'm glad you had a good time."

"We did, but it's good to be home."

Mitch shifts in his seat. "Well, I guess I'll go back upstairs. My clothes aren't going to pack themselves."

We sit in silence as he takes his plate to the kitchen and leaves the room.

I glance at Bolivar. "Did I say something wrong?"

He shakes his head. "No, princess. I do believe he's convinced himself he's homesick before ever leaving home."

"Oh." I can't sit here while Mitch is hurting. "Do you mind if I go talk to him?" I'm not sure who I'm asking. I guess I don't need permission.

Denver kisses my cheek. "I'd say he's hoping you will."

I knock lightly on Mitch's door. "Can I come in?"

"Sure."

I push open the door and glance around the room. There are stacks of clothes, books, and boxes all over the floor. Mitch is sitting on the bed.

I scoot up beside him and nudge his shoulder. "So what's going on?"

He shrugs. "You know. College and all that."

"When are you leaving?"

"Dad says my apartment is ready whenever I am. School doesn't start for a couple of months, but if I want to be close to Taylor, I need to get my ass up there."

"And you don't sound excited. Why?"

"I don't know. I had planned on staying home like Denver. It's a big change and I'm not sure I'm ready. And then things with Taylor are weird."

"Weird how?"

He blows out a breath. "You and Denver made this shit seem easy. I can't even tell if she likes me or not, much less wants to spend the rest of her life with me. I think I freak her out."

"So what? Maybe you do. I mean, it's a lot to take in. Give her time to get used to the idea. Be her friend."

"I'm trying. Do you know how hard it is not to touch her when I'm dying to do so? How bad is sucks not to know how she feels? And she's older and so smart. She has all these goals and plans and they don't line up with mine at all. I want to live here and help Denver with the pack. She wants to live in a big city and work at a trauma center. How in the hell am I supposed to make this work?"

Mitch leans over, face in his hands. I rub his back as I mull over his position. I never imagined there was a scenario where your mate didn't want to be with you. I'm pretty sure I wanted Denver the moment we touched. But this is different. Taylor is not a wolf.

I tug on Mitch's arm. "Hey." He sits up with tears in his eyes. I have to bite my cheek so I don't lose it. "I don't have all the answers, but I think the best thing to do is take it one day at a time. You're losing your shit over stuff that hasn't happened yet. Focus on today. Then tomorrow, focus on tomorrow. Focus on Taylor and showing her what an amazing person you are. And you are an amazing person. I mean you're freaking Mitchell Dean Stone, for crying out loud. She won't be able to stop herself from falling for you. Everything else will fall into place."

"Sounds good, but it's not fail proof."

"No, it's not. But you won't know if you don't try."

"Good point."

I shift around and pull my legs up on the bed. "Tell me what's good about all of this. What will you enjoy?"

"Well, it will be kinda cool to have my own place. I talked Dad into a two-bedroom apartment, and Rieder agreed to be my roommate."

"Mitch, that's awesome! You guys will have so much fun. What else?"

A small smile plays on his lips. "I know what you're doing."

"Humor me."

He laughs and it melts my heart. "I suppose living in a big city will have its perks. There's more to do and good places to eat. College parties will be the bomb. There's some cool clubs, and theaters. I'll already have a group of friends to hang out with since Rieder, Grainger, and Emily will be there. And of course, Taylor is there."

"You're going to do great, Mitch."

"Thanks. I'll miss you though. And Denver..." Mitch clinches his fist. "I don't like to think about not being near my brother."

"I'm gonna miss you too, you little shit," Denver says as he walks in the room.

I eye him suspiciously. "How long have you been there?"

"A while."

Mitch jumps off the bed and walks toward Denver. When I think he's going to hug Denver, he punches him in the arm. "You know I didn't mean any of that sentimental crap, right? I don't even like you."

"Funny. You know, Jada tries to tell me the same thing."

"You're not very likable." I saunter over toward Denver and kiss his cheek. "I mean look at you. You're not even cute."

Denver grabs me and pulls me close. "That's not what you said last night."

Mitch blows out an exasperated sigh. "Hell no, not in my room. Either help me pack or get out."

We spend the next couple of hours helping Mitch clean out his closet. The boy has more clothes than me. No one mentions the upcoming move. Instead we laugh and joke on things that have no meaning or significance. Sometimes avoidance is okay. We'll all face the truth soon enough.

AFTER HELPING MITCH, MY PARENTS' house is our next stop. We spend a couple of hours retelling our honeymoon stories and visiting with my touchy, feely parents. It's weird to say the least. Roland moved back in while we were gone and they act every bit as much the newlywed couple as Denver and I do. It does my heart good for them to be happy. I'm glad my mother has been able to forgive and love again. If anyone deserves to get a happily ever after, it's her. Before we leave, they invite us for dinner later this week and we gladly accept. Roland and Denver speak a moment on business. My father wants to become a part of the pack once again. It appears all things are right in the world, which is nice compared to the previous months of uncertainty. The universe has settled into a calm balance. For how long, no one knows, but we'll enjoy it while we can.

"BABY, are you almost ready? We need to leave for the restaurant."

I walk out of the bathroom freshly made over. My Maui tan is evident in the white sundress I've chosen for the evening. My curled hair is in a clip, with loose strands around my face, and I'm sporting a new pair of strappy sandals Denver bought me in a boutique on our honeymoon.

"I'm ready. Let me grab my earrings and purse."

Denver struts up behind me as I push in a pair of earrings. I regard his handsome face in the mirror. Desire dances in his glowing eyes. He kisses my neck and I shiver.

"Damn, baby. Why'd you have to go and look so hot?"

"I wasn't aware I looked hot." I bite my lower lip.

"Like hell. You're trying to torture me."

"Perhaps. But for now, looking is all you get. We need to go."

A deep growl escapes him as he backs away. "Fine, but be prepared to make it up to me later."

"I have no problem with that whatsoever."

The drive to Diamond Hill goes by quickly. Denver voices his concern over the Mitch situation and we try to come up with a way to help him. In the end we decide it's up to him. We can't make Taylor fall in love with him—as much as we want to. Denver felt like Taylor was interested in Mitch the day he met her in the infirmary, so it makes us wonder what happened inside her head to be so resistant now. We agree to visit often and try to befriend Taylor in hopes she'll come around.

Denver pulls up to the valet and hands off his keys.

"Did you text Emily?"

"Yes. They're at the table."

Denver guides me with his hand on my back as we make our way to the host stand. He gives the name of our reservation and she leads us to a table with a waiting, and smiling, Grainger and Emily.

Emily jumps up the second I'm close enough for a hug. "Jada, you're gorgeous! And so tan!"

"Thanks. You look good too." And my goodness, but she does. She's also been in the sun, and her blonde hair is lighter because of it. Her cheeks are rosy and her smile spreads across her entire face. She's beaming from the inside out.

Denver greets them both as I walk around the table.

I kiss Grainger on the cheek before taking my chair, which Denver is patiently waiting to push in. "Hey, Grainger."

"Hey you." He glances back and forth between Denver and me. "So…how was Hawaii?"

It's not lost on me how close Grainger and Emily have pulled their chairs. I have to know what's happening. "Oh no. Not so fast there, mister. I want to know what's going on here. And by here, I mean with you two."

Grainger winks at Emily and her face reddens. "We've decided to make things official. We're dating now. Boyfriend and girlfriend. Whatever you want to call it."

My insides explode in pure joy. "Oh my gosh, you guys, that's awesome! How did this happen? I need details!"

Grainger rolls his eyes. "I'll give you the guy version and you can get the girl version from Emily later. So basically, we hung out while you were gone and I think she's pretty amazing. Last night I asked Emily if she would be good with dating me exclusively and she said yes."

"Yeah, that was pretty terrible. I definitely need more than that. But holy cow, I am so pumped about this."

Emily laughs and grabs my hand. "Don't worry. We'll have a girls' night soon and catch up."

"Will there be ice cream?"

"Only in moderation. No puking, I promise."

"It's a date."

As the meal is served the conversation jumps from one thing to another. We talk and laugh and then laugh some more. My face hurts from all the smiling.

My two best friends are a couple. Sure didn't see that one coming. They complement each other and bring out the best in each other. I can't wait to watch their story unfold. In two months they'll be heading off to college and starting a new chapter. Life is funny sometimes. Taking twists and turns, leaving us wondering what's around the next bend. Turning out completely different than what we had planned in our head. I'm discovering it's not always a bad thing that my initial dreams didn't come true. About the time I've got it all figured out, I've got it all wrong. But what I get right makes the journey oh so worth it.

IT'S 3:00 a.m. and we've been home for twenty-four hours. The last few of which I've spent making it up to my husband for the "abuse he suffered" by my hotness. He'll make any excuse, to which I reply that he doesn't need one. Silly man.

Speaking of my silly man, he hands me a water and climbs back under the covers. I take a drink and place the bottle on the nightstand. Denver is lying on his back, so I curl up next to him in the crook of his arm. He stares at the ceiling lost in thought.

"What are you thinking about, babe?"

"You."

"You mind being a little more specific?"

His chest vibrates with his laughter. "I was thinking about how blessed I am. I realized something tonight at dinner."

"Oh yeah, what's that?"

"I realized you chose me. You chose us. In the beginning, you could have walked away, but you didn't. You could have never given me another thought and lived your life the way you'd imagined it. You could have decided to go after Grainger and the relationship he was offering. I was thinking about what a miserable wretch I would have been if you'd chosen him. My life an endless loop of loss, sadness, and regret. I'd spend the rest of my life alone and broken-hearted. I'm so thankful you gave us a chance."

"Hmm. I suppose I did have a choice to make, but it wasn't hard. It took me about a second to decide that you were the one for me. Plans be damned, because one touch from you and I knew. And I'm the one that's blessed. I'll never do enough good to deserve your love or the life I've been given."

"Ah baby." Denver tucks his hand under my chin and pulls my lips to his. "It may not always be easy."

"I know."

"I might drive you crazy."

"I know."

"We may fight."

"I know."

"There will be demons. Literally."

"We'll fight them together, side by side." I sit up and grab Denver's face with both hands. "Are you trying to talk me out of this?"

"Hell no!"

"Then stop talking and practice making babies with me."

LIFE IS SO UNCERTAIN. There is no promise of tomorrow, and the only thing we know for sure, is we know nothing for sure. At any moment the ground can shift and shake and our whole world can be turned upside down. I don't know what will happen with Mitch. I can't say for sure if my parents will stay together. I don't know if Emily and Grainger will make it.

The only thing I do know is the power of love. It's a power like no other. Real love is sacrifice and forgiveness. Real love is humble and gentle. Real love never dies and it never gives up. Real love changes things.

REAL LOVE NEVER FAILS.

THREE THINGS WILL LAST FOREVER—FAITH, hope, and love—and the greatest of these is love.

ACKNOWLEDGMENTS

I thank God every day for His goodness and His faithfulness. He will always receive the opening recognition and highest praise for any and all of my accomplishments. To Him be the glory!

This is not the book I intended to write. Initially, no wolves or demons were included. Just regular people, dealing with regular stuff. After a few chapters were written, I woke up one morning over spring break and wondered what would happen if the characters were shapeshifting wolves. And so it began. A completely different story was born, and thanks to quarantine, it came to life in five short months.

I owe a huge amount of gratitude to several people. Every writer needs a team of willing bodies to read their material and give honest feedback. This group of lovely ladies has undoubtedly made me better and has improved the quality of this story with their invaluable input—Karrie Green (my cheerleader), Marlena Dixon, Janae Maksymtsev and Natalie Buell. I'm honored that each of you spent your precious time not only reading, but rereading, texting, emailing and meeting for coffee to give me sound advice and the encouragement I needed to keep going. I love you all!

When writing a book, some things you can do for yourself. For me, editing is NOT one of those things. Saying thank you doesn't begin to cover what you've done, but regardless, THANK YOU! My hat is off to you, Jessica Nelson with Rare Bird Editing, Karen Robinson with Karen Robinson Edits, and Tiffany White with Writers Untapped. You gals are the bomb.com.

The next shout-out goes to Kelsey Keeton with K Keeton Designs for a wonderful cover. Every book deserves a beautiful shell, but when you've spent months or even years creating your book, you want the best. I appreciate your God-given, creative talent and am glad to share it with my readers.

That brings me to a very important group of people. I can't name each and every one, but thank you to all of you who read *Just A Kiss* and asked for what was coming next. I write for the joy and satisfaction it brings, but obviously it's fun to share the story with others. Thank you for checking in and being gracious enough to inquire about my next story. Please know it brought me a great amount of confidence and helped spur forward *Beautiful Boundary*. Your love and support mean everything.

And last but never least is my awesome family. My husband, Johnnie Spivey, deserves a gold medal. Not only has he put up with me for twenty-seven years, he lets me hide in the bedroom for hours on end to do what I love—write. Your love keeps me going, and I'm blessed to have you by my side. Cheers to our newest season, the empty nest, and all the adventures it will bring. To the four people running around who call me Mom, you are the greatest gift on God's green earth, and I'll cherish you always. I've dedicated this book to you in honor of who each of you are and all you will become. Cheers to you and your families and to the many wonderful memories you've yet to make. And of course I must mention my two sweet grandbabies, Jackson and Everleigh, who expand my heart and make me smile.

Many others have shown support and encouraged me along the way. My mom, in-laws, church family, friends, co-workers, and a slew more. I can't mention you all, but I'm grateful for the people God has placed in my life. We all press on toward the prize, but man am I glad I don't have to do it alone.

ABOUT THE AUTHOR

Carol Spivey is an emerging author of romance novels. She lives in corn country Indiana with her high-spirited husband and their four grown children, and two precious grandchildren. When not spending time with family, you can find her writing, reading, working out, driving her Jeep, traveling to the beach, or dreaming of traveling to the beach. She is the author of Just A Kiss.

facebook.com/Godisgoodwriterslife

Made in the USA
Middletown, DE
24 November 2022

15612097R00213